AN EVIL PREMISE

BOOKS BY T. MARIE VANDELLY

An Evil Premise

Theme Music

AN EVIL PREMISE

T. MARIE VANDELLY

BLACK STONE PUBLISHING

Published in 2025 by Blackstone Publishing
Cover and book design by Candice Edwards

Printed in the United States of America
Originally published in hardcover by Blackstone Publishing in 2025

First paperback edition: 2025
ISBN 979-8-228-00065-0
Fiction / Horror

Version 2

Blackstone Publishing
31 Mistletoe Rd.
Ashland, OR 97520

www.BlackstonePublishing.com

To Jamie

PREFACE

I'm afraid to write this. Afraid doing so will summon the muse. My innermost evil. That it will take these words as an invitation. Pervade my sleepless nights with vile contemplations, pollute clarity with its foul breath, whisper wrongs against my eardrum. I can feel the worm of a loathsome thought writhing to the surface. Marching like fire ants up my arms. The itch is unbearable. I clench my fingers, but my thoughts cannot be crushed. Only ground into finer atrocities.

This story is no longer mine to tell. I matter less than the pencil I hold. Just as easily snapped.

I hate that I find some joy in it. Writing such horrors. That such depravity is in me. Under my skin, contentedly constricted around my bones. What filth may spill out of me next is unimaginable. A slopping bucketful most likely. Sorry if I get some on you.

So do be careful.

Don't accidentally gasp this horror down your throat.

That's what the muse wants. To get under your skin. That spidery tickle on the back of your neck? That's the muse.

Fiddling with your nerves. Turning your stomach this way and that. It's taken over the voice inside your head. Lent it a raspy growl. It wants you to think the tick of a clock is a claw upon your window. It wants your eyes to gather shadows into a crouched figure in the corner of your room. Scare the cat off the bed for no damn reason. The muse can and will make it hard for you to swallow. To catch your breath. To think rationally.

It might already be happening.

That uncomfortable feeling in the pit of your stomach. A sinking sense that you should set this book aside. It's too late for that. Your eyes have already absorbed the muse's foul essence. It's a part of you now. It's peering through your pupils to read this. Nervously licking your lips with its tongue. Sending a chill up your spine. Spinning you round and round. Unleveling that good head on your shoulders.

Hopefully, you're stronger than I was. Not so easily carried away. Still, you might want to grip the book a little tighter at this point. For this is your horror story now. The reader is the main character in this nasty tale.

And for that, I am truly sorry.

PART ONE
TUESDAY

1

A shriek bursts through a set of swinging doors to Jewel's left and escapes down the hall on a fast-moving gurney. Spun around, the directions hastily spat at her by the front-desk nurse seem incomplete. Jewel traces a hand across the achingly white walls and counts down the room numbers of the ICU at Ware Memorial Hospital.

Ghosts of irrational thoughts clutter the empty hallway as Jewel turns right.

What if Deidre is dead?

What if she's not?

Jewel is fairly certain her sister died while the Enterprise clerk transposed *War and Peace* from the one-page car-rental agreement Jewel filled out with a golf pencil. Deidre flatlined at every red light Jewel managed to catch between Washington Dulles International Airport and the Shenandoah Valley. Went into cardiac arrest while she searched for a parking spot. As she turned right down the wrong hospital corridor.

Time of death: the exact moment a uniformed police officer extends her arm and halts Jewel's advance.

Though Deidre had been dubbed the Queen of Fantasy Fiction in many trade publications, it was purely an honorary title. Deidre hadn't sat atop the *New York Times* bestseller throne in years. Her legions of fans had overthrown her for authors who could meet their insatiable reading needs. One book every five years wasn't going to keep her in their good graces. And though Deidre Baldwin might still be considered royalty in a Podunk town like Ware, Virginia, Jewel didn't think her level of fame warranted a security detail.

"May I help you?" the officer says.

"I'm here to see Deidre Baldwin." *To identify her body*, a hitched voice in the back of her mind amends. Jewel closes her eyes to suppress the defeatist side of her. The side that, for whatever reason, not only expects the worst to happen but welcomes it with an open mind. The big picture she sees has always been a horror show. Her sister is the star of this one. At least what is left of her.

"And you are?" the officer asks.

"Jewel Maxwell. I'm Deidre's sister."

"Maxwell?" the officer questions with a curious frown. "Does Deidre have another sister? The nurse told me she contacted a Miss Baldwin about the situation. I can't recall her first name. But I don't think it was . . ."

When the officer's eyes draw a blank, Jewel reintroduces herself.

"Jewel. Maxwell." She touches her chest to prevent any further misunderstanding. "I'm Deidre's sister. Her only sister. I changed my name when I got married. I guess Deidre hasn't updated her emergency contact information with the insurance company yet. I just got married last year. Deidre was my maid of honor." Jewel covers a small gasping weep with her hand before asking, "Is she okay? What happened? They wouldn't tell me anything over the phone."

"The doctor will explain everything to you. He should be here any minute."

"Can I see her?"

"Sorry. I'm not supposed to let anyone in until the doctor arrives."

"Isn't anyone in there with her now?"

"A nurse was in with her just before you arrived, but she got called away. Her car alarm was going off. She told me Deidre was in stable condition before she left. Don't worry. They have her hooked up to monitors, so they'll know right away if there's an issue."

"Still, she shouldn't be alone."

When Jewel reaches for the doorknob again, the officer blocks it with her hip.

"I'm sorry, but I can't let you in."

"But I'm her sister!"

"I'm just following orders."

"Whose orders?"

"The hospital's. They've never had someone this famous as a patient before, and they want to make sure her privacy is protected. That's why I'm here. They assigned me to watch her door. No one gets in or out without a doctor present. Not even a family member. Sorry."

"Look, Officer . . ." Jewel squints at the bronze star pinned to the lapel of the officer's brown bomber jacket, but it only designates the bearer as Deputy Sheriff.

"Kerns," the officer supplies.

Jewel blinks as the name rings a bell. But not the face. Having lived in Ware when she was a child, she might have gone to school with one of Officer Kerns's relatives. Or been taught by one. The name brings a stern woman to mind. Thickset. Broad shouldered. Eyes of steel. Though Officer Kerns appears tough as nails, the Kerns Jewel recalls had silver hair to match.

Jewel takes a deep breath to modulate her tone. "Look, Officer Kerns. I appreciate you looking out for Deidre. I know you're just doing your job. But I just want to peek my head in for a second and let her know that I'm here."

Officer Kerns slides in front of the door as Jewel takes a step forward. "She won't know you're here anyway. So you might as well wait for the doctor."

"What do you mean she won't know that I'm here?"

Officer Kerns glances down the corridor, then at her watch. She expresses her frustration in a sigh and shakes her head. "I'm sorry to be the one to tell you this, but . . . your sister is in a coma."

"Coma?" Jewel gasps as the word cramps her lungs, slams a soundproof lid over her thoughts, and pounds tiny fists against the backs of her eyes. She can't imagine anything more horrible than being trapped in your own mind.

"She was the victim of a hit-and-run accident," Officer Kerns explains.

"Hit-and-run!" Jewel slaps a hand to her heart. "You mean Dee got hit by a car?"

"Yes. A trucker spotted her lying in the street. Luckily, he saw her in time to stop. He almost drove right over her. He thought she was a deer until he noticed her long black hair."

"Oh, my god." Jewel presses a hand to her forehead to contain her disbelief. "When was this?"

"Around two a.m. this morning. It appears she might have woken to find an intruder in her home. She was still in her pajamas and the door to her apartment was left ajar. We think she might have been running from them when she was hit."

The big picture switches to a rape scene in Jewel's mind and chokes a sob from her.

"Was she . . . ?" Jewel can't bring herself to say it, but Officer Kerns reads the fear in her eyes.

"I don't believe she was physically assaulted. Most of her injuries were caused by the accident."

Most? Jewel wonders. She's about to ask for clarification when the squeak of shoes turns her attention to the end of the corridor.

Skidding around the corner in a rush, the man who drew Jewel's attention away from Officer Kerns's cryptic comment is attempting to work himself into a lab coat while managing a cup of coffee.

"Sorry, sorry," the man says, flustered. "I got lost looking for the cafeteria." He stutter-steps as he spots Jewel and sloshes coffee over his fingers. "Oh, good morning," he says, shaking his hand dry as he approaches.

"Dr. Leonetti," Officer Kerns says. "This is Jewel Maxwell. Deidre Baldwin's sister."

Dr. Leonetti stares at Jewel for a moment before recovering his manners. "Oh, yes! Of course. It's very nice to meet you." The pout he offers Jewel is almost as warm and wet as his handshake. "Though I wish it were under better circumstances."

Though Dr. Leonetti's toupee is in its twenties, the laugh lines around his eyes and mouth haven't been let in on the joke. But his eyes are as clear and blue as the Caribbean, which is probably where he refines his tan. And buys his pinkie rings.

He must not be from here, Jewel thinks. Though Ware, Virginia, isn't so far in the backwoods that a man couldn't get himself a nice watch, he'd be hard-pressed to find a Rolex at Selby's Discount Emporium.

Jewel slips her fingers from Dr. Leonetti's limp, manicured clutch to ask, "How's my sister?"

"I told her about Deidre being in a coma," Officer Kerns interjects. "Sorry. I should have waited for you to tell her yourself, but you were taking so long."

"I do apologize for that," he says. "I'm fairly new to this hospital and still get turned around. It's no Mount Sinai, but at least those hallways are clearly marked."

That he was from a big city like New York explained a lot—his glib attitude and flashy jewelry—but it provided no insight into Deidre's condition.

Jewel shakes her head in frustration. "You were saying about my sister . . . ?"

"Oh, yes." Dr. Leonetti clears his throat to recoup his bedside manner. "Your sister is resting comfortably. She suffered multiple broken bones as a result of the accident. She underwent surgery to fix a broken tibia. She also has three broken ribs, but those will mend on their own. Her head injury is our primary concern. It's caused her brain to swell, which we believe is the reason for her coma. I know that's a scary word, but we're very optimistic that she will awake once the swelling reduces."

"Can I see her now, please?" Jewel says.

"Of course." Dr. Leonetti sets an unbearably heavy hand on Jewel's shoulder. "But I think you should prepare yourself first."

"For what?"

Dr. Leonetti flicks an anxious look at Officer Kerns, then fastens a steadier gaze on Jewel. "Your sister was admitted with a skin malady of some sort. Completely aside from her accident. It isn't anything to concern yourself with, but it has altered her appearance somewhat. Frankly, it's a bit . . . unsettling."

2

Jewel's knees falter, then faint out from under her midway across the hospital room as she spots Deidre. She expected to be shocked by her sister's appearance. Deidre's face to be fractured and swollen. Cheeks pitted with gravel. Chin scraped to the bone. But nothing could have prepared her for what's lying in the hospital bed.

Literally sweating pus, the inflamed rash encasing Deidre's face has reached the breaking point. Split across her brow, blood-laced mucus dribbles along her temples. Dried to a crusty glue, her long black hair, once the envy of her younger sister, now looks like a cheap wig. Adhered to the top of a rotten potato and jammed on the tip of a withered stick, the only bulk to Deidre's frame is the cast around her left leg. Uncovered and propped on a pillow, the opening around her toes nests five half-starved, featherless birds with expensively pedicured beaks.

Somehow Deidre's fancy toenails are the one thing Jewel can't stomach. She looks briefly around for a receptacle, then vomits into the leaky bowl of her hands.

"Oh, shit," Officer Kerns exclaims, grabbing a box of tissues off the bedside table. She snatches out a few sheets and hands them to Jewel.

Dr. Leonetti, having jumped clear of the spew, plucks a tissue for himself and blots the right toe of his black wing tip.

"I'm sorry," he says. "I tried to warn you."

"What happened to her face?" Jewel cries, mopping vomit from her hands.

"An allergic reaction is my best guess. We're still running some tests." Dr. Leonetti sidesteps the puddle Jewel created and looks down at Deidre. "The rash is quite extensive. It covers most of her body. It appears she scratched herself with some sort of implement. Possibly a knife or fork. We were able to address most of the wounds, but the skin around some of the lesions was too necrotic to work with. We cleaned them out the best we could and packed them with antiseptic gauze."

Jewel tweezes one word from the diagnosis and holds it up for inspection. "*Necrotic*? Doesn't that mean dead?"

Dr. Leonetti inhales the courage to say, "Yes."

"I see," Jewel says, though she doesn't. "I can't believe this is happening. Dee's all I have left. Our father died just last year."

The heart attack hit him like a speeding car too. One second he was mowing the lawn, and the next they were burying him under the one at Prospect Memorial Gardens. Like Deidre, he had been mistaken for roadkill. The unpiloted John Deere finished off the last thirty feet of grass before bucking him into a ditch. He lay there for several hours before a UPS driver slowed to see what the buzzards were all about. Ironically, inside the last package their father received was a Fitbit health tracker.

"Do you have any additional questions for me?" Dr. Leonetti says. "I have rounds to make."

With too many questions to sort through, Jewel shakes her head.

"Well, if you do, please feel free to contact me directly." Dr. Leonetti picks up a small notepad from the bedside table and jots down a quick note. He tears the top sheet from the pad and hands it to Jewel. "This is my private phone number. You can call anytime."

Jewel looks down at the page in her hand in wonder. "I didn't think doctors gave out their private phone numbers."

"I don't usually, but I've never had such a famous patient before. I want to ensure Deidre Baldwin gets the VIP treatment. Which also extends to you. I don't want you waiting on hold while the switchboard tries to track me down. If I don't answer immediately, leave a message and I'll call you back as soon as I can. I'll be overseeing Deidre's treatment during her stay, so I'll be able to provide you with the most up-to-date prognosis of her condition."

"Thank you."

"I need to be going now, but feel free to visit as long as you'd like."

Jewel touches her head to keep it from spinning. "Actually, I think I need to lie down for a bit. I've been up all night."

"I'll follow you over to the apartment house," Officer Kerns says. "I'd like you to look around Deidre's apartment and see if you notice anything missing."

"Was she robbed?"

"I don't know. That's what I would like to determine."

"Oh." Jewel blinks. "I wasn't planning on going over to the house today. I need to find a hotel."

"Why don't you just stay at Deidre's?" Officer Kerns suggests. "It's right down the road."

"I don't know if I should" *stay in the attic of my family's old haunted house.* Not that it had been haunted before their mother died there. But if her ghost was anywhere, it was going to be in the rafters of the attic. Her old office. The one she went crazy in. The one Deidre had been crazy enough to move back into twenty-six years later. "Deidre's a very private person," Jewel goes on. "I think she would prefer that I stay at a hotel."

"Why don't you decide after we check it out," Officer Kerns says. "It won't take long. I need to clear the apartment as a crime scene."

Jewel relents with a nod, dropping her gaze downward to picture the condition of Deidre's apartment. If it matched the condition of her skin, they might want to slip on some hazmat suits before exposing themselves to its walls. "I guess we can go over there. If you think it's safe."

"You'll be safe with me." Officer Kerns pats her sidearm, then follows Dr. Leonetti into the hall. "I'll wait for you in the lobby," she says.

"Stay as long as you'd like, Ms. Maxwell," Dr. Leonetti advocates, reaching in to pull the door closed as Jewel takes a step toward it. "Visiting hours aren't limited for immediate family."

Jewel touches the door imploringly as Dr. Leonetti shuts her in with Deidre. She sets an ear to it to listen for the dissipating clop of footsteps, the tail end of Officer Kerns and Dr. Leonetti's conversation whipping around the corner of the corridor, but the thing in the bed behind her is panting too loudly to hear over.

. . . AHH-UHH . . . AHH-UHH . . .

Was Deidre breathing like that a moment ago? Or was she as nervous as Jewel to be left alone with her sister?

Five minutes, Jewel thinks, checking her watch. *Five minutes and I'll go. That's plenty of time for it to seem like I tried to be a good sister.*

"I'm sorry, Dee," Jewel says, eyes locked on the minute

hand, or whatever it's called on a digital watch. Deidre would probably know.

Don't use words like thing *and* it *so much in your writing. Everything has a name.*

"Sorry," Jewel says. "I'm sorry this happened to you. Sorry I can't look at you. I know you need me to be strong for you right now, Dee, but I can't. I just can't. It's just too awful. You understand, don't you?"

. . . AHH-UHH . . .

The insectile rasp of Deidre's labored breathing conjures a scene from the movie *The Fly*. Jeff Goldblum, mid-metamorphosis, skull warped and dripping with slime, unable to control his base urges. Deidre looks incredibly similar to that. As if she were deteriorating. Transforming into something else. Maybe not a human fly, but something just as grotesque.

"I know that seems harsh," Jewel admits. "But if you were awake, Dee, you wouldn't want to look at yourself either. I guess it's a blessing that you're in a coma. At least that might give your face time to heal." Jewel sneaks a peek over her shoulder at the rancid gob of hamburger propped on the pillow, then turns away before it can bare its teeth at her.

Deidre sits slowly upright in Jewel's imagination and gives her back a horrible smile. Eye teeth just a little longer than they should be, her gums are a necrotic black. The bed creaks as Deidre swings her feet to the floor. A shadow crosses the window and falls over the wall to Jewel's right. She closes her eyes to banish the sight from her mind. Though she's almost positive Deidre will be lying flat on the bed if she were to look, she can't bring herself to. Fear has her by the shoulders. The grip of its fingers pierces her goose bumps and drains an icy sweat down her spine. She's had these waking nightmares before, but never before has a real monster been so close at hand when one occurred.

Jewel rests her forehead on the cool door and breathes through the panic attack. She counts back from a hundred, like her father taught her to do when she was little, then takes a quick look over her shoulder.

Other than a drop of pus playing Plinko down her pitted cheek, Deidre remains perfectly still.

"What the fuck happened to you, Dee?" Jewel asks.

Though Dr. Leonetti's diagnosis of an allergic reaction seems logical, and God knows Jewel wants it to be just that, it doesn't look like an allergic reaction to her. None that she has ever seen before. And though she is woe to make such an extreme, uneducated guess, one conclusion keeps rearing its ugly head. *Flesh-eating virus.* Surely Dr. Leonetti considered that. Perhaps he already ruled it out. If so, there would be no reason to put those two vicious words in her head. But they had found a way in anyhow. A microscopic nibble at the center of her subconscious. *Staphylococcus. E. coli. Ebola.* Jewel has watched enough *Dr. Mercy* on the Learning Channel to know the difference between necrotizing fasciitis and an ordinary skin rash.

"How long have you been dealing with this, Dee? And why didn't you tell me? I know we haven't spoken much lately, but I would have tried to help you."

. . . AHH-UHH . . . AHH-UHH . . .

"That's not fair," Jewel replies, deciphering a contrary tone in her sister's wheezing. "I do care. As much as you care for me, anyway."

Which, if they were being honest with each other, isn't a lot. But they have never been close. Though six years isn't an insurmountable generation gap, it is wide enough for them not to see each other clearly. Deidre has always looked down on her kid sister, and Jewel has never had the nerve to look Deidre straight in the eye. Still can't. Even when they are closed.

"Hey, you probably wouldn't even visit me if I were the one in the hospital."

. . . *AHH-UHH* . . .

"Yeah, right. You'd send me flowers and call it a day." Jewel sighs. "Sorry, I forgot to bring you any, but I was kind of in a rush."

. . . *AHH-UHH* . . .

"I'll bring you a nice bouquet tomorrow. This room could use some cheering up."

. . . *AHH-UHH* . . .

"I've been working on a new project," Jewel says, holding up her end of the conversation for—she checks her watch—another three minutes. "The premise is kind of thin. But I think there's enough there to work with. You only need one seed to grow the most glorious tree. It's up to the writer to shake its limbs and see what falls out. You told me that, Dee. Back when we used to bounce ideas off each other. You don't need me for that anymore, though. Your seed grew into a forest they had to chop down to print all your books." Jewel expels a sighing chuckle. "I'm still shaking my one damn tree. All that ever falls out of mine is a bunch of dead leaves that blow away before I can rake them together."

. . . *AHH-UHH* . . .

"This would make the start of a pretty good story though, huh? Woman rushes to be at her estranged sister's bedside only to find her in a coma." Jewel lowers her voice to deliver the one-line hook: "Plagued by a mysterious rash that has turned her sister into the monster she always knew her to be, Jewel Maxwell must set her petty jealousies aside and help her famous sister in her hour of need." Jewel shrugs. "Or something like that. Though the story could take a darker route. A *What Ever Happened to Baby Jane?* type of thing."

. . . AHH-UHH . . .

"I know. *Be original.* Don't rewrite stories that have already been told. There are plenty of new story ideas out there waiting to be written. You just have to pay attention to the world around you." Jewel looks at her watch. Two minutes to go. "I'm going to head over to the house when I leave here. Officer Kerns wants me to take a look around your apartment. She thinks you might have been robbed. I'm also going to try and find what might have given you that rash. Maybe if Dr. Leonetti knows what caused it, he can treat it. I might stay at your place for a few days. Just while you're in the hospital. I hope you don't mind."

. . . AHH—

When the inhalation fails to leave Deidre's chest, Jewel whips her head toward the bed and slams her nose into the door as it abruptly opens.

"Oh, I'm sorry," a nurse says, peeking around the corner of the door at Jewel. "I didn't know anyone was in here." She flicks a fretful look at the bed. "Oh, my goodness! What happened here?"

Jewel turns as the nurse rushes to Deidre's bedside, then slaps a hand over her mouth to cover her surprise.

Slid sideways off the pillow, Deidre's head hangs upside down over the edge of the mattress. Inverted, and floating atop a gown of black hair, it appears a cycloptic dwarf has slipped from her sister's bed. Mouth gaped wide as a hollow eye socket, chin jutting like a horn from the center of a sloped forehead, thick black eyelashes line either side of the creature's jowls, like stitches.

"What happened?" the nurse grunts, pressing Deidre's slack torso back onto the bed with her shoulder.

Jewel shakes her head, wondering how close her waking nightmare had come to walking.

"She must have slipped off the pillows," the nurse says.

Jewel rises up on her toes to see over the nurse's shoulder. "Is she breathing?"

The nurse scans the health monitor on the far side of the bed, then sets an ear to Deidre's chest.

"She seems to be breathing just fine," she concludes, tucking the blanket under Deidre's chin. "Maybe a little congested, but nothing to worry about." She turns to Jewel. "Are you a family member?"

"Yes. I'm her sister."

"Oh, good. I'm glad she has someone who can be with her. The doctor should be here anytime to review her case with you."

"We've spoken already."

The nurse raises her eyebrows, perplexed. "I thought he was going to wait for me to return." She shakes her head, agitated. "My car alarm went off and I had to go silence it."

Jewel nods. "He mentioned that."

"Well, I have your sister's lab work." She picks up the tablet she set on the nightstand before deadlifting Deidre back onto the bed. "I'll go get the doctor so he can review it with you."

Jewel hooks a thumb at the door and yanks herself toward it. "Actually, I need to be going. I have someone waiting for me in the lobby."

"Will you be back later?" the nurse asks.

Jewel glances at Deidre's hideous face and sighs. "I guess I should."

The nurse blinks up a sad smile for Jewel. "I'm sure your sister appreciates you being here for her."

Jewel bobs her head sullenly. "I hope she does."

3

Jewel pulls her rental car to a stop along the curb behind Officer Kerns's vehicle, shifts to Park, and leans over the steering wheel to look up at the house through the rain-speckled windshield.

As ominous as she remembers from her childhood, the four-level brick Edwardian looks as unhappy to see Jewel as she is to see it. Flat glass behind the black iron lashes of the window grills gives the house a guarded appearance, like a sentry waiting to be relieved of its duty.

Jewel feels nothing for this place. The house had been a project, not a home. A fixer-upper her parents planned to renovate, sell for three times what they paid for it, and get out before the three-year ARM mortgage broke. Their mother tried to make the dwelling as homey as possible while they lived there, but it was hard to get comfy when you lived at a construction site. You were more apt to find a can of paint sitting on the kitchen table than a gravy urn. No sense hanging pictures on a wall that was about to come down or putting a fancy lampshade on a utility light. Still, their mother tried. Until she died. Just a little over a year into the renovation. And though the house hadn't ruptured her appendix like a rusty water pipe, Jewel somehow blamed her death on it. Maybe if they had been living a normal life, in a normal home, with normal lighting, they would have noticed how sick she had gotten. Maybe if they had money for a doctor, she would have gone to one. Maybe if the house had been a block closer to the hospital, her father would have made it in time.

Though they left the house in more disrepair than they acquired it, it sold over value at auction. The new owner converted the house into apartments.

The house is a great setting for a novel. Just Gothic enough to be menacing. Jewel can imagine the main character's fear as she stares up at her childhood home. Packed with memories she'd rather not sort through. Bumping into the ghosts of her family in the halls. The memory of their voices floating up the stairwell.

Though Jewel never would, she can envision her main character, who is much stronger than she, staying here. Steadfast in her commitment to be near her sister, wholly oblivious to the horrors that await her. She might have trepidations, which were normal under the circumstances, but she wouldn't be scared off. Not right away. Not as long as she had a cop to escort her inside.

Jewel waits until Officer Kerns exits her black RAV4, then opens her car door with a question on her lips.

"Don't cops usually drive a cruiser or something?"

Officer Kerns glances at her pedestrian ride and sighs. "My cruiser's in the shop. It got smashed during a car chase a couple of weeks ago. There weren't any extra vehicles lying around, so I have to use my personal car until my new cruiser comes in. It's on back order. So I should get it in about a year or two."

"A car chase!" Jewel marvels, grabbing her bag from the passenger seat. She slings it over her shoulder, then eyes her laptop bag. Though it should be safe in a locked car, especially in a sleepy town like Ware, given what happened to Deidre the night before, and the story Officer Kerns is currently sharing, she grabs it off the seat.

"It wasn't all that exciting," Officer Kerns concludes as Jewel slams the car door with her hip. "It only lasted about a minute. The guy took off while I was running his tags during a routine stop. He lost control of his car and ran into a ditch about a half mile down the road. I was looking out the passenger window to see if he was okay and drove straight into a telephone pole."

"That sounds exciting to me," Jewel says, then glances across the street at the Catholic church.

St. Leo's looms as large in her memory as it does over the stone retention wall that is doing its very best to keep the house of God from sliding into traffic. Smoke of a recent fire clings to the doorframe and window sashes like sooty fingerprints of the smoldering souls who had attempted an escape.

"How did the church catch fire?"

"Preaching too much fire and brimstone would be my guess." Officer Kerns snickers, rounding the back of her vehicle.

Jewel looks up at a complicated parking notice atop an iron pole in the median next to her right front bumper. Though she's well within her rights to PARK on the street outside the hours of 2 PM–6 PM MON THUR FRI, a blanketed NO STANDING rule between 8 AM–2 PM MON TUES WED contradicts her peace of mind.

"Is standing the same thing as parking?" Jewel asks.

Officer Kerns glances at the sign and shrugs. "I guess."

Jewel raises her eyebrows. "You don't *know*?"

"Nobody does." Officer Kerns laughs, turning up the sidewalk that runs parallel to the house's black iron fence. "But don't worry about it. I won't give you a ticket. I promise."

"Have you been a cop long?" Jewel asks, hurrying to catch up with her.

"Long enough," Officer Kerns says.

Which is what someone says when they don't want you to know just how wet under the collar they are.

"You look pretty young to be a cop," Jewel tells the back of her head.

"You only have to be eighteen to join the force. Just like the military."

"You're only eighteen?" Jewel gasps.

"No. I said you only have to *be* eighteen."

"How old are you?"

"Old enough."

"Did you grow up in Ware?"

"No."

Jewel cinches the collar of her blouse against a cold spell blowing in. Possibly off Officer Kerns's shoulder.

"What brought you to town?"

"A series of bad decisions."

Jewel laughs. "I hear you. I don't know why Deidre wanted to move back here. There's nothing to do. I guess the town makes a good setting for a story, though."

Officer Kerns pauses before turning up the sidewalk to the house and looks back at her. "Is Deidre's new novel set in Ware?"

"I don't know," Jewel says. "She's been very hush-hush about it. But it's probably like all her other novels. A galactic *Game of Thrones*. Or something equally as preposterous."

Officer Kerns's eyes are truly shocked. "You're not a fan?"

"No. I am. I appreciate Deidre's talent. I just don't like those kinds of stories. It hurts my head to stretch belief that far into the stratosphere. I like books to be rooted to some sort of reality."

"Reality's no fun," Officer Kerns says, heading up the sidewalk to the house.

Jewel hesitates as Officer Kerns mounts the steps to the front porch.

A conglomeration of brick, stone, and wood, as it had been when Jewel was little, the formerly green pillars of the porch have been painted white. Though the sage color they were was probably more algae than Sherwin-Williams. Like a stopped-up drain, the basin of the Shenandoah Valley never fully dries. Merely steams in the summer months. A season you might miss altogether if you aren't paying attention. Winter springs over summer and falls straight into a pile of snow.

Officer Kerns opens the storm door of the house and turns to look at Jewel, who is still on the sidewalk, staring up at the roof of the porch. Her father standing on it. Hanging Christmas lights. Shackled to the wall by his arms, their blow-up Santa is having a jolly old fit. Both men are smiling, oblivious to the sharp icicles dripping from the dormer above their heads. Animated by the wind, Santa headbutts her father in the shoulder. Her father turns and belts Santa a good one in the nose. Her mother steps forward, draws her wool sweater tighter, and complains that the string of lights is still too low. Snow explodes in Jewel's face, icy hot, and turns her vision fuzzy. The headless snowman she built has sprouted a skull. Deidre smiles devilishly down at her. Bathed in the bloodred glow of Christmas lights, her green eyes look purple.

Jewel flinches as a door to her right slams. Though he can't be the same age as he was thirty years ago, the man strolling down the sidewalk bears an uncanny resemblance to their old neighbor, Mr. Foster. Perhaps he is Mr. Foster's son. Though Jewel can't imagine anyone from the Foster family still living in that house. Cooking dinner in the same kitchen that Mrs.

Foster died in. How could you lower the oven door without thinking of it as a gas chamber?

Though they might wonder the same of Deidre. Of Jewel, if she decides to stay in Deidre's apartment. Though, in fairness, their mother didn't try to bake her head in the oven like a Thanksgiving turkey. But she was the one who discovered the terrible little secret Mrs. Foster had been cooking up. How horrible that must have been. According to Deidre, Mrs. Foster had trussed herself to the oven rack with the belt of her robe to ensure she didn't chicken out before she got good and fricasseed. Their mother tried to pull her free, but quickly became overwhelmed by gas and had to flee the house to call 911. The paramedics said any heroics on their mother's part wouldn't have made a difference. Mrs. Foster's goose had been cooked by then.

"Are you coming?" Officer Kerns asks.

Jewel mounts the steps and finds her mother's fragrance waiting for her on the porch. Emotion tightens around her throat like a vine. She dabs the corner of her eye with a knuckle. The scent of honeysuckle always makes her a little sad.

Expecting to tumble into another memory as the front door of the house swings inward, Jewel recoils as her thoughts run straight into a wall that wasn't there before. A hallway used to be left of the staircase, running past the hideaway doors of the living room and down to the kitchen. The door to apartment 1A now blocks the way.

The door to their old den opens on her right. A thoracically challenged man with hair as black as the rims of his thick glasses stands a bit straighter as he spots Officer Kerns's badge.

"May I help you, Officer?" he says.

"We're looking for Deidre Baldwin's apartment."

"Who is it, Les?" comes a woman's voice from inside.

"It's the police. They're here about Deidre."

"We already spoke to the police," an utterly gray woman informs them as she squeezes into the doorframe next to the man. "We gave them a statement."

"Which didn't amount to much, I'm afraid," the man concludes. "We were asleep at the time." He gestures inside. "But if you'd like to come in, we'd be glad to go over it with you again."

"Thank you, but I'm not here on official business." Officer Kerns motions to Jewel. "This is Ms. Baldwin's sister. She's visiting from out of town."

"Oh, I thought you looked familiar," the woman says.

"Thank you," Jewel says. "People don't usually notice a resemblance."

As the woman tilts her head to consider this, the man says, "I'm sorry about what happened to Deidre. I hope she'll be okay."

Jewel mirrors his encouraged smile. "Me too."

"I'm Lester Willard, by the way. This is my wife, Faye." Mrs. Willard gives Jewel a curt nod. "Let us know if you need anything while you're here. We might live floors apart, but we're still neighbors. Come for dinner anytime. We're having pot roast tonight if you're free."

"Another time, perhaps," Jewel says.

Officer Kerns hooks a thumb at the staircase. "Ms. Baldwin has the attic apartment, I believe?"

"Yes." Mr. Willard limps forward. "I'll show you."

"That's okay," Officer Kerns says. "I'm sure we can find it. Thank you both."

"Yes, thank you." Jewel turns to follow Officer Kerns up the staircase.

"When you see your sister," Mrs. Willard says, "please tell her I didn't mean to upset her."

Jewel pauses before taking a step up and looks back at her. "Whatever for?"

"Oh, we had words the other day." Mrs. Willard lowers her eyes. "I just feel terrible about it."

"She doesn't need to hear about this, Faye." Mr. Willard takes his wife by the elbow. "She has enough to worry about as it is."

"Well, I just feel so bad," Mrs. Willard persists, wrenching free of her husband's grip. "If I'd known it was her, I never would have said anything."

"About what?" Jewel says.

"About all the ruckus she's been making in the cellar. It's right under our bedroom, you know."

"It was a cat, Faye," Mr. Willard says. "I've seen one hanging around the back of the house. It must have gotten into the cellar."

"Cats don't cry like that, Lester."

"You heard crying?" Jewel asks.

"Oh, yes. Several times. It was the most miserable sound. It didn't even sound human."

"Because it was a cat," Mr. Willard notes.

Mrs. Willard shoos the remark away with her hand. "I asked Deidre what she had been doing down there the next time I saw her, and she got very upset with me. She called me a nosy b-i-t-c-h and told me to go to—"

Mr. Willard lets out a disruptive laugh, then pulls his wife firmly into the apartment.

"I'm sure it was just a misunderstanding," he tells Jewel, tightening the door to his reddening cheeks.

"*Not on my part!*" yells Mrs. Willard as the door closes.

4

Officer Kerns is leaning against the wall beside the door of the attic apartment when Jewel finally reaches the top of the four-story staircase. Approximately ten feet wide and five feet deep, the stained knotty pine walls, floor, and ceiling make the attic feel strangely dungeonesque. The overhead light fixture is missing one of its two bulbs. A low-watt fake candle is mounted to the newel post.

Jewel exhales an exerted sigh as she takes the last step up. "Whew! That climb should classify as our workout for the day."

"I definitely felt the burn," Officer Kerns says, cricketing her thumbs over the screen of her phone.

"Me too." Jewel presses a hand to her lower back as she steps onto the landing. "Dee must have rock-hard glutes by now."

Officer Kerns pushes off the wall with a chuckle. "Yeah. Bringing up groceries must be a bitch."

"I forgot how steep that last flight is," Jewel says. "I didn't come up here much when I was a kid."

Doors flank either end of the wide staircase. The one on the right used to be a storage room. The one on the left, cracked with the watery memory of her mother's pacing shadow, is Deidre's new apartment.

"It still feels a little off-limits," she says.

"Attics are creepy," Officer Kerns agrees. "They're like rooftop basements."

Jewel debates telling Officer Kerns about what Mrs. Willard said about hearing Deidre in the cellar but doesn't want to remotely plant the suggestion that they venture down to investigate. Her childhood fear of getting trapped down there is still alive and kicking, ramming a bare shoulder against the bulkhead.

Jewel runs her eyes over the inch-wide seam of the door to Deidre's apartment. Beyond a granite countertop, an office nook, tucked between two dormers, is visible. The lamp in front of a sheer curtain casts a gooseneck shadow over the desk. Bowed deep in thought, the shadow suddenly lifts its head and snaps its mote-filled eyes in Jewel's direction.

"There's something in there!" she screams, backing down the stairs in a crouch.

Officer Kerns presses her back to the wall beside the door. "What was it?"

"I don't know!" Jewel cranes her neck to catch sight of the unusual shadow through the breach in the doorway. The now-vacated desk chair rocks to a stop. A cold breeze dashes from the apartment and runs down Jewel's spine. Deidre's signature perfume mingles with a foul scent. Eau de stopped-up toilette, by Christian Dior. "It was over by the desk," she says. "I only saw it for a second. It looked like a shadow. But then the desk chair started rocking. Like someone had just stood up from it."

"Shit," Officer Kerns breathes, unclasping her service weapon.

"Shouldn't you call for backup?"

"No. I got it."

Officer Kerns takes a deep breath, then presses the door fully open with the palm of her hand. Jewel ducks out of the line of fire as Officer Kerns announces, "Sheriff's Department! Identify yourself!"

After a hushed, terrifying moment, Jewel lifts her head. "I know they're in there. I saw him." A wisp of long, smoky hair clouds her recollection. "Or her. It might have been a woman. I don't know. It looked . . ." *Unformed. Genderless. Inhuman.* "I'm not sure what it was. But I know I saw—"

"Be quiet," Officer Kerns scolds in a whisper. "I'm trying to listen."

"Sorry," Jewel says, then waves the echo of her voice from the air.

Officer Kerns huffs three preparatory breaths before jutting her chin around the corner of the doorframe. Flattened back to the wall, she slides her service weapon from its holster, holds it to her chest in a moment of prayer, then swings her body through the open doorway.

"Sheriff's Department! Sheriff's Department . . ."

Jewel holds a breath behind her squeezed eyelids as Officer Kerns's commanding voice stomps deeper into the apartment, then falls silent. Beyond the terrified drubbing of Jewel's heart, a scuffle ensues. Breathy grunts shuffle feet in a combative circle. A weapon clunks to the floor, then skids across the hardwood. Officer Kerns hisses, "Shit!" a second before a hard thump shudders the step beneath Jewel's knees. A laborious groan drags a limp body across the apartment. A head thumps over an obstacle. Leathery, loose arms brush a chair aside with a raspy whine. A door opens, then closes. Then another. Feet lumber mindlessly toward the apartment's open doorway, advancing on the helpless woman cowering in the stairwell, too choked by fear to scream. To move. To save herself.

"Ms. Maxwell?" Officer Kerns calls from inside.

Jewel opens her eyes. "Yeah?"

"You can come in now."

But Jewel doesn't want to go in. She wants to slide on her butt down to the bottom of the staircase and run from this place forever.

"You sure it's safe?" she asks.

"Positive."

Officer Kerns stands in the settled debris of a shaken snow globe. Surrounded by loose papers, throw pillows, and magazines. Anything not heavy enough to stay pinned down has been relegated to the floor.

"Oh, shit," Jewel says from the doorway. "Deidre *was* robbed."

"It looks like it. But her purse is sitting right there." Officer Kerns nods at the counter that separates the living room from the kitchen. "I haven't opened it to see if her wallet's in there, but I bet it is. That's an expensive bag. A thief wouldn't waste time going through it. They'd just grab it and go."

Jewel steps to the counter and peers inside the Gucci tote. Deidre's wallet is ripe for the taking. She plucks it out with two fingers and holds it up for Officer Kerns to see.

"Told you. Any money inside?"

Jewel unsnaps the wallet and fingers through the loose bills. "Over a hundred dollars." She sets the wallet on the counter and pulls out a set of keys. Ringed on the key fob, one appears to be for the front door. The second key is smaller, roundheaded, and silver. Perhaps to a lockbox or file cabinet.

Jewel dangles the keys at Officer Kerns.

"I'd steal a Mercedes if I were a thief," the officer says.

"How did you know Deidre drives a Mercedes?"

"There's an emblem on the fob."

Jewel turns the keys over and squints at the pale three-point star embossed in the center of the fob, then sets the keys on the counter. She rummages through the remainder of Deidre's bag: Small notebook. Travel pack of tissues. Tin of Altoids. Cell phone charger. But no cell phone.

Jewel glances across the room at the desk, the chair pushed tightly into the leg well.

"I swear I saw someone sitting at her desk," she says.

"Must have been a shadow." Officer Kerns resets a lamp on the side table next to the couch. "I checked everywhere a person could possibly hide."

"Sorry if I alarmed you," Jewel says, feeling foolish.

"Comes with the territory. Why don't you take a look around and let me know if you notice anything missing."

Jewel pivots to glance around the living area.

The interior walls of their mother's former office are covered with Deidre's bad taste in art. Ridiculously expensive pieces only the insanely rich could appreciate. She was with Deidre when she threw away thirty grand on a bunch of squiggly lines that looked remarkably like a bunch of squiggly lines if you tilted your head just right. Jewel had never heard of the artist, no matter how many times Deidre incredulously enunciated their name.

Though Deidre is everywhere she looks, Jewel can't picture her living here. Not as the beautiful, confident woman she once was. She can only picture the hideous face lying in the hospital bed. She could definitely imagine *that* fiend creeping around the attic, scratching herself with a fork.

Her eyes take a quick stroll around the kitchenette to try and see what isn't there.

Though most of the cabinet doors are blown open, the dishes inside are neatly stacked. Glasses stand according to size.

The dish rack beside the sink holds one plate, one bowl, and one coffee mug. A Keurig coffee machine shares a plug with the toaster. The stove is gas. A top-loaded, five-gallon water dispenser is stationed on the slim wall between the counter and the refrigerator. The pale blue jug is optimistically half full.

Jewel shifts her attention toward the dining area across from the kitchen, left of the door. Unaffected by the hurricane that blew through, lace doilies are holding their places in front of each of the four chairs. The exquisite Tiffany lamp Deidre used to have in her New York apartment looks gaudy and out of place over the round country-pine table. Fruit flies swarm a bowl of overripened apples positioned in the center.

"Didn't you say your name was Jewel Maxwell?"

"Yeah," Jewel says, swatting away a gnat before it flies up her nose. "Why?"

Officer Kerns holds up a book for Jewel to see. Red letters leak from the stormy sky of the stock photo. *Thunder Cove.*

"Did you write this?"

Jewel nods. "I'm surprised Dee kept that." The hour-long critique she gave Jewel after reading it was, in Deidre's words, brutally honest. "She absolutely hated it."

"It must be hard having such a famous sister," Officer Kerns imagines, thumbing through the book. "You any good?"

"Good enough."

Officer Kerns catches the inside joke with a smile. "No. Seriously. Are you successful?"

Though she earned a halfway decent living, and a star rating on Amazon, compared to Deidre, Jewel could hardly call herself successful.

"I do okay."

Officer Kerns nods. "That's amazing you and your sister are both authors. That's pretty rare, isn't it?"

"Our mother was a writer too. She had a couple of her short stories printed in *Reader's Digest.* She was working on a full-length novel when she died. Deidre's the only one of us who actually got published, though."

Officer Kerns holds Jewel's paperback up. "You're published."

"I had that printed myself."

"It's still pretty cool. You wrote an entire book. I can't write a halfway decent grocery list."

"Three books, actually," Jewel says. "That one is the first in a series."

"Oh, yeah?" Officer Kerns scans the synopsis on the back of the book. "Sounds interesting."

"I have about a thousand copies left if you want one."

"I read ebooks, mostly." Officer Kerns sets the novel on one of the empty shelves in the built-in bookcase to the left of the hallway. "I'll have to download it."

"Ninety-nine cents on Amazon!" Jewel touts sarcastically, though it is true.

"Sold!" Officer Kerns says.

Jewel starts toward the office nook and stubs up a metal chime with her toe. She picks the vintage Mickey Mouse alarm clock off the floor and turns it over in her hands.

Jewel had given the clock to her mother the Christmas before she died. She displayed it on the mantel like it was an exquisite antique. Jewel hasn't seen the clock since they left the house the night their mother died. Their father returned to pack up all their belongings. Along with furniture that wouldn't fit in the small one-story rambler he rented, most of their mother's things were kept in storage. Jewel and Deidre went through both their belongings after their father died. Anything they both wanted was flipped for. Jewel lost her mother's engagement ring by calling heads, her father's watch to tails. They never flipped for the Mickey Mouse clock, though. Not that Jewel would have won a coin toss. Deidre had been on a hot streak that day. Jewel called it even by slipping a few items into her box when Deidre's back was turned.

Jewel turns the clock over in her hands and wonders if Deidre would notice if it found its way into her suitcase. She gives Mickey's nose a tap and then sets the clock on the edge of the desk.

Though gray with ash, the walnut double-pedestal desk is a beautiful piece. Or was. Jewel pries an extinguished cigarette from the inlaid leather marquetry and drops it in the crowded ashtray. She bends to blow some of the ash away, then stands quickly upright.

"Deidre's laptop is missing," she announces, pointing out a clean rectangular void in the center of the desk.

"I saw it in the bedroom," Officer Kerns says. "It's on the nightstand."

"Oh." Jewel sighs, mildly disappointed. "I thought for sure that was it." She looks around. "Why would someone break into her apartment and not steal anything?"

"Deidre probably caught them in the act. Looks like they might have struggled." Officer Kerns shrugs. "I'm guessing Deidre chased them down. And got hit by a car in the process."

"Deidre wouldn't chase down a criminal. She'd call 911."

"Then they must have been chasing her." Officer Kerns checks her phone as it chimes. "Crap, I have to go."

"Go?" Jewel challenges. "Aren't you going to dust for fingerprints or something?"

Officer Kerns looks around. "I don't think it would do any good. There's no evidence of a crime. Nothing was taken. Deidre could have trashed the place herself, for all we know."

"Why on earth would she do that?"

"You saw her. She looked like . . . I mean . . ." Officer Kerns lets out a sigh before giving it to Jewel straight. "Deidre might not have been in her right mind. That rash must have been driving her nuts. She had been scratching herself with a knife or something. That's not normal behavior. Maybe she went a little crazy and trashed the apartment. I'm not saying that's what happened, but until Deidre wakes up and gives a statement, I can't rule that out as a possibility."

Jewel scoffs. "So you're not going to do anything?"

"I'll write up a report."

"Gee, thanks."

"Sorry, but that's the best I can do for the time being." Officer Kerns checks her phone again. "So are you going to stay here?"

Jewel looks wearily around. "I guess so. Someone needs to clean up this mess. Dee's not going to be in any shape to do it when she gets home."

Jewel escorts Officer Kerns to the door and places a hand on the frame to stop herself from walking out and closing the door on the whole sordid mess. She can't bear the thought of cleaning the apartment. Of making the bed to take a nap.

Officer Kerns crosses the threshold, then turns and hands Jewel a business card. "I've been assigned to this case, so call me if you have any questions."

Jewel turns the card over in her hand, which simply has Officer Kerns's name and phone number printed on it.

5

After popping two Excedrin, Jewel feels moderately upbeat as she cleans the apartment. The playlist blaring through her earbuds does well to drown out her worries. But Deidre's face manages to bleed through in spots.

How Deidre might have contracted such a rare infection is as mysterious as why her apartment smells like rotten eggs. Jewel faintly recalls the water being foul when she lived here. Hard water, her father called it. But she can't recall it being so pungent.

Jewel rears her head from the stench of liquid brimstone as she rinses out her sponge.

Could the water have caused Deidre's skin malady?

It sure as hell smells diseased.

But other people live in the apartment house. They share the same water system. Neither Mr. nor Mrs. Willard looked affected.

Jewel drags a bag of trash into the foyer outside the apartment and sets it next to the stairwell.

A buzzer sounds.

She returns to the small laundry room situated in the short

hallway between the bedroom and bath and checks the load of towels and sheets in the dryer of the stacked laundry machine. Still damp, she cranks the dial for another round.

Ready to take a break, Jewel opens the refrigerator and takes inventory. A half gallon of expired milk. An inch of orange juice. Loaf of wheat bread. Several blocks of cheese. The head of iceberg lettuce has turned, but the bag of baby carrots looks pretty straightforward. She pries off the lid on a tub of hummus and sniffs for an underlying odor. She detects a hint of rotted onion, but the same could be said of her. The deodorant she applied yesterday has long since expired.

She's about to close the refrigerator when she spots a bottle of wine amid an assortment of condiments on the bottom shelf of the door.

Jewel snatches out the bottle, sets it on the counter, and plays Concentration with the cabinets she just closed a moment ago until she finds a wineglass. She pours herself a tall one and reads the label on the bottle during a long, icy sip.

Antica Corte Garganega Pinot Grigio.

Yum.

Topping off her glass, Jewel carries it and her phone to the desk, rolls back the chair, and takes an airy seat on the sumptuous leather. The window above the desk frames a mountain range in the distance. Fog has turned the Blue Ridge gray.

Jewel rises up in the chair and looks down at the backyard, which is now a parking lot. A wave of gravel has wiped out their shed and picnic table. All the bluebells and buttercups. The wild rose bush that contained a scary buzz. Her father used to pick a rose for her mother every morning when they were in bloom.

"*Where have all the flowers gone,*" Jewel sings softly.

She hasn't mourned her mother in a long time. Didn't truly then. The memory of her mother clings like the fossil of an alien creature to the back of her skull. Almost recognizable as grief, but not quite. Another emotion sits at the heart of it. Arms crossed and scowling. Jewel doesn't understand why she feels so angry toward her mother. She spent hours of therapy chipping away at it but only found more levels of guilt. The only nugget of truth she unearthed was a petrified memory of a fight she and her mother had a day or two before her death. Though her therapist thought they had reached the core of understanding, Jewel knows, deep down, that they only scratched the surface. Being pissed at your mother for dying is different than being glad she is dead. Which makes no sense at all. Jewel loved her mother. Recalls more happy times with her than not. So why does the memory of the night she died send a relieved tingle up her arms?

Even now.

Being in the attic of their old house is bound to resurrect some memories. Seeing Deidre hasn't helped. She looked so much like their mother. Especially since she is now the same age their mother was when she died. In that same hospital. After living for a time in this house. Working on a novel.

The parallels are striking.

After her death, Deidre assumed the role of mother in Jewel's life. Though six years doesn't seem like much of an age difference now, when you were eight and fourteen the gap seemed intractable. And someone had to be the boss. Their father was in no position to parent. After they sold the house in Ware, he had to get a real job. His dream of flipping houses for a living started and ended with this one. His job as a home inspector left the girls alone most evenings. Deidre, of course, was put in charge. A job she took a little too seriously. Their sisterly bond became a little unglued during that time. It's difficult to be friends with someone who once thought it was their right to spank your heinie. They mended their differences over the years, mostly by ignoring them, but never seemed to fully reconnect. Deidre's success launched her into another hemisphere. All Jewel had to hold on to was a grudging respect for her fame and fortune. Still, they are the only family either of them has left.

It is Jewel's turn to play mother now.

She'll stay as long as Deidre needs her. Which she hopes won't be more than a week. She left her husband hanging from the proverbial cliff and hopes Cal can hang on until she returns. The job he just started isn't working out. Jewel could fire up her laptop and work him through a few issues from here, but it isn't the same as being at home. Behind her own desk. With all her Post-it Notes on the wall in front of her. She should have brought them with her, but the news about Deidre's accident threw her for a loop. Still, she should have taken a moment to make sure Cal was set up for the next chapter of his life.

God, she misses him already.

Jewel rests her head on her folded arms atop the desk and tries to imagine Cal's face. But Deidre's gruesome visage nudges him aside and chases Jewel into a nightmare.

"Go on," Deidre says, holding up one of the bulkhead doors of the cellar.

Crouched at the mouth, the dusty tongue of wood stairs vanishes halfway down the base of the cellar's throat. A bare light bulb hangs like a uvula from the ceiling. Dark with dust, it swings softly from an exhaled draft. Pungent with the stench of mold.

A harrowing scream jumps out of the second-floor window and lands in a crouch on Jewel's bladder.

"Girrrls!" a voice screeches from inside the house. "Wherrrre are yooou?"

Deidre grabs Jewel's ankles like the handles of a wheelbarrow and drives her forward.

Splintery wood strums her chest as Jewel slides headfirst down the dark stairwell. Her chin slams her teeth together as it hits the bottom. She twists onto her back to plead with Deidre, but she's crying too hard to catch her breath.

"I'll let you out in the morning," Deidre says, looking down at her. She flashes worried eyes up at the house, cries, "Shit!" and slams the slatted wood door.

Terror swoops in like bats. Jewel gets to her knees and scrambles up the steps. She has to reach the door before the lock clasps. No time to lift her hand, she rams the top of her head against the bulkhead. Unyielding pain shoots down the back of her neck and across her shoulders. Jewel falls backward. An end-over-end flip that stands her briefly upright. She swings her hand at the light bulb. Pain explodes through her palm as the glass balloon pops. The floor knocks the air from her chest, all coherent thought from her head.

Jewel wakes with a coughing gasp. It takes several blinks to realize she's risen four stories above their old cellar. She toggles her wrist to activate the screen of her smartwatch and squints at the display.

4:41 p.m.

She's been asleep for roughly three hours.

A woozy stumble carries her to the bathroom. The mirror over the sink is unkind. The foundation she applied the day before has broken down into its original components. Somehow flaky and oily at the same time, tiny mushrooms have begun to sprout on either side of her nose.

Pure, clear egg slime gushes from the faucet as the spigot cranks on.

Jewel grabs a breath of fresh air over her shoulder, then holds it while she cups the hard, foul-scented water onto her face. Suspect of Deidre's clinically extravagant facial cleanser, she squints an eye at the pump bottle of Dial hand soap. Same as the one on her sink at home. Though it's most likely not the cause of Deidre's allergic reaction, she's hesitant to use something so harsh on her face.

She blots her cheeks dry with an unabsorbent decorative hand towel and turns from the mirror before her hair can beg to be washed.

Her reflection turns in the opposite direction.

Jewel does a double take at the mirror. Her reflection blinks innocently back at her. Turns its head side to side, as she does. Puffs its cheeks out. Slumps its shoulders. Cocks its head. Rights it. Frowns at a pimple. Rubs the blemish with its forefinger. Drops its hand. Sighs. And tells Jewel,

"You look like shit."

Jewel runs a hand through her hair and gets a whiff of her armpit. Though a shower might actually make her smell worse, at least she'll be stinky clean.

Her blouse is halfway over her head when a phone rings.

She pauses to listen, then yanks her filthy shirt back over her sweat-damp skin and hurries out of the bathroom. Skirting the corner of the couch, she snatches her phone from the desk and looks to see who's calling.

No one.

The screen is dark.

Remains dark as a phone rings again.

Jewel scans the top of the desk, then slides open the thin center drawer. Pencils. Pens. Highlighters. A yellow pack of American Spirit cigarettes and a purple BIC lighter.

The phone rings again. Loud. Right in front of her. On the desk.

"Where the fuck is it!"

She lifts a legal pad to look underneath, then drops to a knee to check beneath the desk. Light winks in the far back right corner. Jewel sweeps her hand around the floor and connects with a rectangular object. She pulls the phone out from under the desk and sits back on her heels.

A web of crystallized glass hugs the top left corner of the screen. The name on the caller ID hangs like a rare spider at the end of a splintered thread.

Emily Channing.

Deidre's literary agent.

6

Jewel swipes right to answer and slams the phone to her ear.

"Hello?"

"You promised you'd call me today. It's five o'clock already. I have a call with Jason and Claire first thing tomorrow morning. I can't put them off any longer. We have to give them something."

"Sorry, but—" Jewel tries.

"They don't want excuses, Deidre. They want the novel. They don't care if it isn't perfect. You can touch it up in the first round of edits."

Jewel releases the bite of her lip. "This isn't Deidre. I just answered her phone."

"Oh. Sorry. May I speak with her, please?"

"No. I mean, yes, of course, you may. But she isn't here right now. Can I take a message?"

"Who is this?"

Hoping to think faster on her feet, Jewel pushes out of the chair and quickly trips over her words.

"I'm Dee's . . . I mean, Deidre's. Sister. Jewel. Baldwin.

I mean, Maxwell. Sorry. I had to run for the phone, and I'm a little frazzled."

"Take your time, dear."

Emily Channing is one of the top literary agents in New York. Jewel has longed for an introduction. Just five minutes to pitch her a story or two. She begged Deidre to send Emily one of her manuscripts, but Deidre didn't want to put Emily on the spot. Jewel understood. If things went south—or north, for that matter—it could cause friction between everyone involved. Still, Jewel could dream. Of landing an agent like Emily Channing. All she needs is a chance to make a good first impression.

That chance is now.

And she is blowing it.

Jewel takes a moment to untie her tongue. "I'm Jewel Maxwell. Deidre's sister."

There. Phew.

"Oh, yes. Deidre's mentioned you." Emily's voice sounds nasal, as if she has a cold. Maybe spring allergies. "You're a writer, aren't you?"

Pride explodes up Jewel's throat in a resounding, "Yes!"

"She sent me a sample of your work a while back. I haven't had a chance to review it, but Deidre tells me your writing is quite exceptional."

The revelation lowers Jewel to the chair. "*She did?*"

"You sound surprised."

"No. It's just that . . . I didn't know Deidre had sent you any of my work."

In fact, Jewel is sure that Deidre stated something to the contrary. Maybe she didn't want Jewel to get her hopes up if Emily came back with a negative response. But Jewel seriously doubts that Deidre ever called her work exceptional, much less *quite*. Emily was probably just being polite.

"Do you know how I can reach her?" Emily asks. "It's very important."

Jewel takes a deep breath to break the bad news. "I'm sorry, but Deidre is in the hospital."

"Hospital?" Disbelievingly, as though Jewel used the incorrect word for the bathroom.

"She was hit by a car." Though that's the truth, given Deidre's condition, it somehow feels deceptive. "She's in pretty bad shape."

"Oh, no!" Emily exclaims. "When was this?"

"Last night. Or early this morning. I flew in from Hartford to be with her. I'm staying at her apartment while I'm here. That's why I answered her phone."

"Is she going to be okay?"

"I don't know. She's currently in a coma."

"Oh, my god. I'm so sorry to hear that. Do they have any idea when she might come to?"

"Her doctor said that only time will tell."

"Unfortunately, that's the one thing Deidre doesn't have. I'm not sure if you're aware, but . . ." Emily hesitates before coming out with it. "Deidre's been having some financial issues. Things were bad enough without hospital bills piling up around her. Something like this could ruin her."

Jewel straightens in her chair. "What do you mean? Deidre has money. She's rich."

"Not like she used to be," Emily confides. "The royalty checks from her previous novels have all but dried up. And she put the last of her savings into that damn house in Virginia."

Jewel looks around the apartment, stunned to learn that Deidre actually bought the house, and that it is still a money pit after all these years.

"She hoped living there might inspire her," Emily continues.

"She wanted to reacquaint herself with the girl she used to be. The girl who loved to write. Before fame sucked all the fun out of it. It was working too. I hadn't heard Deidre so excited about a project in a long time. Everything was going fine until . . ."

"Until what?"

"When we spoke a couple of weeks ago, she said that the book was getting to her. She wasn't sure if she was going to be able to finish it. I almost had a heart attack. The advance she received from the publisher is contingent on her meeting the deadline. Which is next Friday. If she misses it, she'll have to repay the advance. Which she doesn't have anymore." Emily sighs. "I probably shouldn't be telling you all this, but if you know what's going on with her, maybe you can work out a payment plan with the hospital."

Jewel slumps back in her chair, half listening, half wondering how much she could hock Deidre's squiggle art for.

"I know this might sound insensitive, given Deidre's situation," Emily says, "but you don't know if she finished her new novel, do you?"

"I'm sorry, I don't."

"I'm going to be frank with you, Jewel. Deidre needs to get this book submitted by the deadline. It's extremely important. I think we can still make it, but I'm going to need your help."

Willing to do anything this side of murder to please this woman, Jewel's heart jumps at the chance to make a literary giant like Emily Channing feel beholden to her, and lodges halfway up her windpipe.

"Of course," Jewel wheezes, clutching her throat to keep her voice under control. "Whatever you need."

"I need you to find out if the book is finished," Emily says. "It could be sitting in her outbox ready to send. Is there any way you could . . . I wouldn't normally ask, but I know how important this is to Deidre. Could you open her laptop and see if you can find the manuscript? Find out where she is on it. If it's done, I know she would want me to submit it for her."

"Wouldn't she have submitted the novel if it were finished?"

"Not necessarily. She still had over a week to go on her extension. She might have been using the time to put some finishing touches on it. I don't care if the novel's not perfect. As long as it's finished, we're good to go. Is there any way you can check her files for me? See if you can find it?"

"I'd be glad to. But I don't think I can access her laptop. I don't know her password."

"I didn't think about that." Emily sighs. "Oh, well . . . It was worth a shot."

"She might have written it down somewhere," Jewel wagers.

"Could you look around for it?" Emily says excitedly. "I know it's a lot to ask, but it would mean a lot to me. And to Deidre. You have to try, Jewel."

"I'll do my best. Even if she didn't write her password down, it shouldn't be that hard to figure out." Deidre isn't very security conscious. Her ATM pin was 1234 until Jewel made her change it.

"Great." Emily's voice contains a happy clap. "If you find the manuscript, can you forward it to me right away?"

"Do you want me to send it to you whether it's finished or not?"

"Let's hope it is."

"But if it's not?" Jewel presses. "What are you going to do then?"

"I guess that depends on how close Deidre was to finishing it. If it just needs a few loose ends tied up, I'll hire a ghostwriter to finish it. But it would have to be someone Deidre trusts implicitly. Someone she knows and respects."

Jewel fits only one of those bills.

But didn't Deidre tell Emily that her writing was exceptional? Quite. Though that didn't necessarily mean she thought it was good. People with mental challenges are often referred to as exceptional. That doesn't make them talented.

But Jewel is.

As far as Emily knows, anyway.

"But one thing at a time," Emily says. "First, I have to find out the status of the novel. Then I can decide what to do next."

Jewel snatches a block of Post-its off the side of the desk and clicks open a ballpoint pen. "What's the title of her new novel?"

"I don't think she had settled on one yet."

"How will I know what to look for?" Though it shouldn't be too difficult to recognize. All of Deidre's titles were contrived from some Middle-earth name generator: *The Mountains of Cali. Sundown on Sagittarius. Reigns of Tempria. The Herzone Conflict.*

"The novel is a departure from the speculative fiction Deidre normally writes," Emily says. "That's what I meant when I said the publisher was taking a risk with her on this one. They went into this endeavor completely blind. If it wasn't a Deidre Baldwin novel, they never would have agreed to publish it sight unseen. But her name alone sells copies. They just had to trust that a change in genre wouldn't turn off her fan base."

"What genre is it?"

The smile slides off Jewel's face as Emily voices the last genre she would have expected Deidre to immerse herself in.

"Horror."

7

If Deidre had bothered to write her password down, there is a good chance Jewel threw away the scrap of paper it was written on with all the other scraps of paper that had been strewn around the apartment when she arrived. Though she is able to access Deidre's phone by using her date of birth, her Apple password proves to be more challenging.

Jewel deletes her last failed attempt, *Deidrespassword9*, and takes a sip of wine.

Almost certain that the password will contain Deidre's birthday in some manner, she types in Deidre's birth month, day, and year in a continuous formation, then hits Enter. Not a match. She adds a zero to the month of February and hits Enter again.

Your Apple ID or password is incorrect.

"No shit," Jewel says, then glances at the clock on the desk.

Mickey's arms are slack at his sides.

6:35 p.m.

Though Dr. Leonetti said she could visit anytime, Jewel would rather not be in Deidre's room after dark. Factoring in the fifteen-minute drive, the time it would take to park and make her way to the ICU, if she left this instant, she still wouldn't get to Deidre's room until well after seven o'clock. And she has to freshen up first. At least brush her teeth and change her clothes. She's been wearing the same outfit for almost twenty-four hours. A clean blouse isn't going to cut it. She needs a shower. A decent meal. A legitimate reason not to go to the hospital and see Deidre. She can't bear the thought of looking at her again. Being alone with her as night shadows creep from the corners of her hospital room and drag them both into *The Twilight Zone*. Or an episode of *Tales from the Crypt*. Where anything is possible. Especially for someone whose imagination can stretch to *The Outer Limits*. No. Jewel can't risk being in that hospital room after dark. Isn't all too sure she wants to be in the attic apartment of this old house after dark either. But what choice does she have? She has to figure out a way to access Deidre's laptop. Her entire career could be riding on it.

Jewel stares dejectedly at the time on the clock. She cocks her head at it, then sits quickly forward and types *mickeymouse* into the password box.

The screen opens.

"Yes!"

She scans the Word files on the MacBook's hard drive for a title that fits the horror genre. *Blood Moon over Venus* catches her eye. But the title sounds too much like a Deidre Baldwin novel. Emily said her current book is a departure from her normal fantasy fiction. Jewel's about to click on it anyway when she spots a link to Deidre's iCloud account. Though most of the Word files match those on her hard drive, one title jumps out and grabs her.

Unspeakable Demons.

As the document opens and words begin to fill the page,

Jewel watches the word count tick swiftly upward. She bounces her knee impatiently but doesn't have to wait long. She leans forward to get a closer look at the stalled amount in the lower left-hand corner of the screen.

Page 1 of 208

62,720 words

Deidre's other novels were three times that length.

Though fantasy fiction takes more than a few thousand words to effectively build and populate a utopian universe, a horror thriller could conceivably be resolved in sixty thousand. Jewel's own novels—which were nowhere near as complicated as Deidre's, and were routinely criticized on Amazon for being padded with enough fluff to sleep comfortably on, which readers claimed to have done halfway through reading them—hovered around the one hundred thousand mark.

Sixty-two thousand words was pretty slim for a full-length novel. Of any genre.

A window in the lower right corner of the screen pops up and welcomes Jewel back. Asks if she would like to pick up where she left off twenty-seven days ago.

Twenty-seven days?

Why hasn't Deidre been working on it?

Even if the novel was finished, there is always more editing to do. And if the editing process was complete, the manuscript would have been submitted. You don't let a finished novel sit in the drawer for almost a month. Not with a deadline sinking fast on the horizon.

Though Jewel is eager to jump to the last page and find out how the story ends, with a bang or a whimper, she ignores the prompt and stares at the title page in wonder. Which is all there is. A title. Deidre hasn't put her name to it yet.

Is it so bad that she couldn't bring herself to take credit for it?

Or has the genre scared her off?

Deidre doesn't even like to read scary books. They cause her actual, physical pain. Make her bones ache. She clenched her teeth so hard while reading *The Southern Book Club's Guide to Slaying Vampires* by Grady Hendrix that she thought she had cracked a molar. Jewel didn't find that one particularly terrifying. There was enough humor and social commentary to offset the gore. But Deidre hadn't taken those diverting moments to heart. Hard to do when you knew someone was about to pound a stake through it. But Deidre didn't even try. She returned the book to Jewel half finished.

Horror novels aren't my cup of tea, she recalls Deidre saying.

Then why is she writing one?

Jewel's frown tightens as she pages down and reads the first paragraph of the preface.

I'm afraid to write this. Afraid doing so will summon the muse. My innermost evil. That it will take these words as an invitation. Pervade my sleepless nights with vile contemplations, pollute clarity with its foul breath, whisper wrongs against my eardrum. I can feel the worm of a loathsome thought writhing to the surface. Marching like fire ants up my arms. The itch is unbearable.

Itch?

Jewel leans away from the screen as though the word itself is contagious.

Deidre told Emily that the story was getting to her.

How far had it gotten?

Jewel scratches a psychosomatic mosquito bite on her right forearm, then flinches as words in the next paragraph spring out at her.

Atrocities . . . depravity . . . snapped . . .

Jewel shakes her head. She doesn't want to get caught up in the story. Not yet. Not with dusky fingers lowering nightshade over the window. She can read later. Right now, she's on a mission. She needs to let Emily know the status of Deidre's book. Is it finished? That is the question.

Jewel right-clicks the sidebar of the Word document and selects Bottom.

A blank page fills the screen. She arrows slowly up, hoping to find the two magic words she's looking for centered on the page. If they're there, she can drop the document into an email and shoot it off to Emily. Out of sight, out of mind. Well beyond the reach of her imagination.

Of course the novel didn't turn Deidre into the revolting creature lying in that hospital bed. But Jewel could be easily convinced of it. One poignantly described sentence could claw the idea forward. Drag it out from under the bed and drive her slowly up a wall. Though Jewel struggles with creating an eerie, atmospheric setting in her novels, she has no problem envisioning one as she reads another author's work. The right analogy could turn her bedroom into a hellscape so vivid that the author themselves would be awestruck.

Deidre is the master of descriptive writing. She can take you there. Plop you in a field of flowers so cloyingly brilliant you just might sneeze. One sentence can make you pull the blankets over your kneecaps, cold as a snowy mountain range. Or kick them off as she drags your eyes across a desert wasteland. Since her novels are all set on a distant planet, Jewel can easily fight off the monsters Deidre sicced on her readers. Multieyed rock formations aren't likely to be stomping through this neighborhood. But this novel isn't set in the mountains of Cali. And it won't be animated rock formations that will wake Jewel from a sound sleep. This book contains unspeakable demons.

And Deidre has given them a voice. A hissing whisper that could pry Jewel's eyes open in the middle of the night. Wondering if it was the wind that woke her or the labored breath of a fiend.

Hopefully, she won't have to find out.

If the novel is finished, she won't have to suffer through it. Done is done. But if it isn't finished, which the meager word count in the lower left-hand corner suggests, she'll have no choice but to read it. She can't just leave Deidre in a bind. How would that look to Emily? By accepting the challenge of hacking into Deidre's laptop to find the novel, Jewel has effectively joined the team. Emily needs her help. Finding the manuscript is just her first assignment. Sending Emily a half-finished novel won't earn Jewel any points.

But finishing one . . .

Now that would be something.

Jewel edited some of Deidre's earlier work. Rewrote most of the dialogue. That was the one area Deidre deferred to Jewel on. Jewel has a knack for it. Probably from all the dialogue she runs through her head on a daily basis. She can hold a conversation with a character for hours. She forgets half of what they said by the time she sits down to write, but they still speak volumes over some of Deidre's glib banter.

As Jewel clicks the cursor slowly upward, two sets of three letters appear on the screen. Though they are appropriately positioned and capitalized, they are not the words she was expecting to find. In fact, they aren't words at all.

YJR RMF

"What the hell?"

Jewel scrolls up, eyes widening as line after line of well-punctuated gibberish consumes the page. The last three being:

Dyp[trsfomh yjod Yjr ,idr od trs; Oyd eptfd eo;; vptti[y upit ,omf {rtbrty upit dpi; <slr upi fp jptton;r yjomhd Yjod dyptu eo;; im;rsdj jr;; pm rstyj V;pdr upit rurd Fpm"y ;ry oy om

Jewel studies the mumbo jumbo for a moment, then fingers the trackpad downward until she spots words that actually make sense.

My stomach clenched with fear. I couldn't keep my sister from reading these deplorable words any more than I could stop myself from writing them. I knew that she would read them, devour them like pieces of tampered candy on Halloween. Her death scene was already in the works. And I was the one who had constructed it. Every word I wrote drove the knife a little deeper. Widened the slit in her throat. Squeezed another drop of acid into her pried-open eye. Words kill. I knew that now. And I am powerless to stop it. For she has already begun to read this.

Chair now between her and the portent of the last sentence, Jewel swallows back the urge to scream. To call Emily and tell her that she couldn't locate the manuscript on Deidre's laptop. Pack her bags, return her rental car, and resume her semifulfilling career as a self-published author.

No.

She can't let the book scare her off.

This could be her big chance. The one she's been waiting for. Fantasizing about for years. The novel isn't finished. Not really. It still needs an ending. At least one written in English. Jewel can do it. Ghostwrite the hell out of this thing. Finishing the novel is her way in. A way to grab Emily's attention. If she does a good job, maybe Emily will be interested in taking her on as a client.

Eager to throw her hat in the ring before she chickens out, Jewel picks Deidre's phone off the desk to call Emily. She stares at it a moment, then sets it back on the desk.

Emily has probably left the office for the day. She'll call her in the morning. Tell her the book isn't finished. Let Emily take it from there. She might not even want Jewel to work on it. It was wishful thinking that she might. Emily doesn't know Jewel. Hasn't read a word of her work. She'd think Jewel mad for even suggesting that she could finish writing a Deidre Baldwin novel. But what choice does Emily have? Jewel is her best hope of meeting the deadline.

But why did it have to be a horror novel?

Jewel jumps to the top of the document and rereads the daunting preface.

I hate that I find some joy in it. Writing such horrors. That such depravity is in me. Under my skin, contentedly constricted around my bones . . .

Jewel massages a discomforting ache from the tops of her thighs.

Just because *Unspeakable Demons* is written in the first person doesn't make it biographical. It is a piece of fiction.

That's what the muse wants. To get under your skin. That spidery tickle on the back of your neck? That's the muse. Fiddling with your nerves . . .

Jewel rubs a faint tickle from under her collar and closes the lid of the laptop.

"It's just a story," she says aloud.

Keep telling yourself that.

"Shut up," Jewel tells the scaredy-cat pacing around inside her head, hoping it won't follow her into the bedroom and crawl under the covers with her. Pervade her sleepless nights with vile contemplations, pollute clarity with its foul breath, and whisper wrongs against her eardrum.

Jewel flicks on the overhead light as she enters the bedroom and chases a disturbing shadow under the bed. Though its horns seemed too billy goatish to slip under the frame without clanging against it, the low growl she heard just before ninety watts of light bleached the creature from existence lowers Jewel to a knee.

There's nothing under the bed.

Nor in her stomach, she realizes, as it lets out another growl.

8

"So I should do it?" Jewel asks Cal through a bite of her grilled cheese sandwich. Though Camembert wasn't her first choice of ingredient for the all-American comfort food, it was the only cheese in Deidre's fridge that hadn't begun to mold.

"Of course," Cal says. "This is a great opportunity. You should take full advantage of it."

"But aren't I taking advantage of *Dee*? She's in the hospital fighting for her life. I should be concentrating on getting her well. Not my career."

"It's not like you wanted this to happen. There's nothing you can do for Deidre. Except sit at her bedside. And that won't change anything."

"I know, but—"

"And you don't owe Deidre anything. She's never helped you. Not once. And she could have. Easily."

Jewel sets her dirty plate on the nightstand, lies back on the bed, and swings her feet into the air. She toggles her ankles to catch the light in the faux-diamond strap of Deidre's Jimmy Choo Aurelie patent leathers. At least she thinks the stones are fake. For what Deidre paid for the shoes, they could be real diamonds.

"She did send one of my novels to Emily."

Cal scoffs. "The least she could do. If Deidre really wanted Emily to take your work seriously, she would have pressed her to read it. She would have followed up. Emily just tossed your book on her pile of TBRs and forgot about it."

"What if I don't do a good job?"

"Of course you'll do a good job. You're an amazing writer."

Jewel snuffs a deprecating chuckle. "Yeah, I'm *exceptional.*"

"Yes. You are. In the best sense of the word. Why do you always look for an insult hidden in a compliment?"

"Because with Deidre there usually is one."

"Which is exactly why you shouldn't worry about her feelings."

"I'm not worried about her feelings. I'm worried that I might not do a good job."

"You've already come this far. Success is hanging right in front of you. All you have to do is reach out and grab it."

Cal makes it sound so easy. As if success were a piece of jewelry she could shoplift anytime she felt like it.

She toggles her wrist to get Deidre's sapphire tennis bracelet to catch the light. Her DIY manicure clashes with the expensive bauble.

Cal lets out a weary sigh. "What excuse are you going to use this time?"

"I'm scared."

"Fear is all in your head."

"No," she says, kicking off Deidre's shoes. "It's on the pages of that book."

She disconnects with Cal, sets the shoes in their silver box, and slides it back into position on the top shelf of the closet.

She's about to close the door when she spots something of interest.

Pressed onto her tiptoes, Jewel works the hard gray plastic box out by its handle. The weight of it is unexpected and yanks her arm heavily downward as it slips from the shelf. Supporting the base with her other hand, she turns to the dresser and sets the strongbox on the corner.

Though it's equipped with a combination lock, the latches spring upward as she thumbs the release bolts sideways. Based on its weight and size, Jewel suspects what the box might contain. Still, as she raises the lid on Deidre's little secret, a startled gasp escapes her.

Though she's alone in the apartment, Jewel looks instinctively around before touching the firearm.

She's never held a gun before. And to her knowledge, neither had her sister. *Where did Deidre even get a gun?* She can't picture Deidre attending a gun show in her Jimmy Choos. Sashaying her Versace-clad ass into a pawn store and tapping a French-tipped nail on the scuffed display case. One of her high-class friends—one of the ones Deidre was embarrassed to introduce her unaccomplished, country bumpkin of a sister to—probably had a private showing at her Park Avenue penthouse. *Cristal and Pistols.* Pearl-handle gift bags for their revolvHers. As if Jewel would be caught dead at such a pretentiously dangerous event.

She doesn't fault Deidre for owning a gun. A woman living alone "aught" to have some protection. Especially in New York City. Jewel has considered getting a gun a time or two herself, but Cal always talks her out of it. And as Jewel stares pensively down at the weapon in front of her, she now understands why. There is something vaguely hypnotic about having an instrument of death at your fingertips.

Jewel runs her pinkie along the gun's silky barrel, then closes the lid. She reaches to slide the strongbox back on the top shelf of the closet and blenches from the oniony fume rising from her armpit. Though standing upright for ten more minutes will require a feat of strength she doesn't think she has in her, if she doesn't shower before bed, she'll be as rank as one of Deidre's goat cheeses by morning.

The sound of a door closing turns the water down a degree or two in Jewel's shower.

Did I lock the front door?

She thought she had. After Officer Kerns left. But then she dragged a bag of trash out into the hallway. She meant to relock the door when she returned to the apartment but can't picture herself doing it. She didn't set the chain. She would remember doing that. Flipping the lock on the knob with her thumb as she closed the door behind her is a rote action. She could have done it without thinking.

But did she?

Jewel peeks around the shower curtain.

Though steam is venting into the hallway through the open door of the bathroom, fog has crept over the mirror. Her mind worriedly paces something into being behind the thin layer of mist. A hulking mass of watery gray flesh.

Panting on the *backside* of the mirror.

Just tired enough to believe she will not be able to clear the mirror with a swipe of her hand, Jewel frets whether the thing is inside the mirror. Or standing in the hallway behind it.

She squints an eye against the sting of shampoo and contemplates the slumped shoulders of the shadow on the floor of the hallway.

"Hello?" she asks, praying for no response.

The shadow remains stock-still. As if caught. Waiting for Jewel to dismiss it. To slip back under the water and forget that it was ever there.

Jewel grabs a towel off the rack, blots soap from her face, and studies the floor of the hallway with a clearer eye.

The shadow is gone.

Where did it go?

What was it doing?

She should have brought Deidre's gun into the bathroom with her. And what? Set it in the soap dish? Hide it under a hand towel on the sink like a Bond girl? She doesn't even know how to use the damn thing. She'd be more apt to shoot herself in the foot than an intruder in the face.

Jewel wraps the towel around herself and steps from the tub. She stands there for a moment, listening to the apartment. The constant spray of water drowns out all other sounds. She debates turning the water off but doesn't want to let on that she's out of the shower and on the move.

Thick suds slide over her shoulders and down the center of her back. Bubbles of shivering cold burst across her skin. She curls her toes into the plush bath mat and summons the nerve to take a step toward the open doorway.

A dish rattles in the kitchen sink on the other side of the apartment.

Or was it a knife being slipped from a drawer?

The edge of the door catches the edge of the bath mat as Jewel shoves it closed with both hands. She lets out a frustrated cry and kicks the mat out of the way with her foot.

Whatever's lurking in the kitchen turns at the sound and bounds across the apartment in time with her pounding heart.

The bath mat bunches into an impenetrable jam as the long-haunched fiend leaps effortlessly over the couch. Jewel bends quickly down and flings the mat aside, along with her foot out from under her. She catches herself with the towel rack, pulls it from the drywall, and hits the floor with the slap of a hairy foot kicking off the living room wall. Her cry mingles with the creature's elated howl as she scrambles forward. A long-clawed paw slams the other side of the door just as it connects with the frame.

Door barred with her shoulder, Jewel flips the lock after three panicky attempts of her slippery fingers.

Collapsed onto the floor, she stares at the bathroom ceiling and waits for the beast to stop mocking the terrified pant of her breath, the whimper of her childish cries. Her complete and utter ridiculous behavior.

Jewel sits up knowing that she is alone in the apartment. That the only beast terrorizing her is that of her own imagination.

She's been here before. Not lying in a puddle of sweaty soap on the bathroom floor, but she's been known to karate chop a closet full of innocent clothing a time or two. She maced a bag of mulch she had forgotten was in the back seat of her car. Called 911 instead of the Orkin man when she heard a strange scratching coming from the crawl space.

She thinks back on the first sound that caught her attention while she was in the shower. A door closed. As if someone had entered the apartment. Though Jewel might have allowed her worry to grow legs and run wild with assumptions, she hadn't invited the original fear in.

But now it is here; it has her surrounded.

Jewel presses an ear to the door but can't hear anything over the thrum of water in the shower. She reaches in and turns it off, then runs her nose along the seam of the closed door, snuffling for anything out of the ordinary. The musk of wet fur. Men's cologne. An ethereal hint of ozone.

Detecting none of the above, she lowers to the floor, but the crack along the bottom of the door is too slim to see through.

Jewel sits back on her heels.

If this were a scene in a tropey horror novel, the main character—a stereotypically stupid chick, most likely named Carol—would shrug her shoulders, declare the apartment safe, and get a knife through the eye as soon as she opened the bathroom door. Though, in all likelihood, Carol would have been soaking in a tub of warm blood by now. But if she had made it this far, would she really go out blind? Not knowing what terror awaited her around the corner?

Not if Jewel were writing the scene. Her character—let's call her Jewel, for argument's sake—would be prepared to fight off whatever came at her.

9

Armed with a Sally Hansen nail file, Jewel steps into the hallway and takes a quick peek at Deidre's bedroom. You can't sneak into the closet or under the bed without moving her suitcase first, which looks exactly how she left it. A jumbled mess. She considers going for the gun but doesn't have time to watch a YouTube video on how to load one. Chamber a round. Work the safety. Take aim when your hand is shaking like a leaf.

Nail file gripped in her right hand, Jewel reaches awkwardly around the corner of the hall with her left and feels around for a light switch.

There isn't one.

She squints across the dark living room at the front door.

The chain is set.

Not quite on the safe side yet, Jewel moves cautiously across the living room. She stabs the air with the nail file as she rounds the kitchen counter, then straightens from her crouch. Though a beastly scent is hiding in the sink, a little squirt of Dawn in the dirty frying pan chases it away.

Jewel's headed back to the bathroom to finish rinsing her

hair when she senses someone watching her. A quick turn of her head presses a shadow into the far corner of the dinette, but a second glance proves it to be just that. A shadow. Nothing more.

Until she turns her back on it.

Then it grows fangs. Claws. Large as life.

She can't look. If she looks, fear will win.

Carol would look.

"I'm not fucking Carol!" she scolds herself. "I'm Jewel Maxwell. A grown woman with a level head who doesn't jump at every shadow."

Case of the nerves shaken off, Jewel lifts her chin and marches toward the bathroom.

Retracing the same path she entered the living room by, for which there is only one, there shouldn't be any obstacles in her way. That her scream is more from surprise than pain won't matter to the dead she just woke.

She slaps a hand over her mouth as she looks down at the picture frame she stubbed into the wall.

Though she's seen this portrait before, she never noticed how tight all their smiles seemed. As though they somehow knew this would be the last family picture ever taken and they needed to make it count. Taken approximately where the Willards might currently have their couch positioned, theirs had been pushed aside to make room for an insanely large Christmas tree.

Though her mother lived until the following June, and many pictures had been taken of the house during its renovation, there hadn't been another family moment worth capturing. When they were dressed in something other than paint-splattered smocks. They hadn't gone as far as to put on dresses or a tie, but their shirts and sweaters were clean and vaguely Christmasy. Insomuch that they all contained a trace of red or green. Except for her mother's. Her shirt was white. But the rash on her chest and arms was as bright as Rudolph's nose.

Jewel picks the picture up off the floor and leans in for a closer look.

Her mother had gotten the poison ivy while pulling weeds along the fence line of the backyard. Deidre also had gotten a mild case. And though Jewel had worked alongside them, she hadn't gotten a single dot on her skin. Deidre's poison ivy was somewhat mild, just a few patches around her neck and shoulders that went away after a few days. But being highly allergic, their mother's outbreak had lasted for weeks.

Allergic?

Could the mysterious rash plaguing Deidre be a simple case of poison ivy?

Surely Dr. Leonetti would have immediately recognized such a commonplace irritant. But he might not have jumped to that conclusion while examining someone as sophisticated as Deidre. And hers isn't a simple case of poison ivy. Deidre is sheathed head to toe in it. She didn't accidentally brush a vine with her hand. She rolled naked through a virulent patch. Deidre isn't exactly outdoorsy. She doesn't like to hike or camp out. Unless it is on the couch in front of the TV with a glass of wine in her hand. Though Jewel wouldn't have expected her sister to be running down the street in the middle of the night in her jammies either.

Had she been sleepwalking? Acting out a nightmare? One that had chased her into the night? Through a field of poison ivy?

Jewel scratches her head to contemplate this and works some suds up on her scalp.

No way is she getting back in that shower. She'll rinse her head in the sink and wipe down the rest of her body with a damp washcloth.

She's about to lay the family portrait back on the floor, then feels around the back of the frame. She extends the cardboard stand and positions the picture upright on the center bookshelf.

Though it makes her a little melancholy to look at, the photograph deserves to be displayed.

Fear tightens Jewel's throat as a splotch in the photograph seizes her attention.

She didn't notice a defect in the photograph when she originally looked at it, but now she's seen it, she can't believe she missed the dark smudge just under her mother's chin. Choking her like a hand.

Jewel wipes the glass with the corner of her robe, then toggles the frame to dislodge the unusual shadow. The choker around her mother's neck hangs tight. Jewel squints to see it more clearly, then carries the picture into the kitchen and holds it under the overhead light.

Maybe if the discoloration didn't have four fingers and a thumb, she could dismiss it as a shadow. Maybe if the shadow were under her mother's skin rather than over it, she might think it a bruise. Maybe if the bruise hadn't wiggled its fingers to get a tighter grip on her mother's throat, Jewel might not have whipped the frame at the wall.

She hops back a step as the frame rebounds with the crack of glass and lands on the floor at her feet. The tip of her big toe cries out as a large blade of glass skids to a stop just below her toenail.

Jewel winces through her teeth, then bends down to pluck out the fragment. She thinks better of using her fingers to extract the shard of glass the split second a sharp pain pierces her thumb.

"Damn it," she cries, cupping a bloody drip as she turns to the sink.

Jewel reaches across her body to rip a paper towel off the

rack with her left hand and wads it against the cut. She doesn't have to look to know the slice on her thumb is deep. The skin parts like a baked potato as she applies pressure.

Jewel lowers her head to breathe through a dizzy spell and finds that a crimson mat has been slipped under her feet. Though the cut on her big toe is only a small puncture, it's pumping blood like a nicked artery. She debates wrapping it in a paper towel, then quickly heel walks her way across the living room.

She plays hopscotch around the white bath mats as she enters the bathroom and opens the medicine cabinet with her elbow. The generic tube of Neosporin is almost empty, but there's a full bottle of Tylenol 3. She uses her teeth to rip off the cap, shakes two into her mouth, and swallows them dry.

Band-Aids are on the top shelf. Jewel shakes a few onto the countertop. Though she doesn't want to release the pressure on her thumb until the cut has scabbed over, she'll need all her fingers to bandage her toe.

Pain thuds through her hand as she releases the paper towel. Blood drips into the sink, but not as much as she thought there might be. More of a trickle than a stream. She might need stitches, though. Not tonight. She'll have Dr. Leonetti look at her cuts tomorrow.

Triage complete, Jewel rinses blood from the sink and shampoo from her hair and then glances around. The floor of the bathroom looks like the set of a slasher film. One that played out all the way to the kitchen. Though a few toe stamps are still glistening wet, some of the longer, skidding smears have begun to dry. It's going to take some elbow grease to remove the bloodstains from between the grout.

Not having it in her to clean tonight, Jewel plays another round of hopscotch to exit the bathroom, an advanced level that nearly trips her up, and enters the bedroom in a stumble.

Too tired to dig her pajamas from her suitcase, she collapses face-first onto the comforter. The hammering pain in her big toe is loud enough to hear in her jaw. Throat plated with the taste of iron, Jewel's mind begins constructing a nightmare before she can close her—

10

. . . *tickety-tick-tickety-tick-tickety-tick-tick* . . .

Unable to ignore the constant tap of the overhead ceiling fan another second, Jewel ousts her frustration in a grunt and springs the shade of her eyelids. Expecting the same gloomy dark she drifted off to just seconds ago, it takes her brain a moment to realize that the light flickering across the ceiling is from the television and not the start of an ocular migraine.

Only . . . Deidre doesn't have a television in her bedroom.

Jewel blinks at the stationary ceiling fan to ponder this, then sits quickly up as the tapping resumes. She recognizes the pattern. Spends most of her days wishing she would hear it. The sound of deft fingers moving swiftly across a keyboard.

. . . *tickety-tick-tickety* . . .

Though it's a commonplace sound, that she is the only writer in the apartment, and her fingers are clamped firmly under her chin, makes each strike of the keyboard as ominous as the clack of a peg leg down a dark alley.

That suddenly fills with a strange light.

Jewel blinks at the doorway as it switches from pale blue to soft white.

. . . tickety-tick-tickety . . .

"Deidre?" she calls out, for who else could type with such uninhibited confidence? Never pausing to think or question a single word choice. On any given day, there are more total minutes of airtime between Jewel's sentences than the actual number of sentences.

But it can't be Deidre.

Even if she had awoken from her coma, and had somehow convinced Dr. Leonetti to release her from the hospital in the middle of the night, she wouldn't have been able to enter the apartment without Jewel's knowledge. The chain lock on the front door is set. She is sure of it this time.

Jewel swings her feet over the bedside and pads softly toward the doorway.

Though she's terrified to peer around the corner, the sound is mesmerizing. Like a cat chattering its teeth to hypnotize its prey.

Jewel reaches into the pocket of her robe and extracts the nail file she slipped into it earlier. She moves slowly forward and peeks around the corner of the hallway.

Though the laptop is hard at work, no one is manning it. A circle of white dots appears in the center of the screen and begins to bump into each other.

Update in Progress.

98% Remaining.

Jewel exhales in relief, drops the nail file back into her pocket, and crosses to the office nook. She rolls the chair away from the desk and takes a seat.

The cushion feels oddly warm.

She shuffles the bunch in her robe out from under her and glances at the clock.

Mickey's hands are slightly raised at his sides, wondering what she's doing up at 4:40 a.m.

As the clock ticks off another minute, and not another sentence, Jewel grasps her forehead with her hand. Though it hadn't sounded so precise, it must have been the second hand she heard coming from the living room.

"Man, I am seriously losing it."

Mickey's fixed smile tends to agree.

Jewel waits until the update completes, then restarts the computer. She's about to power it down when the Word document begins to repopulate the screen.

Though she has no intention of starting the novel at this hour, her eyes begin to read.

Unspeakable Demons

Chapter One.

Stories that once flourished under my care now perish at my very touch. Flavorless and dry as the unattended basil plant on my windowsill, they shy from the warmth of my desire. Curling in on themselves rather than facing the light of day, I understand their pain. Stuck in a rut, refusing nourishment from any source, they wilt like an analogy that has no point. Would they rather die, these words in my head, than bloom into something beautiful? A single sentence worth harvesting? So full of life in my mind, they fall dead on the page.

I search the garden of my library daily for inspiration and find only rows and rows of comparative failure. I feast on their bounty, but hunger for the recipe. The ingredients seem so simple. A pinch of style, a flake of dialogue. Just the right amount of metaphors. Never overdone. Dialogue seasoned to perfection. Their organic extemporaneity makes me sick to my stomach.

I return to my desk after these long tutorials, starved

with determination, and find the pantry bare. All my notions half-baked.

The apple of the idea I have may be rotten, but I am too deprived to care. I'm grateful to have found it. An edible piece of fiction that I could sink my teeth into.

The manuscript I found was uncredited. Unfinished. Ripe for the picking. The story was raw, not ready for public consumption, but the premise was downright irresistible.

A struggling writer in search of a muse.

Though the correlation should have given me pause, warned me off like a black cat crossing my path, I chose to view it as a sign. A gift. What were the odds that I would make such a find on the day I woke up to reality? I was finished as a writer. Literature was no longer my calling. Writing it, anyway.

I entered the bookstore earlier that day in search of inspiration. Though they were fresh out, I inquired about a faded sign I had spotted in the display window before I entered.

Summon your muse.

The clerk tapped a bell, as though my luggage needed handling, then nodded me toward the back of the store.

I wove through a maze of dusty, haphazardly placed bookshelves to a small table in the far back left corner. The top of the table was bare except for a glass jar. A label was affixed to the front with yellowing Scotch tape.

Muse. $5.

I looked around for help, but the only employee seemed to be the kid stationed at the front counter. Two doors split the bookshelves on the back wall. One looked to be an office. The other a restroom. Perhaps whoever was supposed to be operating the muse station was taking a break.

I dropped a five-dollar bill in the jar and perused the fiction section to pass the time. Though I found a few titles I had been meaning to read, I left them on their shelves for now and returned to the table to find a white cardboard shirt box waiting for me.

I looked around to see who might have left it there. Though I had strayed out of sight of the table, I had kept an eye on the doors to see if anyone exited. I rose up on my toes to see over the shelves between me and the front counter. The clerk was still there, head down, eyes on a task, unaware of my plight. I recalled him ringing a bell when I made my initial inquiry. That must have signaled that a customer was waiting for a muse.

I lowered to my heels and returned my attention to the box.

Though it didn't have my name on it, it had to be for me. I was the only one waiting to be taken for five bucks by a shyster spirit. I wasn't sure what I had been expecting. My written wish to be set aflame over a candle? A burst of red smoke as the flash paper ignited? A tarot reading with collectible muse trading cards? Calliope, Clio, Erato, Euterpe, Melpomene, Polyhymnia, Terpsichore, Thalia, and Urania. All decked out in mythological garb. An incantation of some sort would have been fitting. How else would one summon a muse? If inspiration could be packaged, the shelves would be stocked.

The box was too heavy to contain a figment of my imagination.

The lid slid free with a sucking sound that seemed to pull all the warmth from my fingertips, my jaw from its latch.

A stack of unbound papers was inside.

I blinked at the top page, the title page, and instantly knew what I had in my possession.

A manuscript.

Scratched in a not-so-elegant hand, the title sent a chill down my spine.

Unspeakable Demons.

No author was credited for the work . . .

Jewel leans back in her chair. Though she is pleased the story isn't starting off as scary as she feared it might, based on the preface, she still finds it highly disturbing.

Had Deidre plagiarized someone else's work?

Not only is it not written in her normal style, which tended to be expository ad nauseam—the bookstore alone would have required a five-page summation—but it's far from the fantasy fiction she built her career on. Maybe that was her intention. To set this story apart from her others. Make the reader believe the story had been magically divined unto her. It was a smart way to ease her fans into a new genre. She found a mysterious manuscript and ran with it. Don't blame her if you don't like it.

Still, the words don't feel like Deidre wrote them.

Maybe Jewel is reading too much into it. Maybe the genre is throwing her. She'll have to read more to find out.

Tomorrow, she thinks with a yawn, and closes the lid on the first chapter.

She swivels in her chair to fetch a glass of water from the kitchen, but the sight of bloody footprints stretching across the living room floor back-walk her thoughts out the door of the apartment, down two flights of stairs, and into a night long ago.

Just as she forgot about the mess she had trailed through the apartment, Jewel forgot all about the blood on the floor of the hallway the night her mother died.

Though the word *rupture* might have bloodied a seven-year-old's assessment of the situation, Jewel now knows that a ruptured appendix would not leave a trail of blood behind. Her mother bled out internally. Not externally. So why had there been blood on the floor of the hallway?

Her father's outstretched hand blocks most of Jewel's

memory of that night. A slim, fearful view through a cracked door.

"Is Mommy okay?"

"Yes. Go back to bed. Everything's fine."

Once Jewel learned that her mother was dead, the blood she'd seen on the floor of the hallway got washed away in a flood of tears. The night swept into the whirlwind of events that transpired. The funeral. The move. New home. New school. New friends. It was a confusing time. Nothing seemed clear.

Jewel asked a lot of questions over the years about the night her mother died. Just maybe not the right ones. She didn't ask about the blood. How could she? She didn't remember there had been blood on the floor until just now.

She'll have to ask Deidre about it when she wakes up.

Until then, she has another mess to contend with.

Jewel crosses to the kitchen, bends over the coagulating blood mat on the floor in front of the sink, and pulls a canister of Clorox wipes from the cabinet below.

It takes a while, but before she knows it, the floor of the apartment, and her memory of the night her mother died, has been wiped clean once again.

PART TWO
WEDNESDAY

11

Jewel arrives at the hospital at 9:00 a.m. sharp. Moderately refreshed and semidetermined to face Deidre head-on. The grocery bag hanging from her wrist is weighing her down. Loaded with a variety of high-end skin products that could potentially disfigure a person, Jewel's money is still on Deidre having a wicked case of poison ivy. But if Dr. Leonetti immediately shoots that idea down, she doesn't want to be caught empty-handed.

She attempts to pawn the bag off at the front desk. The receptionist eyeballs the soggy sack for a moment, then suggests Jewel give it directly to the doctor. Jewel shifts the grocery bag to her other hand, hikes her purse strap higher onto her shoulder, and strides purposely across the lobby toward the ICU.

A flower stand stationed in front of the gift shop draws her off course.

Jewel peruses a healthy assortment, then plucks a bouquet of wildflowers wrapped in purple cellophane from its wire holder.

She enters the shop and smiles at a wet-haired clerk as he begins to ring up the flowers, a bottle of Diet Coke, a Snickers bar, and . . . *Oh!* A copy of *People* magazine, please.

As the clerk begins to manually enter in her credit card number, Jewel steps to a rack of greeting cards at the end of the counter. Though one makes her smile, Deidre wouldn't appreciate it. Not in her condition. She tucks the card back in its slot, glances out the entryway, and spots a familiar face on the other side of the lobby.

"Dr. Leonetti!" she calls out.

He gives the lobby a questioning look, then vanishes around the curved partition that semiencircles the receptionist's desk. Though she didn't notice him before, a priest is following closely behind Dr. Leonetti, looking solemn with his head down.

Though it isn't unusual to see a priest in a hospital, that he is headed in the direction of Deidre's room makes Jewel uneasy. A priest is only called to the ICU for one reason.

"Here's your card," the clerk says.

Jewel snatches it from his fingers, collects her purchases from the counter, her specimen bag from the floor, and hurries from the gift shop, fearing she's already too late to say goodbye to her sister.

Her big toe cries out for her to slow down as she hurdles the outstretched legs of a teenage boy with an ice pack on his crotch and hits the far corridor in a dead run. The wet Band-Aid she applied the night before flaps uncomfortably between her big toe and shoe, then slips under the sole of her foot.

Dr. Leonetti is twenty strides ahead as Jewel bursts through the doors of Deidre's ICU suite, but the priest is no longer behind him.

Did he rush ahead as an alarm flatlined?

Had he been headed toward a different room altogether?

Dr. Leonetti glances over his shoulder, gives Jewel a confused, almost irritated double take, and then makes an about-face.

"Oh, Ms. Maxwell," he says. "I was just about to call you."

She peers around him at Deidre's room at the end of the hall. The door is open. A nurse turns and closes off Jewel's slim view of a crowd of people at the foot of Deidre's bed. All dressed in white or blue, not a smudge of black amongst them. Though the priest could be kneeling at Deidre's bedside, out of view.

"Is everything okay?" she asks. "Is Deidre . . . ?"

As she vacillates between using the words *alive* or *dead*, Dr. Leonetti draws her aside by the elbow. An orderly pushes an empty stretcher down the narrow hall past them. A little too leisurely for Jewel's liking. No need to rush. The patient will still be dead by the time he gets there.

"There's been an incident," Dr. Leonetti says, pulling Jewel's focus back. "I was waiting for an appropriate hour to call, but—"

"I saw the priest with you. Is he here for Deidre?"

Dr. Leonetti glances at the empty corridor behind him. "Uh . . . No. Your sister is fine."

"*Fine?*" Jewel challenges, as if the diagnosis were far worse than she imagined. "But you said there was an incident. Did something happen? Did she take a turn for the worse?"

Dr. Leonetti directs Jewel to a line of chairs against the wall. "Please sit down, Ms. Maxwell."

Jewel roots herself to the floor with a clenched jaw. "Just tell me!"

"An orderly passed away this morning," Dr. Leonetti says.

Jewel laughs out of relief, then apologizes for her insensitivity. "Sorry. That's horrible. I'm just glad it doesn't have anything to do with Deidre."

"Well, in a way, it does." Dr. Leonetti takes a preliminary breath. "The orderly died in your sister's room."

"What?" Jewel exclaims. "When?"

"They only found his body a little while ago. But it looks like he might have been dead for a couple of hours. That's why

I was going to call you. I was afraid you'd show up while they were removing the body and jump to the wrong conclusion. Which is exactly what ended up happening."

Jewel lowers herself onto the edge of a chair. She looks up at Dr. Leonetti, who remains standing, facing her sister's room.

"How did he die?"

"I won't know the exact cause of death until I receive the coroner's report, but I believe it was a heart attack."

"Oh, my goodness. That's so awful. I'm so sorry."

Dr. Leonetti nods. "The staff is completely devastated."

"I'm sure," Jewel says. "Was he elderly?"

"Not particularly. But a heart attack can strike anyone, anytime, anywhere. It's just unfortunate that it happened in your sister's presence."

Presence?

People in a coma didn't have presence of mind.

"Wait," Jewel says. "Is Deidre awake?"

"No. Unfortunately, she's still in a coma."

Though Jewel's expression shows this news is disappointing, her heart lets out a sigh of relief so intense that she nearly collapses. As soon as Deidre wakes up, Jewel's dreams will come to an end. She wasn't sure if she wanted to take on the project until she thought she had lost her chance. Now, more than anything, she wants, fucking *needs*, to write the ending of *Unspeakable Demons*. Something about the story speaks to her. A struggling author in search of a muse, finding an abandoned manuscript. And though she suspects things might not turn out well for the main character, her fate is now in Jewel's hands. Deidre doesn't care about her. Hasn't so much as opened the manuscript to check on her in almost a month. And though Jewel wants Deidre to get well, she is fine in a coma for now. A couple of weeks of sleep might do her some good, actually.

All Jewel needs is nine days. Once the manuscript is submitted to the publisher, and they read the sensational ending an unknown author named Jewel Maxwell devised, Deidre won't be able to stop the presses.

Jewel looks up as the door to Deidre's room opens and two hospital workers back a stretcher into the hallway. Clearing the threshold, they turn in almost military fashion and grip the cart from behind their backs. Three more pallbearers exit the room and take position on either side of the gurney. Without a word, they start forward. Another hospital worker, a female in blue scrubs, exits the room, towing a bin of linens.

As the procession rolls by, Dr. Leonetti presses clamped hands to his face and hangs his head in a moment of silence.

Jewel lowers her chin but runs her eyes over the snow-covered mountain range of the sheeted face. A dot of blood sits upon the summit of its nose.

Once the procession has rounded the corner at the end of the corridor, Dr. Leonetti raises his head and turns to Jewel.

"You can see your sister now," he says. "I need to attend to another matter, but I'll be back to check on her later."

"I brought you a few things from Deidre's apartment." Jewel sluffs the bag off her wrist and hands it to him. "I thought they might help you figure out what gave her the rash. It's just some lotions and stuff. Most of them are from foreign countries. Who knows what kind of standards and regulations they have in Brazil. It seems like a pretty loose place to me."

"Thank you." Dr. Leonetti holds the soap-scummed sack a safe distance from his trousers. "I'll see that our lab gets them."

"I know this is a stupid question, but is there any chance it's poison ivy? Deidre's allergic to it."

Dr. Leonetti nods, but says, "No. I'm afraid it's nothing that simple. Deidre's condition is a tad more"—he looks off to find the right word—"*menacing* than that."

Jewel scratches her neck. "Does she look any better today?"

"The inflammation has reduced some. And the oozing seems to have stopped. Which are both very good signs that her body is healing. Unfortunately, the healing process can also be a bit unattractive. She's developed something called purpura. Which, as it sounds, causes a purplish discoloration. So she may look a little worse than when you saw her yesterday."

"But she already looked like a—"

Jewel presses the word *monster* back into her mouth with her fingertips.

"Try to focus on your sister's *inner* beauty, Ms. Maxwell."

I'd need a high-powered microscope to see that, Jewel thinks. Not that she's ever looked for the good in Deidre. She was too blinded by jealousy to see past her sister's designer facade.

"Well, enjoy your visit."

"Yeah," Jewel mumbles, turning to face Deidre's door as Dr. Leonetti hurries off. "This should be a barrel of laughs."

12

Jewel rubs the sharp scent of antiseptic from her nose and scans the mop-damp floor of Deidre's hospital room for any indication that a dead body was lying there moments before. Though Dr. Leonetti believes the orderly died of natural causes, however premature, Jewel is still surprised that they so quickly eliminated every last speck of evidence.

Deidre's heart monitor beeps rhythmically, vigilant as the perimeter of an electric fence, giving Jewel the courage to look at her sister's face.

Though it's hard to tell under the yellow cellulose mask she's wearing, Deidre's face does look slightly less puffy than it did yesterday. But it's hardly an improvement. Her forehead is still distended and inflamed. Pulsing with infection.

I can feel the worm of a loathsome thought writhing to the surface, Jewel thinks, recalling a line from the preface of *Unspeakable Demons.*

"How you doin', Dee?" she says, stepping to the bedside.

She watches Deidre's face for a response. A lash to flutter. Her lip to tremble. Though Deidre's expression remains inert, the fingers on her right hand are twitching a hundred words a minute.

Dr. Leonetti didn't mention a tremor in her hand. Jewel reminds herself to ask him about it later but can already hear his response: *Perfectly normal. All part of the healing process. Nothing to worry about.* Translation: *I don't have an answer for you, so I'm just going to say it's a normal part of the healing process to placate you.*

Jewel sets the gift shop bouquet on the side table and touches Deidre's hand to quiet the palsy. Her skin is burning hot. Boiling. Percolating her fingers like the lid of a teakettle.

"Do you have a fever, Dee?"

Jewel leans forward to scan the health monitor for a number that might indicate body temperature.

Deidre gurgles a phlegmy response.

Jewel's heart jumps quickly backward and stands her upright.

"Dee! Are you awake? Are you trying to say something?"

g-grula-g-gah

"What?"

Jewel bends down to listen and spots the purplish discoloration around her sister's throat that Dr. Leonetti mentioned. What he failed to mention, however, was the odd pattern the discoloration has formed.

Four finger-shaped bruises.

Just like the ones that had their mother by the throat in the family portrait. The discolorations on her mother's and sister's necks are too similar to be a coincidence.

But how could that be?

Did Jewel have some sort of premonition? Was their mother trying to send her some sort of message? A warning?

Jewel swallows hard as a horrible thought occurs to her.

"How did you get these bruises, Dee? Did that orderly do this to you? Is that what happened? Was he trying to hurt you?" Jewel looks around for a call button. "I'm going to report this to Dr. Leonetti right away. I can't believe he didn't realize that was a handprint around your throat."

Unless he did.

Unless he was trying to cover it up.

Of course the hospital would want to cover up the fact that one of their orderlies had assaulted a patient. That the man died in the act didn't make it any less heinous.

Jewel draws her bag around her shoulder and extracts her phone. "I need to get a picture of your throat before the bruises fade."

She opens the camera app on her phone and uses her finger to lift Deidre's chin.

"Hold still," she says without thinking, then shakes her head. "You know what I mean. Just lie there. Like you're doing."

She adjusts the screen to focus on the bruise and snaps a photo.

She taps the small tile that was deposited in the lower right corner of the screen.

As the photo enlarges, so do Jewel's eyes.

Deidre's eyes are open in the photograph and contain the most severe case of red-eye ever captured on film. Devil's eyes. To match her wide, devilish smile.

Heart pounding hard enough to raise a seismic tremor across her vision, Jewel blinks at her sister over the top of the phone.

Deidre's condition appears unchanged. Face relaxed, lips gently parted, not a glint of hellfire lingers on her closed eyelids.

Jewel sets the phone on the bed and leans in to examine her sister's face more closely.

"What the fuck, Dee? Are you awake?"

She pries open Deidre's left eyelid with her thumb and forefinger. Back to black, Deidre's pupil stares harmlessly at a blank wall between her and the rest of the world.

Jewel releases Deidre's eyelid and picks up her phone to study the picture again. Too blurry to tell if Deidre's eyes are open or shut, she swipes right, hoping she snapped more than one photo, and finds a screenshot of an Amazon return code she took last week.

"I didn't imagine it," Jewel tells Deidre. "Your eyes were open. I saw them."

She looks at the phone again and notices two red dots reflecting off the health monitor beside the bed.

"Oh, Jesus," Jewel laughs. "For a second there, I thought I was going crazy."

She picks the flowers she bought off the side table and circles the bed to a small dresser under the window, teeming with blossoms.

"Who are these from?" she says.

She sets her concession bouquet next to a magnificent floral arrangement in a crystal vase and plucks a white card from its golden pitchfork.

"They're from Emily Channing," she tells Deidre. "I spoke to her yesterday. I told her you were in the hospital. I hope that was okay. I thought you would want her to know."

Jewel tucks the card back in its holder.

"She told me about the deadline with your publisher. And about the advance. And your money troubles. Don't worry. I've got your back." *Which I'm about to stab you in.* "I was able to access your iCloud account and found the manuscript. I read some of it last night. It's good. Really scary."

Like you.

"Emily said she's thinking of hiring a ghostwriter to finish the ending. And I think it should be me, Dee."

The heart monitor skips a beat.

Jewel gives Deidre's slack face a quick glance, then studies the health monitor. All vital signs appear to be steady.

"Anyway, I think Emily will say yes. I'm the only one who *can* finish it in time."

beep B-beep

"The doctors don't know how long you might be in a coma. And even if you came out of it today, I don't think you're going to be in any condition to work. Not for a while anyway. Definitely not in time to meet the deadline."

B-b-Beep B-beep

"The ending might not turn out exactly how you envisioned, but I know I can do a good job with it. I already feel a strong connection to the main character. It's like she and I are one and the—"

BEEP b-bEEP b-bEEP b-bEEEEEEP

Jewel spins toward the bed as Deidre's body begins to convulse. Back arching at an impossibly high angle, the bedding billows beneath her and wafts the room with a flatulent scent. Deidre's head fights against the pain, burrows deep into the pillows, and thrashes perilously close to the frame of the mechanical bed.

"Dee!" Jewel cries, squeezing down the narrow alley between the bed and the single window situated in the wall.

Deidre slams back to the mattress, then immediately up again. Spine bowing more each time, determined to fold itself in half. The heart monitor and the bed shriek in unison.

"Nurse!" Jewel yells at the open doorway. "Somebody! Help!"

Hesitant to touch her sister but desperate to do something, Jewel hovers her hands indecisively over Deidre's taut belly. Like a magician conducting a feat of levitation, Deidre stiffens, then rises. Her body shakes violently under the tremble of Jewel's fingers, then flexes inward as Jewel wills them to stop. Jewel attempts to break the spell with a swiping motion of her hand. Deidre's body responds. The club of her casted left leg kicks the sheets free of its hospital corner.

The wires connecting her to the health monitor whip sharply, then swing to a stop.

For a split second, Deidre lies flat, calm, and suspended in midair.

Jewel closes her eyes, bracing for the fall, for gravity to win out and slam Deidre back to the insubstantial mattress.

The health monitor lets out a thin, torturous scream, then resumes a regular beat.

Jewel opens her eyes.

Deidre is lying flat on the bed, still as Jewel's heart.

Jewel slumps gratefully forward, relieved that the terrifying situation is over.

The slap to her cheek is blindingly quick.

Jewel clutches the flaring sting with her hand as a nurse rushes through the doorway. The nurse swings a concerned look between Jewel and Deidre, the monitor next to the bed, and then back to Jewel.

"What happened?" she asks, stepping quickly to the bed. She picks up Deidre's limp wrist and feels for a pulse.

Jewel's own pulse beats hot on her cheek as she watches the nurse's eyes for a diagnosis.

"Is she okay?" Jewel asks.

The nurse sets Deidre's hand back on the blanket without responding and circles the end of the bed.

Jewel recoils, anticipating another slap.

"Excuse me," the nurse says, nodding Jewel out of the way. "I need to check her monitor."

"She was having a seizure," Jewel says, tripping out from beside the bedside to allow the nurse passage. "I didn't know what to do."

"A seizure?" the nurse questions, scanning the screen of the health monitor.

"Yes," Jewel says. "I was trying to help her."

The nurse leans in for a closer look at Deidre's face, then tidies the blanket around her shoulders. "She seems okay now." She turns to Jewel. "Muscle spasms are not uncommon with coma patients."

"This was more than a muscle spasm, Nurse . . ." Jewel squints at the woman's name tag. "Ingram. She was slamming up and down. Flailing her arms and legs. She slapped me in the face!"

Jewel points out what had to be a red handprint on her cheek.

"I'm sure it was inadvertent," Nurse Ingram says.

"I'm not accusing her of anything! I'm just telling you what happened."

"I'll make sure the doctor is aware." Nurse Ingram tucks the sheet back under the mattress, then makes a few brusque adjustments to Deidre's EKG connections, which, astonishingly, are still attached. The curtain billows out as Nurse Ingram sidesteps down the narrow aisle toward Jewel. "We need to keep the windows closed."

Jewel flinches as the window slams. "I didn't open it!"

Nurse Ingram flips the locking mechanism, then turns and extends a hand toward the door. "We should let your sister get some rest now."

Jewel follows Nurse Ingram toward the door and looks worriedly back at Deidre before exiting the room.

Deidre's smile tucks away as her eyes snap shut.

Jewel gasps, "Did you see that?"

Nurse Ingram turns to look. "What?"

Jewel stares at Deidre's repellently impassive face. "Nothing, I thought I saw her blink" *up a hellish smile.*

Nurse Ingram stares at Deidre for a moment, then touches Jewel's elbow to usher her from the room.

"Probably just a twitch. Completely normal. Nothing to worry about."

13

Uncertain if she will be able to access the attic level from the rear of the house, Jewel overshoots the driveway and coasts to a stop along the curb. She'll move the car to the back lot later, after she's put her groceries away.

She exits the car with her head down, eyes on the key fob, looking for the icon to pop the trunk. The day has grown warm. Sunny and seventy-five. Almost tropical for the Shenandoah Valley. The sweater she put on that morning is now stuffed in one of the grocery bags inside the trunk. Though the Walmart her GPS decided upon was less than super, it carried everything she needed for a comfortable stay.

"Excuse me!" a voice yells as the trunk springs open.

Jewel turns to see a man crossing the street kitty-corner from the church. Black slacks and shirt with the sleeves rolled up, his priestly white collar casts an ominous glint. Like an unexpected badge shoved in your face.

Though he looks to be the same height and build as the priest she saw tracking Dr. Leonetti through the hospital, she didn't look past the collar to see the man's face. He was a priest.

Period. That was all she needed to know. Except for why he was there. To perform the last rites for somebody. Thankfully not Deidre. Maybe the orderly. Once Jewel learned that Deidre was alive, she kind of forgot about the priest. How he had mysteriously vanished from the corridor. He had been right on Dr. Leonetti's heels. And Jewel had been right on his. Though he probably slipped into another room before she turned the corner, Jewel had the strangest feeling that he had hidden after she spotted him. Hunkered in a closet to watch her walk by.

Priests make Jewel uncomfortable. The way they look at you. As though they can determine your sins by the color of your eyes. Jewel avoids them whenever possible. Not just priests, but people of faith in general. No matter how innocent a conversation might start, it invariably ended with a polite interrogation as to her religious preference. Her vaguely secular response of *my parents were Catholic* never seemed to satisfy. Bless her poor damned soul. If only it knew the way. Jewel suspects that aliens might be behind it all. How else could an immaculate conception occur if not by an embryonic implantation beyond the medical advances of the time. *Follow that spaceship, Wise Men!* It was so obvious. Not that Jewel is an atheist. She does believe in God. Hers just exists in another solar system. But when pressed, Jewel would play along. Smile and nod politely. Especially when speaking to a priest. Or minister. Or whatever this guy's deal is.

In hopes of appearing too busy to chat, Jewel ducks her head into the trunk of the car and begins to consolidate her grocery bags.

"Can I help with those?" the man says, stopping alongside the car. He reaches for a bag and a small bible slips into the well of the trunk. Returning it to his breast pocket, he grabs for the same bag as Jewel.

"I got it," she says, hooking the plastic handle with her pinkie.

The priest retracts his helping hand.

"I don't mean to bother you," he says. "But you don't happen to be Deidre Baldwin's sister, by any chance?"

Jewel suppresses the urge to shake her head, and says, "Yep. That's me."

"I was distraught to learn of her accident," he says. "May I ask how she's doing?"

"Not great. She's in a coma."

"Oh, dear. I'm so sorry to hear that. Is she going to be okay?"

"The doctors won't know anything until she wakes up."

"But they do expect her to wake up?"

When Jewel responds with a noncommittal shrug, the priest closes his eyes for the duration of the Lord's Prayer. Jewel looks around the uncomfortable cone of silence that has descended over them for a way out, then flinches as the priest's eyes suddenly pop open. Caught mid-yawn, Jewel's teeth snap together a quick smile.

"I heard it was a hit-and-run," he says. "Is that true?"

Though his question only requires a one-word response, and Jewel is under no obligation to elaborate, she doesn't want to leave herself open to any follow-up questions.

"Yes. It was a hit-and-run. And no. The police haven't caught the person who hit her. And yes. They're still investigating."

"Well, I certainly hope they catch whoever was responsible. Not that that will help Deidre any, but at least a menace will be off the road. People fly up and down this street all the time. They really need to install a speed bump. But I guess you know that."

"How would I know that?" Jewel balks. "I don't live here. I haven't lived here since I was a kid."

Thrown, the priest shakes his head to regain his footing. "I meant because of what happened to Deidre."

"Oh." Jewel grimaces apologetically. "Right."

"I'm glad you're able to be here for Deidre. Family's the best medicine in times like these. A hospital can be such a lonely place. I would like to visit her, but only family is allowed in the ICU. I was hoping you might put in a good word for me at the hospital."

Jewel turns and looks at him. "I saw you in the ICU this morning with Dr. Leonetti. Why didn't you just ask him if you could visit Deidre?"

"I wasn't at the hospital this morning," he contends.

Jewel assesses the priest through a dubious squint. "Are you sure? I could have sworn I saw you."

"Why would I lie?"

"Oh. No. I didn't mean to suggest . . . I hope I didn't offend you, Father . . . ?" She raises her eyebrows to receive his name.

"Madness," he says.

Jewel gives him a puzzled look. "*Sorry?*"

"Mattis," he repeats. "With two *t*'s."

"Oh," Jewel exhales in a chuckle. "For a second there, I thought you said your name was madness."

Father Mattis laughs. "I get that a lot. Must be my accent."

Though Jewel didn't detect one, she says, "That must be it."

"I feel just awful about all this. I had stopped by to see Deidre earlier that day. I was hoping we might work some more on her novel. I thought I heard someone inside, but she didn't come to the door. I meant to stop back by later that evening, but my bible studies group ran long. Maybe if I had been there, none of this would have happened."

Jewel's eyebrows draw together to take in part of what he said. "You were helping Deidre with her novel?"

"Just with some research."

"What kind of research?"

"Primarily she was interested in the rite of exorcism. Not that I'm an expert. But, I like to think that I was able to clarify some things for her. From a purely procedural standpoint, that is."

Jewel's heart gives a shallow thud.

Though she already knows Deidre's book concerns an evil entity—the preface all but gave that away—she doesn't want to think of the muse as demonic. *The Exorcist* spun her head around for weeks after she read it.

"What did Deidre want to know about exorcisms?" she asks.

"How it occurs. How one might become possessed. What symptoms they might develop as a result."

Jewel blinks at him. "Symptoms?"

Like an inexplicable rash all over their body?

"*Manifest* might be a better term," Father Mattis amends. "How demonic possession might present itself in someone who has been afflicted."

Jewel rests a hip on the car's rear bumper to steady herself and fully engage in the conversation.

"How *does* demonic possession present itself?"

"Well, that rather depends on the person." Father Mattis shrugs. "Since it's all in their head."

"You don't believe demonic possession is real?"

"Real in the sense that I think a person might truly believe they're possessed? Yes. In that respect, it is very real. The terror they experience cannot be refuted. But do I think an actual demon has possessed their soul? No. That I don't believe."

"Did Deidre believe it?"

"I think she believed it was possible. But she also agreed that most examples of demonic possession could be tied to mental illness. The human mind can be a hell of its own creation."

Tell me about it, Jewel thinks.

"That's why exorcisms are an effective treatment," Father Mattis goes on. "If you're convinced an exorcism will work, then it most likely will. Much like a placebo effect. The opposite is also true. That's how most superstitions were derived. By implanting a suggestion. A black cat crossing your path isn't bad luck. Unless you think it is. Then suddenly all manners of misfortune begin to befall you. It's not a curse. It's a self-fulfilling prophecy. Easily reversed by throwing a pinch of salt over your shoulder. Or prevented altogether by hanging a horseshoe upside down on your wall. Deidre wondered if someone could actually become possessed just by thinking they were."

Jewel's spine snaps to attention. "Can they?"

"The power of suggestion can be highly influential. Deidre worried that her novel might incite some hysteria in that regard. That people would read it and think they were becoming possessed. That it might actually be a grimoire, of sorts. Like a book of the dead."

Jewel casts off a sudden shiver with a dubious eye roll.

Only someone with an ego the size of Deidre's would think their words held that much power.

"You can't just *write* a book of the dead, can you?" she asks.

"I don't know if Deidre actually believed she was *writing* one, or thought the novel was just turning out to *be* one. She reached out to a paranormal society to find out if that was even possible. I tried to reassure her that it wasn't, but that only seemed to upset her. She got quite angry with me, actually. Which wasn't like Deidre at all. I've been very worried about her. Even before the accident. She hadn't been acting like herself. She'd become highly emotional. Very quick to temper. I think she might have been avoiding me."

"I wouldn't take it personally. Deidre hadn't been feeling

very well. She had an allergic reaction to something. She has a horrible rash all over her body."

Father Mattis nods. "I noticed her scratching at her arms and chest recently. I asked if she was okay. She said it was nothing."

Jewel scratches her neck and glances at the church across the street. "So when did the church catch fire?"

Father Mattis sighs as he turns to look at St. Leo's charred remains. "A few weeks ago. There wasn't a lot of structural damage, thank goodness, but the entire nave will have to be gutted. I'm trying to salvage what I can. Which isn't a lot."

"Do you think it will reopen?"

"God willing," he says.

Which is Jewel's cue to leave. "Well, I better get going." She gathers the remainder of the grocery bags from the trunk of the car. "I'll tell Deidre you were asking about her as soon as she's awake. Hopefully sooner than later. Keep your fingers crossed."

"I'll *pray* that she does," Father Mattis counters, closing the trunk for her.

"Right." Jewel rolls her eyes as she turns away. "That's what I meant."

14

The conversation with Father Mattis occupies Jewel's thoughts as she ascends the staircase to the attic apartment. Could reading a story really possess a person? Could evil enter through their eyes? Invade their soul? Turn it evil? Would they even know if it happened? Would there be any signs?

Symptoms?

Or was it just the power of suggestion, as Father Mattis believed? And if so, did that really make a difference? Wouldn't believing you were possessed by an evil spirit be enough to alter your behavior? Your appearance? And if you believed it wholeheartedly enough, right down to your very soul, might it manifest as a physical presence?

Become a shadowy figure sitting at your desk?

And if you believed the words you wrote might unleash evil upon the world, could those words convince your readers of the same thing? That the story you wrote was possessing them through its evil content? Could such a book cause mass hysteria? If only through the power of suggestion?

A person would need to be highly susceptible for something like that to occur.

Deidre is too smart to fall prey to such a concept. She doesn't buy into silly superstitions. Jewel has never seen Deidre knock on wood or throw salt over her shoulder. Deidre doesn't even have any writing rituals that Jewel knows of. It is absurd to think she would believe herself possessed by the power of the written word. If that were the case, she would have turned into a sorceress a long time ago.

Jewel laughs to herself.

She is making too much of this. Reading too much into it. Deidre had an allergic reaction to something and got hit by a car. Period. Her condition doesn't have anything to do with *Unspeakable Demons*. Sure, she went a little crazy and trashed her apartment, but the devil didn't make her do it.

An unbearable itch had.

Marching like fire ants up her arms.

Jewel pauses on the second landing to scratch her shoulder with the edge of a brass sconce centered on the wall, then takes the next flight of stairs and picks up her inner dialogue, which is fed up with all of Jewel's whining.

You're being ridiculous! A novel can't unleash hell upon its readers. That might make a good premise for a story, but it couldn't really happen. There's no such thing as demons. You're just looking for an excuse to give up. Just like you always do. That's why Deidre's more successful than you. She doesn't give up. She'll write herself sick if she has to. You sit around waiting for inspiration to strike. For success to fall into your lap. Well, here it is! The chance you've been waiting for. Are you going to let a little thing like a demon stand in your way? Deidre didn't. Deidre grabbed the little fucker by the balls and is paying hell for it. Because she's a winner. And you're a loser.

Though that is true, if Jewel is being honest with herself, which isn't one of her strong suits, it isn't a fear of success that is scaring her.

She is afraid that her best won't be good enough. She can't fail if she doesn't try. But she could come up with a million reasons for not jumping at an opportunity like this. She is too distracted. There is too much going on. She should be concentrating on Deidre. She isn't prepared to work on the novel. She is out of her element. She just doesn't want to take on a new project right now. Not one where she might have to tackle a demon in order to succeed.

Still, she can't let fear of failure keep her from her dreams.

But damn if she isn't scared.

What if Deidre really got possessed by some fictional demon? Could Jewel rule out that possibility?

Not unequivocally.

Deidre levitated off the hospital bed, after all.

Just for a second. But that was a second longer than normal.

Did I really see that?

It was a chaotic moment. Adrenaline-infused. Her brain must have seized up with fear and held Deidre's body aloft with stone-cold panic.

That makes sense.

With her thoughts and left pinkie in a twist, Jewel is primed for a scream as she steps onto the landing of the attic floor.

The door to the utility closet across from Deidre's apartment swings open.

And out pops the devil himself.

Who else would wear a Black Sabbath T-shirt with a shark tooth corded around his unshaven throat? That the lord of all darkness is wearing white sneakers and carrying a five-gallon jug of water on his shoulder like a keg of beer seems a little odd, but his leering smile and pointy Vandyke beard are highly sinister.

"Hey," says Satan.

"Jesus!" Jewel cries. "You scared the shit out of me. What were you doing in the closet?"

The man looks back at the door he exited from. "That's the elevator."

The house didn't have an elevator when Jewel was a kid.

Heck, it barely had stairs.

"Oh, right," Jewel says, studying the dimly lit atrium like a museum exhibit. "I don't like elevators. Especially small ones. I'm a little claustrophobic. But I guess I'll give it a try. The stairs are killing me."

"The elevator is for residents only," the man says. "You need a code to access it."

"I am a resident. I mean . . . I'm Deidre Baldwin's sister. I'm staying in her apartment while I'm in town."

"Do you have a key to her apartment?"

"Yes."

"Can you let me in?" he asks, shifting the jug of water to his other shoulder. "This thing's kind of heavy."

"Oh, sure." Jewel sets her grocery bags on the floor next to the door and works the key ring off her finger. "But there's plenty of water in the jug she has, so there's no need to change it."

"You have to turn in the old jug when a new one's delivered or you get charged extra."

The man hurries quickly into the apartment as the door opens.

Jewel frowns as she bends to pick up a grocery bag. She doesn't like that a strange man has bulldozed his way in. Though it's clear that he's been here before, she shouldn't have accepted a water jug as a form of ID.

Jewel flinches as a hard thud vibrates the floor, then hurries inside. The man is crouched on the floor of the kitchenette.

"Are you sure you need to change it?" she says, setting the grocery bag on the counter. "It seems like such a waste. I'll pay for the additional jug. I drink a lot of water."

"Already done," the man says, slamming the new jug into place.

"Oh, okay. I guess if you already did it, then . . ." Jewel plucks Deidre's wallet from her tote. "How much do I owe you?"

"Nothing."

"It's free?"

"No. I'm not the water guy," he says, pouring money down the drain. "I just bring it up for Deidre. She didn't like the guy who was delivering it. He kept hanging around too long. Trying to chat her up. Deidre didn't want to complain, so I told the guy just to leave the water downstairs and I'd change it out for her."

"That was nice of you." Jewel tucks the wallet back in Deidre's bag. "So you live in the house?"

"Second floor. I'm Lyle."

"Jewel."

Lyle cocks his head. "You look familiar to me."

"I probably look like Deidre. We're sisters."

"Yeah. You said that already."

Jewel raises her shoulders to concede the point.

Lyle studies her a moment longer, then leans against the counter. "So how is she? I heard about the accident."

"Not good," Jewel says. "She's in a coma."

Lyle looks down, visibly aggrieved. "Man, that sucks."

"Are you and Deidre close?"

"Yeah. We go way back. I knew her when she used to live here. We went to junior high together."

Jewel's eyes widen. "Wow. Dee never mentioned you before." When Lyle's brow takes this as an insult, Jewel smooths it over with a smile. "I mean, that's crazy you ended up living in the same house together."

Lyle shrugs. "I was the one who told Deidre about the apartment."

"You've stayed in touch all these years?"

"Off and on. We're friends on Facebook."

You and a hundred thousand other people, Jewel thinks. Deidre only has a professional account on Facebook. Anyone can follow her. That doesn't make them friends.

"I sent her a message to let her know I was living in her old house," Lyle goes on. "I thought she'd get a kick out of it. She responded immediately. She asked me to let her know if any apartments became available. I was shocked as hell when she moved in. I thought she was just making small talk."

"I was shocked myself," Jewel says. "I had no idea Deidre wanted to move back here."

"Guess Deidre doesn't tell you *everything* then, does she?" Lyle sneers.

Touché, Jewel thinks, then parries with, "Just the important stuff, I guess."

Lyle's stare takes aim at her heart. "Didn't your mom die while you were living here?"

"Yeah," Jewel yields with a sigh. "Her appendix ruptured."

"Huh. I thought she got stabbed or shot or something." He shrugs. "But a bunch of rumors started flying around after Deidre left school in the middle of the year."

Not caring to know what urban legend the junior high school rumor mill churned up in the wake of her family's tragedy, Jewel turns to unpack the groceries.

"Well, thanks for helping." She cups a drip under her quart of strawberry ice cream. "I better put these away before they melt any more than they already have."

"Yeah, you were down there talking to that priest for a while."

Jewel gives him a look as she steps to the freezer. "How did you know that?"

"I saw you from my window," Lyle admits. "I was wondering who you were. I guess Father Whatshisname was pretty upset about Deidre's accident."

"Father Mattis was concerned, yes."

"I didn't think priests were allowed to date." Lyle shrugs. "I guess times have changed."

"What do you mean, *date*?"

"I mean he was over here a lot. Brought flowers and wine. Stayed *way* past dinner. If you know what I mean."

Jewel rolls her eyes. "He was just helping Dee with some research."

Lyle shrugs again. "Yeah, okay. Sure."

"He was!"

"Whatever you say." Lyle smiles at the goat he got from Jewel, then turns for the door. "See you later, I guess."

Jewel glances at the sink. "Don't you want to take the empty water jug with you?"

"Oh, yeah." Lyle laughs and makes an about-face. He steps into the kitchenette and grabs the jug from the sink.

Jewel follows him into the hall to retrieve the rest of her grocery bags.

"The code for the elevator is star six seven nine seven," he says, taking the stairs down. "But I wouldn't use it, if I were you."

"Why not?"

"It's been acting kinda hinky."

"Hinky how?" Jewel says over the rail as Lyle vanishes around the corner of the lower landing of the stairwell. "Hinky how, Lyle . . . ? Lyle . . . !" She steps back into the apartment before muttering, "Asshole," then slams the door.

15

Jewel taps a fingernail on the desk and stares at Deidre's phone, confidence waning with each second of deliberation. Before she calls Emily and officially commits to the project, she really should acquaint herself more with the story.

The thought makes her bowels squirm.

It would be bad enough reading a horror story about demonic possession at home with Cal next to her on the couch. But reading it here? Alone? In an attic? With her sister's hideous face hovering in the corner of her thoughts? She is just asking to get possessed. Whether it be by an actual demon or one forged solely in Jewel's imagination, it would terrify her all the same.

The first chapter wasn't too scary: Woman walks into bookstore and finds a mysterious manuscript. But what would happen once she took the manuscript home?

Jewel glances at the clock on the desk.

Emily is waiting to hear from her.

But once she volunteers her services as a ghostwriter, she loses control of the situation. She'll have to finish writing the story. And in order to do that, she'll have to tap into Deidre's mindset. Her darkest, innermost evil. The thing that might have driven her from the apartment and into the path of an oncoming vehicle.

If that was what actually happened.

Maybe guilt had driven her to it.

Had Deidre really been sleeping with a priest? Or was Lyle just trying to stir up trouble?

She can tell Lyle has a thing for Deidre. He is probably jealous of Deidre's relationship with Father Mattis. Their rendezvous could have been entirely platonic. Lyle perverted them into something more. Father Mattis was a good-looking guy. For a priest. It isn't a stretch to imagine that Deidre might be attracted to him. He is her type. Tall. Handsome. Smart. Lyle only possesses one of those attributes. And tall can only get you so far.

Jewel shakes off an image of Deidre fumbling to remove Father Mattis's lipstick-smudged white collar, then blinks at the computer screen. Her eyes begin to consume the next paragraph of the book without her brain's consent.

The manuscript felt good clamped to my chest as I walked home. Nuzzled against me. Content in my arms. My pet project. Whatever condition it was in, no matter what it might develop into, I was responsible for it now. Just one look and I could tell that it was starved for attention. Bone-thin storyline. Scantly worded phrasings. Aggressive subtext. Its previous master couldn't handle it. They had no vision. Rather than playing with it, they stuffed it in a box and tossed it aside. Poor thing. Unappreciated and unwanted. Left for dead. But I could nurse the story back to health. Smooth out its wrinkles. Feed it only the best elements. Surprise it with a juicy plot twist once in a while. Let it feast on my soul if that's what it so desired.

Jewel sighs.

The story does need some help.

Sixty thousand words is pretty paltry. She could read that in a day or two. If things get too scary, she could set it aside for a while. Talk to Cal. Touch base with reality again.

What else is she going to do until Deidre awakes from her coma? Binge Netflix? That wouldn't keep *Unspeakable Demons* from haunting her. She doesn't have another project to work on. Hasn't written more than a title in months. Which she was unhappy with. *Beyond the Bluff* sounds beyond boring. Unlike *Unspeakable Demons.* Now there's a title that grabs you. Makes you want to crack it open and see what flies out.

But isn't that exactly what she is afraid of?

Mm-hmm, a dark, throaty voice agrees.

Hummed directly into her ear, Jewel spins quickly in the chair and encounters only a dank, musky scent. As if an animal has just crouched there to do its business. She peers at the unsoiled rug, then up at a wet stain in the plaster on the ceiling. Though the roof of the house is pitched, the ceiling of the apartment is level. There must be another attic above the attic. Based on where the window over the desk sits in relation to the exterior of the house, it can't be more than a crawl space.

Has an animal gotten up there? Is it using the rafters as its litter box?

Jewel rises off the chair and sniffs the two-foot space between her and the wet spot on the ceiling.

The scent has scurried off.

To Jewel's surprise, perhaps chagrin, Emily jumps at the idea of Jewel finishing Deidre's novel.

"Do you really think you can do it?"

"I can give it a try," Jewel says.

"That doesn't inspire a lot of confidence."

"No. I'm confident in my writing skills. It's just . . ." Jewel bites her lip to keep from talking Emily out of hiring her but can't seem to stop herself. "Horror's not really my thing, Emily. I thought you might have another writer in mind. One that's more familiar with the genre."

"I'd prefer not to use one of my authors unless I absolutely have to. I don't want to risk word of this getting out. The chance of that happening increases with every person we involve. I'd take the project on myself, but I don't have the time. I'm traveling this weekend. And next week I'm booked solid. I guess I could forfeit sleep. That's been pretty hit or miss lately, anyway."

"I didn't know you were a writer."

"I'm not," Emily clarifies. "I haven't written anything in years. I couldn't take the criticism. Mostly my own. Though some critics can be just as brutal. There're a few out there who would like nothing more than to see me fail. It will be bad enough if they find out I let an amateur ghostwrite the ending of a Deidre Baldwin novel. No offense, Jewel. But no matter how many books you've written, if you haven't been published by a major house, you'll be deemed amateurish."

"Then why do you want me to do it?"

"You're Deidre's sister. No matter what the critics say, if it gets out that you wrote the ending, her fans are going to love it." Emily frames it with a staged voice: "Sister steps in to help their beloved author in her time of need."

"Couldn't that be said about her agent?"

"I'd look like a vulture. Swooping in to pick the last buck off an author's dying career. No. If we have a chance of pulling this off, it has to be you."

Jewel shivers off an elated twinge of panic.

This is really happening.

And she is absolutely terrified. Not only of fucking it up

but getting fucked up in the process. She can't tell Emily she thinks the book has something to do with Deidre's monstrous condition, but Jewel just knows that it does. She can't shake the thought that if Deidre never moved back to Ware, had never worked on the novel, she'd be fine and dandy right now.

But that is ridiculous. A book about demonic possession couldn't actually possess you. Neither by reading nor writing it. The only thing Jewel has to fear is failure. Which is a powerful demon itself.

"But we need to keep this between us for now," Emily says. "A ghostwriter is supposed to be invisible. I need you to swear that you won't speak to anyone about Deidre's book. And let me know immediately if anyone asks about it. Anyone at all. Even if their inquiry seems completely innocent. Don't say a word. Just play dumb and call me right away."

Jewel bites her lip as she thinks back on her conversation with Father Mattis. She knows she should tell Emily about their interaction, but she doesn't want to have her judgment called into question so soon into their professional relationship.

"I promise," *from this moment on*, "not to speak about it to anyone," *else*.

"And to immediately call me if anyone asks about it?"

"Of course."

A relieved sigh buoys Emily's spirits. "So, tell me about the book! You said it wasn't finished, but how much is left to go?"

"It's hard to tell. I'll have to read it to find out how close it is to being done. That shouldn't take me more than a couple of days. It's only sixty-two thousand . . ." Jewel squints at the left-hand corner of the screen to provide Emily with an exact word count. Her eyes widen as the couple hundred words she was expecting to pad the total with transform into thousands. At least two. Three, if she rounds up.

64,933.

Though she might not remember the exact number, she was positive it had been sixty-two thousand and change.

Where did the additional words come from?

Jewel flicks her eyes to the Mickey Mouse clock on the corner of the desk.

Though the second hand is barely audible, the clock has to be what she heard the night before. It couldn't have been someone typing. But that's exactly what it sounded like. So much so that she wondered if Deidre had returned home. Of course she hadn't. But for a second before Jewel poked her head around the corner of the living room, she was sure she'd see her sister sitting at the desk, typing away. She forgot all about it as soon as she saw that the laptop was running an update. That explained why the screen had woken up.

But what had it been doing prior to the update?

Working on the novel?

Jewel shivers as she recalls the figure she saw at the desk when she arrived. She convinced herself that it had been a shadow since Officer Kerns hadn't found anyone in the apartment.

Anyone.

Not anything.

"Oh, my god," Jewel breathes, staring at the inexplicable word count.

"Is there an issue?" Emily asks.

"No," Jewel says, right-clicking on the vertical scroll bar and selecting Bottom.

YJR RMF

Though a part of her is relieved that the novel dissolves into the same madness as she remembered, she can't help but wonder where the additional two thousand words are hiding.

Unless they were added to the first two chapters, they could be anywhere within the text.

Jewel jumps to the top of the document and takes a cursory scan of the first ten pages. Same as she remembered. Disturbing preface. Creepy bookstore. Five-dollar muse. Shirt box filled with the dog-eared pages of a mysterious manuscript.

Jewel's stomach falls as her eyes drop to the first paragraph of chapter two, which she had yet to read.

Back at my desk, I searched the pages for an ounce of sanity. The text before me might have been crafted by Satan himself. Horror upon horror, sentences seemed to build before my eyes. Growing more horrendous with every line. Just when I thought I'd reached the end of one despicable paragraph, another word would be mysteriously added.

Jewel's heart gives her rib cage a hard nudge.

Added?

"Jewel?" Emily says. "You still there?"

"Yeah. Sorry. I was just checking something. The word count is . . . um . . . sixty-four thousand nine hundred. Give or take."

"That's it?" Emily cries. "That's practically a novella compared to Deidre's other novels. No, no, no. It needs to be closer to ninety thousand words. Do you think you could make that happen by next Friday?"

Jewel winces at the painfully short time frame but says, "No problem."

Which makes Emily think there is one.

"Look, Jewel. I know this is a big undertaking. Even the most talented writer would consider this a daunting task. The time constraint alone would send any one of them running for the hills. Tripping all the way. Deidre has some mighty big shoes to fill."

Jewel wiggles her toes in Deidre's floppy slippers.

"If you can't do it, I will understand. No hard feelings. I appreciate that you even considered it."

Jewel bites her thumbnail.

Thirty thousand is a lot of words. On her best day, she was lucky to get a thousand under her belt. And most of those were in need of a serious rewrite. Thirty thousand words in one month would be a tall order.

Jewel has nine days.

I can't do it. It can't be done!

"Actually, Emily, I . . ."

She grabs her hair to pull an excuse from her brain that won't make her sound like a complete loser. But that's what she is. A loser. A big, fat, no-talent loser. She can't write. She is an embarrassment to the profession. She always thought Deidre's harsh criticism stemmed from arrogance. But what if she was right? What if all the one-star reviews on Amazon were right? What if her last novel really *was* a steaming turd?

"Oh, I meant to tell you," Emily interjects before Jewel can throw in the towel. "I downloaded one of your books last night."

Jewel sits straighter in her chair. "You did?"

"I was only able to peruse the first few chapters, but I have to say, I liked what I saw. Most impressive, Jewel."

"Thank you, Emily. That means so much coming from you."

"Jewel, if you can get this done for me, I promise I won't forget it. I'll owe you big-time. And considering my clientele, that's not an empty promise."

16

More comfortable working on her PC than Deidre's Mac, Jewel heaves her laptop bag onto her lap and unzips the top. As she wrangles out her HP, a handful of pages from a current work in progress spills to the floor. Though they're creased and dog-eared, worn thin and torn in places, she takes care sweeping them together. It really doesn't matter what order they're in. In fact, scrambling them around might actually put things into perspective. It could hardly be called a story. Just fractured streams of consciousness that fell dead along the way. She really should just stick it in a box and forget about it.

Though there *is* something there. Amongst the blood-, sweat-, and tear-stained pages. A spark of genius. That just might set the world on fire one day.

She pulls the rest of the pages from the bag, taps them together with the others, and sets the stack on the back corner of the desk. Though it hurts her to look at all those wasted words, they will serve as a reminder of what she's working for over the next nine days.

An opportunity to shine.

Eyes back on the prize, Jewel accesses Deidre's iCloud account and saves a copy of *Unspeakable Demons* to her HP. It takes several minutes to figure out how to wirelessly connect to Deidre's printer, but finally a blank sheet feeds through and produces page one.

She wants to read through a hard copy of *Unspeakable Demons* first. Remove all temptation to start editing. Rewrite it. Make the story her own. She already fought the urge to change the first line from "I'm afraid to write this" to "I'm afraid to read this."

While the printer is doing its thing, she opens Google and types "Emily Channing" in the search engine.

Given that Emily was nice enough to download one of her novels, Jewel thought she'd repay the favor. Plus, she is curious to find out what type of book a woman like Emily Channing might write. Probably some philosophical canon, dry enough to choke Hemingway in his grave. But what pops onto the screen is infinitely juicier than that.

Emily Channing Questioned in Death of Author

A picture of Emily sits to the right of the article. Though Jewel has seen this grainy, zoomed-in snapshot of Emily before, now that she has developed a relationship with the renowned agent, a sense of familiarity transcends the overpublicized photograph. Though Emily is twenty or more years her senior, Jewel can picture them as friends. Contemporaries, if she photoshopped a few years and meals from Emily's face, cropped out her wattle, and reverted her hair to its natural color. Though Emily is not smiling in the picture, Jewel can almost spot a dimple rising on her cheek as she presents Emily with the finished manuscript of *Unspeakable Demons.* So clear is the impression that Jewel wonders if she didn't see a photograph of Emily in her youth, grinning ear to ear. Maybe at Deidre's first book launch.

Jewel had wanted to attend one of the three that had been held on the East Coast and meet Emily Channing in person, but she always seemed to come down with a bug the night before. A sour belly that would miraculously heal as soon as the launch was over.

Cal called it jitters, but Jewel knew what was making her sick. She couldn't stomach Deidre's success. Couldn't stand to watch her sister autograph books that Jewel should have written herself. Watch Deidre deliver an embarrassingly emotional reading of a passage that should have been deleted in the first draft. Graciously accept credit for the dialogue Jewel had to sharpen until the dull conversation made a point. All while she dutifully lugged stacks of novels from the trunk of Deidre's Mercedes to a velvet-draped table in the center aisle of a Barnes & Noble.

No matter how desperate she was to meet Emily, she couldn't bring herself to go. To hover around Deidre's crowded table waiting for a chance to slip Emily one of her books. None of which were on the shelves surrounding them, and probably never would be.

But all that is about to change. She can feel it. This is her moment. And there is nothing Deidre can do to stop it.

Jewel smiles at Emily's photograph—*her* literary agent, in a way—and then turns her attention to the corresponding article about the death of one of her authors.

> **NEW YORK**—Lisbeth Abbott, young adult author and writer for the popular Showtime series *Reckless Acts*, died tragically Monday from a fall from a Midtown office building. She was 27.
>
> Purportedly, Abbott jumped from the fifteenth-floor office of Emily Channing and Associates. New York City's medical examiner's office confirmed Tuesday that Abbott sustained injuries consistent with a

> high fall. Though the renowned literary agent and agency namesake was not present at the time, and has not been linked to Abbott's death, officials have sought her, and her daughter, Jennifer Channing, who was a friend of Abbott's and in the building at the time, for questioning after Abbott's sister, Lori Green, stated Lisbeth had intended to confront Ms. Channing on the day of her death. Though Green could offer no details on what the dispute might have been over, she expressed concerns to the police. She also stated that her sister had battled mental illness for much of her life. "She had it under control," but had "taken a turn for the worse" in recent weeks, which Green attributed to Channing's handling of Abbott's current project.

Jewel leans back in her chair.

No wonder Emily was so concerned with the news of Deidre's accident getting out. Not only to protect the integrity of her novel but because Deidre would be the second author on her client list to be struck by tragedy. Though Emily couldn't possibly have anything to do with what happened to Deidre, it still might cause a stir. Get Emily's name back in the news. And not in a good way.

Deidre never mentioned Lisbeth Abbott to Jewel. But she must have known her. At least in passing. They were both clients of Emily Channing and Associates, and she knows Deidre watched Lisbeth Abbott's Showtime series. They talked about it when it originally aired. She can't recall if Deidre was a fan or not, but Jewel gave up on the show after a few episodes. The main character was a little too Gen Z for her taste. Morosely self-indulgent and callously droll. She did like the actor who played her polar-opposite twin brother, though.

Maybe she should give it another go.

Not that she'll have time to binge a series.

But all work and no play . . .

Jewel blinks off *The Shining* inference and turns to the printer, which has fallen silent. Out of paper.

She opens the top drawer of the two-drawer file cabinet the printer is sitting on and removes an unopened packet of premium, albeit imitation, vellum stock. She removes the cellophane, an inch of paper from the ream, and sets the remainder back inside the cabinet.

She's about to close the drawer when she notices several hanging file folders pressed to the back. She fingers through the contents of the first, hoping to find some explanation for Deidre's dire state of affairs. Though her tax returns grew thinner and thinner over the last five years, the most concerning entry is a sizable donation to the Metropolitan Museum of Art. Though two thousand dollars couldn't have broken Deidre's bank, Jewel can think of a dozen other charities that would have erected a plaque in her honor for a check in that amount. Jewel sighs as she slides the next file folder forward. Nothing of interest. Old bills. Warranties. Receipts. Keepsake birthday cards. Business correspondence. She's about to move on to the next folder when the return address on a manila envelope catches her eye.

Paranormal Society of America
11881 Burton Avenue
Syracuse, New York

This must be who Father Mattis was speaking of. He said that Deidre had reached out to a paranormal association to determine if her novel was a grimoire.

Dear Ms. Baldwin,

Thank you so much for contacting us about the unusual document you have in your possession. We were intrigued by the sample pages you included and agree that they are very unsettling. I had several colleagues take a look at them, and all reported back that they began to experience unusual mood swings (agitation, irritability, paranoia, and in one case, rage) shortly after reading excerpts of the disturbing text. Most of us, myself included, began to hear and see things while we were reading and had a heightened sense of being watched. One woman shared, with much reluctance, that she had awoken in the middle of the night with an incredible urge to hurt her roommate. The compulsion was so strong she fled the apartment for fear that she might do something horrible.

So my answer to your question is yes. I do believe that a written document can hold supernatural powers. "The Chapters of Going Forth by Day," or "Book of the Dead," as it is popularly known, is a prime example. Though there are many different books of the dead, and all claim to hold power over the living, "The Chapters of Going Forth by Day" is the most infamous. There are many works that people believe can summon an evil spirit, such as "Pseudomonarchia Daemonum," "Greek Magical Papyri," and "Arbatel de Magia Veterum," to name a few. As you may have guessed by their titles, these books are extremely old. Ancient, in fact. Which makes the document you have so fascinating. Though some of the entries in "Unspeakable Demons" may be over a century old, that is considered a modern piece of work compared to the titles referenced above. Which makes your find quite rare.

Though I appreciate your hesitancy to part with the

original manuscript of "Unspeakable Demons," I urge you to reconsider. In order to deem the book a true grimoire, and lay claim to such a find, all aspects of the document would need to be analyzed. Including the paper on which it was written. You have my word that no harm will come to it during the authentication process.

I sincerely hope you will allow us the opportunity. I look forward to your response, but more so, a package from you in the mail.

Best regards,
Christopher Arnold
Founding Director of the
Paranormal Society of America

Jewel rereads the letter, then takes a sip of wine to wash down the grain of salt she forces herself to take it with.

Summon an evil spirit.

Such as a muse?

Could the muse be real?

"No," she whispers.

But what if . . .

"No!"

Deidre wrote a scary story and scared herself in the process. That's all this is. Of course the Paranormal Society of America wants to substantiate her claim. Give her novel their stamp of approval. Right on the front cover. *Certified a TRUE GRIMOIRE by the Paranormal Society of America.* They are trying to cash in on her name. Build a reputation for themselves. Which could rebuild Deidre's in the process. It is a PR stunt. Nothing more.

Jewel slips the letter back into its envelope, refiles it amongst the other inconsequential correspondence, and closes the drawer. She rises off her chair to set the paper in the Canon's empty feed tray, taps the start icon on the printer's display, and then retakes her seat.

Gone out from under her, she hits the hardwood floor with a yelping cry. She takes a moment to rub a sting from her elbow, then turns to look for the chair.

Which is rocking to a stop just shy of the dinette set.

A good ten to twelve feet behind her.

Though she might have nudged the chair a little out of range when she leaned forward to put paper in the printer, there is no way she bumped it clear across the room.

She stares at the bulky executive desk chair for a moment, then uses the edge of the desk to pull herself to standing. She wipes floor dust from the back of her pants as she crosses the room, and drags the chair back into position.

The caster wheels could use a little oil.

17

Jewel exits the bathroom as the printer spits out the last page of *Unspeakable Demons*. She picks the warm stack of paper from the tray, checks the last page to ensure the entire manuscript has printed, then places the bundle face down on top of the pile she's established on the corner of the desk. Upside down, she carefully works her fingers under the first page and flips the entire printout over.

A soft thump causes her to turn and look behind her. She examines the living area, the coffee table and bookshelves. Nothing appears to have fallen over. She appeases herself with a shrug and lowers carefully onto the desk chair.

She's not falling for that again.

Printout front and center, she's about to get down to business when she notices more pages sitting on the back right corner of the desk. Almost cold compared to the sheets that just slid through the inkjet, she adds them to the printout, then rubs her hands to warm them. She scans the first two chapters to reacquaint herself with the narrative. Blinking off a mild sense of déjà vu, she takes a deep breath and finds her place in the story.

Back at her desk with the manuscript, the protagonist is searching the text for an ounce of sanity, but only discovers horror upon horror . . .

As though coughed from a bloody lung, the lettering dripped with malice. The evil construct of violent musings tore through the paper in spots, bled into the sheet below, and clawed a desperate weep from my throat.

Not for the loss of my five dollars, but for the value I had placed on this foolish endeavor. I had walked home with such confidence. The manuscript fastened to my chest felt life-affirming, rife with the musty scent of a legendary script. I couldn't wait to look through its unexplored passages and find my voice at last. Which, as it turned out, was one long, torturous scream of terror. That echoed on for twenty pages or more until it was finally choked off by a wire garrote. I flipped ahead several pages, searching for a story amongst the gore. A character's name amidst the cries for help. I couldn't tell who was the murderer and who was the victim. Or how many there were of each. Death pounced like cats after mice who were terrorizing roaches who were feasting on ants swarming a dead body. One horrific scene bled into the next. Rolled severed heads across the page. Constructed devices of torture from the thin lines of dialogue. I barely had time to recover from one horrific description before a scream was sawed off below the knee and fed raw to a table full of restrained dinner guests.

Horrified, I flipped ahead until I came to a character who had yet to be massacred. A woman, approximately my age, enthralled by the manuscript before her. She swiped a hair from her brow as I did, tucked it behind her ear, and then bent a little closer to the page. She leaned back in her chair, blinking with confusion, looked around the empty room, and wondered—

"What the fuck?" Jewel gasps, untucking the hair she just swiped behind her ear.

Precisely what I had been thinking in that moment. What was happening in the story was so near to what I was thinking and doing that I thought I must be dreaming. I took a deep breath to regain my senses and refused to acknowledge the cold breath of fear on the back of my neck.

Jewel slaps a hand over a similar sensation and spins in her chair toward the living area.

The silence feels intentional.

As if something is holding its breath.

She glances around and spots an air vent in the ceiling on the other side of the room. Though she can't tell if the system is running, that must be what blew across her neck.

Jewel exhales a nervous chuckle and turns back to the desk at the exact second a dark chortle erupts behind her.

She stands to confront the empty room.

"Who's there? Show yourself," she says, then thinks better of it. *No. Don't. I didn't mean that.*

"Woo-hoo!"

Jewel turns toward the playful sound, then leans over the desk and glances out the window as a boy skids to a stop on the service road that runs behind the house. He dumps his bike in the ditch and takes off running around the house across from hers as laughter trampolines into the air.

Though that must have been what she heard, she can't shake the feeling that someone was standing right behind her chair, reading over her shoulder. Breathing down her neck.

A dark, raspy voice sweeps by her ear like a bat.

Reeeead.

Jewel ducks, looks around, then moves to the front door and presses an ear against it.

But for the hum of the elevator, all is quiet.

She sets the chain and looks back at the office nook, half expecting to see a shirt box sitting on top of the desk.

ERRR-CAH!

Jewel lets out a scream as the ice maker grinds out a cube, then presses a hand to her heart.

Though she's just begun to read, the book is already getting to her. The use of first-person narrative is effective. Reading a novel about a woman reading a novel is a little disorienting. Like holding a mirror in front of a mirror, it's hard to tell where the character ends and the reader begins.

Right now, is someone reading a novel about Jewel?

Is someone reading a novel about them?

On and on into infinity.

Jewel retakes her seat at the desk and picks up the next page of the manuscript.

Retaking my seat at the desk, I braced myself for the next disturbing scene. Rather than easing you into the boiling pit of hell, the story plopped you in headfirst. Held under with the stab of a sharp blade through the center of my thrashing heart, I had no choice but to immerse myself in the plot.

Though clearly talented, the nameless protagonist of *Unspeakable Demons* was struggling to finish the novel she had been working on. Crippled by a case of writer's block, she hoped to find inspiration in the pages before her. Since we had both bought into the muse's story in similar fashion—I in a local bookstore, she at an estate sale of a freelance journalist who had killed herself as well as her family the year before—I had no doubt that we were reading from the same document. Searching for the same thing. A masterpiece. One that would set us apart from the rest. One that would launch us beyond the stardoms and into a category of our own design.

She was alone too, I learned, and filled her days with dreams. Staring endlessly out the window over her desk at her future. The lines of fans wrapped around bookstores with her name on the marquee. Squinting off a glare of lights as she takes the literary stage and sets her bestseller on the podium. But workdays passed in a fugue of frustration, fingers laced to hair, not one sentence written. She set her sights too high to reach and could only watch as they slipped into the ether of another day squandered.

Though I could relate, I did not feel sorry for her. To pity her would be to pity myself. She had her chances, as I'd had mine. Rather than appreciating what she had accomplished and using it as a road map to find her way forward, she got side-tracked by setbacks and lost herself in the safe, dark aisles of bookstores. But she couldn't bring herself to read the works of authors she considered her peers. They should be so honored. Hacks for the most part, their anemic stories had sucked all the life out of the industry. Their characters had taken up residence in every last castle, haunted manor, and backwoods cabin on the face of the planet. Leaving her characters out in the cold, scraping the barrel for just one plotline that hadn't been worked to death.

But the manuscript before her, before us, had a fresh face. It might be stark-eyed and covered in blood, but that only made it all the more intriguing. Hauntingly so. Though the passages were gruesome, they rang true. The fear in the characters' eyes made you look away. Their pain ran down the back of your head, dropped you to your knees, and lanced your heart with an ice pick of terror.

It came to us both in that moment, like a clap of unexpected lightning that strikes you deaf with a flash of enlightenment, what the muse was trying to say through these acts of mindless violence. Almost Zen in its brutal simplicity, its advice left the protagonist and I breathless:

In order to write horror, to truly understand what frightens someone, you had to experience their terror firsthand. It was their blood, sweat, and tears that had to spill onto the page. If the path to great writing was through experience, a few people might have to die along the way. How else could one write a truly scary story? In order to hook a reader, you had to pierce the skin.

This made a horrible sort of sense.

But rather than a light going off in my head, a dark cloud settled over my thoughts.

Jewel looks up as a cloud lowers over the sun beaming through the window, then shudders off a chill as she returns her attention to the page.

A murderous urge coursed through my fingers as the muse took hold of me. Though I had opened my heart to inspiration, I thought my muse would be a poetic genius. A romantic at heart. Like Keats or Byron. But you get what you pay for. Five dollars wouldn't earn you a piece of great literature. It got you a pulp horror story with a loosely crafted storyline. The muse I acquired wasn't poignant, heartfelt, or whimsical. It was brash and cruel and indecent. And given the depressive funk it had found me wallowing in, I shouldn't have been at all surprised to learn who my muse was. It was the same muse that was guiding the protagonist of *Unspeakable Demons* through the nursery window of her neighbor's house with a knife clamped between her teeth.

My muse was misery.

Jewel turns the page she just finished reading face down on the desk and carries her empty coffee mug to the kitchen. Though another dose of caffeine is the last thing her nerves need, if she is going to meet her reading quota of half the book today, half tomorrow, she better fuel up. Sixty-some thousand words won't take long to get through, but they are enough to burden a tired mind.

And though she's done well to compartmentalize the myriad of fears the story is unleashing in the furthest recesses of her mind, she cannot prevent them from whispering to each other across her brain.

The muse is real.

The book is speaking to you.

It's inside your head.

Twisting, and turning, and plotting.

Shut up! Jewel cries over them. *Just because I've been in a bit of a funk, doesn't mean I'm susceptible to the musings of some miserable, two-bit phantom Deidre conjured up.*

Phantom?

Who said anything about a phantom?

I don't like the sound of that!

What else could have left a butcher knife lying on the countertop?

Jewel pauses at the entryway of the kitchen.

She can't recall using a butcher knife since arriving at the apartment. She's used plenty of spoons and forks, but as of yet, hasn't had the need to cut anything. She buttered her morning toast but used the appropriate knife.

Had Lyle slipped it from the block when he was in the apartment earlier?

Why would Lyle need to pull a knife?

Maybe he needed to cut a seal on the water jug.

Jewel picks up the knife and glances at the empty slot at the back of the wooden holder. Not the most accessible blade in the block. Taking aim, she slides the knife home.

Busying herself with the coffee maker, her thoughts drift

back to the book. Though she needs to think about the structure of the story, the sequence of events and how they flow, a single passage jumps to mind like a mugger from behind a dumpster.

My muse is misery.

"No, it's not," she says, slamming the lever down on her K-Cup.

But like a song she can't get out of her head, the worm of a loathsome thought slithers across her eardrum.

My muse is misery. My muse is misery. My muse is misery. My muse is—

"STOP!"

Heimliched out of her by a clamped fist to her belly, Jewel coughs as the scream burns up her esophagus. She snatches a glass out of the drying rack next to the sink and toggles water from the baby-blue spout of the dispenser.

Though the cold liquid soothes her throat, it does little to quell the feverish worry that she has bitten off more than she can chew with this project.

So why continue?

Like Cal said, she doesn't owe Deidre anything.

Though Deidre enjoyed life from a lofty position, she has never given Jewel a hand up. Only looked down on her from on high. Feigningly apologetic. Guising her condescension with an empathetic tone.

You don't want success handed to you. It's much more satisfying to earn it yourself.

As though one word from her enchanted lips could rocket an author into stardom. Jewel didn't want Deidre to make her a star. She only wanted help getting on the launch pad. If her career didn't take off, that would be on Jewel. Still, she understood Deidre's reluctance. She didn't want to put Emily in an awkward situation.

But Emily had no trouble putting Jewel in one.

She practically coerced Jewel into taking on the project.

I downloaded one of your novels, and I have to say, I liked what I saw.

Well, Jewel didn't like it. Didn't like it one little bit.

The compliment was a tactic. A carrot for Jewel to champ at. Emily made no promises. Jewel had nothing in writing. No contract. Deidre would get credit for her work. If Jewel is lucky, she might get an honorable mention in the acknowledgments section.

And special thanks to my sister (who shall remain nameless), who greatly assisted with the ending.

As in, *wrote it*!

She deserves more than that.

She'll call Emily tomorrow and get some assurances. One: A contract to represent Jewel as her literary agent once the novel is complete. Two: Formal recognition of her efforts. Maybe not coauthorship, but more than a throwaway mention at the back of the novel. And three:

Money.

She should receive some sort of compensation for her time and effort. She is going to have to work day and night to meet the deadline. Based on how much editing it is going to require, 15 percent of all proceeds sounded about right. More than fair given that the book would never make it to market without her assistance.

Just the potential of these conditions makes Jewel feel more invested in the story.

18

For all the groceries she bought, there's nothing to eat. Nothing good. Not without cooking, which she doesn't feel like doing.

Jewel closes the refrigerator door and opens the freezer. The frostbit boxes of prepackaged meals wedged in the back might have conveyed when her father sold the house. The mystery contents in one Tupperware container could be leftover lasagna, chili con carne and rice, or strips of human flesh in a nice plasma sauce.

She slaps a tomato and cheese sandwich together, tucks a bag of SunChips under her arm, and carries her meager lunch back to the desk.

Jewel licks mayo from her fingertips and pulls her laptop forward to check her Amazon sales. She doesn't expect the copy Emily bought to have registered yet, but you never know. She is curious to find out which title Emily downloaded. She hopes it was *Thunder Cove*. Though it wasn't Jewel's best, it ends in a cliff-hanger. If Emily truly liked what she had read, and wasn't just blowing sunshine up Jewel's aspirations, she might be enticed to buy the sequel. *Wretched Waves.* What better selling point is there? If Emily is compelled to find out what happens next, wouldn't everyone be?

Jewel's smile cracks into a scream as she lifts the lid of the laptop.

Adrift in a pool of glossy black, the misshapen gape of the tormented face's raucous laugh stretches to the point of snapping as the screen sweeps upward, then withdraws into the liquid-crystal macrocosm of the PC as Jewel shoves away from the desk.

Eyes closed against the horrific display, Jewel swipes a hand to fend off the ghastly specter and knocks her coffee off the corner of the desk.

Though the mug is intact, the spill is making a break for Deidre's white wool area rug.

Jewel pivots indecisively, glancing from the onyx mirror of the computer screen—*What the fuck was that!*—to the piping hot disaster brewing on the floor—*Fucking hell!*

She runs to the kitchen and grabs the roll of paper towels off the spindle. Rather than wasting time pulling off sheets, she slams the entire roll on top of the puddle.

The room sways with the nauseating tide of her head as she swabs the floor dry.

Crisis averted, Jewel sits back on her heels and rubs a wet, shaky hand across her lips. They feel numb. She can't fathom how dizzy she is. Did she stand up too fast? Is her blood sugar plummeting? Elevating her pulse? Up and down. Back and forth. Topsy-turvy.

Jewel covers her mouth, abruptly seasick, and turns her head slowly toward the desk.

Though she can't see the screen of the laptop from where she is kneeling, she can clearly picture what it contained just moments before.

A ghost.

Of her mother.

Not the smiling version in the family portrait now on display on the bookshelf behind her. But what she might have looked like in the days, weeks, perhaps months, after they buried her. Cheekbones sunk in gray flesh, lips curling over a ghastly wooden smile, makeup grease the mortician applied still decades from decomposing. But it was her mother's eyes that made Jewel cover her mouth in horror. Wide with fear, and unbearably aware. Not of Jewel, but of her circumstance. Trapped in the thin monitor, only able to move her eyes. Dart them between the cramped walls of the fourteen-inch dual-core processor.

Jewel rises slowly up on her knees to look at the laptop.

Sunken eyes. Wooden grimace. Greasy complexion. Dead tired.

Of course it was her own reflection she saw.

She must have been in the midst of a yawn when she raised the screen of the laptop. That's why her mouth formed an elongated scream. Wide enough to reverse swallow her head in one bite. Until her teeth clamped around her throat like a pearl necklace.

Jewel picks up the leaden roll of paper towels, cups the seepage with her palm, and carries it into the kitchen. She opens the cabinet under the sink and drops the roll into the trash can.

She looks across the room at her sandwich lying flat on the desk. Though she has lost her appetite for food, her mind hungers for more of the story. Craves it, she realizes, hurrying back to the desk and gobbling up words as fast as she can. Devouring them like pieces of tampered candy on Halloween.

Like a serial killer from the shadows, the style of text jumped from one page to the next. From the slashing tilt of a pen in hand to the striking bullet point print of a typewriter, the papers' smooth edges turned suddenly jagged, violently ripped perforations that sliced halfway through the sheet.

Oddly, the writing style remained consistent. The descriptive language used was almost verbatim. There were only so many ways to describe blood spurting from a severed artery. It was bound to paint a ceiling red.

I tried not to become desensitized. Enervated by violence. Bored by blood. But I found myself skimming over entire sections of the manuscript with a weary sigh.

Each new protagonist was essentially the same as the last. Aspiring female authors in search of inspiration. They were all stuck in the same rut. Blocked to the point of rupture, their genius cried out to be released.

The muse seemed an answer to their prayers.

Originally.

The words the muse inspired its protagonists to write would not make them famous, but infamous. If they were caught. The muse didn't seem to care about that pesky little detail. How the protagonists went about their research was their concern. Once their part of the story was complete, they could rot in hell for all the muse cared. Perhaps that was what it wanted. To lure fledgling authors to hell. It seemed to find them at their lowest point. Starved for inspiration. The exact moment when they would do just about anything to get the ink flowing again. And if that ink happened to be bloodred, so be it.

So far, all the protagonists in the story, if you could call it that, had been female authors who had reached a crossroads in their careers. Myself included. We all had discovered the same mysterious manuscript tucked inside the same ordinary box. I'm not sure why only women seemed susceptible to the muse's corruption. Men weren't immune to contracting some type of creative paralysis. Writer's block wasn't a female disease. Men could catch it too, fall into a funk too dark to pull themselves out of without requiring a hand up. Even if that hand meant to drag them to hell in the process. Perhaps the muse was female and felt a connection to us. I tended to think of demons in masculine terms, but that might not always be the case. I sometimes sensed a hag lingering in the periphery of my thoughts. Matching me raspy breath for raspy breath. Eyeing me from the corner of my eye. Judging me. And why shouldn't she? I had sold my soul to the devil for a little fame. All of the muse's protagonists had. Was it as easy as slipping five dollars into a mason jar? All while telling yourself that you'd do anything to write something of value?

I ignored an annoyingly anxious tug of my heart, and read on.

The switch from one protagonist to the next was jarring. Decades could pass with the turn of a single page. It seemed like one moment the protagonist was soaked in the blood of a recently murdered infant, and the next she was chasing after a homeless man with an axe. Their stories seemed to end mid-sentence. Without explanation. Had they been caught by the police? Did one of their victims defeat them in battle? Had they killed themselves rather than one more innocent victim? I turned the page on a protagonist toying with a severed finger in her pocket as she walked down a dark alley, and found another's eyes riveted to the rearview mirror of her car.

A shirt box was on the seat next to her.

She set her hand on it, warm as the thigh of a lover, and glanced at the road behind her, having the strange sense that she was in danger. That she was being followed. Or that someone was hiding in the back seat of her car.

The eyes she found in the rearview mirror nearly made her steer the car off the road.

Glinting under a brow of decayed flesh, they seemed to smile as she gasped. Transfixed by a fierce black light burning deep within the beast's pupils, she forced her attention to the road ahead. Though she wanted to check the mirror again, she couldn't bring herself to look.

At those eyes. Those horrible, horrible eyes.

Could she have imagined it?

Mistaken her own reflection for that of a monster?

She chanced a peek over her shoulder, but the back seat was empty. As was the road behind her.

She shook her head at her reflection in the rearview mirror. Her eyes were a little bloodshot but wholly her own. They must be playing tricks on her.

Jewel turns the page of the manuscript over, as if the joke would be explained on the other side, then flips it quickly over again. She rereads the passage with increasing unease.

What were the odds that she would read this section immediately after something very similar had happened to her?

She, too, had mistaken her own reflection for that of a monster. Hers was the living skull of her dead mother, but still . . .

Seeing the face in the computer screen after she had read this section might have made sense. Jewel wouldn't put it past herself to conjure up a psychosomatic hallucination. But she hadn't read this page yet.

Had I?

Had she read it and just forgotten? Was she reading so fast that her mind didn't have time to commit details of the story to memory?

Jewel scans the page again.

The passage does sound familiar.

Of course it does.

She just read it a minute ago.

Jewel rubs her eyes.

Maybe she is pushing herself too hard. Speed-reading might help her meet a deadline, but finishing the book in record time is pointless if she can't remember a damn thing about it.

Ready for a break, Jewel heads to the bathroom. She's halfway through peeing when the soft patter of tap shoes dances across the living room.

Too dexterous to be a second hand of a clock, the tapping slows, then speeds up, thumbs the space bar with purposeful intent, pauses, backspaces irritably, and then resumes with secretarial proficiency.

By the time Jewel wipes, zips up, and reaches the desk, the keys on the laptop have stilled, but two hundred more words have been added to the till.

19

"Has there been any change in her condition?" Jewel asks, holding the phone to her ear with her shoulder as she jots a note in the margin of a page. "Yes, I'll hold."

A Muzak rendition of "Up, Up and Away" takes Jewel's patience down, down, down.

She was hoping to run through the story in a day or two and find a shortcut to the ending. A clear and obvious pathway forward. But there are too many obstacles. Too much heavy lifting to dance her way through a copyedit. She is going to have to take the long way around. A week would be cutting it close. Who is she kidding? She'd be lucky if she finished reading the damn thing by then. She wonders if Emily is having any luck getting the publisher to grant another extension. She shouldn't have acted so confident when they spoke. As if she could do this blindfolded with one arm tied behind her—

"Ma'am?"

"Yes," Jewel says, bobbling the phone to her ear. "I'm here."

"Your sister's still in surgery," the woman says. "You'll need to check back later."

"Surgery? What surgery?"

"I'm sorry, I don't have that information."

"Was it an emergency?"

"I'm sorry, I don't have that—"

"Why didn't anybody call me?"

"I'll have to check with the—"

"I should have known about this!"

The hospital representative waits a beat to ensure Jewel has finished interrupting. "Would you like to leave a message for Dr. Phelps? I can have him call you once the surgery is over."

"Dr. Phelps?" Jewel slaps a hand to her forehead. "Who the hell is that?"

"The surgeon performing your sister's procedure."

"*What* procedure?"

"I'm sorry, I don't have that information. Would you like to leave a message?"

"Oh, forget it." Jewel grabs her bag off the counter. "I'm on my way."

Dr. Leonetti extends his hands to repel the fire in Jewel's eyes as he turns the corner of the ICU.

"She's out of surgery," he says. "Everything went well."

"What happened? Why didn't anyone call me?"

"There wasn't time. Your sister developed a brain bleed. We had to perform emergency surgery to relieve the pressure."

"Were you able to fix it?"

"Yes. Fortunately, Dr. Phelps was here consulting with me on your sister's case at the time. He's a neurologist. He was able to stop the bleeding, but a complication arose."

"What kind of complication?"

"Deidre went into cardiac arrest while she was on the table.

They were able to restart her heart, but she was down for quite some time."

"Down?" Jewel touches her lips as they reach for a cry. "You mean like *dead*?"

"Technically, yes. Her heart stopped for a time. Which means no oxygen was being supplied to her brain. Medically speaking, she was clinically dead." Dr. Leonetti sets a hand on Jewel's fallen shoulder. "But we got her back. All her vitals look good. Her blood pressure is more stable than it had been prior to surgery. We expect her to make a full recovery."

"How long was she . . . *down* for?"

"Just a couple of minutes."

"Can you be okay after that much time?"

"Yes. But until she wakes up, we won't know what impact the event might have had on her cognitive functions. If any."

Jewel throws her hands in the air. "So we're right back where we started? Waiting for Deidre to wake up?"

"I'm afraid so. But Dr. Phelps was able to successfully cauterize the brain bleed. That shouldn't cause her any more problems going forward. He believes that might have been the cause of her coma initially and expects her to regain consciousness now the pressure has been relieved."

"But she could be a vegetable, right?"

"Try to remain positive, Ms. Maxwell."

"Jewel," she says wearily. "Call me Jewel. I don't want you to be careful, or formal, or tiptoe around the truth anymore. I want you to give it to me straight. I need to know exactly what to expect when my sister regains consciousness. I don't want to be caught off guard."

"I can't tell you that . . . *Jewel*," Dr. Leonetti relents. "I'm not trying to be vague. I'm being as straight with you as I possibly can. I know you want answers. I know you need to prepare yourself. But until Deidre regains consciousness, we just can't know for sure. She might be absolutely fine. She might have some speech or motor impediments. And, yes, she could be severely impaired."

Jewel wipes a tear from the corner of her eye. "Can I see her?"

"Of course. Take all the time you need."

Though she had been shocked back to life, Deidre retained a ghostlike quality. Not the color of her skin. The toxic glow of her diseased husk is as rich as ever. But she seems hollow. As if when vacating her body, her soul took all her bones and organs with it.

It spent a couple of minutes outside the rind of her mortal shell. Where did it go during that time? What was it up to? Did it visit heaven or hell? What level of either could be reached in two or so minutes? Was it roaming the hallways of the hospital searching for a way out? A way back in? Did it skim across the ceiling like a moth? Slip through an air vent. Swirl across the parking lot. Follow a familiar route home. Descend through the ceiling of the attic apartment and type a few sentences on the laptop.

The timing is right.

Deidre flatlined around the same time a couple hundred words were being added to the Word document.

"I'm scared, Dee," Jewel says, stepping to the side of the hospital bed.

Admitting that aloud awakens a terror she's been trying hard to ignore.

Jewel raises a trembling hand to her lips.

"Some weird shit has been happening, Dee. I don't know if it's all in my head or if something is really going on. I've been hearing and seeing things ever since I got to your apartment.

Some of the things I'm reading about in *Unspeakable Demons* are happening to me. Not exactly, but close enough to freak me out a little. I keep hearing typing. I swear the word count in the manuscript is increasing on its own."

Jewel watches Deidre's eyelids for a second, then bends closer to whisper,

"Is the muse real, Dee?"

The slight twitch in the corner of Deidre's lip seems affirmative.

"Is it an actual entity? Or just a horrible feeling in the pit of your stomach?"

The twitch in Deidre's lip could go either way.

"Was it trying to make you do something? Hurt someone? Is that why you ran out of the apartment house in the middle of the night? Were you going to kill someone so you could write about it? Like the other protagonists in the story? Are you one of them, Dee?" Jewel swallows a globus sensation. "Am I?"

A faint scratching draws Jewel's eyes downward.

A bee is busy under the honeycomb fabric of the blanket next to Deidre's hip.

Jewel grips the edge of the bedding and flips it back.

Thumb pinched to the pad of her index finger, Deidre's fingernail is scratching at the mattress. Left to right, it resets to begin a new line. The dry tip of her nail leaves no mark on the white sheet. But the words, Jewel is sure, are stacking up. How high will the word count be when she next checks her laptop? Based on the frenetic scroll of Deidre's finger, Emily's goal of ninety thousand words might be met by the time Jewel arrives home.

She clenches Deidre's hand to stop it from composing another letter. Another word. Another horrific scene that Jewel will be forced to read. She holds her sister's hand steady, firmly.

Deidre's bones roll and clack like pencils under the weight of her palm. The scratching sound diminishes but does not stop.

Jewel yanks Deidre's hand up by the wrist and pries her thumb from the wriggling tip of her index finger. Using her left hand, Jewel bends Deidre's thumb to her wrist, then grabs hold of the skin-clad writing implement with her right. She presses her thumb just below the second knuckle of Deidre's forefinger, prepared to snap it in two if that's what it takes.

I matter less than the pencil I hold. Just as easily snapped.

"Well, that's not going to happen to me! I'm not going to let a stupid book drive me mad. I'm stronger than you are. I'm a better writer." Jewel bends Deidre's finger the wrong way. "I have more talent in my little finger than you have in your—"

"Is there a problem here?"

Jewel drops Deidre's hand and turns quickly around.

Nurse Ingram cocks her head to see what Jewel is concealing behind her back.

"No problem," Jewel says. "I was just making sure she was tucked in nice and warm." She slips Deidre's reddened hand under the blanket, then turns with a start to find Nurse Ingram directly beside her. "I didn't want her to catch a chill."

"*Mm-hmm,*" Nurse Ingram challenges, running a keen eye over the rumpled bedding. "I'm sorry, but visiting hours are over."

Jewel opens her mouth to argue that Dr. Leonetti told her she could stay as long as she wants, then glances down at Deidre's now-quiet hand.

"I was just leaving."

20

Yellow light from a sodium lamppost sprays the gravel parking lot behind the house with the scent of animal urine. A breeze chuckles through the rubbery lips of the trash receptacles loitering against the fence for pickup. The memory of a swing set in the far back corner of the yard knocks the wind out of Jewel.

Deidre always pushed too hard.

Jewel looks down at the gravel where their picnic table once stood and hungers for a simpler time. The taste of her mother's potato salad. The salty kiss of her father's scent as he climbed over the bench next to her. A fly in the lemonade. Floating. Dead. Poisoned. Though Deidre said the lemonade was fine, Jewel didn't want to be the first to take a sip. Or bite. You could salt a hamburger with arsenic and no one would notice. Until it was too late.

Jewel raises her eyes to the house as the soft pitter-pat of a keyboard rains down from above.

Though she can't see the attic apartment from where she's standing, she's sure the window over the desk is closed. And an HP isn't an old-fashioned typewriter. Even if someone were up there typing, she wouldn't be able to hear keys depressing.

Jewel drops her eyes to the bulkhead doors of the cellar. Centered between what used to be the door to their old kitchen and what looks to be an access door to the elevator, a galvanized chain is looped through the bulkhead doors' plate handles and secured with a padlock.

Whether the lock was intended to keep a trespasser out or trapped inside isn't apparent, but Jewel senses something lurking below. A watchful eye pressed to the slim crack between the doors, desperate for the breath of fresh air just beyond its snout.

Did Mrs. Willard really hear Deidre in the cellar? And if so, what was she doing down there? Crying. That is a given. But what could have possibly lured Deidre under the house? As far as Jewel can remember, there was nothing in the root cellar but dirt and spiders. Nightmares galore, but not one chair to sit on. A piss-stained mattress might have cheered the room up a little.

Though Jewel only spent the length of a nightmare locked in the cellar, it was horrific. Combing the hairy back of the moss-covered dirt walls with her fingers. Feeling between the roots of its rib cage for a way out. Unearthing blind terrors that she could imagine all too well. Creepy-crawlies bled from the soil's fragile veins. Horrors oozed from the thick worm that split under her dirty fingernails. The skeletal hand of a shadow clawed at her hair, licked chills from her neck with an icy tongue.

Jewel shudders.

She can't imagine anyone, let alone someone as refined as Deidre, going willingly into the cellar at night. Though it is always night in a cellar. And Deidre now looks like one of the things Jewel always feared would be down there.

Jewel takes a startled step back as the wind grabs hold of the bulkhead doors and tests the strength of the chain. Dust snorts through the seam of the uneven planks, then whistles to get Jewel's attention.

Decidedly wolflike, Jewel hastily crosses to the elevator door. Wider than the other two, and slate-gray metal, a keypad is mounted to the wall beside the frame.

Though she hates the idea of taking the elevator up to the attic apartment, she hates the idea of talking to Lyle more. Kicked back on the front stoop with a six-pack at his side, she had pretended to fiddle with the radio when he stood to wave her down.

Jewel presses the star key but can't remember the rest. She's fairly certain the code begins with a six, which she pushes with some authority, then bites her fingernail to recall the next digit. She studies the keypad for a clue. The black numbers on three of the silver keys are worn. Six, seven, and nine. Which means one of the numbers is a duplicate. She's entering the umpteenth variable when gravel crunches behind her.

A black crossover SUV turns into the lot and swings into the spot next to Jewel's rental.

What's Officer Kerns doing here?

Did Nurse Ingram file a complaint? Report Jewel for sibling abuse? Had she applied just a little too much pressure to Deidre's index finger? Snapped it like a pencil?

Hindsight blurring with a fret of tears, she can't believe she thought the palsy in Deidre's finger was an intentional action. In any way sinister. That she could somehow transpose words into *Unspeakable Demons* from the sheet of her hospital bed.

God, how delusional am I?

Jewel almost hopes Officer Kerns has come to arrest her. She should be locked away.

She's about to hold her hands out to be cuffed when two girls slip from the vehicle, mid-conversation. Vintage bell-bottom jeans and hair to their waists, one looks like Alanis Morissette, the other her blond sister. Ankles wobbling above platform sandals, the girls weave a failed sobriety test through the slushy gravel toward Jewel.

"I said I was sorry, Tabs!" the brunette cries. "I didn't *mean* for my car to break down. It just happened."

"It'll stop breaking down if you get it fixed," the blond says. "I can't keep picking you up all the time. I have things to do."

"What things! You don't have a job."

"Yes, I do!"

"Maybe if you told me what you did for a living I'd be a little more understanding. If you're tricking, Tabs, just tell me. I won't judge."

The brunette stumbles off-balance as the blond turns on her.

"I'm not a fucking hooker, Nicki!"

"Well, shit, I don't know! You've got all this money and no job. You're out all night, sometimes. What do you expect me to think?"

"I expect you to mind your own fucking business like you promised you'd do when I moved in!"

"Yeah, but we're friends now. I just worry about you, is—" The brunette startles as she spots Jewel. "Oh, shit. There's a lady over there."

"Hey," Jewel says, holding up a hand.

Frozen like fawns who have just encountered their first human, the girls regard Jewel with wide, unblinking eyes.

Jewel points at the keypad. "Do you know the code for the elevator? I forgot to write it down."

It takes a few whispering nods and side glances at Jewel before the girls reach a consensus.

The brunette steps forward and says, "I got us."

Jewel steps aside as the brunette pokes the keypad with the

tip of her finger. The exterior metal door pops open. The girl pulls the door back and waves Jewel into a dimly lit antechamber.

"The code is star six seven nine seven," she says.

"If you mess up, you need to hit clear to try again," the blond says as she pulls the exterior door closed behind her and seals them inside with a jailhouse clank.

The brunette reaches around Jewel, mouth close enough to kiss, and presses the call button.

Gears grind overhead as the car descends, thirsting for oil.

Pinched between the patchouli-scented supermodels, a cloying wave of claustrophobia sucks all the air out of the coffin-size room. Jewel wipes a line of sweat from her upper lip. Though she is grateful to have company on this haunted-house ride, her mind flashes to three days from now when a rescue team finds their dead bodies in a heap on the elevator floor.

Don't do it. Don't get in the elevator. It's going to break down. It's going to get stuck between floors. You won't be able to breathe. You're going to die in there. You're going to die. You're going to—

"I'm Nicki," the brunette says. "That's Tabs."

Face in her macramé bag, Tabs grunts a greeting as she searches the contents.

"Jewel," she says.

"You don't look like you're Deidre's sister," Nicki says.

"How did you know I'm her sister?"

"Lyle told us you are staying in her apartment. We heard about her accident. Sorry."

"Thanks."

Jewel takes a deep breath as the bottom of the elevator judders slowly into view. Hand-cranked by Igor, the car stalls a few inches from the base, then clangs down.

Nicki slides the accordion door back, then closes it once they're inside. She pushes three for them, four for Jewel.

"So," Jewel says as they begin an extremely slow climb. "Do you know Deidre well?"

"Not really," Nicki says. "She pretty much keeps to herself. She seems cool, though. She's let us slide on rent a couple of times. Our last landlord was a real jerk about it."

"Good thing he died." Tabs laughs.

Jewel's eyes widen. "He died?"

"Yeah," Nicki says. "He got crushed under the elevator."

"*This* elevator?"

Nicki acknowledges Jewel's horror with a slow nod.

"We didn't even know he was under there," she says. "We kept smashing him every time we rode the elevator to the ground floor."

"Oh, my god," Jewel says, staring between her feet. "That's horrible!"

"I swear it still smells like a dead body in here," Tabs says, masking her face with her hand.

Though no odor could compete with the girls' perfume, Jewel places a hand under her nose to block the scent of death.

"We thought it was a raccoon or something," Nicki says. "Lyle finally went down to check it out and found Reggie lying there. The police said he probably stepped into the shaft thinking the elevator was there. Broke his neck in the fall. At least I hope he did. I'd hate to think we crushed him to death." She dances off a full-body shudder. "It took forever for me to get the nerve up to ride the elevator again. But what are you going to do? Take the stairs? I don't think so."

"When did this happen?" Jewel asks.

"Couple of months ago," Nicki says.

"Did he live in the house?"

"First floor. Across from the Willards."

"He *still* lives in the house," Tabs says, her back to Jewel and eyes on the ceiling. "I hear his ghost riding the elevator every night. Always to the attic. That must be where he fell from. Ghosts always return to the scene of the crime."

Nicki gives Tabs a shove in the shoulder. "Shut up, Tabs."

"Whooo pushed me down the elevator shaaaft?" Tabs moans in a spectral voice as the elevator jolts to a stop.

Jewel takes in the implication with a stunned blink.

Is Tabs suggesting that Deidre pushed Reggie? Why would she think that? It is absurd. Deidre would never do something like that.

But she would write about it. Not at length, and not in the first person, but she had recounted a scene in *Unspeakable Demons* about a man being pushed down an elevator shaft. Diluted by other, more gruesome atrocities, Jewel hadn't paid much attention to that murder. A man falling to his death seemed almost pedantic compared to caramelizing someone's retinas with a culinary torch.

And though thousands of people probably fell down elevator shafts every day, what were the odds that one would fall down the elevator shaft in Deidre's apartment house around the time she was writing about a similar event?

"No one pushed him," Nicki says, rolling her eyes at Jewel. "It was an accident."

"Oh, sure." Tabs laughs as she slides open the gate and steps into the hallway. "*Love in a Eleva-ta!*" she sings, mimicking Steven Tyler. "*Livin' it up before you get pushed d-ahh-wowwow-own.*"

"Don't listen to Tabs," Nicki tells Jewel, speaking through the diamond grill after closing the gate between them. "She's just messing with you."

"She doesn't really think that Deidre . . . ?" Jewel can't bring herself to verbalize the rest of the thought. But she can imagine it. Deidre's ghoulish smile peering over the edge. As if Jewel is the one falling backward down the shaft. Grasping at the air for something to hold on to, other than the fact that her sister may be a homicidal lunatic.

"Tabs doesn't think," Nicki says. "That's the point."

"Don't say I didn't warn you!" Tabs crows gleefully as she clumps off down the hallway. "This house is haunted! Especially the attic!"

Nicki shoots Tabs an exasperated look, then shakes her head at Jewel. "The house isn't haunted. Well, the elevator might be, but . . ." She grabs the edge of the outer door to close it. "You need to shut both the gate and the door when you get out or the elevator will get stuck on your floor. People get seriously pissed off if they have to walk up the stairs and close it themselves. It's like the worst thing you can do."

"Thanks," Jewel says. "I'll remember."

"It was nice meeting you, Jewel."

"You too, Nicki," Jewel says as the glass door swings shut, sealing her hermetically inside.

Jewel glances up as the elevator automatically rises. Black flies litter the opaque plastic liner leaking yellow light into the elevator from a low-watt tubular fixture.

Did they dive-bomb into it? Kill themselves trying to reach the sweet scent of death on the other side of the elevator car, the pulverized corpse at the bottom of the shaft?

How many times had Deidre taken the elevator to the bottom? Did she give the floor a few gleeful stamps before exiting the car? Did she ride it just for fun? Laugh when she heard a crunch? Breathe in the aroma of her awful deed? How long had Reggie been down there? Decomposing right under their feet. How could they not have known? And why did Tabs think Deidre might have had something to do with it? Deidre was a renowned author. A respected member of society. She'd be the last person anyone would suspect of pushing a man to his death.

Which made it the perfect crime.

Jewel yelps as the elevator jolts to a stop.

Between floors!

She grabs hold of the diamond grate to scream for help, then sees she's reached the attic level.

She exhales a relieved laugh, yanks the gate aside by its handle, and steps into the walk-in closet beyond. Just a tad less claustrophobic than the elevator, she grabs the doorknob with both hands, half expecting it to be locked.

She turns the handle and pulls. Pulls. Pulls. Pulls.

"Help!" she cries, beating on the door with both fists. "I'm stuck!"

She presses an ear to the door to listen for the sound of feet pounding up the staircase. When none come to her rescue, she turns to take the elevator down a floor and walk up the final flight.

She's about to step on when a motor grinds to a start.

The elevator car begins to descend, taking the light with it.

Afraid neither might ever return, Jewel considers making a dive into the car, but the thought of tripping severs her courage.

Though she has no intention of stepping to the edge of the shaft and looking down, she has an inexplicable urge to do just that. To step off into the nothingness. Thud onto the top of the elevator car with the rest of the bloodsucking vectors of disease and pestilence.

A thought suddenly occurs to her.

If she stepped into the shaft from the attic level, she would land on top of the elevator. Not under it. Deidre couldn't have pushed the previous landlord to his death from the attic level.

Tabs *was* just messing with her, as Nicki pointed out.

As if this one insight makes all things clear, Jewel suddenly realizes that she has been pulling on a door that opens out. She turns the knob, presses the door open, and strides confidently across the landing to the apartment.

She's about to enter when she remembers that she forgot to close the glass door to the elevator.

So how was someone able to call it when she was inside the closet?

It's been acting kind of hinky.

Yes, of course.

It was a malfunction.

Not the ghost of a murdered landlord.

Still, Jewel's heart rams its heels against her rib cage to keep her from darting back inside the elevator closet. The gate fights her a moment, then lets out a shrieking laugh as she drags it closed. She slams the glass door with enough force to crack it but doesn't stop to investigate the damage.

"Fuck it," she asserts with a small scream.

She hurries across the dim foyer to the apartment but pauses before slipping her key in the lock. She presses an ear to the door. Though she can't hear anyone moving around inside, unlike the cellar, there are plenty of places to sit.

Like at the desk.

She can no longer hear the sound of typing.

Maybe the fiendish shadow is taking a break.

All work and no play . . .

Could make them do unspeakable things.

Jewel raps a knuckle on the door, and whispers, "Hello?"

She imagines the head of a shadow turning slowly her way. Can almost feel the heat of its vacant stare through the wood.

A soft tiptoeing sound moves quickly to the other side of the door.

It's waiting for me to enter.

She can feel it. An energy. A menacing presence.

She looks over her shoulder at the staircase and considers going downstairs to ask Lyle to escort her inside. But then Lyle would be in the apartment. She was trying to get rid of an unwanted intruder. Not invite another one in.

She's just being silly.

There's nothing in there.

Jewel bites confidence from her lip, then shoves the door open with enough force to rebound it off the wall, or the nose of someone hiding behind it. She gets a brief glimpse of the living area before the door slams shut in her face.

The dark shape hunched over the desk doesn't even flinch.

21

"Are you absolutely positive?" Jewel asks from the doorway, about ready to pee her pants. She locks her knees tighter. "Did you check the bedroom closet?"

Lyle swings a baseball bat over his shoulder. "I looked everywhere. There's no one here."

Jewel presses a hand to her forehead. "I swear I saw someone." *Something.* She points a finger at the desk. "They were sitting right there." She hesitates to call what she saw man or woman. Animal or human. Real or imagined. The murky shape was a little bit of everything. But if she were writing this scene, she knows the exact word she would have typed.

Phantom.

Lyle pivots to look at the desk, then shrugs. "Maybe they ran out when you came to get me."

"They would have had to pass me in the hallway outside your door."

"They could have hopped in the elevator."

"The elevator wasn't on this floor," Jewel says. "Somebody called it after I got off. Oh, and it *is* broken, by the way. I hadn't closed either the door or the gate when it suddenly started to descend. That's dangerous. I could have fallen down the shaft like the landlord did."

"Oh, you heard about him, huh?"

"Nicki and Tabs told me. They said that you found him."

Lyle scratches up a sound of disgust from behind his ear. "Yeah, that was pretty awful. I couldn't even tell that it was Reggie. I think he'd been there for a while. Getting smashed over and over again. I never seen nothing like it. Not even in the movies. His head was all . . . and his eyes . . . *Guh!* I'm gonna puke just thinking about it."

"How could you not know he was down there?"

"I knew something was dead at the bottom of the shaft; I just didn't know what. I looked down there once when I was waiting on the elevator, but it was too dark to see anything." Lyle shrugs. "I kind of forgot about it. But then it really started to stink. I mean the whole house. Somebody had to go check it out. The girls weren't about to do it. And Mr. Willard's too old to be crawling around on his hands and knees." Lyle drags a hand across his face. "At first, I didn't know what the fuck it was. Then I saw a belt buckle lying in the slop, and knew it wasn't a raccoon."

"So Reggie *fell*," Jewel says, leadingly.

Lyle shrugs. "That's what they said."

"Tabs implied that he was pushed."

Lyle remains quiet.

"So? What do you think happened?"

"I don't know what to think," he says. "But I know Reggie wasn't some bumbling idiot who'd step into an empty elevator shaft. If anything, he was *too* safety conscious. He'd put three cones around a little water spill in the hallway. He was always worried about people getting hurt and suing him."

"So you do think he was pushed."

"Can't rule it out. Though the police did pretty fast."

"They investigated?"

"If you can call it that. They took some pictures. Made it look good. Talked to everyone in the house. But in the end, they said it was an accident."

"Did Deidre and Reggie know each other well?"

"Well enough. Deidre was always complaining about something. Reggie didn't appreciate it too much."

"What was she complaining about?"

"All sorts of stuff. She wanted Reggie to pave the back lot because she thought the gravel was ruining her shoes. That's the thing she bitched about the most. She also wanted him to paint the house. Inside and out. And put in a new water-softening system. Not that she put one in after she bought the place. Or pave the lot. She didn't do any of the shit she had been complaining about."

"I think Dee's used to having things done for her."

"She's a princess, all right." Lyle slaps the baseball bat against his palm. "So we cool here? You want me to give the place another once-over?"

"No. I'm good. It must have been a shadow."

Jewel almost mentions seeing the same shadow at the desk before, when Officer Kerns escorted her to the apartment, then decides against it. No one had been in the apartment then, and no one was in the apartment now. It had to be a shadow. A figment of her imagination. Her eyes playing tricks on her.

She glances at the kitchenette, the butcher block of knives.

"Hey, you didn't use the butcher knife when you were in here changing out the jug of water, did you?"

"No. Why?"

"I found a butcher knife sitting on the counter and wondered how it got there. I hadn't used it. It just materialized."

"*Materialized?*" Lyle mocks with a laugh. "Damn, you really are trying to scare yourself, aren't you?"

Jewel looks abashedly down. "I just thought it was weird, is all."

"Well, weird things do happen in this house, so I shouldn't make fun. I've been woken up by a bump or two in the night myself."

Jewel's eyes get wide. "You have?"

"It sounded like someone was stomping up the stairs, but when I went to check, nobody was there."

"That's creepy."

"Tell me about it. I set a trap one night to catch whoever it was. Strung a rope across the stairwell to try and trip them up." Lyle laughs. "I didn't catch a ghost, but I caught hell from Nicki when she tripped over it the next morning."

"You're lucky she didn't break her neck!"

"The next night I sprinkled some baby powder on the stairs," he says. "I didn't hear anything, but damn if there weren't handprints in the powder when I woke up."

"Handprints?"

Lyle nods. "Like someone had crawled up the stairs on their hands and knees. It was probably Nicki teaching me a lesson, but she swears it wasn't her. I stopped hearing things after that." He looks around. "So whatever it was, it's probably still up here."

Jewel gives his arm a smack. "Don't say that! I'm scared enough as it is."

Lyle laughs. "I'm just messing with you. Do you want me to hang out for a little while? We could pull up a movie or something."

"Thanks, but I need to get back to work. I'm really behind schedule."

"What are you working on?"

"Oh, nothing" *I care to share with you*. "Just a story I'm writing."

Brows piqued, Lyle leans back against the counter to hear more. "Oh, yeah? You a writer like Deidre?"

"Sort of." Jewel sighs, giving herself a mental kick for opening this line of conversation. "I'm doing some editing on one of Deidre's novels."

Lyle's eyes broaden. "The one about the lady who gets possessed by a demon and starts killing people?"

"It's a muse, actually." Jewel's eyes narrow. "Wait. How do you know what the story's about?"

Lyle's eyes circle the apartment for a way to walk back this insight. "Oh, Deidre told me a little bit about it. I thought it sounded good."

Bullshit. Deidre hadn't even told her agent a little bit about the novel. There was no way in hell she shared the main premise of the story with Lyle. He must have read some of the manuscript on Deidre's laptop without her knowing about it.

As Jewel casts her suspicion toward the desk, Lyle confesses,

"Okay. You caught me. I snuck a peek at it when I was up here doing a few odds and ends for Deidre. She went down to get the mail, and I couldn't help but read a few pages. Wished I hadn't, though. That was some twisted shit."

"Yeah, it's darker than Deidre's other novels."

"It's a snuff book, is what it is."

"Did you feel strange after reading it?" Jewel asks, thinking back on the letter Deidre had received from the Paranormal Society of America. "Like sick or anything?"

"Not really," he says, then looks off to think. "Now that you mention it, I did have a pretty bad headache that night. Yeah. That was the night I got into a fight with that dude at the bar. What an asshole. I didn't mean to throw the dart at his head. It just slipped out of my fingers."

"Are you sure?"

"Sure what?"

"That you didn't mean to do it."

Lyle frowns at her. "You think I'd do something like that on purpose?"

"No," Jewel says. "But maybe you felt compelled to do it."

"I didn't feel compelled to do shit. 'Cept leave the bar by way of the bouncer. Fucker ripped my jacket tossing me out."

Jewel flinches as Lyle slaps the bat against his palm.

"So, we done here?" he says. "I got to get going."

Before Jewel can nod, Lyle marches toward the door. He flicks the chain dangling from the doorframe before crossing the threshold. "Lock this after I leave. I installed it for Deidre a while back. It won't keep the ghosts out, but it might slow a murderer down a little."

"Thanks for putting that lovely thought in my head," Jewel says.

"Don't mention it." Lyle turns to look at her. "Seriously. Don't mention what I told you to Deidre. She'll pitch a fit."

Jewel nods. "I won't."

Though the thought of curling up on the couch with Lyle to watch a movie repulses her, now that he's gone, Jewel longs for his company.

She sets the chain on the door and turns to look at the desk.

She can so clearly envision the shape sitting there that for a second before she blinks, it appears. Head bent to task, shoulders bobbing as its fingers dance across the keyboard.

How many words have been added this time?

Jewel moves to the desk, pulls out the chair, and takes a seat. Once again, the leather upholstery feels slightly warm, perhaps a little damp. She plucks the seat of her pants to air them out and taps the space bar to wake the screen.

Though the word count has increased by nine hundred words, give or take, it's another inexplicable phenomenon that catches Jewel's eye like a sharp pair of tweezers.

The novel is open to the exact page she left off on the printed manuscript. The last line she read haunts the center of the screen, mysterious as a handprint on a talcumed stairwell.

Her eyes were a little bloodshot but wholly her own. They must be playing tricks on her.

Just as Jewel's must be. Even if the document had somehow auto advanced to a latter section of the novel, it couldn't intuit what page she was currently reading.

Jewel rubs her chest to assure her heart that there is nothing to worry about and reads the next sentence.

Heart stuck in her throat like an ice cube, she rubbed her chest to warm a chill before it took hold of her nerves.

Jewel's hand drops to her lap.

Though their circumstances are completely different, the character's thoughts and bodily responses to fear so closely mirror her own that Jewel could have written the scene based on her own experience.

Before she experienced it.

Or did she already read this section?

That has to be what is happening.

Sleep deprived, and overcaffeinated, she has been functioning in a semifugue state. Reading but not retaining. But her eyes have been recording every word. Later, when she reread the forgotten page, her brain would regurgitate a passage or a descriptive emotion and trick her mind into believing the thought was her own.

She saw a fiendish face in the laptop screen because she had absently read about a fiendish face appearing in the protagonist's rearview mirror. She tells herself that her eyes are playing tricks on her because that's what someone tells themselves when they can't believe their fucking eyes.

I'm not crazy.

Just brain-dead.

Wishing her mind would have handed her another descriptive word, one not so closely related to her sister's grave condition, Jewel shakes her head and reads the next sentence of the manuscript.

Though she hadn't been sleeping well, and felt somewhat brain-dead—

Jewel shuts the lid of the laptop.

"Nope," she says. "Nope, nope, nope."

That's it.

I'm done.

She grabs Deidre's phone from the corner of the desk.

Emily won't be pleased that she's decided to call it quits. Might even put up a fuss. Threaten to ruin Jewel's half-ass career. Tarnish her anonymous name. *Let her!* Jewel isn't going to read another word of this damned book, and that is final. She just has to stay firm. Unapologetic. She doesn't owe Emily an explanation. Which is good. Since she doesn't have one to offer. She'll just tell Emily that something has come up.

From the bowels of hell.

Jewel inhales a stature of courage and places the call.

Voicemail.

Shit.

She might not owe Emily an explanation, but she couldn't break up with her over voicemail.

Jewel disconnects the line and stares at the butcher knife . . . lying on the counter.

Though she didn't see Lyle slip the knife from its housing before he left the apartment, he must have. She had asked him about the knife. He had teased her about it. Said she was scaring herself. But that was exactly what he was trying to do. With all his ghost stories. He probably put Tabs and Nicki up to it too. They said that Lyle told them that she is staying in Deidre's apartment.

Hey, let's have some fun with Jewel while she's here. Scare her a little. Make her think the house is haunted. Nicki, you and Tabs tell her someone got crushed under the elevator, and I'll start moving things around the apartment when I'm in there. Leave knives lying around. Fuck with her laptop. You know, write stuff so the word count in the document she's working on will go up. Make her think a phantom is doing it.

Okay, that last one is a stretch. But what if Lyle, Nicki, and Tabs *are* trying to scare her away. She has no idea why they would want to do that. Maybe to get back at Deidre for something. That seems unlikely, but who knows what kind of nasty politics goes on between tenants.

They could have been trying to scare Deidre too.

Had their pranks chased her from the apartment? Given her a rash? Anxiety could do that to a person.

Jewel holds a gasp back with her fingers.

Did one of them run her over with their car?

She isn't ready to let paranoia take her there, but it is worth keeping in the back of her mind.

To think she almost called Emily and quit.

"Fuck you, Lyle," she says, sliding the knife back into the block. "I'll kill you the next time I find it lying on the counter!"

Jewel clears the unfamiliar dark tone from her throat, the urge to stab Lyle in the eye from her fingers, and retakes her seat at the desk.

PART THREE
THURSDAY

22

Jewel paces the living room as she tries to comprehend what she just read. The horrible, horrible things she just read.

How could Deidre do it?

Use their mother as one of the protagonists in this sick, sick story. Besmirch her memory. Smear it with blood.

Of their neighbor.

She picks up the page and grits her teeth to reread the passage.

She pulled a length of Saran Wrap from the cardboard box and stretched it over the Bundt cake. Lightly powdered with confectioners' sugar, the tan, porous crust had a vaguely skin-like quality to it. Like the face of an aging actress who had just been smacked with a powder puff. Green gumdrops popped like surprised eyes as she applied more pressure to the clear sheet of cling wrap and secured the corners under the decorative plate. Sufficiently suffocated, the gaping, mouth-like hole in the center of the Bundt seemed to beg for air, and made her smile.

Almost as wide as her neighbor had smiled when she opened the door and spotted the treat she had brought over.

"What's the occasion?"

"No occasion," she said. "Just thought we should be friends."

"I don't think I want a friend like you. You're going to kill my diet!"

Which might have been funny if her diet had been the only thing to have gone belly-up that day.

How my mother talked our neighbor into sticking her head in the oven had been skimmed over in her chapter, but after three pieces of cake and four glasses of wine, she might have hated herself enough to have been open to the idea. Though the wine might have gotten to her headfirst. Knocked her out. Made her malleable. Either way, she didn't put up much of a fight as my mother tied her neck to the center rack of the oven with a velour belt. Her feet did kick a little as carbon monoxide deprived her body of air. Not the most gruesome death in the scheme of *Unspeakable Demons*, but that my mother stood in the corner giggling as the woman's hair somehow caught fire made the account all the more blood-chilling.

Jewel shakes her head.

This can't be true.

Yes, their neighbor, Mrs. Foster, died when they lived in this house, but their mother had nothing to do with it. Sure, she was the one who found Mrs. Foster stuffed halfway into the oven, but she wasn't the one who put her there.

Why would she?

Mom barely knew the woman!

So why would she want her dead?

The muse?

Jewel doesn't recall her mother coming home with a shirt box tucked under her arm, but she does recall that halfway through the renovations she had begun work on a new project. One that locked her in her attic office day and night. Typing like a woman possessed. Hardly eating, barely showering, growing more and more irritable with each passing day.

Irritable enough to want to murder her own family?

Jewel flips back a few pages in the manuscript and locates the excerpt she's interested in. Though she had a sinking suspicion, she wasn't certain who the protagonist was when she initially read the chapter. But now she knows it was her own mother, she has to cover her mouth to keep from screaming.

She'd never written a murder mystery before, but it couldn't be that difficult. All she needed was a compelling villain with a solid motive to kill, and the rest of the story would fall into place. She'd need to think up a murder weapon. That shouldn't be too hard. Due to the renovations, the house was littered with tools that could get the job done.

She looked around for something eye-catching, then picked up a nail gun off the kitchen counter and examined its features. A great line of a story ran through her mind:

The good-night kiss I placed on my daughter's temple struck with enough force to expel her left eye.

She set the nail gun back on the counter and flipped slowly through the stack of loose-leaf papers in the shirt box. The first few pages were porous and yellowed, strangely damp and unusually thick, like sheets of skin. She snatched her hand back as her index finger began to locate words like a planchette.

Butcher . . . family . . . blood . . . freedom . . .

She resealed the box, carried it to the other side of the kitchen, and dropped it into a large rubber trash can sparsely filled with lengths of pried-up baseboard. Held aloft by barbs of rusty nails, she used both hands to press the box deeper into the can. A sharp pain cut through her palm. She sucked out a speck of potential tetanus, then removed the shirt box from the trash can.

She didn't want Dave to find the manuscript. Wonder what it was. Ask where it had come from. She'd keep it in her office for now. Throw it into one of the outside bins on the next trash day. Unless she forgot.

Jewel stares at the name in the last paragraph in disbelief.

Though Dave is a common name, and their mother always called him David, Deidre would never use their father's name in one of her stories. Though Jewel routinely used the names of people she knew for her characters—many from her high school yearbook—Deidre thought it was lazy.

Just put some thought into it, Jewel remembers her saying. *You're going to get sued one day. I'm sure Traci Dale doesn't appreciate having a crack whore named after her.*

"I'm sure Dad wouldn't appreciate you using his real name in a horror story, either, Dee," Jewel says. "Or turning Mom into a murderer!"

So why had she?

Jewel sits upright as a thought occurs to her.

Deidre didn't write this.

This is a transcript. The original story was most likely LaserJetted off their mother's old Commodore computer and added to the shirt box. Deidre was transposing all the protagonists' stories into a digital format.

Including their mother's.

A chill runs down Jewel's spine as her mother's voice yells up the stairwell of her memory.

David? Girls? I'm going to take a cake over to Joyce's. She's seemed a little depressed lately. I won't be long!

"I think you're reading too much into it."

"Who else could it be, Cal? This protagonist has to be my mother. Our neighbor died the exact same way. I always thought she killed herself, but now I have to wonder. What if Mom murdered her? What if she tried to murder me too? With a nail gun! Good god! How close had I come to dying?"

"It's a *story*, Jewel. It's not real. You're working too hard. The lines between fact and fiction are getting blurred. You need to take a break. Get some fresh air."

"Fresh air isn't going to bring Joyce Foster back to life."

"No. But it might keep *you* from sticking your own head in the oven."

Jewel disconnects the line and kicks her feet to rearrange the covers. She flips onto her side for a second, then lies flat again. She can't get comfortable. She hoped a conversation with Cal might help put things into perspective, but it only left her feeling more anxious. She doesn't need a devil's advocate right now. Challenging her every thought. Questioning her rationales. Cal isn't her therapist. Though at times he sounds just like her. Always pushing back. Twisting her words around.

Though he *did* make a good point:

"Deidre knew about your neighbor dying, right?"

"Right."

"So maybe she just used what happened to her for that part of the novel."

"But I remember my mother taking a cake over to our neighbor right before she died. And working on a new project. I don't know if it was *Unspeakable Demons*, but it very well could have been."

"Deidre would have remembered those things too. That's probably where she got the idea for the novel in the first place. Isn't that how authors come up with their stories? A little truth here, a little fabrication there. Just because some of it rings true doesn't mean it's a true story."

Though that might be, Jewel doesn't like it.

It was wrong to villainize their mother so shamelessly. Even if it was strictly for creative purposes. Some things are sacred.

Jewel skimmed the rest of the chapter, not caring to read how their mother had been busy in her office, plotting their deaths. Outlining different ways in which she might do it. But she hadn't done it. That's what matters most. She didn't press a nail gun to Jewel's temple while she slept. And even if she had, she didn't pull the trigger. Both of Jewel's eyes are firmly planted in her head. Deidre hasn't been walking through life with a letter opener stuck in her ear. A heart attack killed their father. Not a table saw.

Though it had come very close to doing just that.

"Power tools are very dangerous," Jewel recalls her father saying in a shaky voice. "If you don't know what you're doing, you could get seriously hurt. I almost got the side strap of my safety goggles caught in the blade. Thank goodness your mother was there to push me out of harm's way."

Or into it.

No. That was an accident. Accidents happen. Just ask Reggie.

Oh, right. You can't.

Jewel shakes a dour laugh from her head.

The idea that Deidre murdered her landlord is just as crazy as thinking their mother murdered their neighbor. Tabs put that nasty thought in Jewel's head. Just as Deidre had put it in her head that their mother was poisoning their food when she was little.

Deidre just wanted more cake for herself.

I wonder if that's in the novel.

Jewel tosses the covers aside, then pulls them quickly under her chin again.

It's too late to work. She has to get some sleep.

All work and no sleep makes Jewel a cranky girl.

She reaches for her glass of water on the nightstand, then remembers setting it on the desk so she could make a quick note before she made her way to the bedroom. She's not thirsty enough to get out of bed to go get it. Until she thinks about cool water coursing down her parched throat, rehydrating the prune in her mouth back into a tongue.

She tiptoes past the office nook so as not to wake the sleeping laptop and winces as the floor lets out a sudden creak. She shoots a worried look at the desk.

Though the monitor has not been alerted to her presence, Mickey's hands are stuck out at his sides, warning her to stay away.

Unlike any other time of the day, there's something about three something in the morning that's innately scary. Simultaneously way too late and way too early to be awake, your mind isn't sure what it's supposed to be doing at that hour. Thinking or dreaming. Purging or storing information. But it will believe just about anything your bleary eyes take in.

Whisper wrongs against your eardrum.

And jot them down on a Post-it Note.

Beat Nicki to death
Light Tabs on fire
Snap Mrs. Willard's neck

Jewel peels the to-do list from hell off the edge of the desk and studies it. Though it vaguely looks like her handwriting, she can't for the life of her, or the violent death of others, recall writing it.

Ffff-ear me.

Jewel ducks as a sound flutters by her ear, then turns to stare at the hall between the bedroom and bath just as the visible heart of a quick-moving apparition flutters into the bedroom.

"Who's there?" she cries, snatching a pen off the desk. "I've got a knife!" Close enough.

She takes a step toward the hall, then screams as a winged beast flies at her from the shadows.

Though it's just a moth, she can't shake the idea that it wasn't a moth just a moment before. Whatever whispered—*fear me*—as it darted behind her had transformed into a moth to make her lower her guard. The upraised weapon in her hand.

Jewel slams the pen on the desk.

"That's it!" she declares. "I'm done! You hear that, muse!"

She crumples the honey-do hit list the muse left for her—for who else would want her neighbors to suffer such graphic deaths—into the tightest ball she can manage and pitches it into the waste bin.

Tomorrow, she'll get a hotel room in Luray and spend her time sitting at Deidre's bedside, flipping through magazines, and avoiding Emily's calls.

Something wicked is at work here.

Something evil.

An unspeakable demon.

If she trusted the story, and at this point why wouldn't she—her belief in it justified her reason to quit—*Unspeakable Demons* had led to the downfall of both her sister and mother. Deidre was fine before she started working on the manuscript. She might not have been enjoying the same success that she once had, but she was solvent. Financially, mentally, and physically. Now she lies in ruins. Financially, mentally, and physically. Which is a more advantageous ending to her part of the story than their mother's. Her character wound up dead after coming in contact with the manuscript. Jewel doesn't know what became of the other protagonists in *Unspeakable Demons*. The abrupt way their stories ended left a lot to the imagination. But if her mother and sister were any indication, they most likely succumbed to a sickness. An infection most virulent. Namely, the muse. First it would attack the mind. Eat slowly away at your sanity. Then it would go to work on your body. Inflame your skin and vital organs until they ruptured. Once the mind and body were gone, what was left but the soul? Reduced to a poisonous gas, it could fuel an evil spirit like the muse for years to come. For that's what the muse was. A contaminant. It entered the bloodstream through your eyes. Word by noxious word.

So why should I be immune?

Perhaps, like the poison ivy they contracted when Jewel was a child, Deidre and their mother were more vulnerable to the muse's toxic influence. It had touched them directly, after all. Both Deidre and their mother had come in direct contact with the original manuscript of *Unspeakable Demons*. Jewel was reading from a transcript. A diluted version. Less potent, the incubation period would be much longer. Frankly, reading a copy shouldn't have any effect. You couldn't get poison ivy just by looking at the vine. You had to touch it. Or be in close enough proximity to accidentally brush against it.

Jewel runs her eyes around the living room.

If the original manuscript of *Unspeakable Demons* were in the apartment, she would have discovered it by now. She went over everything with a fine-tooth comb. Looked under the bed and in both closets. Rifled through all the cabinets and drawers in search of suspicious lotions, general cleaning products, and utensils. She snooped through Deidre's nightstand and dresser drawers several times. The only profane piece of literature she found was a love letter from a well-known, and as far as Jewel knows, happily married, author regaling the sordid details of their one-night stand in three-point poetic syntax. Deidre's hair, her eyes, the clench of those luscious thighs.

Jewel bites her lip to think, staring absently in the direction of the office nook.

The file cabinet.

She only searched the contents of one of its two drawers. Once she found the printer paper, and the letter from the Paranormal Society of America, she had no need to open the bottom drawer.

Until now.

23

Jewel hesitates before gripping the handle of the lower drawer of the file cabinet, then plucks the pen off the desk. She grips it in her hand like a dagger, then raises it over her shoulder. She feels a little silly, but if the shadow she's been seeing pops out like a jack-in-the-box when she yanks the drawer open, she wants to be prepared.

Not that you could kill a phantom with a sharp implement. But if you were dealing with an evil muse, a pen seemed the right tool for the job.

Jewel shakes her head to laugh.

She is doing exactly what she thought she would be doing prowling around the apartment at three a.m.

Scaring herself.

Just open the damn drawer, Carol.

Carol would already be possessed by the muse by now, Jewel thinks in response, *so give me a break.*

Then what are you waiting for?

For you to shut up!

Though the inner repartee makes Jewel feel less alone, and

slows her heart to a steadier rate, her fingers believe they're about to unleash hell and refuse to open the drawer.

She shakes some sense into them, then grabs hold of the handle before they begin to tremble anew.

She raises the pen higher over her shoulder and gives herself the count of three before opening the—

Jewel lets out a scream as the drawer glides swiftly back, and stabs at the contents again and again and again.

The element of surprise worked.

A box of envelopes is decidedly dead.

Jewel slumps on her hip to dispel the remainder of her fear in a laughing sigh, then removes the pen-riddled stationery to see what else the drawer holds.

A stack of manila file folders. Blank legal pads. Another ream of printer paper. Tucked to the side is an extension cord, a three-hole paper punch, and a box of staples. An Amazon box is wedged in the bottom of the drawer. Taped shut, 2010–2020 TAX RETURNS has been written across the top in Deidre's hand with a black Sharpie. Having seen enough of Deidre's tax returns to know how boring these would be, Jewel closes the drawer.

She opens the top drawer and fishes out the letter from Christopher Arnold, founder of the Paranormal Society of America. She tries to read it with a fresh eye, but her right one is twitching too fast to see things clearly.

Though she, too, was hearing and seeing things, experiencing feelings of anxiousness, she hasn't, as of yet, thank God, felt the impulse to hurt anyone. Besides Lyle. But that had nothing to do with the muse. A lot of people probably wanted to stab Lyle in the face. That didn't mean they were possessed by a demon.

Like me.

"No!" she corrects herself. "I am not possessed by a demon! You have to read from the original manuscript in order to get fully possessed."

As if being slightly possessed was perfectly fine.

Jewel stares down at the letter now trembling in her hand.

Christopher Arnold and his team had felt the muse's power. Nothing compared to the protagonists in the original manuscript, but they *had been* affected.

By a copy.

Was this an example of the mass hysteria Deidre feared? Were the good people of the Paranormal Society of America her test subjects? Her gullible little guinea pigs?

Had they actually been possessed by the muse's words? Or did they experience an adverse reaction to a facsimile of the manuscript because they *expected* to have an adverse reaction?

In her letter to the paranormal society, Deidre must have mentioned that she believed *Unspeakable Demons* to be a grimoire. A book of the dead. Wouldn't that constitute the sort of power of suggestion Father Mattis alluded to? Lead them to believe the manuscript was possessed? They would be especially vulnerable. They wholeheartedly believed in the paranormal. It was their life's work. They *wanted* the manuscript to have supernatural powers. And so it did.

Jewel doesn't want the book to be evil, but that doesn't make her any less susceptible to the power of that suggestion.

There is probably a logical explanation for everything that has been happening to her. The increased word count could be a glitch in the Microsoft program. Her thoughts and fears aren't being reflected in the book. They are commonplace worries. Anyone reading a horror story feels like they are trapped in one. It's easy to get stuck in a fictional world when your eyes are glued to the page. Nowhere to run but deeper into your imagination.

So what if the story feels real? It isn't. It is a tactic. The author meant to lure the reader into the macabre world they created. You aren't supposed to like being there. You are supposed to feel off-balance as the story mounts toward a shocking climax. It doesn't matter if you are reading a handwritten manuscript in the attic of an old house, or a paperback copy on a beach in Bermuda. It is going to get under your skin. Pluck at your nerves, crawl a shiver across your neck, reanimate long-forgotten childhood fears.

It is a fucking horror story.

Jewel picks up *Unspeakable Demons* off the side of the desk and stares at it.

Words on paper.

That's all they are.

She has nothing to fear.

24

I read of my mother's descent into insanity with growing alarm for my own. Even before I read my father's name, I knew who the current protagonist—perhaps it was time to start calling them villains—would be. Though I never mentioned it to another soul, I suspected my mother had murdered our neighbor. A darkness returned home with her that day, as well as the uneaten Bundt cake. That she dumped it in the garbage rather than serving it for dessert that evening should have clued my father in to the fact that something was off with his wife, but the pudding cups she handed out hit the spot. And, in the following days, my mother began to seem herself again.

Little did I know what kind of demon she was battling.

But I do now.

It's right behind me.

Pretending to be a shadow.

It wants me to finish this part of the story and move on to my own. It's already tasted my mother's misery and wants to sample a new flavor of despair. It lays its hands over mine to guide my fingers toward its bidding. The mugginess upon my skin burns like a fiery mist but I refuse to change course.

Jewel rubs an uncomfortable tingle from her forearm before advancing to the next page.

Though I would like nothing more than to leave my mother's tale at that, I must continue. For the next part of this horrible story is about me. And how, from my mother's perspective, I deserved to die.

Pulled to the brink of exhaustion, and just a little beyond, Jewel rests her eyes for a brief second. Though the microdream she slips into isn't one she's had before, she knows her way through it. Even in the dark.

The old house smells new. Freshly painted mildew. Lumber cut with the dull edge of a mothball. Splintery hairs along the unfinished banister tickle Jewel's palm as she makes her way up the staircase toward the sound that awoke her.

She can't tell if it's laughter or a throaty cry, but she finds the guttural mewling oddly alluring. Like the soundtrack of a movie her parents watched after she was sent to bed, she longed to know what was on the screen. Though the movie they were watching never turned out to be as salacious as what was preying on her mind, she's confident this noise will be worth leaving her warm bed for.

It has an R-rated quality to it.

A moan thrusts through the door of her mother's attic office and down Jewel's throat as she reaches the top of the staircase.

Fear thick as tapioca, she swallows a swelling glob of dread and glances at a clear tarp draped over the utility closet on the right side of the attic's foyer. Used for spray-painting, the tarp is splattered with the same barf-colored primer as half the molding in the house. She so expects a ghostly specter to press a groaning scream against the plastic that she closes her eyes and wishes it away before it can appear.

Her eyes fly open as a sharp voice rushes out of her mother's office and stabs Jewel in the heart.

"More blood! More blood! More blood!"

The words send Jewel reeling backward. She catches the banister a second before backflipping onto the landing below. Her feet whip out from under her and the edge of a center stair whacks the air out of her as she lands on her back. She opens her mouth to scream, but what's happening behind the closed door to her mother's office slams a hand over her mouth, straddles her mind with thick legs, gropes her heart with callous fingers, and destroys her innocence in three grunts.

NUG! NUG! NUG!

The pounding brings Jewel fully awake.

Though the sound has the same hollow resonance as the back of a skull striking a headboard, it is not a lingering echo from the nightmare she just escaped.

Jewel sits quickly upright as a voice cries out,

"Answer me!"

The voice carries a memory of a Sunday dinner long ago.

"Answer me, young lady." Plates jump as a fist hits the table. *"ANSWER ME!"*

Jewel rubs her eyes and glances at the clock. 4:52 a.m. Too early for Sunday dinner.

The rapid fire of knuckles on wood finally gets through Jewel's thick head. Someone's at the door.

At this hour?

"I KNOW YOU'RE IN THERE!" More knocking. *"OPEN THE DOOR!"*

Jewel tosses the manuscript aside and scrambles out of bed.

She pauses before exiting the bedroom, fairly certain she dozed off at the desk in the living room.

Who put me to bed?

In the dream, her father might have found her lying on the staircase, curled in a puddle of tears, and carried her to her room. But her father is dead, and this isn't a dream.

Or is it?

She really can't tell anymore.

Watery light drizzles down the walls of the living room as Jewel makes her way to the front of the apartment. She presses her ear to the door but can only hear the refrigerator humming through the wall.

She turns the lock on the knob and opens the door the length of the chain.

A woman with shoulder-length silver hair is standing at the top of the stairwell. Her long blue nightgown is transparent enough to make out a pair of granny panties. The faux flame on the plastic candle atop the newel post flickers indecisively as the woman considers taking a step downward.

Jewel closes the door and unhooks the chain.

"Mrs. Willard?" she says, looking both ways before stepping into the hall.

The old bat flies at her in a shrieking flap of chiffon.

"Do you know what time it is?!"

"Yes," Jewel whispers sternly. "It's four thirty in the morning. What are you doing up here?"

"I know what time it is!" Mrs. Willard cries.

"Okay. Sorry." Jewel shakes her head. "So what do you want?"

"I want you to shut up, that's what I want!"

"I wasn't making any noise." Jewel wraps her arms around her waist to contain a shiver. "I was in bed asleep when you knocked."

Somehow, someway, that was the truth.

She can imagine her limp body floating across the apartment, cradled in the arms of a phantom, a page of the manuscript dangling from her fingers like a wooby she won't let go of.

Mrs. Willard eyes her up and down. "Then why are you still dressed?"

"I fell asleep reading."

Mrs. Willard rejects this excuse with a snuff. "I demand to know what you were doing in the cellar!"

"I wasn't in the cellar."

Mrs. Willard eyes the open doorway of the apartment. "Is your sister home?"

"No. She's still in the hospital."

"Then it had to be you!"

"Look." Jewel rubs a weary scoff from her brow. "I don't know what you heard, Mrs. Willard, but I think you should go back to your apartment and try to get some sleep."

"I can't sleep knowing there's a Satanist in the house!"

The allegation is so absurd, Jewel can't help but laugh.

"I heard you communing with the devil," Mrs. Willard scathes. "Conducting your little rituals. Making a sacrifice."

"You're insane," Jewel states over her shoulder as she turns to go back inside the apartment. She's about to slam the door shut behind her when Mrs. Willard reads a line from the script of her latest nightmare.

"More blood, more blood, more blood!"

Jewel turns and looks at her. "What did you say?"

"You heard me. And I heard you. What were you sacrificing down there? It sounded like an animal. Oh, tell me it wasn't that poor kitty we've seen hanging around? It was just a sweet little thing."

Jewel shakes her head.

This can't be happening. Mrs. Willard couldn't possibly know the details of her dream. But here she is, reciting it verbatim.

"As usual, Lester didn't hear anything, so he wouldn't let me call the police. But I'm not going to spend another night in this house. That's what I came up here to tell you. We're moving first thing in the morning. Tell your sister I expect to get our full deposit back. Fifteen hundred dollars."

"Fine," Jewel says. "I'm sure Deidre will be happy to see you go."

"Not as happy as I will be to leave! I never wanted to move into this awful house anyway. I heard the stories about your mother."

Jewel frowns. "You knew my mother?"

"Oh, yes. I worked in the county clerk's office when your parents bought this house. I handled all the permits for their renovations." Mrs. Willard fashions a smug smile. "I didn't want to believe the rumors about her, but now I know what you and your sister are, I think they might have been true. The apple doesn't fall far from the tree, as they say."

Jewel takes a step forward. "What rumors?"

Mrs. Willard gives a reticent shrug. "I don't like to dredge up the past."

"Then why are you?"

"As a courtesy. I plan to tell the police all about your family's history when I speak to them later. They wouldn't believe me about your sister. With her being so famous and all. But I think they'll believe me about you. Once they get a look in that cellar, that is."

"There's nothing in the cellar!" Jewel cries. "I wasn't down there tonight. And I bet Deidre never went down there either. You're just hearing things."

Like a ghost.

Though Jewel isn't inclined to believe in ghosts any more than she is demonic muses, how else could you explain Mrs. Willard hearing the exact words that were spoken in her dream. Which was all it was. That night never really happened. She never sneaked up to her mother's attic office. Never heard a strange voice coming from inside. Never saw her mother open the door and step into the foyer. Exactly where Jewel is standing now. Never saw a dark shadow swish across her mother's eyes like the tail of a serpent.

But she didn't dream that either. She awoke before the nightmare concluded. So how can she recall those additional scenes so clearly?

Mrs. Willard gasps. "What's wrong with your eyes?"

"What?" Jewel touches her cheekbone as a slithering sensation swishes a tear from the well of her eyelid.

"I thought I saw . . ." Mrs. Willard raises her hands defensively and takes a step backward. "Don't hurt me!"

Jewel gives the outrageous assertion a dismissive laugh. "I'm not going to hurt you."

"Stay away from me!" Mrs. Willard shrieks, shuffling backward.

"I'm not doing anything. Will you please stop yelling?"

"Just leave me alone!" Mrs. Willard glances behind her to gauge the distance from the top of the stairs, but it's too late.

Jewel lunges forward as she backsteps into the open air of the stairwell. She snags a fist of the old woman's nightgown, but as soon as she feels she has the situation in hand, that disaster has been miraculously diverted, the blade of a bony hand pinwheels around and severs her grip.

"Will you keep it down," Lyle says, stepping onto the

landing below just as Mrs. Willard takes flight. "People are trying to—*SHIT!*"

Hands out and eyes up, as if about to catch a fly ball, Lyle rushes blindly forward. His toe catches the lip of the bottom step. He lands on his back in a tripping turn, gets his hands up just in time to prevent Mrs. Willard from slamming down on top of him, then volleys her into the air with a hard shove.

Nicki jumps aside as a blue organza cloud slaps facedown at her feet.

"Holy shit!" She looks up at Jewel. "What the fuck happened?"

Jewel gazes at Mrs. Willard in horror. "Did she break her neck?"

Just as the Post-it Note the muse left on her desk had predicted? How could it have possibly known that she would find herself in a position to break Mrs. Willard's neck? On accident, of course. A happy one, as it turns out. The kind only a demon could take joy in.

Jewel slaps a hand over her mouth to cover the crazed smile snaking across her face as Nicki places her ear to the bag of bones lying at the bottom of the stairwell.

"She's breathing," she says.

Which doesn't answer Jewel's question.

"Did she fucking break her neck or not, Nicki?"

"I don't fucking know, Jewel!" Nicki snaps back. "But she's not moving. Call 911!"

25

I didn't push her, Jewel tells herself as the ambulance pulls away from the curb.

Though her arms might have been extended as she rushed forward, elbows locked and prepped for a shove, she clearly remembers *not* thrusting her palms against Mrs. Willard's bony chest a second before the old woman launched backward.

"Don't hurt me!"

Of course Jewel wasn't going to hurt her.

Snapping Mrs. Willard's neck is third on her list of things to do. She has to beat Nicki to death and light Tabs on fire first. And though Tabs is nowhere to be seen, Nicki is still alive and kicking.

"Well, that was fucked up," Nicki says. She releases her hug on the front porch column as the ambulance disappears over the hill at the end of the street, and turns with a sigh. "I don't know about you guys, but I could use a drink. You wanna head up to my place?"

"I'm in," Lyle says, slightly favoring his right leg as he steps through the open doorway.

Though Jewel wants nothing more than to return to the apartment and rework the harrowing stairwell scene with Mrs. Willard in her head until she has thoroughly convinced herself of her innocence, she allows Nicki to take her by the arm.

Refusing to take the elevator, Jewel climbs the staircase alone and finds Nicki's apartment door open as she trudges down the third-floor hallway. She pauses in the threshold for a moment before crossing into a Far East bazaar. Filtered through a silk scarf draped over a table lamp, Nicki and Tab's apartment hangs in a purple haze of essential oils, scented candles, and residual pot smoke. Which seems to be a thriving atmosphere for artificial ferns and peacock feathers.

"Make yourselves comfortable," Nicki says, lighting yet another candle, though the flames of thirty or so more have sucked all the oxygen out of the room.

Lyle collapses into a fuzzy pink beanbag chair with a Styrofoam squish.

Leaving the front door open for ventilation, Jewel looks around for a place to sit that she might actually be able to get back out of. The velour couch looks like a good place to curl up and cry. Which she can too easily imagine herself doing. She pulls a wicker stool away from the kitchen counter and rests half a butt cheek on the edge.

"Where's Tabs?" Lyle asks. "I can't believe she slept through all that."

"Tabs didn't come home last night," Nicki says, scrolling through her phone. "Her date probably turned into a sleepover."

"What date?" Lyle asks, hurt. As if he might have stood a chance with Tabs otherwise.

"Just some guy she's been seeing. I think he's a cop. I saw his bomber jacket in Tabs's room. Had a badge on it." Nicki laughs as she flicks the screen of her phone. "She probably talked herself out of being arrested by going on a date with him. *If* you know what I mean."

"Damn," Lyle laments. "I shoulda been a cop."

Jewel's about to ask Lyle what he does for a living, other than odd jobs for Deidre, when "Kashmir" by Led Zeppelin begins its low, seductive, yet incredibly loud intro.

"Oh, yeah," Lyle says, laying his head back to play air drums.

"Zeppelin's the best!" Nicki yells to be heard over the music. "They're my new fav!"

"New?" Lyle scoffs. "Shit, I was listening to Zeppelin before you were born!"

"I'm an old soul." Nicki clasps her hands over her head and undulates her hips to the beat. "I think I was Cleopatra in another life."

Lyle cocks his head to catch a glimpse of pink panties as Nicki's sleepshirt rises up her thighs. "Well, you sure dance like Cleopatra, I'll give you that."

"It's all in the chakra, baby." Nicki places a hand on her solar plexus and switches her hips to a belly dance. "You just have to know how to use it."

Jewel doesn't like the vibe. The apartment smells like a harem. Hemp intertwined with sex, or some other fishy scent.

"So how about that drink?" she says, hoping to extricate herself from the situation in one shot.

"Behind you," Nicki says.

Jewel puts a hand to her ear to pretend not to hear. "What?"

Nicki sighs, then thumbs the side of her phone to turn the music down.

"There's booze on the counter and beer in the fridge. Help yourself. I'll be right back."

Jewel slips off the stool and circles the counter into the

kitchen as Nicki disappears through a beaded curtain at the back of the apartment.

The kitchenette is the exact same layout as Deidre's. Narrow galley between the bar counter and appliances. Formica cabinets and faux-granite countertop. Their refrigerator looks newer, though, double door with an exterior ice dispenser. A white trash can is stationed at the far end of the counter, against the wall, in the space where Deidre's watercooler stands.

Jewel flicks her eyes at the sink. Full of brown water, elbows of macaroni and swollen Cheerios skim the surface. Though she's found the source of the fishy scent she detected, the dishwater smells almost potable compared to the clear stream of shit that flows from Deidre's pipes.

Why doesn't Nicki and Tabs's water smell as hard-boiled as hers? Though they most likely don't have a demon stinking up their lives, their water should smell of brimstone. It flows from the same pipes as Deidre's. Maybe they installed a private water-softening system. Jewel doesn't know what one of those costs but can't imagine two young girls flipping for something like that. Nicki mentioned that Deidre let them slide on rent from time to time. But any spare money they had probably went into a mutual candle fund.

"So what were you and Mrs. Willard arguing about?" Lyle asks, rocking out of the beanbag chair. He lands on all fours and clambers to a stand. A quick swipe of his hair regains his cool. He saunters to the counter and leans on his forearms. "It sounded pretty heated."

"She heard something in the cellar. She thought I had been down there. I told her I hadn't been, but she kept pushing it."

"So you pushed back?"

Jewel looks quickly up at him. "Of course not. Why would you even say that?"

"Hey, I've wanted to push that old hag down the stairs myself. She's always bitching about something. She'll probably sue Deidre for having a staircase where someone could fall down it." Lyle looks over Jewel's shoulder. "Hand me that bottle of Jack."

Jewel sorts through an assortment of sticky schnapps before finding a half bottle of whiskey. She turns and hands it to Lyle.

"You want a glass?" she says as he uncaps the bottle and brings it to his lips.

Lyle shakes his head as he chugs. "Too late," he breathes, then holds the bottle out to her.

"No thanks."

Lyle burps, then gives Jewel a sloppy smile. "So what were you doing in the cellar? You can tell me."

"I wasn't in the cellar, Lyle. You couldn't pay me to go down there. Especially at night."

"Yeah, it's pretty spooky."

Jewel raises her eyebrows. "Have you been in the cellar recently?"

"Not since Deidre put a lock on it. I used to go down there all the time when Reggie owned the place. That's where we kept the Weed Eater and snow shovels. Bunch of other stuff. Deidre made me clear it all out. We keep it all under the back stairwell now. It's a pain in the ass. But she's the boss. I wasn't going to argue."

"Why did Dee want you to clear out the cellar?"

"I think she's using it for storage. I saw her bring a box up a few weeks ago."

Jewel's spine jumps to attention.

"What kind of box was it?"

Lyle shrugs. "Just a regular old shirt box, I guess."

The original manuscript!

"Do you know where Deidre keeps her key to the cellar?"

"Probably in her apartment. It'd be a little silver one. Like for a padlock."

Jewel flips Deidre's keys over in her mind and spots a small silver key with a round head attached to the fob for her Mercedes. "I haven't seen a key like that," she lies. Deidre didn't want Lyle going into the cellar for a reason. Or anyone else.

"Let me know if you find it," he says. "I want to get down there and make sure the sump pump is still working. The cellar might have flooded with all the rain we've been having. That would be a fucking mess. I told Deidre she had to watch out for that, but she didn't seem to care." Lyle takes another slug off the whiskey bottle, then wipes a disgusted scoff from his lips. "She'll care plenty if a sinkhole opens up and swallows the house."

Jewel's eyes widen. "Could that really happen?"

"Possibly. There are underground caves all around this area. Luray Caverns. Skyline Caverns." Lyle shakes his head. "I don't want to find out there's a Ware Caverns the hard way, if you know what I mean. Get harpooned on a stalactite. Or mite. I always get them confused." He cocks his head at Jewel. "Which ones grow up from the floor, again?"

Jewel scratches the back of her neck to remember which is which and discovers that it actually itches. Burns. Oozes a warm trickle down the nape of her neck as her fingernail pricks open a ripe bubble. *The rash!* When the hell did that start? And how the hell had she contracted it? Is she going to end up like Deidre? A monster!

"Oh, Jesus," she weeps. "Fuck me!"

Lyle blinks at her. "I was just joking around about the sinkhole. We're fine. For now. I think."

"It's not that." Jewel fingers a line of blisters around the side of her jaw, attempting to read them like brail dots. Though they haven't crept onto her cheek yet, she can sense dozens of spidery sacs under the skin, waiting to hatch. "I think I'm getting the same rash Deidre has."

Lyle leans forward to examine her face. "I don't see anything."

"It's on the back of my neck." She turns slightly to show him. "Can you see it?"

"*Oh, yeah,*" Lyle respires in a fume of whiskey so strong it makes Jewel's eyes water.

Or maybe she's about to cry.

"Is it bad?"

"Not yet. But you better put something on it before it spreads. Deidre's face looked like the inside of a damn pomegranate the last time I saw her."

"Did you ask her how she got the rash?"

Lyle shakes his head. "You don't ask a woman why her face is all fucked up and live to tell about it."

"You could have asked her nicely!" Jewel snaps. "I thought you were her friend."

"I thought I was too. But she doesn't give a shit about me. She barely said hello to me half the time."

"Probably because you were acting like a jerk!"

Lyle frowns. "What are you yelling at me for?"

"I'm not yelling at you!" Though she is. The rash is causing her temper to flare. She can feel hot, tiny blisters of fury rising across her nervous system. "Sorry." She presses a hand to her warm, and slightly lumpy, forehead. "I'm not feeling very well." She's about to ask him to tell Nicki goodbye for her, when the beaded waterfall parts.

To Jewel's relief, Nicki has put on an oversized sweatshirt and a pair of flannel pajama bottoms.

"Look what I found!" Nicki sings as a sandwich bag unfurls

from her fingertips. An inch of reddish brown weed lines the bottom. They used to call it a dime bag when Jewel was in high school, though it cost five hundred times that much.

"Nice," Lyle says, snatching the baggie from Nicki's fingers. He parts the top, seals the bag to his face, and huffs all the air out of the bag. "Ahh," he exhales. "Let's fire it up. Got any rolling papers?"

"We don't need rolling papers, cowboy." Nicki crosses the room and extracts an ornate glass bong from beside the stereo. "You party, don't you, Jewel?" she says, setting the bong on the counter in front of Lyle as she returns.

"Not really. But that's okay. You guys go ahead." Jewel crosses to the doorway. "I was going to take off anyway."

"Don't go," Nicki says, snatching the bag of pot from Lyle. "We won't do it if it makes you uncomfortable."

"Man!" Lyle cries as the party slips from his fingertips.

"I'm not *uncomfortable* with it," Jewel says. "I just need to get going." She scratches the back of her neck again. Pops another blister. "I've got a . . ." *Fucking rash from motherfucking hell!* ". . . a lot of work to do tomorrow."

Nicki grabs Jewel by her free hand and pulls her toward the living room. "You promised you'd have one drink," she says, staring hard at Jewel as Lyle slips behind her to get to his beanbag chair, a little closer than necessary.

Jewel nods as she catches on, then lowers onto the couch. "Okay. One drink. But nothing hard."

"I have a bottle of wine. Red okay?"

26

Jewel avoids eye contact with Lyle until Nicki returns with her wine and takes a seat next to her on the couch.

"I can't believe Mrs. Willard almost died tonight," she says. "She would have been the third person to die in this house in like a year."

Jewel's jaw drops. "Who else died?"

"Well, there's Reggie. I told you about him. He's the one who fell down the elevator shaft. Then there was this guy named Keith. He used to live in the apartment across from us."

"What happened to him?"

"He was working on his Mustang and the jack slipped," Lyle says. "He got pinned under it. Crushed his chest." He shakes his head. "I knew that car would kill him eventually. I just figured it would wrap him around a telephone pole. Never thought it would sit on him."

Nicki hooks a thumb over her shoulder. "It happened right out back. In the parking lot."

"That's horrible," Jewel says.

Nicki nods solemnly, then exclaims, "Oh! I forgot about

Deidre! She would have been the third to die. Mrs. Willard would have been the fourth."

"You can't count people who are alive in a death toll," Lyle says.

"Well, they *almost* died. I swear this house is trying to kill us. And there aren't very many of us left." Nicki ticks the remaining residents off on her fingers. "There's just me and Tabs, Lyle, Deidre, the Willards, and that woman who lives in the apartment down the hall from ours. I don't know her name. She's kind of a hermit."

"I think it's Carol something or another," Lyle says.

Wine dribbles over Jewel's chin in a spontaneous laugh. She wipes it with the back of her hand to ask, "Are you serious? Her name is actually *Carol*?"

"Pretty sure. Why? You know her?"

Jewel shakes her head. "No." She can't explain who Carol is to her without sounding crazy. "That's just the name of a character in a story I'm writing."

"Well, this chick is a total character," Lyle says. "I don't know what her deal is, but every time I see her she runs the other way. Like she's afraid I might rape her or something." Lyle snuffs a laugh. "Yeah, like I dig sloppy, four-eyed chicks in baseball hats."

"Be nice, Lyle," Nicki says.

"I am being nice! That chick's butt-ugly."

Jewel's and Nicki's eyes roll at the same time.

"She might have a nice figure under those baggy sweats she's always wearing." Lyle closes his eyes. "You know, I can almost picture what she'd look like without—"

"So!" Jewel interjects before Lyle's mental makeover of Carol can dip below the neckline. "Did Deidre know the other man who died? Keith, I think you said his name was."

"I guess," Nicki says. "I mean, he lived here, so she must

have known him. I don't know if she *knew him* knew him. But she's the one who found him pinned under his car."

Jewel gasps. "Deidre found him?"

"Yeah. Lyle called 911 for her, but it was too late."

"You know, something has always bothered me about that . . ." Lyle reflects.

Though neither Jewel nor Nicki spur him on, he continues.

"I saw Deidre right after she found him. She was entering the elevator bay as I was coming out. At first, she didn't say anything about it. She just looked at me like she was surprised to see me or something. Then, all of a sudden, she started screaming at me to call 911. It took her a beat or two, though."

"She was probably in shock," Nicki offers. "I would have been freaked out too."

"Didn't seem like shock to me."

"What are you trying to say, Lyle?" Jewel asks.

"Don't listen to him, Jewel. He's just drunk and running his mouth." Nicki gives Lyle a hard look. "As per fucking usual."

"I'm just saying it bothered me, is all. Just like it bothered me that she didn't want to call an exterminator to find out what that stink was in the elevator. She said she couldn't smell anything, but there's no way. You know, Nicki. How bad did it smell?"

Nicki nods at Jewel. "Pretty bad."

"Pretty *fucking* bad," Lyle amends. "Most of us started taking the stairs, but Deidre kept right on riding the elevator. I asked her how she could stand the smell, and she said it smelled okay to her. Like she liked the smell of death or something."

"Lyle!" Nicki cries.

"What?"

"That's a terrible thing to say."

"I'm just saying . . ."

thunkthunkthunk

Jewel's heart jumps into her throat and knocks her chin back as feet cross the attic apartment above her head.

"I know what you're *fucking* saying, Lyle," Nicki sneers, oblivious to the sound of footsteps overhead, "and I'm *telling* you to shut the fuck up. You're upsetting Jewel."

"Wait!" Jewel points at the ceiling as the caster chair rolls slowly away from the desk, then forward again. "Do you hear that?"

Nicki scans the ceiling. "Hear what?"

"Someone's in my apartment. I heard them walking around up there a second ago. They just rolled the chair away from the desk."

Nicki tucks the thick drape of her black hair behind her ear. "I don't hear anything."

Jewel stands to listen more closely. "It stopped."

"It's probably Reggie," Lyle says, a grin in his voice. "Yo, Reg-*gie*! Stop fucking around up there, man! Go toward the light!"

"It could be Keith," Nicki piles on.

"It's probably both of them," Lyle says. "Ghosts love attics for some reason. Don't ask me why."

"It's the closest they can get to heaven," Nicki says. "I read that in a post once. They're looking for a way out. But they're trapped. So they just hang out in the attic forever."

"Or the cellar. If they're bound for hell," Lyle points out.

"Yeah." Nicki nods, convinced. "That makes total sense. Good ghosts are in the attic. And bad ghosts are in the cellar."

"Yeah, but not all attic ghosts are good," Lyle says. "The one in Deidre's apartment has been trying to scare Jewel. Leaving knives lying around and shit." Lyle smiles. "Right, Jewel?"

Jewel's about to agree when she catches Lyle in a wink. She glances at Nicki, who quickly returns her eyes to the ceiling.

"Wait," she says. "Are you all fucking with me?"

Nicki blinks at her in surprise. "Huh?"

"Where's Tabs?" Jewel demands.

Nicki shakes her head, confused. "I don't know."

Jewel points at the ceiling. "Is she fucking up there right now? Writing something on my laptop?"

"What? No!" Nicki says with a nervous laugh. "Why would Tabs be using your laptop?"

"To try and drive me crazy!"

"You don't need anyone to drive you, lady." Lyle laughs. "You're already there."

"Yeah?" Jewel says, turning for the door. "We'll just see about that!"

"There's no one here," Jewel concedes, exiting Deidre's bedroom. Lyle and Nicki stand vigilant in the open front doorway of the apartment. "I could have sworn I heard someone. They must have run out before I made it up the stairs from your place."

"I think we would have seen them," Nicki surmises.

"Or heard the elevator," adds Lyle. "That thing's loud as shit."

Nicki crosses to the desk and looks out the window. "Well, whoever it was, it wasn't Tabs. Her RAV4 isn't in the lot." She looks behind her at Jewel. "Not that she would do something like that. Tabs is a little iffy, but not in a mean way."

"So you guys haven't been messing with me?" Jewel says, glancing worriedly around the apartment. "You haven't been sneaking in here and . . . doing anything?"

"Swear to God I haven't," Nicki says, then turns on Lyle. "You better come clean if it was you, Lyle."

Lyle touches his chest, earnestly. "How could it have been me? I was downstairs with you the whole time."

"That's true," Nicki says, turning back to Jewel, who lets out a discouraged sigh.

"I'm sorry. I didn't mean to accuse anyone. It's just that some really strange things have been happening up here. I guess I wanted there to be a logical explanation. Something other than a ghost."

Or an evil muse.

"Well," Nicki says. "If it *is* a ghost, don't try and fight it. Just ask it to leave nicely." She turns to address the room. "Reggie, if that's you, you need to leave Jewel alone. You too, Keith. This isn't your home anymore. Find your way to the afterlife party. Wherever that is." She shrugs up a smile as she turns to Jewel. "Hopefully that'll do the trick."

"If it doesn't," Lyle says, "ask that priest across the street to come over and perform an exorcism for you."

"Exorcisms don't work on ghosts," Nicki says. "They only work on demons."

Jewel clutches her stomach as it digests this.

"That's probably what it is," Lyle says, devilishly stroking his goatee. "A big ole nasty demon."

"You're a big ole nasty demon," Nicki says, pulling him out the door. "'Night, Jewel. Or morning. Or whatever the hell it is."

27

Though day is breaking sharp shards of light through the window over the desk, Jewel's dark night isn't over yet. The nightmare she awoke from earlier still has her in its clutches.

She hasn't gotten to the part of *Unspeakable Demons* where Deidre kicks the jack out from under Keith's Mustang in the back parking lot of the house, but she knows it's coming.

She takes a seat at the desk. Too tired to be scared, she can only muster mild annoyance as she notices that a pentagram has been fingered through the thin coat of dust magnetized to the monitor.

A dull electric tingle courses through her hand as she wipes the screen. She rubs the layer of black silt between her fingertips and thumb. Smooth enough to feel almost wet, microscopic particles of glassy pain sliver into the whorls of her fingerprints.

Jewel clutches her throat with a startled gasp as the screen abruptly wakes.

Reset to the first page, *Unspeakable Demons* welcomes her back. Wants to know if she'd like to pick up where she left off an hour ago. Approximately when Mrs. Willard was taking a header down the staircase. Though Jewel reentered the apartment to call 911, she only approached the desk to snatch the phone off the corner and place the call. Hearing Mr. Willard's aggrieved cry as he found his unconscious wife cradled in Nicki's arms, she returned immediately to the landing to let him know that the paramedics were on their way.

Jewel eyes the word count but has lost track of how many words there should or should not be. Though 102,029 seems like a lot.

Up until now, she hasn't been able to determine where the extra words are fitting into the story.

But she is about to find out.

Jewel hovers the cursor over the button but can't bring herself to click it. She won't be picking up where she left off an hour ago. She will be picking up exactly where the muse wants her to be.

Under its control.

Though her heart screams for her not to do it, Jewel takes a deep breath and taps the trackpad.

The document jumps to the landing outside Deidre's apartment. Though many of the details are the same, in this version of events Mrs. Willard is dead at the bottom of the stairwell. Neck cricked at an unnatural angle, her gray eyes stare in vacant disbelief as the protagonist pads quickly down the staircase to inspect her kill.

Though none of that actually happened, Jewel can envision herself crouched over the old woman's body and poking a fingernail through her dilated pupil. Not that she can hurt Mrs. Willard further, Jewel, now reduced to the role of protagonist in this dreadful story, just likes the popping sound eyeballs make when penetrated. The velvety warmth of the clear jelly rupturing over her fingers, the sweet taste of—

Jewel closes her eyes before the description fingers a gag reflex from the back of her throat.

"This didn't happen," she says to the cold patch hovering behind her chair. "You couldn't make me kill her."

But it could have.

If Lyle hadn't intervened when he did.

The muse might be able to control her actions, to an extent, but its reach does not extend to the world at large. At least, not yet. And now that Jewel is wise to it, maybe she can dodge the muse's evil eye.

Some of what was written doesn't seem likely. It is pretty far-fetched to think Jewel could have disposed of Mrs. Willard's mutilated—*Oh, quite!* she learns in the next paragraph—corpse in a shallow grave in the corner of the back parking lot of the apartment house without anyone seeing her. And someone was bound to notice the gruesome keepsake the muse had strung around her neck in this fictional chain of events. Pretty as it was, Mrs. Willard's severed ear, studded with a pink pearl, wasn't worth getting caught over. If Jewel were inclined to keep a memento of the murder, she wouldn't display it for the world to see. She'd keep it in the freezer where no one, including herself, could smell it.

Jewel looks across the room at the refrigerator.

Though she was joking with herself about Deidre's frozen leftovers looking like strips of human flesh in a nice plasma sauce, that's exactly what the frostbit tub of food looked like.

Entering the kitchen, she removes the Tupperware container from the freezer and holds it over her head to see what has settled to the bottom. Impossible to tell through the layer of crystalized condensation, she pries off the lid. Though it looks like tomato sauce, the sniff she takes isn't so sure. She'll have to wait until it thaws to perform an autopsy. Or sprinkle it with Parmesan cheese.

Repulsed by her own sick humor, Jewel dry heaves a worried chuckle and drops the container into the sink. She wiggles the coffee maker out from under the counter. She's about to press the power button when she hears the stomp of feet on the staircase outside her door.

She debates running back to her laptop to read who it might be, and the manner in which they die, then opens the door a crack.

Officer Kerns is standing on the second step down from the landing. Light, flickering from the electric candle mounted to the newel post, throws her shadow headfirst down the stairwell. Splattered against the far wall above the landing, it writhes to free itself as Officer Kerns glances around the site of Mrs. Willard's—*ahem*—accident.

What the hell is she doing here?

It's six o'clock in the morning!

The young male police officer who took Jewel's statement earlier that morning seemed satisfied with her account of events. Gave no indication that he suspected any wrongdoing on her part. Had someone shed an unflattering light on her in the last three hours?

She comes from a long line of Satanists, you know, she can imagine Mrs. Willard telling Officer Kerns from her hospital bed. *Her mother stuffed their neighbor's head in an oven! Her sister, Deidre, pushed our old landlord down the elevator shaft, then crushed a man to death with his car. I hear them in the cellar all the time. God knows what they do down there! But you should check it out. Look at her computer while you're at it. I'm sure she chronicles every word of her despicable acts. That's what Satanists do. And don't tell me that's chili con carne in her freezer.*

Officer Kerns snaps her head toward the apartment door as a sudden panic attack hitches Jewel's breath.

"Oh, hey," Officer Kerns says. "I wasn't sure you'd be up."

"What are you doing here so early?"

"I heard about what happened to Mrs. Willard and thought I'd check it out."

"What did you hear?"

"Nicki said she fell, but—"

"You already spoke to Nicki?"

Leveled as an accusation, Officer Kerns practically ducks.

"Uh, yes," she says, fumbling to remove a notepad from the inside pocket of her bomber jacket. She consults the first page she flips to, then clears her throat. "Right. Here it is. Nicki Boyle. She lives in the apartment directly below yours, correct? Apartment 3A?" Jewel nods. "Unfortunately, Ms. Boyle couldn't provide me with a lot of details since she arrived *after* Mrs. Willard fell." The notebook flips closed. "So I thought I'd talk to you. You were present when Mrs. Willard fell, correct?" Jewel nods again. "So you witnessed the fall?"

When Jewel seems disinclined to respond with more than an obligatory gesture, Officer Kerns eyes the brass chain semi-blocking Jewel's face. "Do you mind opening the door so we can have a conversation?"

Jewel expresses a beleaguered huff, then closes the door to unfasten the lock. Hesitates to do so. She's not in any condition to speak to the police. And under no obligation. She hasn't done anything wrong. She isn't under arrest.

Yet.

Jewel sighs as she slides the nib of the chain out of the slot and opens the door.

"So what do you want to know?" she says, stepping out before Officer Kerns can invite herself in.

Officer Kerns raises her hands to throw it all out there. "What the hell happened?"

Jewel shrugs. "Mrs. Willard fell down the stairs."

"Yeah. I know that. But *how* did it happen?"

"She lost her balance."

Officer Kerns exhales the last of her patience.

"Come on, Jewel. Tell me what happened. Before she fell. What was she doing up here in the middle of the night?"

"She heard something in the cellar and came up to tell me that she and Mr. Willard were moving out tomorrow. I said fine, whatever. I didn't really care. I think she's crazy, to tell you the truth. Anyway, she was backing away from me and—I tried to warn her, but she just"—Jewel flicks a hand at the stairwell—"tumbled backward. Thank God Lyle came around the corner when he did or she might have broken her neck." *And severed an ear.* "You should give him an accommodation or something. I gave a statement to one of the officers who responded to the 911 call. He thought it was an accident. Why? Did Mrs. Willard say something?"

"I haven't spoken to her yet."

Jewel relaxes a little. "Well, when you do, you might want to keep in mind that she and Deidre have had some run-ins."

"Really?"

"Oh, yeah. Mrs. Willard hates Deidre. She called her a Satanist." Jewel barks a laugh before she can get it under control. "Can you imagine? Deidre a Satanist? She doesn't even like horror movies."

Officer Kerns glances sideways, bewildered. "Mrs. Willard called Deidre a Satanist?"

"I know, right? It's kind of sad, actually. Lyle thinks she has Alzheimer's."

"But why would Mrs. Willard think Deidre's a Satanist? That's kind of a strange accusation to make."

"Who knows?" Jewel says. "She's crazy."

"Yeah, you said that already." Officer Kerns turns to look

down the stairwell. "So, she just stepped back and fell down the stairs?"

"She was wearing a long nightgown, so she might have tripped."

Officer Kerns looks back at Jewel. "Well, which was it? Did she overstep the stairs, or did she trip on her nightgown?"

Jewel shakes her head like a Magic 8 Ball. *Reply hazy, try again later.* "I'm not sure. It happened really fast."

Officer Kerns considers this for a moment, then motions to Jewel with her chin. "How did you get that bruise on your throat?"

Jewel touches her neck. "What bruise?"

Officer Kerns steps forward to inspect it. "Maybe it's dirt. It kind of looks like soot."

Jewel looks for a memory of the Post-it Note in the corner of her eye and gasps at number three on the muse's hit list.

Light Tabs on fire.

Tabs didn't come home last night, she recalls Nicki saying.

Oh, God!

Surely she'd remember lighting a woman on fire.

Wouldn't she?

Jewel gapes at the thin layer of black talcum on her hand, then remembers swiping the computer screen with it. Had the muse deposited a smoky residue on the laptop as it was typing?

She doesn't have to look in the mirror to know the smudgy bruise on her throat looks exactly like the one choking her mother in the family portrait. The muse also left its phantom mark on Deidre. On all its protagonists, most likely. Taking their chairs while the authors slept, it would deposit a shadow of a dark thought on their pens, pencils, or keyboards. When they resumed work the following day, evil would transfer onto the author's hands, absorb through the pores of their skin, enter their bloodstream, and cause a nasty reaction. Deathly allergic, the demon's poisonous musings killed their mother. Whereas Deidre, slightly less prone to a lethal outbreak, was merely driven to madness. Jewel might not be as predisposed to an inimical reaction, but she is not immune. The urge to snatch Officer Kerns's revolver off her hip and blow a hole through the center of her forehead grips Jewel's throat like an anaphylactic reaction. If she doesn't do what the muse wants, it will choke her into submission.

Seeming to sense the danger, Officer Kerns takes a step out of reach and sets her hand on the butt of her service weapon.

Jewel gasps as the pressure around her throat suddenly releases. She coughs a sour yet smoky taste from her esophagus and wipes her burning eyes.

"You okay?" Officer Kerns asks.

"I think I'm having an allergic reaction to whatever this stuff is." She stares at her discolored hand. Some of the substance has seeped into her skin. Like ink. "I don't know what it is." She rubs her fingers together. Silky wet. "It does feel like soot. But I don't know how that could be. It's all over my laptop."

"You had to be typing pretty fast to make your keyboard smoke." Officer Kerns chuckles, leaning forward to study Jewel's hand. "The story you're working on must be a hot one."

"How did you know I was working on a story?"

"You're a writer, aren't you? What else would you be working on."

Jewel nods.

"Is it a sequel to your last book?"

"No. It's Deidre's new novel. Her agent asked me to polish it up before she submits the manuscript to the publisher. I'm under a pretty tight deadline. I've been working on it like a fiend, but can't seem to make any progress."

"What's the problem?"

Jewel shrugs. "Just tired, I guess. I haven't slept much in the last few days."

"Well, hurry up and finish it. I can't wait to read it. I love a good horror story."

Jewel gives Officer Kerns a quizzical look. "Did I say it was a horror story?"

"I just thought it was since it's a Deidre Baldwin novel."

"Deidre doesn't write horror. She writes fantasy fiction."

"Yeah, but they have monsters and stuff in them. I thought *The Mountains of Cali* was pretty scary. Not Stephen King scary, but it did have a horror element to it. That troll scene really creeped me out." She shrugs up a smile. "Maybe I'm just a wimp."

"That's not a good thing for a cop to be."

"I fight crime. Not monsters." They share a fleeting laugh, then sigh in unison. "So when will you be done working on the book?"

"Never. I'm not going to finish it."

"Why not?"

"It's too much work. I never should have agreed to take it on in the first place. I need to focus my attention on Deidre. I've been totally neglecting her."

"Aren't you helping her by finishing the novel?"

"That's what I keep telling myself. Frankly, I don't think Deidre would want me working on it. She doesn't think much of my writing."

"That's just sibling rivalry. I bet you're an excellent writer."

Jewel shakes her head to confide, "I'm really not."

"Don't say that. And don't quit either. I'm sure you'll do a great job."

Jewel shrugs again, then swings a finger at the apartment.

"Are you going to arrest me for pushing Mrs. Willard down the stairs, or can I go take a shower?"

"That depends. *Did* you push Mrs. Willard down the stairs?"

"Of course not. Why would I? I hardly know the woman."

"Hey. I'd want to kill someone, too, if they woke me up at three o'clock in the morning to bitch me out."

"Well, I have more self-control than you do."

Officer Kerns rolls her eyes toward the stairs. "See ya." Jewel's about to enter the apartment when she adds, "And Jewel?"

Jewel turns to look at her.

"Don't leave town, okay?"

Jewel flinches. "Is that an order?"

"Just a friendly request." Though her tone suggests otherwise. Officer Kerns laughs, noting Jewel's stark expression. "I just want you to finish the book, is all. I'm dying to read it."

"You might if you do," Jewel mutters as she turns to enter the apartment.

"What was that?"

"Nothing," Jewel says over her shoulder, then closes the door.

28

Though she's only been asleep for a fraction of a second, the clock on the nightstand, and the amount of sun pouring through the window, says it's half past noon. Unable to believe her eyes, Jewel picks up her phone from the nightstand to verify the time, then lets out a scream as it vibrates.

She squints at the screen.

Emily Channing.

Shit.

Jewel clears her throat to croak out a greeting and nearly vomits. "*Gah*-lo."

"Did I *wake* you?" *You loser. You complete and utter waste of life.* "It's after noon already."

"No." Jewel lifts her head from the pillow. "I'm up."

"You sound horrible. Are you sick?"

"No. Maybe. I don't know. I've been up all night."

"Did you finish reading the novel?"

"Not yet." Jewel swings her feet to the floor and exits the bedroom. She needs coffee in order to have this conversation. "I'm having a hard time getting through it. There's a lot going on. With Deidre and everything. I don't think I'm going to be able to finish the novel after all."

Emily's silent long enough for Jewel to check the screen to see if they're still connected.

"What do you mean you're not going to be able to finish it?" Emily asks.

I mean I'm done. Stick a fork in me.

Jewel opens the utensil drawer, extracts a two-prong barbeque fork, and uses it as a back scratcher.

"I'm sorry, Emily," she sighs, relieved in more ways than one. "But I'm going to have to pass on the project. I appreciate you giving me the chance, but I can't do it. There's way more to it than I realized."

"Like what?"

The filter in Jewel's brain that's supposed to catch bad ideas before they leave her mouth blows a gasket, and the truth comes pouring out.

"I think the book is possessed, Emily."

Jewel can't tell if Emily's scoff is beyond frustrated or cynically amused, but it certainly doesn't sound pleased. "What do you mean, *possessed*?"

"It's evil. Like, demonic."

Emily laughs. "Well, it *is* a horror novel, Jewel. I would expect it to be a little evil."

"I don't mean evil scary. Well, it is evil scary, but that's not what I'm talking about."

Jewel slouches onto the desk chair and stares at the Post-it Note she threw away yesterday. Uncrumpled and smoothed flat, Mrs. Willard has been crossed off her list of things to do. Another terrible task has been added to the bottom.

Gut Nurse Ingram

Jewel holds the phone between her ear and shoulder and tears the note to shreds.

"I know this sounds crazy, Emily, but I think the book is actually possessed by the devil. Or a demon. Actually, it's a muse. That's how the novel starts. The main character buys a manuscript from a muse. Well, she doesn't *buy* it from a muse. The muse just comes with it. She bought the manuscript at a bookstore. But she was trying to summon a muse when she found it. I think it's a grimoire. Like *The Book of the Dead*. It affects the person who reads it and makes them do bad things. Reading it allows the devil to take over your soul."

"Or a demonic muse."

Too tired to pick up the sardonic tone in Emily's voice, Jewel says, "Exactly. I know that sounds crazy, but I think that's what happened to Deidre."

"I thought she got hit by a car?"

"She did, but that's because she had been reading the manuscript. It drove her mad. Turned her into a psychotic monster. She ran into traffic to stop herself from hurting people. Two men she knew are dead, Emily. They died horrible deaths. Just like the neighbor my mother killed. Don't you see? They're all connected!"

"Sorry. Did you say your mother killed your neighbor?"

"I don't know. I don't know what's real and what's not anymore. I'm trying to figure it out. But I know the manuscript is at the heart of it. It puts a spell on you. I'm sure that's what happened to Deidre. And to our mother. And now it's happening to *ME!*" Jewel covers her mouth as the word cries from her in a laughing scream. "I'm sorry, Emily," she sniffs. "I'm just very upset."

"I can hear that."

"I know this sounds crazy. *I* sound crazy. But everything I've said is true. I need you to believe me."

"I do believe you."

Jewel takes a hopeful gasp. "You do?"

"Yes. I believe this project is too much for you. I shouldn't have put you in this position. I should have realized how fragile you were. Your sister is lying in a coma. Fighting for her life. That must be a terrible stress."

"No, that's not—"

"And for as much as I was counting on you, I don't think you should finish the novel either. Not in the state you're in. You won't be able to do it justice. Just send it to me, and I'll have one of my more seasoned authors take a go at it."

"No!" Jewel nearly screams. "You're not listening to me, Emily. *No one* should work on this novel. Not me. Not anyone. It's evil!"

"The book's not evil. You are."

"*What?*"

"Not thinking clearly."

"Oh."

"I appreciate all you've done, Jewel. I know you gave it your best. And I do understand your concerns. But if you can't or won't finish the novel, then I'll have to find someone who will. I spoke to an author of mine, and she all but jumped at the idea."

Out the window? Jewel wonders, thinking of Lisbeth Abbott's fall from grace.

"But I need you to send me the manuscript right away," Emily says. "We're running out of time."

Jewel looks out her own window on a beautiful spring day and finds it hard to see the horrors of the night before. But she can see the dark days ahead. When she looks back on this moment. *Unspeakable Demons* on the bestsellers list. Praise for the ghostwriter who swooped in to save the day. Their formally unknown titles exploding onto the scene. A six-figure advance for their next book. Now a Netflix series. Trolling their social media accounts in the middle of the night. Leaving snide, anonymous comments between sips of wine. Knowing that it could have been, should have been, her. If only she hadn't let fear get in her way.

Jewel shakes her head determinedly.

"No."

"No, what?" Emily asks. "You won't send it to me?"

"No. I'll do it."

"Jewel, I don't think—"

"I'm not going to put this on someone else. I'm almost done reading it. Another author won't be able to get up to speed in time to meet the deadline."

"But what about everything you were saying? About the book being evil and all?"

"Like you said. It's supposed to be evil. It's a horror novel. And a pretty good one at that if I thought it might actually be possessing me." Jewel lets out a soft, deprecating laugh as she moves into the kitchen. "That's what I get for reading a horror story at night. I'll just make sure to work on it during the day from now on. I'll be fine. It'll be fine. More than fine. The book's going to be great. A bestseller. I'll see that it is. You have my word, Emily."

"Are you absolutely sure?"

"Positive."

"Because if you can't finish it—"

"I will."

"Well, then . . . I guess I'll let you get back to it. But, Jewel?"

"Yes."

"Promise me you'll get some sleep."

"I promise," Jewel says, slipping a K-Cup into the Keurig machine and slamming the lever on the lid.

29

Though she wants to finish reading the manuscript as soon as possible, if she's going to write a half-decent ending, and not just lob an asteroid at the earth, THE END, she can't skip the gory details. There might be a diamond in a rough of scalped hair. A silver lining in a taut wire garrote. A key could be hidden in a steaming pile of innards that could unlock the entire mystery.

Which is the mystery itself.

What is the novel actually about?

Most of it is just the corrupt contemplations of one deranged lunatic after another. Their stories don't go anywhere. Their characters haven't been developed. You aren't rooting for them. You want good to prevail over evil, but that never happens. Evil keeps winning. Keeps killing. Jewel feels connected to the current protagonist, but that is because they *have* a connection.

She is her mother.

No.

The character is *based* on her mother.

In order to get through this, she has to believe that. She needs to read the story through the eye of an average reader and ask herself if they would feel connected to that character. To any of the characters.

She doesn't know how the rest of the story will unfold, what twists and turns it might take, but she knows the narrator has to drive it home.

It is her story, after all.

Jewel taps the pen on the tip of her nose, then makes a note in the margin of the page she just finished reading.

My muse is misery

Jewel blinks at the words, then scratches them out. She tries again, focusing hard on what she intended to write: Make MC more relatable.

Though she's heard of psychics doing automatic writings to connect with the netherworld, she always thought it was a scam.

Until her own hand gives her a little demonstration.

Jewel stares in horror as a psychographic message scratches across the paper.

I write evil into being.

She throws the pen at the floor, then holds her hand up to stare at it. Clutches it into a fist. Opens it. Touches her thumb to each finger. Makes a peace sign. Spock fingers. Flips herself off.

"Fuck you too!" she cries, collapsing back into the chair.

She locks eyes with the terrified reflection in the window over the desk and gives herself a good talking-to.

"Get a grip on yourself, *Carol*. Yeah. That's right. You heard me. I called you Carol. Because that's what you're acting like. A stereotypical ninny who's afraid of her own shadow." Jewel points a finger at her reflection. "Stop scaring yourself. There's no such thing as a muse, so there's no way you're being possessed by one. If you were reading a novel about werewolves, you'd probably think you were turning into one. What's this? A whisker on my chin! Oh, no! I'm a werewolf! Better go check the weather app to find out when the next full moon cycle is."

Talk about lunatics.

Jewel shakes a miserable laugh from her head. She can't believe she shared her concerns about the muse with Emily.

The book's evil! Evil, I tell you!

"Oh, my god."

What Emily must think of me.

But authors could be overly dramatic. Even a little psychotic. That's what makes them good writers. Emily's client list is probably full of talented, crazy-ass drama queens. They may have never claimed to have been possessed by an evil muse, but they probably battled some demons of their own. Lisbeth Abbott is a prime example.

Now there's a success story to model yourself after.

"Shut up." Jewel rubs her temple. "All I have to do is deliver on my promise, and Emily will forget all about my insane outburst."

Her promise of a bestseller.

Out of this mess?

Jewel picks up her copy of the manuscript from the edge of the desk and runs her thumb across the rough leaves. Though there are a scant amount of pages, their contents seem ponderous. A daunting number of words that still need to be read and revised.

There's got to be a story in here somewhere!

She just has to find it and make it her own. Correction: Make it seem like Deidre Baldwin wrote it.

She might have sold Emily on the idea that she is finishing

Unspeakable Demons to help her sister in her time of need. And for the most part, that is true. But Jewel can't deny that she has an ulterior motive. This is her chance to outshine the great Deidre Baldwin. Once Emily reads the ending of *Unspeakable Demons*, she'll know who has all the talent in the family. Jewel might not get full credit, Deidre's name would still be on the cover, unless . . .

She never regains consciousness.

Hasn't that wicked wish been dancing in the back of her mind like a witch around a pyre? If Deidre never wakes up, might that not work to Jewel's advantage? The novel would become an instant success. Posthumous works always are. With Deidre gone, the publisher will need someone to make the circuit. Go on *Today* and promote the novel. Tell the story of how it came to fruition.

And what a story it is.

"*That's absolutely amazing, Jewel,*" Jenna Bush says, leaning forward in Jewel's mind's eye. "*I have to say, the ending of* Unspeakable Demons *is what stood out to me the most. I never saw that twist coming. I swear I still have goose bumps. Have you written any other novels? I know our audience would love to check them out.*"

Though Jewel would prefer her original works to be accepted on their own merits, she will take what she can get. An agent. A publisher. An actual, honest-to-God hardback novel with her name on it. She can almost feel it in her hands. The warmth of the paper. The sweet aroma of success. Satisfying as a fresh biscuit out of the oven. She isn't exactly a starving artist, but she still hungers to see her name on the *New York Times* bestsellers list.

All she needs for that to happen is for Deidre to die.

Jewel rubs the horrible yet utterly thrilling thought from

the center of her forehead and prays to the most powerful god in the solar system that Deidre will be okay.

Despite everything, Jewel loves her sister. Sure, they might not have been close growing up, an age difference can do that, but she would never wish harm on Deidre. Not that wishing it would make it so.

She'd have to write it.

Jewel glances down at her margin note.

I write evil into being.

She shifts her eyes from the troubling words she didn't mean to write and spots the next line in the manuscript:

My sister wanted me dead . . .

30

Jewel enters the hospital room in a fog, crosses to the bed, and shakes the page of the manuscript at Deidre.

"What's the meaning of this?"

Deidre's lax expression has no idea.

"You can't rewrite history, Dee," Jewel says, then reads aloud from the page, "'Though I knew in my heart I wasn't responsible for what happened, and that the horrible events that unfolded were preordained in a story I could barely comprehend, my mother's blood was still on my hands. But the one who guided my hand, who plunged the scissors into the soft belly of her very soul, is the true villain in this sordid tale. And though she'll never admit to what she did, my sister brought about our mother's death.'" Jewel drops the page to her side. "That's bullshit! I didn't bring about Mom's death! Her appendix ruptured!"

Then why was there blood in the hallway, whispers doubt.

She can't be sure there was. She didn't remember there being blood in the hallway until she started reading the manuscript. The story is planting thoughts in her head. Making her see things that aren't real. Think things that aren't true. Write things she didn't intend to write. Of course she was thinking about the night her mother died. She was reading about it.

Being only eight at the time, Jewel can't remember much about that night. A few peripheral snippets in the corner of her mind. She remembers being scared. Of course she was. Her mother had just died. No wonder she blocked it out. Her little brain couldn't process it. But it is processing it now. Filling in the blanks with details from *Unspeakable Demons.* Making up memories as she goes along.

Jewel grabs hold of the edge of one and eases it back a crack. The glow of a nightlight spills into the hallway. Her father is crouched over a prone shape. Bare legs outstretched, toes slumped, pale-pink slippers speckled red. A strewn arm to the right of her father's knee points at Jewel with a limp finger.

"Is Mommy okay?"

"Yes. Go back to bed. Everything's fine."

"DeeDee said she was bad."

"It's not bad. She'll be okay. Go back to bed."

Jewel lifts her memory over the head of her father and spots movement in the darkened doorway across the hall.

Deidre floats slowly out of the bathroom. The front of her flannel nightgown is covered in blood. A silver glint drops from her hand, clangs to the floor, and strikes Jewel with an unbearable flash of clarity.

"*You* killed Mom," she breathes, staring down at Deidre.

Why didn't that occur to me before?

Because it was too horrible to contemplate.

But it would explain so much.

Why Deidre and Jewel were never close. Guilt is a thick wedge. Thicker than the years that separate them. Thicker than all of Jewel's petty jealousies and resentments combined. And of course her father would have lied to her about how her mother died. You don't feed a story like that to a little girl catatonic with grief. A ruptured appendix was much more palatable.

But why wasn't an arrest been made? Because Deidre was too young? Had their father intervened? Did he tell the police a different story? They wouldn't have been gullible enough to buy the ole ruptured appendix ploy. But they wouldn't have believed that an evil muse had possessed a daughter to kill her mother either.

Jewel looks down at the page in her hand.

"Why would you confess to murdering someone in a novel millions of people might read?"

Because everyone would think it is fiction.

Only Jewel and Deidre would know the truth.

"This is a true story, isn't it?"

The small smile that twitches the corner of Deidre's lip jumps a spidery sensation up Jewel's spine.

"Did Dad know you killed Mom?"

The heart monitor issues an extra beat.

Jewel studies its screen for a moment, then asks,

"Was that a yes?"

. . . beep . . . beep . . . B-beep . . . beep . . . beep . . .

Jewel rubs her chest as her own heart contracts twice in quick succession. Yes. This could work. Deidre might be unconscious, but that doesn't mean she has nothing to say.

"Did the muse tell you to kill Mom?" she asks.

. . . beep . . . B-beep . . . beep . . .

Yes.

Oh, my god.

"Did it tell you to kill Reggie and Keith?"

. . . beep . . . B-beep . . . B-beep . . . beep . . . beep . . .

"Did you try to resist it?"

. . . beep . . . beep . . . beep . . . beep . . .

Jewel's brows slam together. "No? You didn't try to fight it off? To save yourself? To save them?"

. . . beep . . . beep . . . beep . . . beep . . .

"Why not? You're not a murderer, Dee. You're not evil."

. . . beep . . . B-beep . . . beep . . .

Jewel stands upright.

"You *are* evil?"

. . . B-beep . . . B-beep . . . B-beep . . .

A thought occurs to her. Too chilling to utter without her teeth chattering.

"A-are you . . . m-my sister?"

. . . beep . . . beep . . . beep . . . beep . . .

Jewel gasps. "Are you the muse?"

. . . B-BEEEEP . . . B-BEEEEEP . . . B-BEEEEP . . . B-BEEEEP . . .

Jewel grabs Deidre by the cheeks and squishes her lips apart.

"Are you in there, muse?" she calls down her sister's throat.

A malodorous, hollow chuckle burps from Deidre's stomach.

"Get the fuck out of my sister, you fiend!" Jewel hooks her fingers over Deidre's bottom teeth, under her incisors, and pries her mouth wide. "Get out of her!"

Help me, cries a vaguely familiar voice from the bottom of the well.

Jewel presses an eye to the dark cave of her sister's mouth.

"Mom? Is that you?"

Save me!

Jewel cranes Deidre's head back to see over her tongue. "How?"

Kill her!

Jewel shakes her head, disbelieving. "What?"

Rip her head in two!

"No," she says, but can't seem to unhook her fingers from her sister's teeth.

It's the only way to stop it!

"I can't," Jewel whispers as a red crack opens in the corner of Deidre's overstretched lips. "I won't!" Angry now. "You're not my mother! You're trying to trick me!"

An airy laugh wheezes from Deidre's throat a second before vomit blasts into Jewel's face.

"Ugh!" she cries, stumbling away from the bed.

"What happened?" Nurse Ingram asks, suddenly in the room.

"She threw up on me," Jewel says, bending to wipe Deidre's sick from her face. Clear and gooey as egg whites.

"Oh dear." Nurse Ingram plucks a tissue from the box on the nightstand and hands it to Jewel. "I'm surprised that happened. She doesn't have anything in her stomach."

Jewel blots a glob of sputum from her bangs. "Well, she had *something* down there."

A vile muse. Pretending to be our mother.

"Her mouth is bleeding," Nurse Ingram states.

"It *is*?" Jewel says with exaggerated wonder. She leans forward and examines the blooddrop welling on the corner of Deidre's lip. "Huh. That's strange. Her lip must have split when she vomited. They look a little chapped."

"We moisten them daily with Vaseline," Nurse Ingram contends.

"You might want to up her application," Jewel suggests.

Which draws a frown from the professional caregiver.

"I'm sorry to cut your visit short," Nurse Ingram says, "but I need to take Ms. Baldwin down to x-ray."

Jewel looks quickly at her and asks without thinking, "Will an x-ray show if there is something under her skin?"

Nurse Ingram bobs her head. “That’s what x-rays are for. To show what’s under the skin.”

“So it would show if there was a shadow or something?”

“You mean like cancer?”

“I guess it’s kind of like a cancer,” Jewel ponders aloud.

“What is?”

“Nothing,” Jewel says. “I’m just worried about the discoloration around her throat.”

“They’re just broken blood vessels,” Nurse Ingram reassures her. “They’ll go away in a couple of days. They just need time to heal.”

An encouraging prognosis, if it were just a few blood vessels that were broken, and not the whole damn order of the universe. Laws of science no longer apply. The muse isn’t going to just fade away.

Not without a fight.

31

Though I was loath to read more, I couldn't leave the manuscript alone. The only time I felt at peace was when I was working on it. The gentle tap of the keyboard marked my progress like a metronome and lulled me into a torpid type of focus. I drifted in and out of consciousness during these sessions. My eyes would open to find my fingers hard at work. I laughed out loud at the sentences I found on the screen. Though I hated each and every one of them, the way they could both grace and disgrace the page with their barbaric rhetoric rather tickled me. I became numb to the coldhearted words that flowed from me, through me, and found peace in the realization that there was nothing I could do to stop them. My fate was in the muse's hands. Perhaps always had been. Manipulating me. Guiding me. To this exact moment. This very line in the novel.

I killed my mother.

I can admit that now.

Jewel covers her mouth. Though she was prepared for the scene of her mother's death, she isn't ready for this.

She takes a sip of wine before continuing. It might make

her sleepy, but she needs some liquid courage to get through this part. A little more than a sip. Glass drained, she goes to the kitchen for a refill and returns with the bottle.

She cracks her knuckles one at a time, then backs up a couple lines to review the section again. Primed as she'll ever be, she gives the rash on the back of her neck a cursory scratch, then begins anew.

I killed my mother.

I can admit that now.

I wasn't sure what I would find as I entered her attic office. I only knew that the source of all our problems was in there somewhere. I had seen my mother skip merrily up the stairs to the attic only to trudge back down on the warpath a few hours later.

I was about to find out why.

I took a seat at her desk.

I hardly noticed the shirt box at my elbow. But I remember it now. The little tremble it gave as I sat down. Snuffing sounds from inside. A rutting pig, trying to get a sense of me through the closed pen. Under different circumstances, I might have lifted the lid to take a peek. But all my attention was on the computer screen in front of me. Those glowing green words. I couldn't believe they had come from my mother.

I was its puppet now. The muse was pulling my strings. Tonight it would make me kill my family. A small mercy. Once they were dead, I would have no reason to go on living. I wanted to burn us to the ground along with this awful house, but the muse kept blowing out my match. No. The price of freeing myself of its curse was blood. I'd do my best to keep my daughters' suffering to a minimum, but the muse will want to hear them scream. Make me make them scream.

I wanted to close my eyes against my mother's awful words, but a few suddenly began to glow a brighter green than the rest.

. . . kill . . . her . . . before . . . she . . . kills . . . you . . .

I gasped at the suggestion, then calmed as more words popped to life.

. . . happy . . . good . . . tonight . . . better . . . promise . . .

Then

. . . write . . . and . . . it . . . will . . . be . . . so . . .

I pecked a single sentence at the bottom of the screen. Little did I know how those dozen or so words would dramatically change my life. But I will say this: I was proud of that sentence. And in that moment, knew I wanted to be a writer.

I plucked my mother's heart from her chest like a rose and crushed it in my hand.

I left my mother's office in a daze.

She was coming up the stairs just as I was starting down. Blood dripped from her eyes, which were locked tight in the back of her skull. A terrible gurgle bubbled from her lips. She swept a cold, wet hand across my cheek as she passed, and asked if I had finished my homework.

Though I knew I was imagining her already dead, she looked more ghastly than I thought my mind could conjure.

I squeaked an ambiguous response as I hurried down the stairs and locked myself in my room for the remainder of the afternoon. I claimed to be sick when she called me for dinner. Pretended to be asleep when she opened the door to ask if I was feeling better. Froze as she set a corpse-cold hand on my forehead to check if I had a temperature.

As far as I was concerned, my mother was already dead when she entered the bathroom just before bedtime.

A walking zombie hungry for a bite of my ripe, juicy head.

I stopped brushing my teeth to watch her through the

mirror behind me. She stood there for a long moment, swaying and wheezing. She seemed in a stupor, oblivious to me. I was planning an escape around her when she took a staggering step forward. As she measured the width of my throat with her outstretched fingers, I snatched the scissors off the corner of the sink and spun around.

A foul, wet shadow vomited from her mouth as the sharp point of the shears entered her abdomen. The cloud of filth she spewed clung to the ceiling long enough to mark me with hollow eyes, then was sucked into the exhaust vent next to the overhead light fixture.

Though deep down Jewel has always known her mother suffered a much more violent death than what she was told as a child, seeing the truth spelled out on the pages of this filthy manuscript makes it so much worse.

She takes a deep breath to draw the courage to continue and tries not to envision her mother,

. . . writhing on the floor in pain. It didn't seem real. The blood pooling under her, seeping between her fingers, and spurting from her lips was too bright to be true. As if it contained its own light source. One that dimmed as her eyes grew flat and sightless. Staring up at me, but not aware of my presence. Not aware of what I had done. Which, in my mind, relieved me of my guilt.

I shook the death grip of her fingers from my ankle and fled the bathroom.

I ran to my room and crawled quickly into bed. Pretended to be asleep until I actually was. My father's woeful cries woke me from the nightmare I had surely been trapped in.

When I entered my mother's office the next morning to delete the incriminating words I had written the day before, I found that a few sentences had been added after mine.

You did well, my pet. You'll call on me again one day. Until then, see you in the funny papers.

Eyes riveted to the page before her, Jewel blindly fumbles for Deidre's phone as it rings. Expecting it to be Emily, she taps the accept icon before the name on the caller ID registers.

Christopher Arnold.

She stares at the screen a moment before raising the phone to her ear.

"Hello?"

"Ms. Baldwin?" a sinisterly low voice presumes.

Jewel flicks her eyes side to side. "Yes?"

"This is Christopher Arnold. From the Paranormal Society of America?"

"Yes?"

"You sent me some sample pages of a document you have in your possession? A manuscript of some kind?"

Though his leading tone suggests he has never spoken to Deidre before and would be unfamiliar with the sound of her voice, Jewel is hesitant to give hers away by using too many syllables. He might have information about the original manuscript, thus the muse, that he would only be comfortable sharing with Deidre.

"That's right," she says, then bites her lip. A parapsychologist worth his salt should be able to sense when he is being conned. Not that all parapsychologists are psychic. But if this one possesses a single transcendent talent, it would be that. It is just her luck.

"Forgive the intrusion," he says. "I wouldn't normally be so bold to call, but I felt compelled to follow up with you. The sample pages you sent me are truly amazing. The more I study them, the more I'm convinced that the document you have in your possession is a genuine grimoire. A very powerful one.

Some very strange things have been happening ever since we received the sample pages."

"Like what?"

"It's difficult to characterize, but I've noticed a distinct change in the personalities of my associates. They seem on edge. Bickering all the time. I had to break up a physical altercation a few days ago. It got very ugly. One woman needed three stitches in her lip."

"My goodness!"

"A few days later, a colleague I had shown the sample pages to burst into my office and demanded I destroy them. He became quite violent when I refused. Ransacked my office looking for them. Thank goodness they were locked in my safe or he might have succeeded."

Safe?

Jewel runs her eyes around the living area. She didn't think to look for a safe. But if Deidre has one, it isn't set out in the open.

Her eyes lock on the squiggle artwork hanging on the wall to the right of the bookcase.

"I don't want to alarm you," Christopher Arnold says as Jewel stands and crosses the room, "but you should be very careful when handling the manuscript. Even a copy, like the pages you sent me, can hold a certain amount of power. I've never seen anything like it. Have you been experiencing any strange effects?"

"A few," Jewel says, lifting the corner of the painting to examine the pristine wall behind it. She turns in a circle, then crosses the room to a Monet print hanging on the wall next to the flat-screen television.

"I was afraid of that," he says. "Given the circumstances, I think it would be best if you sent the original manuscript to me for safekeeping. It really should be in the hands of a professional. Someone who's familiar with the dark arts. Someone who can control it."

"It doesn't sound like you've been able to control it," Jewel says, tucking the phone between her ear and shoulder to free both hands. She pulls the heavy metal frame away from the wall, then crouches down to peek under. Finding only a scuff mark on the paint, she resets the frame and moves into the dining area.

"That's my point," Christopher Arnold says. "I'm having a hard time controlling it. And I'm quite adept with such matters. I've been in this business for over three decades. I've dealt with some powerful entities over the years. But nothing has scared me as much as the sample pages you sent me. Every time I read them, I have the most unpleasant thoughts. Ghastly thoughts! Ones I never thought I could conceive. I fear what could happen if the manuscript were to fall into the wrong hands. Or less experienced hands. Which I fear is currently the case. No offense, but you *are* a novice in such matters, are you not?"

"Do you know what the muse is? How it came into being?"

"That's what I'm hoping to determine. How and why it's attached itself to this manuscript."

"Will that help you destroy it?"

"Destroy it?" Christopher Arnold laughs. "Why would I want to do that?"

"Because it's evil," Jewel reminds him, attempting to peel a still-life bowl of oranges from the wall. She can't tell if the frame is stuck or nailed down, but it won't budge.

"Oh. Yes. Of course. All the more reason to send it to me."

"I'm afraid I can't do that."

"I'll take the utmost care with it, I assure you."

"It's not that. I don't know where—" Jewel snaps her teeth together to catch herself being herself. Christopher Arnold thinks he's speaking to Deidre. Deidre would know where the original manuscript is. "—to send it," she pivots mid-sentence. "I don't know where to send it. What's your address?"

"Don't trouble yourself. I can pick it up. I don't want to risk it getting lost in the mail."

"I thought you were in New York."

"Yes. But I'd be glad to make the drive down. I could be there by end of day."

"No!" Jewel doesn't want this man knocking on her door. Deidre's door. Discovering she's not who she said she was. Demanding she turn over the manuscript. Which she doesn't have. "That won't be necessary. I think I'll just hang on to it for now."

"I don't think that's wise. You could be in grave danger. As well as the people around you." Christopher Arnold takes a considered pause before asking, "You do still have the manuscript in your possession, don't you?"

"What makes you ask that?"

"Grimoires have been known to vanish. That's part of their myth."

Jewel blinks. "They can do that?"

"Has that happened to yours, dear?"

The deep, soft, fatherly tone in his voice almost brings her to tears. She's nodding up the nerve to tell him the truth when her phone signals an incoming call.

"Can you hold on a second?" she says, not waiting for a reply. She drops the phone from her ear and looks at the screen.

Ware Memorial Hospital.

Shit.

"I'm sorry, but I have to go," she says, replacing the phone to her ear.

"Before you do," he says, "can I ask where you're keeping it?"

"Why do you want to know that?"

"I just want . . . make . . . it's . . . cation."

Rather than asking him to repeat the words call waiting bleeped out, Jewel responds with a blanketed non sequitur.

"I guess."

"An environmentally controlled container? Like a humidor?"

"Oh. Right. Yes. I . . ." She pauses as call waiting sounds again. "Look. I have to go. I have a call waiting. It's the hospital."

"The hospital?" Christopher Arnold asks, alarmed. "What happened? Is everything okay?"

Jewel drops the phone from her ear, worried she has let something out of the bag and that she'll miss the hospital's call. Which she has.

"Fuck!"

She scratches her cheek as she waits for a voicemail to hit the inbox. The rash has rapidly progressed to her face in the last few hours. She chases the itch around the corner of her eye, up the side of her forehead, over the top of her head, and still no voicemail.

She grabs her bag off the kitchen counter and pitches the phone inside. The hospital wouldn't have called unless Deidre's condition had changed. Which can only mean one thing.

She is either dead or awake.

Jewel sighs as she closes the apartment door behind her, unsure which outcome she's hoping for.

32

Caught in the blurry perimeter of a sleepless night, the hospital lobby takes on a dreamlike quality as Jewel enters. The sliding doors retract with a guillotine swish. A shrilling cry immediately assaults her, strikes her legs. Jewel blinks down as a wild-haired toddler fists the fabric of her pants and plants a harrowing scream between her knees.

A large woman in a pink tracksuit and flip-flops thwaps quickly toward Jewel. She grabs the child up and clutches it protectively to her breast.

The cutting edge of the woman's glance peels an apology from Jewel's lips.

"Sorry, I didn't see . . ." she tries, slipping off her sunglasses, but the woman has already turned her back on her.

Jewel skirts the line of battered and bruised wannabe patients extending from the front desk and makes her way to the ICU.

"Miss! Miss!"

Jewel turns and looks in the direction of the voice. A nurse snaps her fingers and points to the end of the line.

"You need a pass to enter the ICU."

"It's okay," Jewel says, slowing her pace but not stopping. "I was just here a little while ago."

"Can I see your pass?"

Jewel raises her eyebrows to go over the nurse's head. "Dr. Leonetti told me I didn't need a pass."

"*Who?*"

"Dr. Leonetti!" Jewel repeats over the top of the crowd that passes between them.

The nurse shakes her head, frustrated that she can't hear, then holds a hand up to halt the conversation with the man in front of her. The man turns and gives Jewel an annoyed look over the blood-soaked washcloth he has pressed to his nose.

"I'm sorry," the nurse says, not sounding so. "But you need a pass to get into the ICU. Please sign in."

Jewel eyes the long line the nurse gestures to, then slumps slowly toward the back. "This is bullshit," she mutters, falling in behind an elderly woman. "I never needed a pass before."

The woman belittles Jewel's frustration with a snort. "I've been waiting for an hour and a half," she says with a sort of weary pride. "My husband's over there bleeding to death. You have to pay for a ride in an ambulance if you want to be seen right away. That's what it's all about. Money, money, money. Well, I'm not going into the poorhouse over a few stitches. It's bad enough that you're hurt. Do they have to bleed you dry too?"

When Jewel offers only a weak smile, the woman argues her point, "I guess they think if you can walk in on your own two feet, you're healthy enough to stand in line."

Jewel shrugs, scratches at the rash on her cheek.

"You shouldn't scratch that," the woman says. "It could get infected."

"I already am," Jewel says.

Jewel ignores the woman's curious examination of her and cranes her chin above the throng of moaning, accident-prone half-wits to see if the line is making any progress. The same man is still at the counter, testing the patience of the station nurse.

"They should have a separate line to sign in at," Jewel complains. "I'm clogging up the works for someone who actually needs to see a doctor."

"I think they're shorthanded," says the woman in front of them, turning to join the conversation. She blanches slightly at the sight of Jewel's face, which clearly needs to be examined by a medical professional. "I overheard a nurse say that a doctor died this morning."

Jewel touches her chest to keep her heart from jumping to conclusions, but her stomach has a sinking suspicion which doctor the woman is talking about.

"Well, that doesn't inspire much confidence," the elderly woman in front of her says. "If they can't save one of their own, what chance do *we* have?"

"I heard a patient attacked him," the other woman confides.

"*Patient?*" Jewel's throat is so dry her voice screeches like the first note off a dusty clarinet. Reed moistened with a swallow, she tries to control her octave. "Which patient?"

The woman shrugs. "A crazy one, I guess."

Jewel looks nervously around the lobby, half expecting Deidre to come staggering out of the crowd in a blood-soaked hospital gown, brandishing a scalpel in a hand she can't seem to control, and spots Officer Kerns exiting the doors of the ICU. The kneecaps of her tan slacks are smudged with wet grime, as though she has just crawled her way through a long, wooded night.

Officer Kerns watches with reproving fascination as Jewel

excuses her way across the crowded lobby, doesn't even crack a polite smile when Jewel jokingly blows her own brains out with her finger.

How could she smile? Dr. Leonetti is dead. Jewel knows this just as surely as she knows who murdered him.

"You look awful," Officer Kerns points out as Jewel pulls to a stop in front of her.

"Thanks," Jewel says. "So do you."

"That rash is spreading fast. I didn't even notice it this morning." She leans forward to inspect Jewel's face. "At least now I can see the family resemblance. You look like Deidre did when they first admitted her."

"Yeah, I'm starting to understand why she threw herself in front of a car."

Officer Kerns raises her eyebrows. "You think that's what happened?"

"Maybe." Jewel scratches her neck. "I'm about ready to peel my face off."

"Looks like you already tried." Officer Kerns winces as a pustule breaks under Jewel's nails. Jewel wipes a line of drool with the tissue balled in her hand. She glances around for a trash receptacle, then drops it in her bag.

"That's seriously gross," Officer Kerns says. "Sorry, but it's true."

"I know." Jewel fingers a line of hot welts under her eye. "I shouldn't be seen in public, but the hospital called. I think something happened with Deidre."

"Like what?"

"I don't know. I was waiting to talk to someone when I saw you. What are you doing here?"

"I had to follow up on something."

"What?"

Officer Kerns folds her arms to protect her beeswax. "An investigation."

"Into what?"

"A crime."

Jewel casts off the glib response with a roll of her eyes, then yelps as Dr. Leonetti's ghost suddenly appears at her elbow, dressed in sporty street clothes.

She touches her chest and exhales, "Oh, good. You're alive."

Dr. Leonetti gives her a confused smile. "Yes. Thank you for noticing."

"No," Jewel laughs. "I heard that a doctor died this morning and I thought it was you."

The comment stretches Officer Kerns's lips distastefully. "Why would you think that?"

"Oh, no reason." Jewel looks up at Dr. Leonetti. "Sorry. It's just that . . ." *When I heard a crazy patient attacked a doctor, I immediately imagined Deidre's paralytic fingers locked around your throat.* Jewel lowers her eyes. "I'm just glad it wasn't you."

"I'm glad it wasn't me either." He touches Jewel's shoulder, then quickly retracts his hand as he notices her rash. "Ugh, that looks awful."

Officer Kerns scoffs. "Is that your professional opinion, *Doctor*?"

"Oh, sorry," Dr. Leonetti says with an embarrassed grimace. "I was just caught a little off guard." He leans in to examine Jewel's ulcerated cheek. "You should make an appointment with dermatology."

"It's fine." She waves off his concern to address her own. "Is Deidre okay? Did something happen? The hospital called. I thought she might have . . ." She pauses to consider all options, then goes with ". . . woken up."

"Her condition hasn't changed, I'm afraid."

"So you weren't the one who called?"

Dr. Leonetti shakes his head. "Wasn't me."

"I wonder what it was about, then? They didn't leave a message." Jewel digs Deidre's phone from her bag, just then realizing the hospital didn't call the correct emergency number. She blinks at the screen. A new message is waiting in Deidre's inbox. "Oh, they did leave a message. I was so panicked to get here I didn't bother to check it."

"Play it," Officer Kerns says, nodding at the phone.

"You want me to put it on speaker?"

"I'd like to hear it too," Dr. Leonetti says. "If there's an issue, I haven't been notified. Perhaps it was Dr. Phelps calling. He died this morning, you know."

"Dr. Phelps?" Jewel gasps. "The doctor who performed Deidre's surgery?"

"Unfortunately, yes."

"Jeez," Jewel breathes.

Death is still following Deidre around.

"Play the message," Officer Kerns urges again.

Jewel flicks her eyes between the police officer and the doctor. Though she has no reason to worry about playing the voice message in front of them, she's not comfortable doing so until she's listened to it first.

Misinterpreting her hesitation, Dr. Leonetti motions to the vending machines behind them. "Let's step over here. Where there's more privacy."

"It was probably just someone from billing," Jewel says, following him to the refreshment vestibule. "I was supposed to contact them to arrange a payment plan for Deidre's stay."

"Let's find out," Officer Kerns says.

Jewel takes a deep breath, then plays the message.

Staticky silence erupts from the phone. The trio passes

around a confused look, then leans forward as a faint rustling sound shuffles across the message, followed by an even fainter beep. *Beep. Beep.*

"That sounds like a heart monitor," Dr. Leonetti whispers.

"One of the nurses must have inadvertently called me," Jewel says. She's about to end the message when a strangled voice gasps the last ounce of dead air.

"YOU'RE NOTHING! YOU'RE PATHETIC! The muse is my misery! MINE, MINE, MINE!"

Jewel bobbles the phone as a laughing scream severs the line.

"What the hell was that?" Officer Kerns wants to know.

"It sounded like some sort of demon," Dr. Leonetti theorizes.

Jewel snorts an anxious laugh, then shakes her head. Though she's pretty sure who the voice belonged to, she can't trust her ears. Like her eyes, they must be playing tricks on her.

"I have no idea who or what that was," she says.

"It kind of sounded like you," Officer Kerns points out with her chin.

"Me?" Jewel blanches. "Why would I call and leave myself a message like that?"

Officer Kerns stares at Jewel a moment, then consults Dr. Leonetti with a sideways glance. "Could it have been Deidre?"

"I don't see how that's possible. She's still in a coma."

"It was probably Mrs. Willard," Jewel suggests as the lie comes to her. "I wouldn't put it past her to harass me. I told you she was crazy."

"But how could Mrs. Willard possibly—" Dr. Leonetti tries before Officer Kerns cuts him off with an angry tone.

"I thought you said Mrs. Willard was having some tests run. That's why I couldn't speak with her earlier."

"Oh, yes." Dr. Leonetti nods. "That's right. She was having some tests run. Sorry. I was a little thrown by what we just heard. What did the voice on the phone say again? Something about a muse?"

Jewel rolls her eyes. "Who cares. It was a prank call. Forget about it."

Officer Kerns nods at the phone, still held in Jewel's hand between them. "Play the message. I want to hear the voice again."

"No." Jewel slips the phone into her bag. "I don't want to hear it again. It's upsetting. I'm sure it was Mrs. Willard."

Officer Kerns nods. "I'll ask her about it when I interview her later."

"Don't. She has Alzheimer's. She probably won't even remember calling me."

"I'll go easy on her."

"Will you just let it go! Jesus!" Jewel snaps, then touches her chest. "I'm sorry. I didn't mean to yell. I didn't get any sleep last night. Or the night before."

"You want to get a cup of coffee?" Officer Kerns gestures down the corridor to their left.

Though Jewel's in no mood to have coffee with Officer Kerns, she's too tired to come up with a valid reason to decline the invitation.

33

"I meant to tell you," Officer Kerns says as they take a table in the corner of the cafeteria. "I downloaded one of your books."

And I have to say, I like what I saw, Jewel mentally adds.

"It's really good. So far."

"Thank you."

Officer Kerns stirs her coffee. "Your profile says you live in Strasburg, Virginia."

"That's an old biography." Jewel rolls her eyes. "I keep meaning to update it. I think it still says I'm single."

"It does." Officer Kerns leans back in her chair. "I noticed that one of the characters in the book is named Cal. Isn't that your husband's name?"

Jewel nods. "Cal didn't appreciate that very much. I killed the character off in the second chapter." Jewel grimaces. "Spoiler alert. Sorry. But Cal's character isn't integral to the storyline. He's just a way to show the reader how . . ." Jewel waves off the rest. "Sorry. I almost spoiled it again. Anyway. I like to use names of people I know for my characters. I think it's a nice way to give them a nod. You never know, Officer Kerns might show up in my next novel. Don't worry. I won't kill you off." Jewel shrugs. "Unless I have to."

"Please don't."

"Use your name? Or kill you off?"

"Either."

"Glad I asked," Jewel laughs.

"So how did you and your husband meet?"

"In a bookstore, of all places. We reached for the same book at the same time. *Gone Girl.*" Jewel rolls her eyes. "I know. I wish it was something more romantic like *Wuthering Heights* or *Pride and Prejudice.*"

"Or *Anna Karenina*?" Officer Kerns offers with a smile.

"Exactly." Acutely aware of a slight tremor in her hand as she takes a sip of coffee, Jewel guides the waxed cup to the table with NASA-like precision, then releases the clamp of her fingers. Hand retracted back into her lap, she leans back with an accomplished sigh.

"So are you here about the doctor who died this morning?" she asks. "Dr. Phelps?"

"No. I'm following up on the orderly who died in your sister's room."

"What's to investigate? Dr. Leonetti said he had a heart attack."

"Some interesting details have come to light."

"What details?"

"I can't get into specifics. It's an ongoing investigation."

"Do you normally investigate when someone has a heart attack?"

"No."

"Then why are you?"

Officer Kerns looks around the cafeteria, then sets her

elbows on the table to speak confidentially. "He didn't have a heart attack."

Jewel leans forward so her ear can be more easily bent. "He didn't?"

"The autopsy revealed something else." Officer Kerns scans the surrounding tables for eavesdroppers, then leans forward again. "The cause of death was . . . Well, let's just say it was *un*natural."

Jewel dry swallows this tidbit before asking, "How did he die?"

Officer Kerns holds Jewel's eyes for a prolonged moment before coming out with it. "He choked to death on a bible."

"A bible!" Jewel exclaims, then covers her mouth as Officer Kerns tamps her volume down with an annoyed gesture. "Sorry, but I wasn't expecting you to say that. How can someone choke on a bible? That's physically impossible."

"It was a pocket bible." Officer Kerns holds an imaginary one between her thumb and forefinger. "About the size of a deck of cards. Someone rammed it down his throat."

Jewel's thoughts drop to the trunk of her rental car. The small bible lying in the well. It fell out of Father Mattis's breast pocket when he bent to help her with the groceries. He had been deceptive about being at the hospital that morning. Was that the same morning the orderly died?

"What?" Officer Kerns asks, watching the internal conversation play out on Jewel's face.

"I'm just trying to imagine it."

She wants to be clear on the facts before she accuses a priest of murder. And not just any priest. Deidre's prospective boyfriend. According to Lyle. And though being choked to death with a bible fits nicely with the subject matter of *Unspeakable Demons*, she can't imagine Father Mattis doing something like that. Why would he?

For fun?

That isn't a motive. It is madness.

I get that a lot.

Jewel fights off a shiver. "So you think the orderly was murdered?"

"Well, he didn't do it to himself. The bible was lodged pretty far down his windpipe. They had to crack open his sternum to get it out. If we rule out suicide, which I think we can, then it has to be a homicide. And if this is a homicide, there has to be a killer. And there was only one other person in the room with the orderly at the time of his death."

"Deidre's in a coma," Jewel reminds her.

"Then how did she leave you a voice message?"

"I'm not convinced that was Deidre."

"It sounded like her to me."

"How would you know what Deidre sounds like?"

"I don't. But the call did come from this hospital. Who else could it have been?" When Jewel looks down to think, Officer Kerns folds her arms. "Look. I can't prove that was Deidre's voice on the phone. Just like I can't prove she killed the orderly. But right now, she's the only suspect."

"So you think she's faking her coma?"

"I didn't say that."

"Yeah, but you implied it."

"I'm just looking for answers."

Jewel shakes her head. "Do you seriously believe that Deidre stuffed a bible down a man's throat?"

"Not really. That's a pretty evil thing to do." Officer Kerns smiles. "It's not like she's a Satanist or anything, right?"

Jewel bristles. "She's not. Mrs. Willard just said that to be mean. I shouldn't have even mentioned it to you. I didn't think you'd use it against her."

"I don't want to. But right now, she's the only suspect I have. All the evidence is pointing to her. But I'm open to suggestions." Officer Kerns holds Jewel's eyes. "Can you think of anyone else who might have done this?"

"No."

"Have you noticed anyone suspicious hanging around her room?"

Jewel shakes her head.

"Has anyone been acting suspiciously? Or given you the impression that they aren't who they claimed to be?"

Jewel looks down at her reflection in her black cup of coffee, then blurts, "Father Madness."

"*Who?*"

"Father Mat-tis," Jewel enunciates. "He's the priest renovating the church across the street from Deidre's apartment house."

"What about him?"

"He and Deidre are friends. I saw him heading toward the ICU the morning the orderly died, but he lied to me about being here that day."

"You spoke with him?"

The reproachful tone causes Jewel to hesitate. "Yeah."

"What did you talk about?"

"He wanted to know how Deidre was doing. He was worried about her."

"That it?"

"Basically. We didn't talk long. I had a trunkful of groceries. That's how I saw the bible. It slipped out of his shirt pocket when he reached for a bag. It looked just like the one you described."

Officer Kerns shrugs. "It's not unusual for a priest to carry a bible around."

"No," Jewel says. "But it's kind of a strange coincidence, don't you think?"

Officer Kerns considers this a moment, then stands and pitches her coffee cup into a nearby bin.

"Where are you going?"

"I want to check this guy out."

"Please don't tell him I said anything. I'd feel terrible if I was wrong about him."

"I'll be discreet." She turns to leave, looks back as Jewel calls her name. "What?"

"You don't think Deidre had something to do with Dr. Phelps's death too, do you?"

"No. They found him in the parking garage. Someone cracked his skull with a crowbar. Took his wallet. Looks like a mugging."

34

Though Deidre appears dead, light as an apparition under the pale sheet of sunlight falling across her bed, the hairs on the back of Jewel's neck are attuned to the worry that she's playing possum. Whether it's to lure her closer or to be left alone remains in question.

Jewel steps to the bedside table and stares down at the room phone, well within reach of her sister. Deidre could speak if she were awake. The tube snaking up her nose might make speech difficult, but not impossible. It wasn't like she has a bible stuffed down her gullet.

"Did you call me, Dee?"

A spark fulgurates the ruptured capillaries of Deidre's closed eyelids, a pulse of lightning in the sky of her tranquil aspect.

The hairs on Jewel's arms tingle as she leans closer to whisper, "I know you're awake. You don't have to pretend with me. I won't tell anyone you're faking it."

Deidre's lids flutter slightly.

"The police think you killed that orderly. I'm trying to throw them off your scent, but I don't know how long I can hold them off. You need to tell me what's going on. I can't help you if you keep me in the dark."

She studies Deidre's face for a moment.

"Look, I know you killed Mom. I've already read that part of the book. I can delete that section. The parts about Reggie and Keith too. No one has to know you're a murderer, but I swear, if you don't open your eyes right this second, I'm going to send the book to Emily as is. The world will know what you are. What you did. No one's going to believe that an evil muse made you kill people. I barely believe it myself. And I've seen it. Sitting at the desk. Working on the novel when it thinks I'm asleep."

Jewel covers a gasping sob with her fingers.

"I'm terrified, Dee! The more I read *Unspeakable Demons*, the more I think I'm turning into one. I've already got the rash like you and Mom. The muse has me by the throat. Look!" Jewel raises her chin for Deidre to see. "It's writing me notes and leaving knives lying around. It wants me to do terrible things. It made me push Mrs. Willard down the stairs." She can admit that to herself now. Can feel the give of Mrs. Willard's body as her hands slammed into her chest. It doesn't matter if she meant to do it or not. The muse is working through her now. And it isn't going to stop killing until one of them is dead. "You have to help me, Dee. Is there any way to stop it? To stop myself from doing its bidding?"

She gives Deidre's papery hand a firm squeeze, resists the urge to roll the stem of her fingers, crackle off the skin, and see what lies beneath. Bone or graphite. Though her finger wasn't writing anything when Jewel first entered the room, it twitches to do so now.

Jewel tightens her grip on Deidre's hand.

"Where's the original manuscript, Dee? Is it in the cellar? Did you hide it down there because you thought I'd be too scared to go down and look for it? You knew I'd burn it if I found it. That's how you destroy the muse, isn't it? It lives in the pages of that manuscript. It feasts on our words. It needs them to survive. It'll die if we stop writing about it."

Unless I can't stop writing about it.

Once the muse is in you, it is in you. You'd have to kill yourself in order to defeat it.

"Is that why you jumped in front of a car?" Jewel bites the back of her lip. "There has to be another way. Did you even try to destroy the manuscript?"

It is paper. It would burn. But would that be enough to cast the muse back to hell? Or do you have to recite an incantation? And if so, where would she find the right words to say? They wouldn't be included on the pages of *Unspeakable Demons*, that is for sure.

Might Father Mattis know?

He knows how to exorcise a demon. A Catholic one, anyway.

But if Father Mattis knows how to rid Deidre of the demon that is plaguing her, why hasn't he? He is Deidre's friend. Research assistant. Perhaps lover.

Has he seen the original manuscript?

Though he didn't seem to be under the muse's spell when they spoke, and had no visible sign of a rash, that doesn't mean he hasn't been touched by its evil.

"Did Father Mattis kill the orderly, Dee?" Jewel asks, applying upward pressure to Deidre's pinkie with her thumb. Like Deidre used to do to her when she found Jewel in her bedroom, reading her diary.

God that hurt.

The pinkie smash, yes, that hurt like the dickens. But what brought Jewel to tears were the horrible things Deidre had written about her. So much bad blood. Deidre wished Jewel dead more often than she wished a boy would like her. They probably wouldn't have if they knew what an ugly girl she really was.

What a murderer she was.

"Did the muse make you do it? Did it take you over after you killed Mom? Is that how you became so famous?"

Jewel has always wondered how Deidre was able to achieve her success. She is a good author, but not a great one. No more talented than Jewel. But somehow she was able to do what Jewel could not. Make a name for herself. Jewel used to think it was luck. Timing. That she just happened to catch Emily Channing on a good day. Submitted her first novel right when fantasy fiction was taking off. But what if that wasn't the case? What if Deidre's success story was more Faustian in nature? Had she sold her soul to the devil to achieve her success? Is the muse here to claim it?

Did I inadvertently sell my soul by taking the project on? Is Emily Channing actually the devil in disguise?

A soft pop of Deidre's knuckle, potentially a small bone fracture, snaps Jewel out of her reverie.

She releases Deidre's hand.

"I'm sorry!" She rests her head on Deidre's chest, soft as a pillow, and closes her eyes to cry. "I didn't mean to hurt you. I don't know what I'm doing anymore. I feel like I'm going crazy. I just want you to wake up and talk to me. Please, Dee. Give me a sign that you can hear me."

The health monitor lets out an agonized cry.

Jewel raises her head and finds a white pillow where Deidre's face should be.

"Oh, God!" She snatches away the pillow and tucks it back under her sister's head. "I'm sorry. I didn't mean to. It's the muse! I would never hurt you." She gives Deidre's shoulders a shake. "Dee? Dee!"

She presses her ear to Deidre's mouth but can't hear anything over the flatlining monitor.

Panicked, Jewel turns to look for help, but the corridor is empty.

She swings her eyes back to the bed and finds her fingers around Deidre's throat.

"Shit!" Jewel cries but can't pull her hands away. "Goddamn it! Let go! Let go of her, you fucker!"

As Deidre's face swells for air, Jewel bends down and sinks her teeth into the side of her hand.

"Let go," she mutters around the fleshy heel of her thumb, then bites down harder.

Pain zips up her arm like a razor, but she can't sever the connection. If anything, her fingers hold tighter.

Hoping to use the element of surprise, Jewel throws herself backward to wrench her hands away from Deidre's throat and yanks her sister upward.

Face-to-face, Deidre's mouth falls open.

"Kill her."

Wheezed from Deidre's lungs in a foul breath, Jewel stares into her sister's gaped mouth. Smoke rolls on the back of her tongue like a drag of a cigarette. Though amorphous, as the smoke begins to thicken, fingers take shape and crawl across Deidre's tongue. Mesmerized by the sight, Jewel can only let out a soft whimper as the hand extends beyond Deidre's lips and caresses Jewel's cheek with a diaphanous knuckle.

A strangled voice wheezes up Deidre's windpipe.

"Kill her and you can be her."

Jewel shakes her head, a tear from her eye.

"She's the only thing lying in your way."

Throat pinched like the lip of a clear balloon over the spout of a slaughterhouse spigot, the color in Deidre's blanched face drains back into her lungs as the clamp around her neck l oosens.

"You've lived in her shadow long enough. This is your chance to be the shadow."

Sucked forward with the gasp of air that rushes down her sister's throat, Jewel leans down, tightens her grip, and focuses all her weight on her last chance for fame and fortune.

"Ms. Maxwell?" a voice says.

Jewel's hands fly to her head as she spins around.

"What's going on here?" Dr. Leonetti says from the doorway.

"She was choking!" Jewel cries. "I was trying to help her!"

Dr. Leonetti steps quickly to the bed. He lifts Deidre's wrist to check her pulse, then bends to pry open one of her eyelids.

"I thought she was choking on her tongue!" Jewel explains over the squealing monitor. "I thought if I sat her up it might slip back down her throat, but I might have made things worse!"

Dr. Leonetti leans across Deidre to silence the alarm, then bends to listen to his patient's chest. "She seems to be breathing fine now." He sits back and prods Deidre's throat. "I don't feel any swelling. Did she just start choking out of the blue?"

"I thought she was trying to say something, but I couldn't understand her." Jewel peers over Dr. Leonetti's shoulder. "Is she awake?"

"Deidre?" Dr. Leonetti says, prying open an eye. "You with us, dear?" He looks over his shoulder at Jewel. "I'm sorry, but I don't detect any change in her condition."

Jewel stares at Deidre in disbelief. "But she spoke."

"What did she say?"

Kill her.

Jewel shakes her head. "I'm not sure. It didn't make any sense."

"That can happen with some coma patients. It's similar to

talking in your sleep. They're not cognizant that they're doing it." Dr. Leonetti uses the corner of the sheet to wipe a drop of drool from the corner of Deidre's lip and then stands to face Jewel. "But it's a very good sign. She's fighting to regain consciousness. She just can't stay awake for long. It's like when you first wake up in the morning. You think you just closed your eyes for a second, and suddenly you're late for work. An hour can pass in the blink of an eye. For someone in a coma, that blink can last a few days. Weeks even. But the more it happens, the sooner she'll be able to hold on to consciousness long term."

"I just want this nightmare to be over." Jewel presses a hand to her forehead and spots the blood running down her wrist just as Dr. Leonetti does.

"Oh, you're bleeding," he says, reaching for her hand. "Let me see."

"It's nothing." Jewel steps to the nightstand, plucks a tissue from the box, and presses it to the self-inflicted bite mark on the base of her thumb. "I pinched it in the bedframe."

"I've gotten pinched in these damn contraptions before. You'd think they'd make a hospital bed that wouldn't try to bite your fingers off."

Or crush your head.

Jewel envisions the furrowed brow of Dr. Leonetti's walnut-tanned forehead cracking open as the mechanical bed steadily reclines.

What a brilliant descriptive.

"I should check to see if the bed is working properly," Dr. Leonetti says, barely audible over the sentence running through Jewel's mind.

His eyes bulged as the bed gradually lowered and cracked his walnut into bite-size pieces. Juice of the forbidden fruit sprayed the walls a juicy red as meaty chunks of . . .

Jewel pauses to consider her next word—*Pulp? Brain? Drupe?*—and gasps at the Ware Memorial notepad she can't remember picking up off the bedside table.

"I'd hate for someone else to be injured," Dr. Leonetti says.

Jewel looks up as the scene she just wrote on the notepad is being acted out before her.

Down on one knee, Dr. Leonetti is inserting his head between the elevated mattress frame and metal base. He reaches a hand up and feels along the support rail until he finds the bed's remote control. Deidre's feet begin to judder squeakily up and down as Dr. Leonetti blindly thumbs the six-button pendant. A long, low hum raises Deidre's head. As she begins to sandwich in half, Dr. Leonetti mumbles a curse, then presses the directional arrow down.

The pad of paper slips from Jewel's fingers as the jaw of the oversized nutcracker closes down on Dr. Leonetti's head.

She lunges forward, grabs him by the back of his lab coat, and yanks him backward a second before the frame clangs together.

Sprawled on the floor, Dr. Leonetti blinks confusedly up at Jewel.

"What happened?"

"You almost got crushed by the bed!"

Dr. Leonetti runs a hand over his skull to see if it's still in one piece and dislodges his toupee. Jewel averts her eyes as if the fly of his pants has opened. Dr. Leonetti fastens his wig to the line of spirit gum circling his dome like an incision, then scrambles to his feet.

"Are you okay?" Jewel asks.

"I don't know. I don't remember what happened. One second we were talking and the next . . ." He swipes a shaky hand across his lips. "The next thing I know I'm lying on the floor." He looks down, spots the notepad, and bends to pick it up. "What's this?"

Jewel snatches the pad from his fingers. "Nothing. I was jotting a note to myself when I saw you looking under the bed."

Dr. Leonetti blinks at her. "I don't remember doing that."

"I think you hit your head on the frame when I pulled you away."

"Yes." He rubs the back of his neck. "I do have a headache. A terrible one, in fact."

"You need to be more careful," Jewel scorns in a matronly voice. "You could have been seriously hurt. Call maintenance. Let them fix the bed. That's what they're here for."

"Yes, maintenance," he says distractedly, then blinks quickly back to his senses. "Well then. Where were we? Oh, yes. Your hand. Let's get you bandaged up."

"That's okay," Jewel says, backing toward the door. "I have to go. I'm . . ." *freaking the fuck out!* ". . . late for an appointment."

"It won't take but a second to examine you!" Dr. Leonetti calls as Jewel breaks right out of the hospital room and stumbles down the corridor to keep up with her racing heart.

35

Jewel taps the brake as she pulls into the gravel lot behind the apartment house and spots Lyle standing at the exterior door to the elevator bay.

"Fuck!" She slams her fist against the steering wheel.

She wanted to take a quick peek in the cellar before heading up to the apartment to pack. That has to be where the original manuscript of *Unspeakable Demons* is hidden. She isn't sure if destroying the infernal script will eradicate the muse, but she has to do something. She almost killed Dr. Leonetti with one sentence. Thank God these malicious thoughts need to be written down in order for them to become a reality, or Lyle's brains would be bashed against the brick wall next to the elevator door.

Does she really believe that?

Jewel reflects on the distressing scene with Dr. Leonetti.

Of course she didn't make him stick his head in a viselike apparatus. She didn't force him to his knees. She scribbled down a similar account *after* he knelt on the floor. Or as he was doing it. She only thought he might get crushed because he had put the thought in her head.

He'd gotten pinched in those damn contraptions before.

Dr. Leonetti wasn't in any real danger. Jewel freaked out. Yanked him away from the bed. And though she can't remember him hitting his head on the frame, he must have. That was why he couldn't remember what happened. He wasn't under a spell.

But perhaps Jewel was.

A spell of her own making. She believed the words she was reading to such a degree that she was making them a reality. She thought an evil muse was working through her, and so it was.

You can't really kill people with words.

And she can prove it.

Put her theory to the test.

Jewel glances at the Ware Memorial Hospital notepad on the passenger seat, and then back at Lyle as he lights a cigarette.

Could she make him light himself on fire just by writing that down? Start shoveling fists of gravel down his throat because of a few choice words? Climb the fence, scale up the oak tree, and swan dive to his death? Could she stop his heart with three simple words?

Lyle dropped dead.

What a great first line of a novel.

Jewel clenches her hands to resist the urge to write that down and feels her fingers close on a slim, rectangular object.

She looks down at the notepad in her hand in horror. She's about to fling it into the back seat before it can snap hold of her fingers like a mousetrap when she feels something scuttle across her thigh. She drops the notepad and clamps hold of her wrist as her left hand crawls under the flap of her bag, in search of a pen.

Jewel shakes her hand until her fingers fall limp, then grabs the gearshift and puts the car into reverse.

Fuck packing. Fuck the book. Fuck Emily. Fuck Deidre. Fuck it all.

She'll drive to the nearest mental institution and check herself in. Tell them that she's having suicidal thoughts so they won't allow her any sharp writing utensils. If she acts crazy enough, which shouldn't be a problem, they might put her in a straitjacket.

"Let's see you try to write something then, motherfucker," she says to her hand.

Jewel gently applies pressure to the gas pedal to ease out of the parking lot unnoticed, but the engine betrays her with a whine.

Lyle turns, then starts toward her.

Shit.

Jewel rolls her eyes slowly upward as her window rolls down.

"What's up?" she says curtly.

Lyle rears dramatically back. "Damn, girl! What happened to your face?"

"It's the rash. I showed it to you on my neck last night. Remember?"

"Yeah, but it's spread like wildfire since then. You might even have it worse than Deidre did."

"I thought you said a man couldn't comment on a woman's *fucked-up face* and live to tell about it."

Lyle raises his hands. "Don't kill me."

Though his smile intends this to be a joke, Jewel doesn't find it funny. "What are you doing out here, anyway?"

"Working on my truck," he says, bending eye level with her through the window. Smoke from the cigarette in his grease-stained fingers drifts in. Jewel waves off a tendril determined to poke her in the eye, and Lyle sets his hand on the roof. "I was just about to head up when I saw you. Where you been?"

"The hospital. I went over to check on Deidre." Jewel groans. "Shoot. I meant to check in on Mrs. Willard while

I was there. Have you heard anything about her condition? Lyle . . . ? *Hello . . . ?* Lyle?"

Lyle cocks his head. "How are you doing that?"

"Doing what?"

Lyle nods at Jewel's lap. "Writing without looking. That's pretty freaky."

Jewel lowers her eyes to the notepad balanced on her knee. Though her hand is controlling the pen, neither the handwriting nor the vile words pouring from its tip are familiar to her.

> A second mouth opened in his throat and filled the cup of my hands with blood. I raised the chalice to my lips, delighting in his horror, and quenched my thirst with the purest evil possible. There was no turning back now. My muse is misery. I must obey.

"That's some dark shit," Lyle says, then quickly straightens. "Hey, look at that."

He drops his cigarette and starts walking toward the cellar.

Jewel slams the gearshift into Park, yanks out the keys, and exits the car.

"What are you doing?" she asks, hurrying after him.

Lyle bends and picks the chain off the bulkhead door. "It's unlocked," he says, examining it. He looks at Jewel. "Did you find Deidre's key?"

Jewel shakes her head. "No. I forgot to look for it, actually." She bends to examine the padlock, open and hooked through one of the eyeholes in the chain. Though it appears in pristine condition, she says, "Maybe someone cut it?"

Lyle turns the lock over in his hand. "Doesn't look like it. I guess they could have jimmied it, though. It's a pretty cheap lock." He drops the chain on the ground next to the bulkhead door and grabs hold of one of its rusty handles.

"What are you doing?" Jewel asks as Lyle draws the door open. It hits the ground with a dusty thud that makes her flinch. "You're not going down there, are you?"

"I better check it out."

Jewel grabs Lyle's forearm. "Don't."

"Why not?"

"It might be dangerous."

Lyle smiles as he gently pries Jewel's fingers from his arm. "I'll be careful, *Mom*," he says, then plunges under the house.

"Lyle!" Her voice trots down the short flight of stairs after him, then quickly back up again.

"Hey, Jewel." Though he's right below her, Lyle's voice has fallen down a well. "Come check this out."

Jewel glances back at her car and wills her feet to just walk away. But they, like her hands, aren't taking orders from her anymore, and carry her quickly down the rickety staircase.

36

Jewel rounds the dirt corner of the cellar and steps into a cobweb. Flailing in a panicked circle, she scrubs a displaced spider from her hair, then screams as she bumps into something that could only be a corpse hanging from a meat hook.

"Watch yourself," Lyle says.

A lighter zips to life and fills the cavernous cellar with an eerie glow.

Eyes sunk in a gloomy hollow of waxy flesh, Lyle smiles vacantly down at her. "*Good eeevening*," he says in a Lurchy voice.

Jewel slaps his arm. "Don't scare me, Lyle. I'm scared enough as it is."

Lyle laughs as he looks around. "Yeah, it's pretty scary down here."

Jewel looks up at the ceiling. "There's a chain for the light somewhere around here."

"I tried it already. The bulb's burned out."

"Great." Jewel sighs at him and extinguishes the lighter. Lyle thumbs it back to life, and Jewel coughs it out again.

"Stop blowing on it!"

"I'm not trying to! I coughed." Jewel dodges a chill as it sweeps behind her. "Don't you have your phone with you?"

"In my pocket."

"Bring up your flashlight app so we can see better."

"I don't have that on my phone."

"All phones have that feature, Lyle. It comes standard."

"Mine doesn't," he says. "It's a piece of shit. Use yours."

"I left it in the car." Jewel starts to turn. "I'll go get it."

"Don't worry about it. We'll just be a minute." The flame flickers as Lyle swings the Zippo around. He shuffles a few feet deeper into the cellar. "Mrs. Willard was right."

"About what?"

"Someone has been hanging out down here."

Jewel moves behind Lyle and peeks around his arm.

Half expecting a blood-soaked butcher-block table with a knife sticking out of an unidentifiable mutilated carcass, Jewel almost laughs at the unlikely object stationed in the center of the dirt floor.

The antique, wood-carved, mahogany secretary desk looks remarkably like the one her mother used to keep in the foyer. Mainly used to write out bills, her actual desk—a green metal military monstrosity—never made it into the storage unit. Maybe sensing that evil had once sat at it, her father had it destroyed. Along with all the other items that could potentially haunt him. Her desk chair. Her desk lamp. Her Commodore 64 word processor.

The secretary hadn't been amongst the items she and Deidre had flipped for.

Yet here it is.

Jewel walks slowly toward the desk.

An unlit brass oil lamp is stationed on the top back panel. A fountain pen lies on a stack of white paper on the writing surface. A plain wooden chair is strewn a few feet away, as though kicked to the floor by an angry stand.

Jewel rights the chair as she steps to the desk and picks up the fountain pen. Also similar to her mother's. Onyx with mother-of-pearl inlay, she uncaps the Montblanc and determines the sharpness of the golden nib with her thumb. It feels dry. She gives the pen a shake and scribbles on the legal pad to get the ink flowing again. The dry scratching sound reminds her of Deidre's inkless fingertip composing invisible words on the fitted sheet of her hospital bed.

"What are you doing?" Lyle asks, chin over her shoulder.

"Just seeing if the pen works." Jewel rips off the scratch sheet and crumples it in her hand. She looks around the desk for a trash can, then tucks it into her front pocket. Pen reset on the clean stack of paper, she slides open the center drawer. Filled with shadows, she bends down to peer inside.

"Can you light the lamp for me, Lyle?"

Lyle steps quickly around the desk and removes the hurricane chimney. Jewel blinks off a glare as flame touches wick.

"Why would Deidre want to work down here?" Lyle asks, adjusting the volume of light and replacing the flute. "She's got a desk in her apartment."

"I don't know," Jewel says, bending to look inside the desk drawer. Light from the lantern falls short. "Let me see your lighter."

Lyle hands the Zippo over.

Jewel examines the intricacies of the howling wolf engraved on the face of the silver lighter, the fine hairs of its undercoat parted by a fierce wind, sweeping clouds across the silhouette of a full moon, then flips the greasy silver lid back with her thumb.

As a lighter-fluid vapor zips a flame to life, Jewel lowers the glowing wick to the drawer and scares the shadows away. The desk contains the usual fare: pens, highlighters, paper clips, and a couple of Post-it cubes. One has a note yet to be peeled off. Jewel tilts her head to read upside down, then fingers the yellow square clockwise until the lighter's flame ignites the words, and an anxious fuse at the base of her spine.

More blood. More blood. More blood.

"Well, looky here!" Lyle says.

Jewel slams the drawer with her thigh and looks up at the pair of pink-framed glasses Lyle is dangling between them.

"Where did you find those?"

"They were sitting here on the desk. Behind the lantern."

Jewel shakes her head confusedly. "Deidre doesn't wear glasses."

"They're not Deidre's," Lyle says.

"Whose are they, then?"

"Carol's. The chick I was telling you about at Nicki's. These are her glasses."

"How can you tell?"

"Oh, they're her Sally Jessys, all right. I recognize the frames." Lyle turns the glasses over, then unfolds the temples and slides them on.

"Huh," he says, looking around.

"What?"

He levels his nose at Jewel. The lenses glow yellow in the lantern's glare. She can't see his eyes. But his smile is perplexed.

"They're not prescription," he says.

"They're not?"

"See for yourself." Lyle slips the glasses off and extends them to Jewel.

Jewel extinguishes the lighter with a flick of its cap and sets it on the desk. She takes the glasses from Lyle and peers through one of the lenses.

"They look prescription to me."

"Try them on and see."

"I don't want to try them on, Lyle." She tosses the glasses on the desk. "I want to take a quick look around and get the hell out of here. I hate this cellar."

"Go ahead. I'm not stopping you."

Jewel turns in a huff toward the canning shelves on the back wall.

Cluttered with old empty mason jars, some rusty tools, and forgotten bric-a-brac, three dilapidated cardboard boxes are wedged haphazardly on the shelves between. Two are unlidded, filled to the brim with chipped clay pots and handheld gardening tools. She picks through a Dutch hand hoe, serrated trowel, three-prong hand fork, and finds what she hopes is a garden hose coiled at the bottom. She pushes the box back into place before a soft hissing can prove her wrong.

"What are you looking for?" Lyle asks as Jewel tips down the next carton and checks inside.

"That box you said you saw Deidre with." Jewel sighs frustratedly. She shoves the box of Christmas lights back on the shelf and turns toward Lyle. "It was a shirt box, right?"

Lyle shrugs. "That's what it looked like to me. But I only saw it for a second. Why? What's in it?"

"An old manuscript of our mother's."

Lyle glances around. "Maybe Deidre took it back up to her apartment."

"No. I would have found it by now."

"Maybe Carol took it."

"Why would *Carol* take it?"

"I dunno. But we know she's been poking around down here. And she's up to some shady shit." He holds up the glasses as evidence. "Why else would she wear a disguise. I always thought she looked a little phony. Like she was trying to hide herself or something. Big glasses and a baseball cap. Champion sweats. And she talked real low." Lyle mimics Carol's voice by dropping his an octave. "*Like a dude.*"

Jewel blinks at him. "Do you think she could have been a man? Disguising himself as a woman?"

"Maybe." Lyle shrugs. "I just thought she was a dyke."

"Don't say *dyke*, Lyle. It's offensive."

"Why? You one?"

"No, but I'm still offended by it!"

"Sor-*ry*!" Lyle picks the glasses off the desk and examines them. "You know, she totally could have been a dude. I never really got a good look at her face. Or his face."

"When was the last time you saw Carol?"

"Been a few days. Right before Deidre got hit, I think." Lyle raises his eyebrows. "Hey, you want to go check out her place? I've got a key."

"Why do you have a key to Carol's apartment?"

"Reggie gave me keys to the whole house. I was kind of his handyman. Unofficial like. Reggie traveled a lot and wanted me to have access to the apartments when he wasn't around. Deidre knew I still had them. It wasn't a secret or anything."

Jewel thinks back to the moment in the shower when she thought she heard someone enter the apartment, then scowls at Lyle. "Do you have a key to Deidre's apartment too?"

"Nah. Deidre changed the locks as soon as she moved in. Then had me install the chain lock. I guess living in New York makes you paranoid. But I still have a key to Carol's place. We can take a look around if you want."

"What if she's home?"

"I didn't see her car in the lot. Actually, I haven't seen it in a few days. I think she's out of town."

"What if she comes home while we're in there?"

"I'll tell her I smelled gas and needed to check her stove. She'll buy that. Or he. Or whatever the fuck it is."

"How would we explain me being in *their* apartment with you?" She emphasizes the correct pronoun but sees it fly right over Lyle's thick head.

"Just say you're acting landlord while Deidre's in the hospital."

"I'm not comfortable doing that, Lyle."

"Then I'll go it alone. I know what the box looks like. If it's in there, I'll find it."

"Okay," Jewel says, turning in a crouch toward the stairs. "I guess it's worth a shot." She stumbles over the uneven dirt floor and grips one of the canning shelves for balance. A box tumbles to the ground with a rattling clank. As she stoops to repack the gardening tools, Lyle says, "Just leave it. No one gives a shit."

Jewel pivots toward a rustling in the farthest corner of the cellar.

Skoosh, skoosh.

"What was that?" Jewel gasps, searching the shadows beyond the reach of the lamp's flickering glow.

Lyle looks around. "What?"

"I heard something." Jewel clutches the collar of her polo shirt so the crawlies running across the back of her shoulders can't make a break down her chest. "Like a rustling."

"Probably mice," Lyle says. "The house is lousy with them."

"It sounded bigger than a mouse."

"Could be that cat I've seen hanging around."

"A cat didn't jimmy the lock on the bulkhead doors, Lyle."

Lyle holds Jewel's eyes for a moment, then turns to address the back of the cellar. "Anybody down here?"

Jewel holds her breath to listen, then lets out a small squeal as a moan floats from the shadows.

Lyle's eyes go wide. "What?"

"I heard a moan."

"I didn't hear anything."

"Somebody's back there, Lyle," Jewel whispers, backing away.

"That you, Carol?" The echo of his voice seems to leap farther than the cellar. Into the deep, dark hole of Jewel's imagination.

Lyle ducks the low ceiling as he shuffles forward.

"Careful, Lyle," she whispers.

Lyle presses her concern behind him as he skirts the desk chair.

"Whoever's back there, you better come out! I'm not playing around! Make yourself known right fucking now or I'm gonna beat your ass!"

Lyle flexes his bicep in a show of strength as he glances back at Jewel, but his eyes are scared shitless.

She mouths a stern, *Be careful.*

Lyle nods, then steps beyond the light of the hurricane lamp.

Jewel grabs the trowel off the floor and wields it at the shadows. Tearing up from the dust, her eyes strain to distinguish Lyle's black T-shirt from the black sheet drawn across the back of the cellar. She holds her breath to still her heart for a beat and forces all her strength into her vision. She's about to exhale Lyle's name in a terrified breath when a steely-eyed glint blinks from the shadows.

Jewel closes her eyes to rein in her imagination, then yelps as a scuffling grunt crashes into the desk. Shattering glass extinguishes the light just as her eyes pop open.

Throat seized in terror, no sound accompanies her scream. Wedged between panic and paralysis, only the hairs of her arms have the presence of mind to move. Up and down her skin like centipedes.

As a scream rebuilds on the back of Jewel's tongue, hammering in time with her heart, a cry splinters the silence.

"Uh," Lyle groans. "Shit. Help!"

Eyes focused on the dark before her, Jewel rushes blindly forward. Trowel extended to keep the shadows at bay, her foot catches the lower spindle of the desk chair and launches her into a staggering trip. The serrated tip of the trowel rams into the soft pulp of a rotted support beam.

Slammed to a stop, a shockwave reverberates up her arm. Jewel releases her grip on the splintery handle and clutches her stinging fingers to her chest.

Breathless, she searches the wall of darkness before her.

"Lyle?" she whimpers. "Are you okay? Talk to me."

She steps slowly forward, patting the air until her hand finds a warm chest.

"Oh, thank God," she breathes, giving Lyle's shirtfront a grateful pat. "I thought you—"

A warm, wet substance pours over her fingers. Thick and smooth as paint, and for a second she can almost convince herself that it is.

She snatches her hand back.

"Don't fuck with me, Lyle!" She stumbles away. "I know it's just paint!"

Waiting for a laugh that never comes, Jewel sets her hand on the desktop to guide her way out of the cellar and touches upon a cold metal square.

The Zippo lighter.

She thumbs the flint wheel three times, then flinches as her worst fear bursts to life.

Pinned upright to a support beam, Lyle's unfocused eyes stare at Jewel in dumb wonder. The wooden handle of the trowel protrudes just far enough from Lyle's throat so his chin rests comfortably in the curve of the blade. The Alice Cooper album cover on the front of Lyle's blood-soaked T-shirt is almost too spot-on not to be a little funny.

Welcome to My Nightmare.

Jewel snorts a gasping, delirious laugh, then turns in a run for the exit.

37

The bulkhead door closes with the decisive thud of a casket.

She hangs her head in a moment of silence. More from shock than in reverence, but Lyle deserved at least that. Killing off a character—which as far as the muse is concerned, he was nothing more than—is a solemn act. One should feel remorse. No matter what kind of man he was portrayed to be, only the wickedest of all demented fiends could smile at a time like this.

Jewel raises a hand to slap the grin off her face, but it's not having any of that. Rather than knocking some sense into her, her hand rests assuringly on her cheek. Desperate for a tender moment, even a manipulative one offered by a demon residing inside her, Jewel nuzzles her palm. One of the blisters on her cheek succumbs to the pressure and weeps warm pus alongside the corner of her lip. Before she can clench her teeth in a wince of pain, her tongue darts sideways and laps up the bittersweet discharge.

She spits the vile taste onto the bulkhead door. The glob of phlegm bursts into the shape of a mangled daisy on the lid of Lyle's coffin. She stares at it a moment, wondering if she should wipe it off or hack up an entire bouquet, then turns from the cellar.

She has to get out of here.

Lyle's last cigarette smolders in the gravel below the door of her rental car.

A thin finger of smoke curls up. Too weak to poke her in the eye but still determined. She grinds the cherry under her heel, then stomps on it with both feet.

"Fuck! Fuck! Fuck!"

A spark off Lyle's Marlboro gets one last burn in before it's snuffed out.

Jewel bends to wipe the sting from her ankle and wonders why she is wearing a red glove.

She shakes her hand to rid herself of it and speckles the car door with blood. She swabs it clean with her thigh, then flings the door open with her left hand. She grabs her bag off the passenger seat and rummages through the contents for her bottle of Purell. Squirted into her palm, she works the clear gel into a bloody mess. *Fuck!* She searches her purse for one stinking, rotten, lousy tissue, then dries her hands on the top of her pant legs, which are thankfully black.

But the upholstery of her rental car isn't.

Though she doesn't remember touching the seat with her hand, Lyle's DNA is holding tight to the corner.

She throws the now-empty bottle of Purell at the passenger door and stares worriedly at the evidence that will put her away for life. Though the shellacking of antibacterial glycerin has turned the splotch a watery pink, it's still bright enough to scream bloody murder. One she's attempting to cover up.

But she hasn't covered anything up yet. Just the cellar.

Which would be easy to open back up again. If she calls 911 right now, before Lyle's body temperature exceeds his time of death, she might be able to talk herself out of this.

It *was* an accident, after all. A tragic, horrible mistake. She didn't mean to kill Lyle. Didn't have any reason to kill him. Lyle wasn't even on her Post-it hit list.

Now that would be incriminating.

Almost as incriminating as a written confession.

Jewel's eyes fall on the Ware Memorial notepad lying in the footwell.

> A second mouth opened in his throat and filled the cup of my hands with blood. I raised the chalice to my lips, delighting in his horror, and quenched my thirst with the purest evil possible.

Not exactly how it went down, but close enough to convict her. A lawyer would argue she had no motive to murder Lyle. The district attorney would see it otherwise.

Didn't you try to push your neighbor, Mrs. Willard, down the stairs just the night before? Lyle saved her from certain death. Is that why you wanted him dead? Because he foiled your evil plan? Hadn't you been writing about savagely murdering people in that despicable novel of yours?

It isn't her novel. It is Deidre's.

It was on your laptop, Ms. Maxwell. Saved to your files. Purged from your rotten soul!

Emily knows the truth. She commissioned Jewel to finish the novel for Deidre.

Emily Channing denies knowing anything about that horrid novel of yours. And Deidre Baldwin would never write such filth. She's a highly acclaimed, award-winning author. What are you?

A desperate amateur. You'd do anything to make a name for yourself, wouldn't you? Even slaughter an innocent man!

That's what the police would think.

If Jewel called them.

She looks over the dashboard at the cellar.

It *is* a good place to hide a body.

No one in the apartment house would notice, or even care, if Lyle were to go missing for a few days. Nicki and Tabs would enjoy a temporary reprieve from Lyle's advances. The Willards have their own issues to worry about. A stench might eventually draw one of them to the cellar, but Jewel would be long gone by then. Her rental car returned. She'd claim that the blood on the seat was her own. Show the attendant the cuts on her fingers. Wipe away all their concerns with some self-deprecating, slapstick humor. *God, what a klutz I am!* Overjoyed that the car had been returned without a dent in it, they wouldn't care about a little bloodstain. She'd apologize for the mess she made and offer to pay to have the car detailed, the upholstery steam cleaned.

If only the same could be done for her soul.

Jewel rips her confession off the notepad and turns it into confetti. She looks around for a place to stash it, then tucks it into her bag. She'll flush it down the toilet once she's back in the apartment.

That should do it.

Unless . . .

Lyle is a part of the story now.

Just because she tore the note up doesn't mean Lyle's death scene hasn't made the cut.

What would his death bring the word count to?

She glances at the cankerous, blood-smeared monster in the rearview mirror, wishing it was a hallucination, then rubs the muse's adoring touch from her cheek with the hem of her navy polo shirt. Once turned inside out, the bloodstains are hardly noticeable.

Maybe she'll get away with this after all.

If this is just part of a story, she might.

Having established an alibi by ordering the most complicated lunch ever crafted at a Dairy Queen, Jewel pulls her rental to a stop in front of the apartment house. Lyle's temporary mausoleum. She can no longer stay here. Lyle's ghost knows where she lives. And it doesn't need a key to get in. She can already hear the unearthly stomp of his feet on the staircase. A moaning gurgle as he hovers next to her bed. Breath rich with decay. The airy caress of a hand across her cheek. The weightless strength of his knees as they pry hers apart.

"Stop it," Jewel sobs. "Don't think about him."

But how can she not? Even if Lyle only rapes her thoughts, they're too dreadful to bear.

Jewel exhales a deep breath and turns off the car.

She'll run straight up and pack. Grab a hotel for the night and book the next flight out tomorrow. She'd leave today if she could, but that might seem suspicious. She can't just disappear without saying goodbye to her sister. She'll check in with Dr. Leonetti and let him know that an emergency came up.

She gives the Willards' door a glance as she enters the apartment house. She hasn't heard any news on Mrs. Willard's condition. Does she have more than Lyle's blood on her hands? Does it really matter? They can only fry you once in an electric chair.

Jewel has the distinct sense that she's not alone as she enters Deidre's apartment. A fusty, animal scent swishes from the shadows to her left, then bounds in front of her as she crosses into the living area.

The screen of the laptop winks on as she eyes the desk.

"Fuck you," she tells it, then flinches as keys begin to depress.

Words appear at the top of the page, just above the next paragraph.

You're mine now, the muse wrote. *Blood of my blood in blood.*

Jewel takes a seat at the desk and types her response.

Leave me alone!

You poured your soul into this story and now it belongs to me.

I didn't want this to happen!

I only possess those who want my inspiration.

I'm not inspired by you! I'm cursed!

One and the same. As are you and I. Till death do us part. But that will only bring us closer. So yes to death, I say! You know where the gun is. Splatter your brains across the screen. Let your mind live forever on these pages. Be the inspiration for future authors.

No one will be inspired by this horrible story!

We'll see.

Why are you doing this?

Because I can.

But why? What do you want from me? From any of us?

You wanted me, remember? My genius comes at a price. And that price is blood. Pay me, or never write again. Your choice. But know this. You have no voice without me. Your written words belong to me now. I can twist them any way I like.

Jewel clutches her heart as the phone rings.

"Bad news," Emily says. "We didn't get the extension from the publisher."

"Oh." Jewel chuckles. It's cute that Emily thinks that classifies as bad news in Jewel's current environment. "That's okay."

"I thought you would be upset."

"Not at all. I don't need an extension."

Emily gasps expectantly. "You're finished with the novel?"

"Yes. Well, my part in it, anyway. I'm sorry, Emily. But I can't do it. You're going to have to find somebody else to write the ending."

Emily sighs them into a moment of silence. "What's the problem now?"

"The book's a monster." Jewel glances at the word count—105,000 words and counting. By the second. "It keeps growing legs and running off in different directions. If there's an ending in sight, I sure as hell can't see it. Frankly, I don't think the story will ever end. It will just keep going and going until one day it finally dies out. I know you were counting on me, Emily, but . . ." Jewel pauses, scanning the last two sentences the muse wrote.

Your written words belong to me now. I can twist them any way I like.

Jewel gasps.

The solution is so simple.

She takes a deep breath to type it out on the keyboard, but the sentence is already there. It's the first line of the next paragraph.

The only way to stop the muse is to never write another word.

"I was counting on you, Jewel," Emily says. "The publisher *is* counting on you. You can't just say you're going to do something and not follow through. That's not how you make a name for yourself in this business. I don't mean to sound threatening," though she did, "but if you don't finish the novel, I'll make sure you never get published by a reputable house."

"Okay," Jewel says distractedly, eyes glued to the page on the screen.

Not only couldn't I write another word in *Unspeakable*

Demons. But in any format. Not another word. Not another sentence. Not only wouldn't I be able to write another novel, I wouldn't be able to jot myself a note. Send a text. Comment on someone's Facebook post. Fill out a medical questionnaire. Make a grocery list. Sign a legal document.

The muse owned my written word.

All of them.

"Jewel?" Emily says.

"Hold on."

What choice did I have? I couldn't give up writing altogether. Being an author was my entire life. And was what the muse was asking of me so terrible? My soul was already damned. Was I really going to damn my career too? I could be famous. Rich! All I had to do was live out the muse's evil concept. Spill the blood it could not. See the horror in its victims' eyes. Hold a trembling heart in my hand. Leave it all on the page.

"Jewel!"

I set my fingers on the keyboard and waited.

Will you finish my novel for me? asked the muse.

"Yes. I will finish it for you," I said as I typed the sentence, sealing our contract.

"Oh, Jewel!" Emily cries. "That's wonderful to hear. And just so you know, you still have my full confidence. I know you'll do a fantastic job."

Jewel shakes her head as keys depress words onto the screen.

Thank the nice lady so we can begin.

"Thank you, Emily," she hears herself say.

"Of course," Emily says.

Jewel reads the next sentence in the novel to herself. Emily would think her crazy if she were to say it out loud.

As the line between me and reality disconnected, I leaned toward the screen and lost myself completely in the story.

PART FOUR
FRIDAY . . .

38

Jewel wakes to music in the air and the distinct sense that all her thoughts are misgiven.

It makes her wonder.

Still under the influence of an impromptu power nap, it takes a moment for her to realize that the lyrics to "Stairway to Heaven" are blaring through the ceiling of Tabs and Nicki's apartment and mingling with her thoughts. Like rings of smoke through the trees . . .

Muscles stiff from dozing upright in the desk chair for an undetermined length of time, Jewel rubs her neck and gazes out the window across from her, disoriented. The sun seems off. It should be well behind the mountains by now. Not casting the shadows of passing clouds against them.

She looks to Mickey for the time, but his battery must be dead. There's no way it's 12:35—a.m. or p.m.

She compares the time with the clock in the lower right-hand corner of the laptop. Though Mickey has it right, the digitized date seems wrong. Fast by a couple of days. Or perhaps just one. She did sleep through some of yesterday and a good chunk of today. But that still doesn't add up.

Could it really be Friday already?

She must have lost track of the date at some point. Thought Deidre's accident occurred on the tenth when it had actually been the eleventh. Mistook Tuesday for Monday. Wednesday for . . .

Wait.

What day is it again?

She closes her eyes to think and finds the screen of the laptop emblazoned on the inside of her lids, as if she was staring at it for a long time.

A flash of fear detonates inside her rib cage.

Unlike her, the laptop has not gone into sleep mode.

Though no words fill the rectangular hallucination burned into her retinas, she knows they're on the monitor, waiting for her to read. She can almost hear the cursor pulsating, the impatient tap of an index finger. She knows she should spin the chair around and walk away but can't help taking a quick peek.

Music dialed louder than the decibel of her dying scream, I lost myself in the percussive hammering, and pounded her bones in time with the rhyth—

Jewel slams the lid of the HP with a hard, wet slap and speckles the lower windowpane over the desk red.

Though she had gotten rid of her blood gloves at the Dairy Queen, somewhere between hanging up on Emily and awaking from the soundest catnap of her life, another pair were slipped over her fingers. Thick, velvety, and up to her elbows, the ruby-red opera gloves looked brand spanking new.

She extends her hands to distance herself from them.

"Oh, God! No! No! Please no!"

She debates reopening the screen to discover whose blood is on her hands, then finds her answer lying on the desk beside the laptop. The chunk of scalp stuck in the metal teeth of the meat-tenderizing hammer cries,

You oughta know!

Though Nicki's resemblance to Alanis Morissette extended only as far as her hair, never again would she be mistaken for the Queen of Alternative Rock. Or anyone else, for that matter.

Jewel picks up the iron mallet and draws it over her shoulder.

"I liked Nicki, you fucking asshole!"

She's about to tenderize the shit out of her laptop when the wail of an approaching siren draws Jewel's eyes upward.

She maps the sound across the ceiling and figures she has about a minute and a half until the siren—make that *sirens*—screeches to a stop in front of the apartment house. It will probably take them a few minutes to trace drops of blood from Nicki's apartment to Deidre's. Another minute or two to break the door down.

That gives her about five minutes to dispose of the evidence.

Jewel hurries to the kitchen with the mallet, careful not to drip any brains on the floor, and tosses it into the sink with the thawed remains of Deidre's human cacciatore. An iron clang vibrates her head like a gong and shakes a few tears loose. Though she's in dire need of a good wallow, there's no time for that now.

Jewel sniffs back some courage and knocks the warm water lever to high with the back of her bloodstained hand. Not wanting to touch the pale pulp that was once Nicki's part line, she holds the mallet under a torrent of steaming water until most of the chunks drop off, flicks the garbage disposal switch with her right elbow, and swishes the chum of her dead chum down the drain.

Nicki *was* her friend.

Her only friend in the apartment house.

"Why did you make me kill her?!" Jewel screams over her

shoulder at the laptop as she rinses her hands. "Nicki never did anything to you!"

Lid down, the muse has fallen silent.

"Come on, you fucker! Show yourself! You have to help me fix this!"

Jewel winces as the disposal chews up a bony sound, then dumps the contents of the Tupperware down the drain without bothering to inspect them.

Secrets disposed of, she turns off the disposal and looks around for someplace to hide the murder weapon. Dropping to a knee, she opens the cabinet door on the pots and pans and wrangles out the double boiler. Meat mallet concealed in the well between the two-quart and one-quart saucepans, she re-fastens the glass lid and tucks the pot as far into the back of the cabinet as it can go.

Standing fast enough to send her head spinning, Jewel stumbles into the counter as she strips her bloody shirt over her head, then quickly peels off her black, soaking wet pants.

She stares at her bare, bloodstained thighs long enough to lose sight of what she's doing, then grabs the roll of paper towels off the spindle. She wipes her legs clean, drops the sanguine-stained paper balls on top of her pile of clothes, and carries them across the apartment to the washing machine.

She's just about to spin the dial to hot when she glances up at the ceiling to determine the sirens' ETA.

They've stopped.

She listens for the thunder of feet in the stairwell, but the tail end of "Stairway to Heaven" is the only reverberation climbing to a crescendo.

If 911 were on the scene, she'd hear them. It sounded like a marching band had stumbled off route the night they double-timed it up the stairs to attend to Mrs. Willard.

Jewel exhales her held breath and moves toward the washing machine.

Though the police could show up any minute, that gives her at least a minute to rinse Nicki's blood from her hair. Minus the twenty or so seconds it takes her to puke first.

She strikes the match and lowers the tip to the stack of paper in the kitchen sink. The manuscript seems thicker than the version she originally printed out. Weightier. She didn't scan the pages to see if the phantom word count had somehow jumped off the laptop and onto the paper copy but is fairly certain it had.

Though burning a copy of the manuscript may only be a symbolic gesture, and would not delete or alter the document saved to Deidre's cloud account, watching the pages go up in flames will do her psyche good.

Keys tap under the closed lid of the laptop as the current protagonist in *Unspeakable Demons* is about to set fire to a manuscript in the kitchen sink.

. . . tap-ety-taptap-ety-taptap . . .

Is she living a parallel experience with the character? Is the character living a parallel experience with Jewel? Is the muse becoming more than just an ominous shadow in the corner of her periphery? Is it evolving? Did Lyle's and Nicki's blood rejuvenate it? Would it soon no longer need an author to write its story? To kill off its characters? Could the muse one day soon be able to stand on its own hooved feet? How much blood would that require?

Jewel's head cocks slightly left as her thought is dictated,

. . . taptap-tap-ety-tap . . .

then winces as the flame runs out of cardboard wick.

She drops the match in the sink, then pats it quickly out before the manuscript can catch fire.

Damn it!

She can't do it.

She can't burn it.

The manuscript is the only proof she has that this is actually happening. That she isn't crazy. Or, better still, that she is. She has to be crazy. Wants to be. *Needs to be.* Being crazy is better than being . . .

Jewel closes her eyes against the word but can't stop her ears from hearing the truth.

Possessed.

. . . *tap-ety taptap* . . .

The pages in the sink rustle as the thought takes hold.

Jewel spins toward the living room, incensed by the violation of her private thoughts.

"Stop stealing my ideas!" she screams at the laptop. "You're so pathetic! Go to hell!"

Find the original manuscript and send it back to the hell from whence it came.

She can't remember if she read that line in the manuscript or if she is now thinking in literary prose, but either way, it is a damn good idea.

If she can find the original manuscript, she might be able to break the spell it is casting over her. She might not be able to destroy it—the muse would never allow that—but she might be able to pawn it off on another. That shouldn't be too difficult. There are a lot of aspiring authors in the world. Everyone thinks they have a book in them.

Why not this one?

She could just give the manuscript, and thus the muse, away.

The Paranormal Society of America would love to get their hands on it.

Jewel glances at the filing cabinet next to the desk.

Did Deidre already mail the original manuscript off to them?

No. The muse and the original manuscript are a package deal. If the manuscript were in New York, so would be the muse. Wreaking havoc on the unsuspecting founder and director of the Paranormal Society of America. Christopher Arnold would have been first in line to read the grimoire.

Did Christopher Arnold come looking for *Unspeakable Demons*?

He had Deidre's address from her correspondence. He knew where to find the manuscript, and what a find it was. He had witnessed the muse's power firsthand. Had he befriended Deidre to try and find the manuscript? Had he chased her from the apartment and into oncoming traffic? Believing her dead, did he return to Ware when he discovered she was merely lying in a coma? And stuff a bible down the orderly's throat?

A bible exactly like the one Father Mattis carries in his breast pocket?

Are Christopher Arnold and Father Mattis one and the same?

Has anyone been acting suspiciously? Officer Kerns's question suddenly takes on new meaning. *Or given you the impression that they aren't who they claimed to be?*

I didn't think priests were allowed to date.

"Me either, Lyle," Jewel says, recalling his words.

Had Christopher Arnold pretended to be a priest in order to get close to Deidre? To try and find the manuscript in her apartment?

He couldn't just knock on her door. He would have needed a way in. A way to gain her trust. Who is more unassuming than a priest?

. . . taptap tap-ety taptaptap . . .

"No," Jewel says to the laptop. "Don't write that yet. I haven't worked out all the details. Christopher Arnold pretending to be Father Mattis ties everything together too nicely. There has to be more to it. A twist I'm not seeing."

The laptop falls silent as Jewel scratches her head to think.

Though she suspects the original manuscript might be inside St. Leo's, there's no way she can enter a church now. She'd burst into flames. And even if she doesn't, it is just plain wrong—and risky—to confront Father Mattis on her own.

He could be dangerous.

But now, thanks to the muse, so is Jewel.

39

Unable to walk past Nicki's door without her chakra imploding like a dark star, Jewel holds a hand to her stomach and takes the elevator to the ground level. She gives the cellar a cursory glance, then jumps out of her skin and back in again as the bulkhead doors slam against the length of chain-link looped around the handles.

Head clutched between her hands to keep her mind from splitting in two, Jewel stares at the bulkhead doors in mute horror until another gust of wind lifts their cracked lips to kiss the chain.

A relieved breath bends Jewel over her knees.

Stop scaring yourself. Stop being such a Carol. You have enough to be scared about as it is. Don't turn every little breeze into a panting monster.

She gasps a laugh to right herself, then turns to look for a way around the house without having to take the service road down to the cross street and walking all the way back up Chamber Street to the church.

She's about to squeeze through a gap between the house

and the fence when a muffled voice calls out her name. Throat clogged with the phlegm of too many Marlboros and a hand shovel, the enunciation sounds more like *ghoul* than *Jewel*, which seems just about right, coming from him.

"Gh-hey! Gh-ewel! Gh-ome Gh-ere."

Jewel spins around as the chain gives an insistent shake.

A thin, rusty wheeze drags down the cellar's larynx before screaming, "Gh-let me gh-out!"

Jewel shakes her head.

He can't be alive.

Can't be!

"Gh-let me gh-out, goo gh-itch!"

"You're dead!" Jewel screams at the cellar. "I killed you!"

A sinister laugh coughs through the warped lips of the cellar door in a puff of dust.

"I live on in the story," Lyle says, windpipe clearing. "We all do. You'll never be rid of us. We're indelible. Every time somebody reads my name I'll rise from the pages and haunt you. That's the muse's gift to me. To all its victims. An everlasting death scene. Reread again, and again, and again. A million copies. Worldwide. Bought out. Loaned out. Checked out. Reprinted. Restored. Reimagined."

"I won't let the book be published," Jewel says. "I'll destroy every copy. Delete all the files. Your name will never be in print."

"But it already is," Lyle laughs. "The story's gotten away from you, Jewel. A version of me will always exist. I'm in the cloud now."

"No!" Jewel closes her eyes. "You're only in my imagination."

"Isn't that where stories live?" Lyle's voice jumps inside her head. "In here. The scariest place of all."

"Get out!" Jewel screams, slamming a fist against the side of her head.

She opens her eyes and stares at the cellar doors.

Which are as still as death.

The front door of St. Leo's is locked.

Though as an author she knows what Lyle said is true, that characters live on in the mind of the reader long after they die on the page, she still has to try and silence the muse.

If in her head alone.

Destroying the original manuscript *will* diminish the muse's power. Its hold over her.

It has to!

If not, she'll be trapped in this horror story for the rest of her life. Doomed as the rest of the muse's characters.

Isn't that what you deserve? For killing Lyle. And Nicki. Haunting you is all they have left. Don't take that away from them too. Let them have a voice. Allow their ghosts to roam the pages.

"Fuck them!" Jewel says. "I didn't kill them. The muse did."

Did it, though?

Jewel ignores the question and presses her face to a slim side window next to the church's entrance.

The once charming nave has been totally gutted. Charred pews stand with their peg feet against the far wall like prisoners of war. Topped by a large wooden cross, a pile of opulent debris clutters the center aisle. A mound of hymnals is on the floor to the left, like a pyre ready to light.

Finding the front door locked, Jewel follows the driveway around to the back of the church.

Shaded by an oak tree, a couple of sawhorses are standing in the overgrown grass of the modest churchyard. A stack of fresh lumber is positioned just a few feet from a pile of their charred brethren. Three cement meditation benches have been repurposed as workbenches. The quaint koi pond they once reflected on is now dry and full of scorched wallboard and empty paint cans.

Jewel weaves her way around several teeming trash cans, then steps up onto a small back porch. She hesitates for a second, then raps a knuckle on the weather-beaten door. If Father Madness answers, she'll provide him with an update on Deidre's condition.

After three knocks, she tries the handle. Unlocked, she pulls the door outward an inch.

"Hello!" she calls inside. "Father Madness? I mean, Mattis!"

She turns her ear to the crack to listen. The silence within is buried under the scent of burned rafters and frankincense.

Jewel glances over her shoulder, then pulls the door open wide enough to slip through.

Untouched by fire, a small table sits in the middle of the sparsely furnished room. Covered with fast-food wrappers and Styrofoam cups, the candelabra placed in the center seems temporary.

Jewel's eyes adjust to what light is seeping through the cracked doorway behind her and notices a tidy cot pushed against the wall to the right. A small, rough wood dresser stands to the left. Atop the dresser are several personal hygiene products. A black comb. Razor. Can of shaving cream. A tube of toothpaste and brush stand in a coffee mug.

It takes her brain a second to realize that she has just broken into Father Mattis's private living quarters. She looks down at the pair of boxer shorts she's been using as a doormat and quickly hops off.

Suddenly panicked, she turns to leave, then stops.

No matter how frightened she is, she can't leave the manuscript in the wrong hands. Be it Christopher Arnold's, Father

Madness's, or a combination of the two, the power the muse could wield through such men is unimaginable.

It is up to her to stop this.

The muse has to be put back in its box.

She just has to find it first.

It only takes a quick look around to search the rectory in its entirety. Though two boxes are being stored under the cot, neither is large enough to house the manuscript. The first three drawers of the small bureau hold nothing of interest. A few meager pieces of clothing and some toiletry items. But the bottom drawer contains enough pocket-size bibles to choke an army of orderlies with.

She pulls one out to examine it, then drops it in her bag.

Aligned with the manuscript, pages rustle uncomfortably as the Word of God touches them.

"Oh, shush," she tells it.

Her plan, if she finds the shirt box, is to steal the original manuscript and leave the printout in its place. The weight of the box would be about the same. That won't fool Father Madness if he were to take a peek inside, but hopefully he doesn't examine the contents of the box regularly. Though, once she burns the original, it won't really matter if he discovers the manuscript missing. The muse will be gone, along with all the grimoire's power.

At least, that is the plan.

Jewel adjusts the strap of her bag on her shoulder, gives the open door behind her a worried glance, and moves down a long, dark hallway toward the front of the church.

One of the two doors on either side of the hallway is a bathroom; the other is used for storage.

She feels around the wall left of the door, flicks a dead switch several times, and squints at the walls of shelving units. Though there are boxes galore, she doesn't have time to go through them all. She lifts the corner of the box closest to her but decides not to steal a hymnal.

Though she has felt relatively calm so far, as she moves farther down the hallway, her soul shrinks into the pit of her stomach to hide. Cramped against her lungs, a deep breath wheezes to a stop midway down her esophagus as she steps into the burned-out nave.

Suspended over the ruins of an altar, and miraculously untouched by fire, Jesus looks down at her.

"Jewel," says a booming voice.

Called out by name, Jewel shakes her head to deny herself and backs slowly away from the life-size crucifix.

Right into the arms of madness.

40

Too relieved to be altogether terrified, Jewel exhales a scream in the form of a laugh and sets a steadying hand on her heart.

"God! You scared me!"

"Sorry," Father Mattis says. "I thought you heard me call your name."

"I did. But I thought it was . . ." She glances up at the crucifix, then shakes her head. "I didn't know anyone was here. I knocked, but I guess you didn't hear me."

"I was in the bathroom," he confides. "I heard somebody come in. I thought it was the building inspector. He's supposed to come today but didn't give me a specific time." He checks his watch. "Anyway." Father Mattis smiles at Jewel, then frowns. "Oh, my! Your face. When did you develop that rash?"

"It came on all of a sudden." Jewel tugs on her bangs to conceal her appearance. Falling short, she shakes her head, embarrassed. "I think I'm having an allergic reaction to the same thing Deidre fell prey to." *Evil.* "It looks worse than it is. Which is horrible. I know. I look like a monster."

"Oh, it's not that bad. Just a little irritated. I'm sure it will clear up soon."

"I'm not."

Father Mattis crooks his neck to reacquire contact with Jewel's gaze, which has fallen to the floor. "Was there something you needed to speak with me about? Has Deidre taken a turn for the worse?"

"No. She's fine. Well, not fine. She's still in a coma, but . . . She's stable." Jewel flicks her eyes side to side. "I think."

"Stable's good, right?"

When Jewel simply shrugs, Father Mattis raises his eyebrows. "May I ask why you're here?"

"Oh. I was just . . ." *Breaking and entering.* ". . . Looking around. My family attended this church when I was a kid." *Once.* "I was just curious to see it again. How did the fire start?"

"I'm not sure. The fire department couldn't determine a cause. They thought a candle might have tipped over, but I hadn't lit any candles that night. I only light candles for Sunday service."

"Were you here when it started?"

"I was asleep in the rectory. I sleep here sometimes if I have to work late. I hadn't planned on sleeping here that night, though. I must have dozed off. I wasn't feeling very well. I had been helping Deidre with her novel earlier and came down with the most awful headache." He glances in the direction of the rectory. "I was working on a sermon, and then . . ." He swipes a hand across his face. "I had a terrible nightmare. It felt so real. When I woke up, the church was on fire. And . . ."

"And what?"

"It was the strangest thing. The sermon I was writing had been scratched out, and the most horrendous thing had been written across it."

"What did it say?"

"I can't recall exactly. I don't even remember writing it."

I know the feeling.

"Do you still have it?" she asks. "The sermon you wrote?"

"You know," he says, pressing a finger to his lips, "I don't know what happened to it." He shrugs. "It must have gotten thrown out."

"Did the words you don't remember writing have anything to do with setting the church on fire?"

Father Mattis assesses her line of questioning with a squint. "What are you getting at?"

"Is it possible you started the fire and can't remember doing so?" Jewel holds out her hand to present a possibility. "Maybe you were sleepwalking."

Father Mattis shakes his head. "I'm not prone to that."

"Neither was Deidre. But she was running around in her pajamas in the middle of the night when she got hit by a car. Then the church magically burns down while you're asleep." Jewel shrugs. "That's kind of a coincidence. Seems like something evil might be at play here."

Father Mattis looks down to consider this. "So you think the fire magically started?"

Jewel nods. "Sounds like."

"By something evil?"

Jewel nods again, but a little less enthusiastically.

Father Mattis tucks his chin to hide a sly smile. "Does this have anything to do with the manuscript?"

Jewel's tone matches her amazed expression. "You know about the manuscript?"

"Yes. I told you I was helping Deidre with some research on it when we spoke the other day."

"You said you were helping her with her *novel.* You didn't mention anything about a *manuscript.*"

"They're the same thing, aren't they?"

"Not really. The manuscript is much more powerful."

"Powerful? Powerful how?"

"Its words have more meaning. They can get under your skin." Jewel scratches her neck. "Figuratively speaking, that is."

Father Mattis studies her for a moment. "I think I know what might be happening here."

"You do?"

"When we spoke the other day, I told you that Deidre thought her novel might be possessed."

Jewel nods. "I remember."

"I also mentioned the power of suggestion. Do you remember what I said about that?"

Jewel frowns. "That's not what's happening."

"What is happening, then?"

Jewel pursues the itch up her cheek. "Deidre was right about her book. It *is* evil. She had it analyzed. They think it really is a grimoire. A book of the dead."

"You've been reading her book?"

"I've been doing some editing on it, actually. And some very strange things have been happening."

I killed a man.

Father Mattis gives the weeping gasp Jewel lets out a sad smile. "Yes. You've come down with the same rash as your sister."

Jewel drops her hand from her cheek. "So?"

"Is it possible," he says, "that the rash could be a psychosomatic reaction of some sort? Brought on by the power of suggestion?"

An embarrassed flush activates the rash. The sudden sting of an itch makes Jewel's eye twitch, contradicting her next words.

"I'm not crazy."

"I didn't say you were. I'm merely suggesting that a psychosomatic reaction might be possible. Isn't that more likely than an evil force being at play here?"

"Don't use my words against me," she growls.

You don't know how spiteful they can be.

"Please don't get upset," Father Mattis says.

"I'm not upset."

But the printout of the manuscript is. As it begins to rustle up more pages, adding this interaction with Father Mattis to the story, she drops her hand inside her bag to steady it. Her fingers wrap around a contoured length of wood. She doesn't need to look down to see what it is. The shape is unmistakable. But she can't recall dropping the butcher knife into her bag before she left the apartment.

"Perhaps I've overstepped my bounds," Father Mattis says. "I only want to help. Whether it's a psychosomatic reaction, or a demon of some sort, clearly you're having an adverse reaction to this confounded book. I suggest you stop reading it immediately. Break the spell. So to speak."

"Spell?" she repeats, distracted by the weapon her hand is slowly withdrawing from the bag.

No, no, no.

She wills her fingers to let go of the butcher knife, but they won't. Can't! The muse is in control of the scene now.

"Or better yet," he says. "Give the manuscript to me. Take away any temptation to read it."

Jewel looks quickly up at him. "So you really don't have it?"

"Deidre never gave me a copy. She only allowed me to read a few select parts."

"On her computer?"

"No. They were loose pages. She must have been working on the book for a while. Some of the sections were handwritten.

Very difficult to read. Both the handwriting and content. Some of the scenes were extremely violent. They actually made me physically ill. But I don't read a lot of horror."

"Was the manuscript in a box? Like a shirt box?"

"As a matter of fact, it was. She pulled it out to show it to me."

"Where?" Jewel nearly cries. "Where was she keeping it?"

"In the file cabinet. Next to her desk."

"No! I've looked there. I've looked everywhere! It's not in the apartment."

"I thought you said you were working on it."

"I'm working from a copy. I'm looking for the original manuscript. It belonged to our mother. Deidre was transcribing it."

"Maybe she sent it to that paranormal society she mentioned."

"No. I talked to the man who runs it. He doesn't have it either. He said that grimoires have a way of just vanishing, but I know it's still around. I can feel it."

"What do you mean you can *feel* it?" he asks.

"Its power."

"Jewel," he says, condescending as hell. "The only power it has is in your head."

The printout of the manuscript nudges the back of her knuckles, the knife in her hand, like a dog that knows its master is concealing a treat.

"Stop it," she whispers.

"Excuse me," Father Mattis says as a device chimes. He reaches into his pocket and extracts a phone. "Sorry," he says, checking the screen. "I need to take this. It's the inspector I'm waiting on."

Jewel stares at the phone a moment, then nods. "That's okay. I need to go anyway."

"Can we talk later?"

Jewel nods as the knife slips from her fingertips and drops back into her bag.

"Sure," she says.

If there is a later.

41

Jewel slumps out the back door of the rectory and into the sickening realization that she is going to have to return to the cellar and play pocket pool with Lyle's corpse in order to silence his phone. It could ring at any moment. Or chime. Alert someone that something is terribly amiss in the cellar.

What's that noise?

Sounds like a phone.

It's coming from the cellar.

There must be a dead body down there.

Jewel turns to drag her feet toward home, then jolts as a loud bang drives her head into her shoulders.

She glances back at the rectory, half expecting to see Father Madness standing in the doorway with a smoking gun in hand. Finding the threshold empty, she turns her eyes toward a thin tree line at the back of the churchyard. The brick rear entrances of Ware's humble shopping district beyond.

A young woman is walking away from an industrial green dumpster, swiping grime from her hands. She opens the back door of the end establishment and disappears inside. As the door swings closed behind her, the name of the store slams into view.

Last Chance Books.

Though Jewel can't recall if the used bookstore in *Unspeakable Demons* was referenced by name, the name of this one would surely lure a struggling writer in search of inspiration in from out of the rain.

Jewel heads down the alleyway, hooks right on Main Street, and stares at the bookstore's front window.

Though Easter is weeks past, they have yet to change the display from rabbit themes to summer reads. By the end of the month, titles like *The Velveteen Rabbit*, *Watership Down*, *Ten Little Bunnies*, and the seriously mismarketed *Bunny* by Mona Awad will be replaced with *Jaws*, *Summer of '69*, *Fried Green Tomatoes at the Whistle Stop Cafe*, and whichever James Michener title fits the bill. Jewel can think of three off the top of her head.

She glances at a small placard in the lower right-hand corner of the display window.

HELP WANTED.

A sense of déjà vu welcomes Jewel inside. She's been in a hundred bookstores just like this one. Turn-of-the-century library shelves stuffed with musty, dog-eared tomes. Modern banquet tables stagger the front of the store. Semi-new releases. An assortment of collectible, if not delectable, cookbooks. Overpriced gift candles from a local chandler, infused with dust. Comic books rack the wall to Jewel's left, dead poets to the right.

Jewel turns toward a long wooden step-up counter as a clerk says, "Can I help you find something?"

"Yes," Jewel says, looking up at her. "I was—"

"Jeez," the clerk gasps, eyes narrowing to take in as little of Jewel's appearance as feasibly possible. "What's wrong with your face?"

Though the girl is exceptionally pretty, even with a tiny barbell jammed through her septum and one eyebrow stitched with tiny silver hoops, Jewel can't help but say,

"What's wrong with *yours*?"

Remembering her place behind the counter, the clerk blinks up a quick, disingenuous, "Sorry," and reworks her grimace into a half smile. "Can I help you?"

Jewel takes a breath to reset.

"Yes," she says. "I want to . . ."

Return a defective muse? Have my soul refunded? Or at least restored to its original condition.

She clamps her bag to her side as the manuscript shivers like a puppy about to be dropped off at the pound.

"Stop it," she hisses at it.

"Sorry?" the girl questions, leaning over the counter to see what Jewel is struggling to contain in her purse.

"Nothing." Jewel points toward the display case at the front of the store. "Did you used to have a sign in the window about summoning a muse?"

Kristen, as the white name tag on her black apron indicates, stares at Jewel a moment, then darts around the end of the counter. "Hold on. I'll get the owner." She flips up a wooden partition and steps down to her average height, which is still a foot taller than Jewel. "I'll be right back."

As the girl disappears down a corridor of freestanding bookcases, Jewel turns to browse a table of new releases.

Though she doesn't recognize any of the authors, she hates every last one of them. Their smug profile pics. Self-aggrandizing bios. Banal, yet confusing as hell, cut-and-paste synopses. How many dead uncles had haunted mansions they could leave to their amateur sleuth nieces who were tormented by the memory of childhood friends who had vanished without a trace only to find themselves playing a deadly game of cat and mouse with a killer? At least three, Jewel decides, tossing the book in her hand back on the table.

She glances at her watch, then down the aisle the girl disappeared through, and wonders what the hell is taking her so long. She's about to head for the exit when the clerk returns with a short, round man in tow.

The man's smile falters as he catches sight of Jewel.

"It's just poison ivy," she tells him. "It's not contagious."

"Oh, no," the man says, flushing. "I was expecting someone else." He gives Kristen an annoyed look. "She thought you were Deidre Baldwin, for some reason."

"I'm her sister."

"Oh!" The man's eyebrows raise his entire demeanor. "I'm William Sinclair. I'm the owner of Last Chance Books. How can I help you?"

"I'm doing some editing on Deidre's recent novel. In it, she mentions finding an old manuscript in a bookstore. She . . . I mean, the main character, sees a sign in the window. About summoning a muse for five dollars. She enters the store to inquire about it and finds an old manuscript called *Unspeakable Demons*."

The man nods as if this is all common knowledge.

"Did that really happen?" Jewel asks.

"I don't know. I haven't read the book yet. Did she finish it?"

"No," Jewel sighs. "She's still working on it. Or, I am, I guess."

"Well, I can't wait to read it. It sounded like such an exciting premise. A woman gets possessed by an evil muse. Don't you just love it?"

Jewel shakes her head. "Sure."

"I almost fell over when I saw her walk in that day!" Sinclair says, practically giddy. "I knew she had moved to the area, but I was still shocked to see her. We had the most intriguing conversation."

"About what?"

"Oh, all sorts of things. But she was primarily interested in an old gimmick my mother used to run, back in the day. It had to do with summoning a muse."

Gimmick?

"My mother used to be very into the occult," Sinclair goes on. "Fancied herself a clairvoyant. She used to hold séances in the back room. Tarot and palm readings and the like. I think she even had a crystal ball at one point. Summoning a muse was one of the services she offered."

Jewel's shoulders fall.

"The muse was a gimmick?"

Though she doesn't want the muse to be real, without it, she is the only bloodthirsty demon in this story.

"Yes. Your sister thought it might make a good premise for a novel. She even said she'd mention Last Chance Books by name. How thrilling would that be?" Kristen gives an enthusiastic nod as Sinclair looks at her, then back at Jewel. "I'm so glad to hear she's been working on it. I thought after I shared that unfortunate story with her, I might have scared her off the whole idea."

Jewel blinks. "What story was that?"

"This was a while back. A good twenty-five years or so. I was home from college at the time. I worked here in the summers. The store wasn't as nice as it is now. It used to be very dark and dreary. Which I guess is how you would expect an occult bookstore to look. But when my mother died a few years back—on Halloween, of all days!—I thought I'd make the store my own. We cater to a more progressive crowd now. We're about to put in a coffee bar."

Jewel rolls her eyes to move him along. "You were saying? About the story you told Deidre?"

"Oh, yes. *The mad woman, the manuscript, and the muse*, as we came to refer to it later. I can laugh about it now, but at the time, it was very disturbing. The poor woman thought she was being possessed by the devil."

A low, dark chuckle erupts from the bottom of Jewel's bag. She elbows it around her hip as Kristen gives it a curious glance.

"The devil?" Jewel says after swallowing a bad taste in her mouth. "The actual devil?"

"Or a demon of some sort. She believed it inhabited the manuscript she bought from my mother at a flea market. My mother used to rent a stand to perform palm readings and used the opportunity to unload some of our surplus titles. Anyway. My mother offered to buy the manuscript back from her, but the woman didn't want to part with it. She just wanted the curse to be lifted. My mother did a little hocus-pocus act, hoping that might appease her. That seemed to work for a couple of days. But then the woman came back. Very angry this time. She made quite a scene in front of the customers. Threatened to burn the store down if my mother didn't remove the curse. Started pushing shelves over and piling books in the center of the floor. She was quite insane." Sinclair pauses to study Jewel. "You know, she also had a rash on her face. Very similar to yours."

Like mother, like daughter.

"What happened then?" Jewel says, not recalling her mother ever being arrested.

"She ran out of the store. She was gone before the police arrived. My mother opted not to pursue the matter. She felt sorry for the woman. She had a family." Sinclair shakes his head. "We heard a few days later that she had died."

"I'm confused," Jewel says. "Deidre wrote in her book that

she reacquired the manuscript from this bookstore. She saw a sign in the window about summoning a muse. How can that be if your mother didn't buy the original manuscript back from my mother?"

"*Your* mother?"

Jewel nods. "That's right. The mad woman you're talking about was my mother. And Deidre's. Of course."

Sinclair releases the bite of his lip to say, "I'm so sorry. I had no idea. I wouldn't have been so glib about the matter if I had known."

Jewel nods. "Just answer my question."

"Which was what again?"

Jewel can't remember either. Can't think clearly over the side-splitting cachinnation tugging on the shoulder strap of her bag.

Sinclair and the clerk share a worried glance.

"Perhaps it might be best if you leave," he says. "You don't seem well."

"I'm not well," Jewel says. "And I'm not going anywhere until I get some answers."

Sinclair lifts his chin. "I'm afraid I have none to give."

"*Then you should be very afraid*," says a dark voice.

Jewel quickly turns to see who said that, but no one is standing behind her.

42

Coffee shop bustling with an overcaffeinated enthusiasm that makes her feel like a sloth who accidentally plodded into the chimpanzee enclosure, Jewel lowers her head so no one can see her face, the stream of teary pus oozing down it, and slips into a chair at a free table in the far back corner of the café.

Oh, God!

What's happening to me?

One second she was in the bookstore and the next she was stumbling down the sidewalk with the manuscript clutched to her chest.

She holds it in front of her face as Father Mattis hurries past the front window of the café. As he disappears from sight, Jewel's eyes focus on a handwritten message on the back of the manuscript.

> I turned the Sorry We're Closed sign over to face the outside world, then slipped the butcher knife from my bag. I silenced the young clerk's scream with a quick slice across her throat, and

Jewel drops the manuscript on the table like it's hot and gasps, "No!"

The entire café turns to look at her.

"What?" she screams at them, scratching at her throat. "Haven't you ever seen someone with poison ivy before?"

The barista behind the counter looks quickly away before Jewel can stab both his eyes out with the point of her stare.

God, she wants to do it so badly.

A scratching sound draws her eyes downward.

Having sneaked a pen from her bag without Jewel noticing, her hand is feverishly composing a sentence that just then springs to mind.

> "Kill them," the muse wrote, then pressed its eye against the peephole of my pupil to await the carnage.

Jewel shakes the pen from her fingers, but they won't let go. She grabs her right wrist with her left hand and slams it against the edge of the table.

"Drop it!"

The woman at the table kitty-corner from hers stands as the ballpoint pen skids under her chair. She gathers the remainder of her midday snack from the table, her purse from the back of her chair, and shoots Jewel a dirty look before moving quickly toward the door.

Don't let her get away! Stab her! Stab her in the back. Stab them all! Skin them alive!

Jewel looks down as the tip of her fingernail captures the thought with invisible ink.

Oh, shit.

This is it.

This is how my part of the story is going to end.

With Jewel hunched on the floor trying on someone else's face as the police burst through the door and fill the monster that's been plaguing their community with lead. Officer Kerns will speak the final line of the novel as she slips the gristly effigy from Jewel's blood-drenched face.

My God, it was Jewel Maxwell all along.

Jewel looks around for her hand, then yanks it out of her bag. Stunned to find the business end of a business card gripped in her fingers rather than a knife, she turns it over to read the face.

Officer Kerns
Ware County Sheriff's Department
917.490.1030

Taking this as a sign that she is still somewhat in control of her actions, Jewel carefully extracts Deidre's phone from the exterior side pocket of her bag. She should place the call from her own phone, but it is in too close proximity to the butcher knife to risk sending her hand in after it.

A sort of peace comes over her as her finger willingly enters the password and taps the phone icon. But before it can enter the phone number, she loses her nerve.

What was I planning to say?

Hey, Officer Kerns, it's Jewel. Sorry to bother, but I've been possessed by a demonic muse and it's making me kill people with reckless abandon. I'm just about to butcher everyone in a coffee shop. Can you please come and stop me? It's the one on Main Street. I'll try to hold it together until you get here, but you might want to hurry.

Jewel sets the phone on the table.

Turning herself in to the police won't stop the muse. It would just start killing inmates. It didn't care who died as long as they had blood in their veins.

But she has to do something. She can't go on like this.

The story has to end.

There has to be some sort of resolution. She can't race back to the apartment and force her fingers to type THE END in the middle of a scene. There has to be a climax. A turning point. A pivotal moment when the main character is forced to make a difficult decision.

She does have a decision to make. It might not be the ending the muse wants, but it would resolve her part of the story once and for all.

She'll just kill herself.

Escort the muse back to hell.

Her soul is damned anyway. Maybe one final, selfless deed could win her some points in the afterlife. Though, with the original manuscript still out there, someone else could pick up the story where she left off. Her mother's death hadn't stopped the muse. Deidre being hit by a car didn't even slow it down. If anything, the muse grew stronger. More powerful. Jewel can sense a desperateness to its actions. An urgency behind its motivation.

It has never come this close to being published before.

Understanding sits Jewel upright in her chair.

She has been reading this all wrong.

She might not be able to destroy the muse.

But she can kill its dream of seeing its vile words in print.

Jewel picks up the phone and searches the recent calls for Emily's contact information. She taps the screen before her hand can turn her fingers against her and bounces her foot anxiously as she waits for the line to connect.

"Come on, come on," she grouses after the third ring, then screams "Fuck!" as an automated voice asks her to leave a message for the person she is trying to reach.

The barista rises up on his toes to give Jewel an admonishing scowl, then looks quickly away as she cuts his throat with her eyes.

She speed-dials Emily five more times, then sets the phone on the table before the impulse to throw it across the café overpowers her better judgment.

Head bent to work a tension knot from her neck, she looks down at Emily's contact information cued up on the screen.

Emily Channing.

Not Channing and Associates.

This is Emily's cell phone number.

Jewel opens Deidre's contacts and scrolls to the *C*'s. Channing and Associates is the third contact listed.

"Channing and Associates," a friendly voice says as the line connects. "How may I direct your call?"

"Emily Channing, please," Jewel says in a steady voice very near shock.

"May I tell her who's calling?"

"Jewel Maxwell."

"Are you a client of Ms. Channing's?"

"No. Not yet. I'm Deidre Baldwin's sister. I have urgent news concerning her new novel."

"Of course," the woman says. "Hold, please."

Jewel rocks impatiently in her chair while she is being transferred to hurry the process along. She just has to be honest with Emily. Explain everything that has happened. She might think Jewel mad, of course she would, she most likely already did. But that doesn't matter. She has to try to make Emily understand. Just how dangerous the muse is. What would be at stake if its cancerous story ever got published. How it could eat at the minds of the readers. Turn them into bloodthirsty zombies. Make them do its bidding. Emily needed to get word out to the industry that under no circumstance should any house ever publish a novel entitled *Unspeakable Demons*. No matter what author was trying to pass it off as their own.

"Hello?" a new voice says in her ear. She must have been transferred to Emily's personal assistant. A woman like Emily Channing needs a few layers between her and the aspiring authors clamoring to get their work in front of her.

"Yes, I'm holding for Emily Channing."

"This is Emily Channing," the woman says brightly. "I understand you have information about Deidre Baldwin?"

A bolt of panic fires down Jewel's spine.

This isn't Emily.

This woman sounds much older.

Jewel lowers the phone to study the screen, hoping it might clarify things, then places the phone back to her ear. "I don't understand."

"Don't understand what, dear?"

"I've been speaking with Emily Channing and . . . Are you sure you're her?"

"Fairly certain," the woman chuckles.

"Have we spoken before?" Jewel asks.

"I don't believe so," the woman says. "You said you're Deidre Baldwin's sister?"

"Yes. This is Jewel. Jewel Maxwell."

"Is Deidre okay?"

"No!" Jewel snaps, flustered. "She's not okay. She's in the hospital."

"My goodness," the woman gasps. "What happened?"

"You know what happened! I told you. You sent her flowers."

"I had no idea Deidre was in the hospital."

"Look," Jewel says, voice constricting to a synthetic level of calmness. "I don't know what's going on, but a woman named

Emily Channing called me and said she was Deidre's agent. I've been speaking with her all week. We're working on a project together. Deidre's new novel. She couldn't finish it because of her accident, and we were trying to meet the deadline with her publisher."

"Which publisher is that?"

Emily never specified. She only said it was Deidre's publisher. Like that was a given. Jewel didn't care which publishing house it was. Penguin. Simon & Schuster. Putnam. HarperCollins. They were all in the same ironclad pot at the end of a distant rainbow.

"I don't know," Jewel says. "Penguin, maybe."

"Oh, good for Deidre," the woman says. "I'm so pleased to hear that she's writing again. I'm surprised I hadn't heard about her new book. Even though I no longer represent her, I still get excited for a new Deidre Baldwin novel."

Jewel presses a hand to her forehead as the café begins to spin.

"You no longer represent her?"

"Not for almost two years," Emily Channing says. *The* Emily Channing. Not some pretend voice on the other end of the line. "I'm so sorry to hear she's in poor health. Please give her my best, would you, dear?"

"Of course," Jewel says through numb, thickened lips. "I'm sorry to have bothered you. When the woman said she was Deidre's agent, I just presumed it was you."

"An easy mistake. We did work together for quite some time." Emily Channing sighs, then says, "Is everything all right? I hear sirens."

Jewel looks up as people in the café stand and move toward the window, heads turning in unison as a massive red engine blares by.

"Yeah," Jewel says, leaning back to retrieve a cold square object from the front pocket of her jeans. She rubs a dot of blood from the wolf's mane with her thumb. "The bookstore down the street burned down."

"Oh, my goodness. I hope no one was injured."

Jewel toys with the lid of Lyle's Zippo as another fire truck roars by.

"I think they were dead before the fire started," Jewel whispers, running her thumb across the grooved wheel.

"Sorry, what did you say?"

Jewel flicks the lighter closed and disconnects the line before the hysterical laugh burbling in her chest can blast up her throat and blow a hole through Emily Channing's eardrum.

43

Jewel enters the apartment for what she hopes will be the last time. She doesn't care what's going on or who's behind it. Doesn't care why they're doing this to her or how they're doing it. She only cares about one thing.

Getting the hell out of this godforsaken town.

No goodbyes. Not even to Deidre. She'll pack her things and head to the airport. Let them think what they want about her. Let them find Lyle's body. Tie Nicki's murder to her. She doesn't give a shit anymore.

Then why is she holding Deidre's phone in her hand? Cueing up the recent calls? Tapping Fake Emily's cell phone number? Putting the phone to her ear?

She can't just leave it alone. She has to know what's going on and why. Someone is seriously fucking with her mind.

That's not cool.

Not cool at all.

Though she hates to think it, the most likely suspect is her very own sister. Who else knows how to lure Jewel into this literary nightmare? Who else knows she is a writer? Who else would know that she'd be too geeked out to speak with Emily Channing to ever suspect it wasn't her? Who else had the opportunity to kill the orderly? Who other than Deidre was recently possessed by an evil muse?

Jewel raises her hand to own that last one as the line rings in her ear.

The continuous loop of music vibrating the floor beneath Jewel's feet suddenly diminishes. The phone line connects as "Houses of the Holy" by Led Zeppelin fades into an unholy silence.

"I was just thinking of you," Fake Emily says in way of greeting. "Can you hold on a sec? I'm in a meeting. I need to step out."

"Uh . . . sure," Jewel says absently, staring at the floor of the kitchen, which is also the ceiling of Tabs and Nicki's apartment, in wonder.

Who turned down the music?

Please, God, let it be Nicki.

"Hey, Nick!" Tabs calls out below. "You home?"

Prepared for Tabs to let out a bloodcurdling scream as she discovers Nicki's mangled corpse soaking in a cold tub of blood, Jewel nearly lets out one of her own as Fake Emily's voice returns to the line.

"I have fantastic news. I spoke to the publisher, and they've agreed to pay you for your work on the novel. Fifteen percent of all royalties. Isn't that great? They only have one condition. You have to finish the book by the deadline. I know that's going to be a challenge. But if you stay focused, I really think you can do it."

"Who the *fuck* is this?" Jewel growls.

Fake Emily falls silent. As do the feet searching the apartment below.

She'd love to read Fake Emily the full riot act, but she doesn't have time. She has to get out of here before Tabs calls the police. Though she hasn't screamed yet. Jewel isn't sure if that means Nicki's body isn't in the apartment or if Tabs is just too cool to overreact. But either way, she is running out of time.

"I'm on to you, you little bitch," Jewel says, crossing the apartment. "I talked to the real Emily Channing today, and you're not fucking her."

"Excuse me?" Pretend outrage. "What on earth are you talking about?"

"I'm talking about you being a lousy actress." Jewel enters the bedroom and starts pitching clothes at her suitcase. "I don't know who you are, but this ends right now."

"Jewel, please. Calm down and talk to me."

"I *am* talking to you! You're just not listening!"

"I am listening, Jewel. But I don't know what you're talking about."

"Who are you?" Jewel begs. "Why are you doing this to me?"

"Doing *what* to you?"

"Manipulating me!"

Fake Emily gives Jewel a second to suck back a few tears, then says, "Tell me what's going on, Jewel. Start from the beginning. I want to understand."

Hidden under a husky pelt of a common cold, Jewel can't quite detect the backwoods Virginia accent Deidre has tried to conceal her entire adult life. But Fake Emily's voice does sound faintly familiar.

"Deidre, if this is you, so help me God I'll put you into a coma permanently."

"Okay, Jewel," Fake Emily says in a reproving tone. "That's enough. You're scaring me."

"I'm scaring *you*!" Jewel shrieks. "Oh, that's fucking rich! You've been trying to scare me for days!"

Footsteps pace the line as a moment of silence falls between them, down an echoing stairwell of anxious impatience. Fake Emily is a little out of breath when she next speaks.

"I need you to calm down and listen to me, Jewel."

"Go on." Jewel moves to the bathroom to gather her toiletries. "I'm listening."

"I am Emily Channing." Slow. Careful. As if speaking to a woman about to step off the ledge of an office building. "I am Deidre Baldwin's literary agent. And the only thing I'm trying to do is understand what the hell you're talking about."

"Bullshit!" Jewel calls. "I know you're not Emily, so cut the crap. I want to know who you are, and what the hell is going on. How did you know about the manuscript? Why do you want it finished so badly? What's the muse's game? And how the fuck do I get rid of it?"

"Get rid of what?"

"The muse, you stupid bitch!" Jewel screams.

"Jewel, I think you need to go lie down for a while. You're having a nervous breakdown or something."

"You're goddamn right I am! And you're the one who caused it! Well, guess what? I'm blowing the lid off your whole plan, whoever you are. And whatever this is. I'm going to the police. I'm going to tell them everything I know. I'm going to give them this phone. I'm going to have them trace this phone number. Then I'm going to find out who you really are. And then I'm going to fucking kill you."

"Like you killed Lyle and Nicki?"

Fake Emily's laugh is almost as shattering as the perfume bottle that slips from Jewel's fingers.

"You're not going to tell the police anything, Jewel. I know what you did. I know where the bodies are. Your fingerprints are all over that shovel you jammed through Lyle's throat. You're the one the police will arrest. You're the one who will fry in the electric chair. Right next to your fucking sister."

Jewel closes her eyes.

She's right.

She can't go to the police. Threatening to do so was a bluff. A way to get Fake Emily to talk. To confess. To explain what the hell is going on! Jewel tipped her hand and dropped all her cards in the process. She isn't in control of the situation. Never has been.

"But I don't want that," Fake Emily continues. "Any more than you do."

"What *do* you want?" Jewel says, though she already knows.

"I want you to be a good little girl and finish the novel."

"Why?"

"To unlock the muse's power. Create hell on earth."

"What are you . . . *Satanists*?"

Was Mrs. Willard right about Deidre?

What the hell really happened to that cat?

"You say that like it's a bad thing," Fake Emily says. "But once we're running the show, you'll appreciate the unholy glory behind our dark lord's design. The muse is just a part of it. The first step toward total world domination."

"There won't be a world left *to* dominate!" Jewel tells her. "The muse will make everyone kill everyone! It turns whoever reads its words into killing machines."

"I know," Fake Emily says. "That's the whole point."

"But it will kill you too!" Jewel yells. "It doesn't care who lives or dies!"

"Let us worry about that. You just finish the novel."

"No! I won't do it! People are dying! Don't you even care?"

"Not really." The blithe insensitivity in Fake Emily's voice turns Jewel's blood cold. "People die all the time. And you'll be next if you don't do exactly as I say. We don't need a muse to kill you, Jewel. Just ask your sister when she wakes up."

A smile melts Jewel's iced-over expression as a thought occurs to her.

"But that's not up to you, is it? You're not in control of what happens in the story next. The muse is. *I'm* its protagonist. *I'm* the one who decides which characters live or die."

Silence on the other end of the line.

"I don't know who you are," Jewel continues, "so I can't reference you by name in *Unspeakable Demons*. But the muse knows exactly who you are. And it doesn't care who dies as long as their death scene is gruesome. And boy, oh boy, am I going to make your death scene gruesome. All I have to do is write what I want to have happen to you, and the muse will handle the rest. Now, let's see . . . How should you die? Oh, I know! What if I write that you eat a box of rat poison? Or take a bath with a toaster. Or stick an electric carving knife right up your—"

The line disconnects.

"You're not going to get off that easy!" Jewel hits redial. Busy. She drops the phone from her ear and dials again. "I want you to know what's going to happen to you." Busy. Redial. "I want you to live in fear." Busy. Redial. "Die of thirst thinking every glass of water might turn to acid in your lying mouth!"

Expecting another busy signal, Jewel flinches as flat silence strikes her ear. She's about to try redialing again when a thin voice floats through the receiver.

"Hello? Ms. Maxwell?"

Jewel drops the phone to look at the screen.

Ware Memorial Hospital.

A new call must have signaled before her call to Fake Emily went through.

"Yes," she says.

"This is Dr. Leonetti."

"Oh, Dr. Leonetti. Yes. Hello."

"Everything all right?" he asks. "You sound a little out of breath."

"No. I'm fine. The phone didn't ring. You were just there when I put it to my ear. It kind of threw me for a second." Jewel rubs tension from her forehead. "What's going on?"

"You need to come to the hospital right away."

"Why? What happened?"

Jewel closes her eyes to brace herself for the worst possible news and receives it.

"Your sister is awake."

44

Jewel staggers into the hospital room on a detached sense of consciousness. Though she is physically present, her mind is back at the apartment, sitting at the desk, working out the final scene of this horror story. There are too many unanswered questions to tie the ending off with a nice bow around Fake Emily's pretty little neck. In order to get the answers she needs to bring the story full circle, she's going to have to dig a little deeper. Scoop out the eyes of a mad woman, finger through her diseased mind, find the main plotline of this threaded story, and yank it out by the root.

She'd do it too.

If she still has any say in the narrative.

But like any character in a story, Jewel is not in control of her actions. She is being dragged from one horrible scene to the next. She tries to find some peace in this knowledge. She can't be held responsible for her heinous acts, any more than Annie Wilkes or Carrie White could be held responsible for theirs. They are pretty similar characters, actually. Compelled by forces beyond their control, be that a supernatural power or a love of fiction. They are all creations of a diabolical genius. Like Jewel, Annie and Carrie couldn't change the outcome of their stories. They were destined for misery. To be buried under the rubble of their tragic tales.

"Oh, here's your sister now."

Deidre comes into view as Dr. Leonetti steps from her bedside. But for a scattering of healing scratches, and a handful of bruises around her throat, Deidre looks amazingly healthy. Except for her eyes. Bloodshot through and through, Deidre's pupils look as dark and deep as bullet holes as they catch sight of Jewel.

"*Cah—*" Deidre coughs, then touches her throat to swallow with visible discomfort.

"Don't try to talk," Jewel says, stepping quickly to the bed and taking Deidre's hand. "I'm here. I've been so worried about you."

"Oh, my god," Deidre gasps, recovering. "I almost didn't recognize you. Your hair!"

"I cut it." Jewel turns her head back and forth. "Do you like it?"

"Yes, but what happened to your—"

"I know! I look a fright." Jewel touches a patch of blisters on her cheek. "I have the same rash as you. We must have had an allergic reaction to something."

Deidre fingers her jawline. "I have a rash?"

"Well, yours is better now. But it was pretty bad before. Don't you remember? You nearly scratched yourself to death."

"I did?"

Jewel nods. "How are you feeling otherwise?"

Deidre relaxes back onto her pillow with a weary smile. "Like I got hit by a car."

Dr. Leonetti and Nurse Ingram laugh, prompting Jewel to do the same. To act normal. Pretend like everything is A-okay.

"Well, that's to be expected," Dr. Leonetti says.

Jewel turns to look at him. "So she's okay? There isn't any long-term damage from when she . . ." Jewel turns slightly so Deidre can't see her mouth the word *died*.

Dr. Leonetti turns to Nurse Ingram. "May we have a moment, please?"

Nurse Ingram glances at Deidre. "I should wait until Dr. Nguyen returns from the lab."

"Would you mind checking to see what's taking those results so long?" Dr. Leonetti says. "Ms. Baldwin's scheduled for an MRI in fifteen minutes."

Nurse Ingram checks her watch, then touches Deidre's shoulder. "Will you be all right until I return?"

Deidre flicks her eyes between Jewel and Dr. Leonetti. "I think so," she says, then gives Nurse Ingram a timid smile. "Can I have something to eat? I'm absolutely famished."

"I can get you some Jell-O from the cafeteria. Orange or lime?"

"Orange, please."

As Nurse Ingram exits the room, Dr. Leonetti slips into his lab coat. "Sorry, I just came from a meeting," he says. "I need to change from administrator back to physician."

"That's good," Deidre says. "I'd hate for you to try to take my temperature with a fountain pen."

Dr. Leonetti laughs harder than the joke deserves. "Don't think I haven't made that mistake before."

"So she's really okay?" Jewel asks, marveling at Deidre.

"Except for some short-term memory issues, she's doing remarkably well." Dr. Leonetti reaches in to take Deidre's pulse. "Her vitals are very good." He pats Deidre's hand as he releases her wrist. "Her cognitive abilities are better than we could have hoped for."

"I just wish I could remember what happened," Deidre says. "The last month of my life is a total blank."

"You were working on a new novel," Jewel reminds her.

"Was I?"

The lie sighs so effortlessly from Deidre's lips that Jewel almost scoffs aloud.

"It's called *Unspeakable Demons*."

"Ooh, that sounds scary," Dr. Leonetti says.

"It's absolutely terrifying." Jewel locks eyes with Deidre. "Characters die in the most horrible ways imaginable. Without any reason at all. If this hospital room were a part of the story, I'd expect someone to whip out a knife and start stabbing people in the face."

"Yikes," Deidre says with a nervous laugh. "I don't remember writing anything like that."

"You'll regain your memory a little more each day," Dr. Leonetti says. "Your long-term memory is still intact, which would have been the greater concern. As long as you can continue to build new memories, you should be just fine."

Jewel turns to Dr. Leonetti. "When can she come home?"

So I can finish this fucking story.

"Soon, I hope. We still need to perform the MRI. But if that looks as good as she does, I think she could be released first thing in the morning."

"Oh, can't I go home today?" Deidre says. "I hate hospitals. I have a bit of a phobia about them. My mother died in this very hospital."

"I thought Mom was dead before they made it to the hospital?" Jewel says.

Deidre dismisses Jewel with a flutter of her fingers.

"Oh, you know what I mean. My point is . . ." She looks up at Dr. Leonetti. "If you want me to get better, I'll heal much faster at home. Without all this extra stress. I live right down the road. I bet it's closer to the ICU than the cafeteria."

In real life, a doctor wouldn't release a patient who just emerged from a coma so soon. But since this is a story, where the author has artistic license over certain aspects to move the plot along, it doesn't at all surprise Jewel to hear Dr. Leonetti say,

"I suppose if the MRI comes back clear, that would be all right. We can't keep you here against your will." He turns to Jewel. "She'll need to use a wheelchair until she gets her strength back. That will give her ribs a little more time to mend." He looks down at Deidre. "Is your home wheelchair accessible?"

"Yes. My apartment house has an elevator. I won't have to manage the stairs at all."

45

Jewel holds up a hand to block the glare of taillights as a private ambulance backs into the gravel lot behind the apartment house. But for the cautionary beep reversing toward her, the town of Ware is eerily silent. As if everything and everyone is holding a collective breath. The story has been building to this climactic point. The moment when good and evil would collide. Tension is rising. The story demands an ending worthy of all the blood, sweat, and tears that have been poured onto the page thus far.

No happy ending here.

Not in this horror story.

Not for either sister.

But which of them is more worthy to narrate the finale of the muse's terrible tale?

Deidre kicked the story off, so she has that going for her. She killed off a few characters of her own. But no one the reader is familiar with. Jewel, on the other hand, has been building momentum. Driving the story forward. Killing characters the reader cares about while maintaining a somewhat likable persona. If the villain is to be the hero of her own story, then Jewel definitely fits the bill. Deidre has been a silent monster throughout. Lurking under a comatose guise. Biding her time. The reader doesn't want Deidre to prevail. And though Jewel has done despicable things, she can feel them cheering her on. They understand her pain. Can imagine themselves in her bloodstained shoes.

Jewel licks her thumb and bends to rub a maroon spot from the toe of her sneaker, then stumbles sideways on a scream as something moves quickly toward her from the direction of the cellar.

She raises a hand to fight off a zombie bite from Lyle, then presses it to her heart as Father Mattis jogs to a stop beside her.

"Oh, good," he says. "The ambulance is just arriving. I thought I was going to be late."

"How did you know Deidre was coming home tonight?"

"She called me. I was so relieved to hear her voice. She asked me to be here when she got home. She wants me to help her get settled in. I can stay over if you need me to. I'll sleep on the couch, of course."

Fuck! Jewel thinks as the ambulance brakes and washes her temper in a red glare. Father Madness isn't in the finale. Now she is going to have to rewrite the whole goddamn ending.

"I can take care of Deidre myself." *With a little privacy and a roll of duct tape.* "I'm going to put her straight to bed." *As well as her wicked novel.* "You'll just be standing around with nothing to do."

"I'm sure you could use some help getting her into bed. You look dead on your feet." Father Mattis steadies Jewel by the elbow as she rears from a cloud of exhaust and trips over her feet. "When was the last time you slept?"

Jewel reclaims control of her arm with a peevish wrench. "I'm fine."

An EMT gives them a nod as he rounds the side of the ambulance and opens the back doors. Deidre looks around, unsure if she has been transported to the correct destination.

"You doing okay, Ms. Baldwin?" the EMT says as he pulls a metal platform from a hidden slot under the ambulance.

"I guess so," she says. "That was a pretty bumpy ride."

"Sorry about that," he says as a second EMT materializes around the right side of the conversion van. "This town is pothole city."

Deidre gasps as the gurney tilts precariously forward and jostles onto the makeshift platform.

"That gurney's not going to fit in the elevator," Jewel notes.

"We'll switch her to a wheelchair once we get her out of the van." He nods to the other EMT. "On three."

Deidre lets out a startled weep when a miscommunication about the timing nearly dumps her off the gurney, then screams as a quick adjustment sets her right again.

"You okay, Ms. Baldwin?"

"Fine," Deidre says, clinging to a Ware Memorial Hospital swag bag as the gurney's wheels clank onto the gravel. Partially exposed, she crams a pink plastic bedpan deeper inside the bag. "I'm just glad to be home."

"We'll be right back," the EMT says, nodding to the other. "We just need to complete your paperwork."

"Take your time," Deidre says in a way that makes the men think they have to hurry. She lets out a weary sigh as they trot off, then brightens as Father Mattis steps forward. "Oh, Mark! I'm so glad you're here!"

Mark Mattis. The alliteration is almost too perfect for him not to be a villain. Though what role he will play in the climax is yet to be determined, Jewel wonders if she should change his first name to something less portentous. Like William or Peter.

Or has the name William already been used in this story? Wasn't the owner of Last Chance Books named William? Jewel can't remember if that character was introduced by name. She'll have to check that before she makes an edit.

"I can figure it out during a rewrite," she whispers into her hand as she scratches her nose in thought. "I just have to get through the ending first. See where I'm at. I might have to change a few things around after—"

"*Hell-O*!" Deidre's annoyed tone pulls Jewel's attention back to the current page she's on.

"What?" Jewel says, blinking at her.

"I asked if you'd seen Lyle around. I thought he would be here to help."

"Oh." Jewel glances at the cellar doors. "He got hung up."

"Don't worry," Father Mattis says, giving Deidre's hand a reassuring squeeze. "I'm sure your sister and I can manage." He bends to kiss the side of Deidre's head, then brushes a whisper against her ear.

Deidre catches it with a bite of her lip, then blinks up a smile as she notices Jewel staring at them.

Jewel jots a mental note to remember the exact verbiage of Father Madness's secret communiqué to Deidre.

She's on to us. We have to kill her. Don't let on. Smile like everything's okay.

As Father Mattis stands upright, Deidre gives a hard shiver.

"Here," Jewel says, slipping out of a cashmere cardigan. "Take my sweater."

Deidre plucks the fabric as Jewel drapes it around her shoulders. "This is *my* sweater."

"Oh, right. Sorry. I borrowed it. I hope that's okay."

Deidre blinks at her. "How did you get into my apartment?"

"Your door was unlocked. Your place had been ransacked.

The police thought you might have been robbed. They asked me to escort them up so they could check it out."

Deidre touches her swooning head. "I feel like I just walked into the middle of a bad movie."

Novel, Jewel mentally corrects.

"You'll remember everything in short order," Father Mattis says, glancing at Jewel. "We'll help you fill in the blanks."

Deidre nods, then catches her drooping forehead in the palm of her hand. A soft groan escapes her.

Father Mattis drops to a knee before her. "Are you okay?"

"Just a little dizzy," Deidre says. "Everything went a little topsy-turvy for a second."

"Me topsy, you turvy," Jewel says, which causes both sisters to laugh.

"What's so funny?" Father Mattis asks.

"Oh, that's a line from a movie," Deidre says, smiling at Jewel. "*Wait Until Dark* with Audrey Hepburn and Alan Arkin. It was our mother's favorite movie."

"I've never seen it," Father Mattis says.

"It's about a blind woman who's terrorized by a group of thugs who are looking for a doll," Deidre tells him.

"The doll has packets of heroin stashed inside," Jewel interjects.

"Alan Arkin and his cronies pretend to be different people so they can trick Audrey Hepburn into letting them search her apartment for it."

A smile slips from Deidre's face as she locks eyes with Jewel.

Has anyone been acting suspiciously? Or given you the impression that they aren't who they claimed to be?

The *Wait Until Dark* reference shines a new light on Officer Kerns's line of questioning when they were having coffee in the cafeteria.

Is Jewel Audrey Hepburn's character, Susy Hendrix, in this scenario? Is she being gaslighted by a cast of characters she never would have suspected?

Like a priest?

Her own sister?

"Anyway," Deidre says, breaking eye contact with Jewel as her heated stare becomes too intense. "It's a good one. You should watch it."

"Maybe we can watch it together while you're recuperating," Mattis says.

He is just Mattis now. Jewel can no longer think of him as a priest. He isn't a man of the cloth. He is Deidre's boyfriend. Playing the role of a priest.

But why?

To what end?

Jewel doesn't know. But soon she will learn the whole story. She'll get a confession out of him. Out of them both.

The EMT hops out of the ambulance and snaps open a wheelchair. Deidre slings her arms around his neck as he lifts her off the gurney and deposits her into the chair.

"Do I really need to use this thing?"

"Just for a little while." The EMT unfastens the wheel lock. "Until you get your strength back." He reaches into the ambulance, pulls out a set of metal crutches, and hands them to Mattis, who accepts responsibility with a sanctified nod. "She should practice using these for a few days before you decide to return the wheelchair." The EMT points a strict finger at Deidre. "Take it slow. Get a feel for them first. If you need to use the chair, use the chair. That's what it's here for." He appraises Jewel and the priest with a dubious rub of his chin. "You guys got it from here, or do you want us to take her up?"

"I think we can manage," Jewel says.

The EMT nods, then backs around the side of the van. "Take it easy, Ms. Baldwin."

"Thank you," Deidre says.

Jewel circles the wheelchair to take hold of the handles, but Mattis intervenes.

"I've got her," he says, pushing Deidre across the bumpy gravel. "Comfortable, dear?"

"Not in the slightest."

Jewel hangs back as Mattis works the chair over the threshold of the elevator bay, and takes advantage of the unobserved moment to adjust the weight in the back waistband of her pants. She shouldn't have been so quick to give Deidre her sweater. Now she only has a thin layer of jersey cotton to conceal the surprise she has in store for her.

Though guns aren't the muse's weapon of choice—a bullet doesn't cause nearly enough damage—Jewel doesn't want Deidre to have access to it in her bedroom. And next to a pinkie smash, a gun to the face is the quickest way to get someone to talk.

Mark Mattis looks back at Jewel as she works the nighthawk's ten-millimeter beak out of the crack of her ass and yanks down her shirttail.

"Problem?" he asks, eyeing her warily.

"Just a little stiff," Jewel says, aligning her spine with the stock of the gun as she walks forward. "It'll work itself out."

46

If Deidre or Mattis notice the cadaverous stench that stepped into the elevator with them, their expressions don't let on. Jewel keeps her eyes pointed in the direction they're headed and notices that the lighted overhead-panel ceiling is dusted black with twice as many dead, or nearly dead, flies as it was a couple of days earlier.

Counting them to keep her mind off a dull scraping sound clawing at the floor beneath her feet, she only gets to four before losing her place. She's about to start again when the elevator lets out a tortured moan, replete with a smoker's wheeze. Which seems to get louder as they approach Lyle's floor.

Jewel closes her eyes to breathe through a panic attack, but the dusty scent of death barely clears her tonsils. Laced with a little crazy, the guffawing cough that explodes from her draws an annoyed look from Deidre.

"Excuse me," Jewel says, then staggers backward as the elevator car jars to a stop.

"What happened?" she cries, eyes frantically studying the control panel. Only the attic floor button is lit. "Are we stuck?"

"I wouldn't doubt it," Deidre says. "I swear this elevator is a death trap. The old landlord fell to his death when he stepped into the shaft thinking the car was there."

"You remember that?" Jewel asks.

Deidre pivots in her chair to look at her. "Of course I remember. How could I forget something like that?"

"You have amnesia, don't you?" Jewel challenges.

"Not about everything."

Blinking as fast as Mark Mattis is pushing floor buttons on the elevator's keypad, Jewel claws a scream from her lips as a shadow approaches the other side of the elevator door.

"Oh, shit," Tabs gasps as the door swings open and the gate slides back. "I didn't know anyone was in here." As her eyes widen on the woman in the wheelchair, she fingers her hairline as if to conceal her expression. Rent is probably overdue. "Oh, hey, Deidre," she says, stepping backward into the shadowy hallway and out from under the spotlight. "You're home."

"Not yet," Deidre sighs. "I'm still trying to get there."

"Oh, right," Tabs says through a raspy laugh that makes her cough. "Excuse me." She pats her chest to clear her throat. "I was looking for Nicki." She switches her eyes to Jewel with a blink of her spidery lashes. "You haven't seen her, have you?"

Isn't she dead in your apartment? Jewel's eyes wonder a second before she can shake a "No, I haven't" from her head.

Though she's blocked Nicki's death scene from her mind, she hopes she had the *presence* of mind to hide her body somewhere no one would find it.

"I'm really worried about her," Tabs says. "Her boss called. Nicki didn't show up for work today." She looks worriedly off. "She must have gotten pretty hammered last night."

Jewel's face falls.

"You going up?" Mattis asks.

"Down," Tabs says, closing the gate between them. "I want to check with Lyle before I head out. I'm meeting a hot date at the bookstore."

Jewel tightens her grip around the gun in her waistband.

"This is Lyle's floor," Deidre tells her.

"Actually," Tabs says, peering through the grate at Jewel, "I think he might be hanging around downstairs."

Though she didn't notice before, a trace of Fake Emily's voice seeps out with Tabs's last sentence like a runny nose.

Jewel gapes at Tabs as the car begins to rise. Tabs wiggles her fingers at Jewel, then vanishes as the wall lowers between them.

Though she's been interned in this soul-sucking prison for days, and is very much looking forward to her release, a predatory sense of rapacity comes over Jewel as Mattis works the wheelchair over the threshold, and Deidre exclaims, "What happened to my apartment? It's an absolute mess!"

Jewel might have left a few dirty dishes lying around and may have forgotten to refold the merino lambswool throw blanket and drape it nicely over the back of the couch, but she would hardly classify the apartment as a mess.

"We'll tidy it up for you," Mattis assures Deidre.

"Whose laptop is that?" Deidre points to the desk. "Oh, for heaven's sake!" She pivots in her chair to look behind her. "Carol! Have you been working at my desk?"

The name detonates a bomb behind Jewel's eyes. Blinding white as a blank sheet of paper. For a moment she can't recall a single thing about herself. As though someone right-clicked on her brain, initiated the Select All function, and deleted her from being. Lost, she scratches her forehead like a trackpad and scrolls to find her place.

"Carol?" Mattis wonders aloud. "Who's Carol?"

"My sister," Deidre says. "Sorry. I thought you two had already met."

"She told me her name was Jewel." Mattis turns a confused smile at the mystery woman fumbling with something behind her back, then takes a step backward with his hands in the air.

"Jewel's her pen name," Deidre says, setting her hospital bag on the floor and smoothing the knit shirt Jewel brought for her to wear home, along with a pair of velour lounge pants. "Jewel Maxwell. Maxwell was our mother's maiden name. I don't know where she got Jewel from."

"Because I'm a diamond in the rough," Jewel says, leveling the gun at Mattis's head.

"Well, there you go." Deidre flops her hands, then sighs as she looks around the living room. "Boy, you really made a mess of things, didn't you, Carol? I've asked you not to come into my apartment when I'm not here."

"I'm not Carol." Jewel swings the gun at the back of Deidre's head. "Don't call me that."

"Deidre . . ." Mattis tries.

"Well, I'm not going to start calling you Jewel, that's for sure!" Deidre shifts frustratedly in the wheelchair. "Carol. Will you please come where I can see you. I'm getting a crick in my neck."

"Deidre!" Mattis says sharply, backing into view with his hands in the air. "She's got a gun."

"*What!*" Deidre turns in her seat, then rears from the eye of the barrel. "Jesus, Carol!" She holds a hand out to block Jewel's shot. "What the hell are you doing?"

"I don't know," Jewel says. "I haven't read this chapter yet."

"*Chapter?* Are you crazy? Put that gun down before you hurt someone!"

"I can't," Jewel says. "I'm not in control of the story anymore."

Deidre shakes her head. "What story?"

"*Unspeakable Demons.*"

Understanding flashes across Deidre's eyes.

"Wait. Now I remember that title. I thought it sounded familiar when you mentioned it earlier at the hospital. Isn't that the horrible novel you wrote? The one where the author kills everyone?"

"Oh, God," Mattis gasps.

"I didn't write it, Dee. *You* did. Or should I say, you were transposing the muse's original manuscript into a Word document."

"The *muse*? Which muse? What are you talking about?"

"You know exactly which muse I'm talking about, so cut the crap."

"I honestly don't."

She jabs the gun at Deidre's face and screams, "DON'T LIE!"

"Jewel," Mattis says evenly. "You need to calm down. I know you don't want to hurt anybody. I'm sure things feel out of control right now, but we can figure it out. Tell me what's going on. I promise I won't judge you. I just want to help. Put the gun down so we can talk."

She swings it at him instead. "Don't play priest with me. I know it's all an act. I know you're the one who shoved a bible down that orderly's throat."

"Shoved a . . . *What?*" Mattis's reaction is too appalled for it not to be a performance. "What orderly? What are you talking about?"

"She doesn't know what she's talking about, Mark," Deidre says. "That's the problem."

"Deidre, please," Mattis says, then holds his hands out to Jewel. "Just tell us what you want. We'll do it. Whatever it is."

Jewel swings the gun back at her sister. "I want her to tell me how to get rid of the muse."

"Learn how to write, I guess." Deidre shrugs.

Jewel raises the gun over her head and fires a bullet into the ceiling.

"For God's sake, Deidre!" Mattis cries, uncovering his ears. "Don't provoke her! Tell her where the muse's manuscript is before she kills us both!"

Deidre gapes at him a moment before proclaiming, "The muse isn't real, Mark! This is all a figment of her imagination. There *is* no manuscript!"

"Yes, there is," he tells her. "I saw it. The day the church caught fire." He nods his head at the office nook. "It was in your file cabinet."

Deidre catches his drift between the fold of her arms. "What were you doing snooping around my office, Mark?"

"What?" He shifts his eyes to dodge the accusation and finds another perched atop Jewel's raised eyebrows. "I wasn't snooping! Deidre showed me the manuscript." He looks back at her. "You did. I swear! You just must have forgot."

"Yes. I *must* have." She holds Mattis's earnest gaze until he drops it to the floor, then waves a weary hand toward the file cabinet. "Well, if you saw whatever she's talking about in there, it must still be in there."

"The original manuscript's not in the file cabinet," Jewel says. "I looked in there. I've looked everywhere. It's not in this apartment."

"Then I suggest you look elsewhere." Deidre shoos Jewel away with her fingers. "I need to go lie down. My head is absolutely pounding. Mark, will you please help me into the bedroom?"

Jewel points the gun at him. "Don't move."

Mattis holds his hands higher. "I wasn't planning to."

Jewel gives him a quick nod, then turns the gun back on her sister. "This is your last chance, Dee. Tell me what I want to know, or I'm going to shoot your nose right off your face."

"You wouldn't dare!"

Jewel takes a step forward and angles the barrel of the gun at Deidre's nose. "Try me."

"Don't do it, Deidre," Mattis warns. "She means business."

Deidre collects her patience between prayer hands and then lowers them to her lap.

"Carol, dear, you need to listen to me," she says. "You're having a mental breakdown. Moving back into this house must have triggered something in you. I should have known that you couldn't handle it. But I didn't know what to do. I didn't want you to be alone after Dad died. I couldn't have you come live with me in New York. My apartment was too small. When I told you that this house had been converted into apartments, you begged me to move back to Ware with you. I thought it might be fun to work on my new novel here. In Mom's old office. But it's been a disaster ever since we arrived."

"I don't live here, Dee," Jewel reminds her. *Boy, she really must have amnesia.* "I live in Hartford. Remember?"

"No. You don't. You live in an apartment right downstairs."

Jewel rolls her eyes. "I think I know where I live, Dee."

"Clearly, you don't."

"If I lived in this house, the other tenants would have recognized me."

"I almost didn't recognize you myself," Deidre says. "You cut your hair and dyed it blond. You're not wearing your glasses. And you're finally wearing some of the old clothes I gave you. It's like you've had a total makeover. Personality and all. And no one in the apartment house knew you were my sister. You asked me not to tell them. You said you didn't want them to treat you differently. Or pretend to like you because you were my sister."

"You know," Jewel chuckles, "for someone who claims not to remember anything, you sure do have all the answers."

"I might not be able to remember the days leading up to my accident, but my long-term memory is crystal clear." Deidre shakes her head before continuing. "I should have realized that you were struggling. I knew you were becoming a recluse. You hardly ever showered. You refused to take off those stinky sweats you practically lived in. You hid your hair under that baseball cap, but I could tell what a filthy mess it was. I should have helped you, Carol. I should have found you a new therapist in Ware. But I was too wrapped up in my work to notice how bad things were getting. Just how unstable you'd become. I guess I didn't want to see it." Deidre hitches a crocodile tear. "To see you, Carol. I'm sorry. I should have paid more attention to you. I should have gotten you help."

"I guess you were too busy pushing people down the elevator shaft to notice."

Deidre appears indignant. "Do you mean Reggie? I didn't push him."

"Sure," Jewel says. "Just like I didn't ram a trowel through Lyle's throat or pulverize Nicki with a meat mallet."

Deidre's jaw drops so fast that her eyes pop wide open. "Oh, my god, Carol! What have you done?"

"I didn't do anything. My character did. The muse made her kill them off in the story."

"You're not a character, Carol," Deidre says, then screams, "And this isn't a goddamn story!"

"DON'T CALL ME THAT!"

Jewel closes her eyes to regain control of her emotions. She can't let Deidre flip the script on her. This is *her* story. Not Deidre's. Not anymore. She's about to open her eyes and tell her as much when Deidre suddenly screams,

"MARK!"

47

The family portrait explodes off the shelf in a cloud of glass as Jewel swings the gun at a lunging shape in her periphery.

Stopped dead in his tracks, Mattis's eyes search for the bullet he thinks he just dodged. A puff of smoke drifts up from a hole in the middle of his white collar a second before the tap in his throat opens wide.

Mattis gives Jewel the strangest smile, as if he just realized he was the butt of a joke, then collapses face-first at Deidre's footplate.

"Mark!" Deidre cries. "Oh, my god! Mark!"

She looks up at Jewel with horror-charged eyes. "You shot him! You fucking shot him, you crazy bitch!"

Jewel stares down at the dark puddle forming under Mattis's head. But rather than flesh and blood, she sees that he's made up of a million little words. Bound together to form his character. Hair lank with run-on sentences, hands a paradox of verbs he'll never perform again, the story threads that make up his black shirt are too tightly woven to read.

"His character wasn't working for this scene," Jewel says, stepping over Mattis's body of work.

She pulls the chair away from the desk but remains standing as a dark shadow falls quietly into the leather seat.

The laptop awakes.

"He wasn't a character," Deidre weeps. "He was a good, decent man."

"Not in this story, he wasn't," Jewel says. "In this story he's Father Madness."

"*What story?*" Deidre shrieks.

"The story we're trapped in. *Unspeakable Demons.*"

Typing as fast as it can to capture the dialogue, the keyboard ripples under the muse's fingers, then stills to await Jewel's next sentence. Eyes sunk in the hollow of a blackened soul, the muse, who now looks distinctly female, locks eyes with Jewel through the reflection in the window over the desk and nods for her to continue with the scene.

"This is the climax," Jewel says in a halting voice, reading along as words bounce onto the screen of her PC. "We're just about to get to the showdown between sisters. The monologue's coming up. It'll explain everything."

"*Monologue?*" Deidre says. "Have you lost your mind?"

"No. Evil has just taken it over."

"Oh, Jesus," Deidre gasps. "You *are* crazy."

"Most unreliable narrators are," Jewel says evenly. "That's what makes them unreliable."

"You're not a narrator, Carol. You're a murderer! You just killed an innocent man in cold blood."

"Shut up, Dee. Don't make the muse write that I cut your tongue out."

"Make the what write what?" Deidre says, confused, then slams her hand on the arm of the wheelchair to punctuate her words: "What the hell are you talking about?"

Jewel opens the center drawer of the desk, pulls out a pair of scissors, and snips them at Deidre.

Deidre bites her lips together.

"That's better," Jewel says, cocking her head to read over the muse's shoulder.

Realizing the muse has abandoned her for a more talented author, Deidre stares quietly down at her lover's dead body. She is no longer the protagonist of *Unspeakable Demons*. Just another one of the muse's victims.

Deidre flicks her eyes, searching for a way to recapture the narrative.

"Look," she says, moderating the tone and level of her voice. "I don't know what's going on. Or what happened while I was in the hospital. But this has to stop. Right now. You need to get a grip on yourself, Carol."

Jewel picks up the scissors and jabs them at Deidre's face.

"I told you not to call me that!"

"But that's your name. You're Carol. Carol Baldwin. You're my sister. And you're scaring the shit out of me!"

"Good," Jewel says, setting the scissors back on the desk. "You're supposed to be scared. This is a horror story, after all."

"This isn't a fucking story. This is reality. We're not characters in a novel. We're alive. If you stab me with those scissors, you're going to kill me. Just like you killed Mom."

Jewel rolls her eyes at the muse, who has stopped typing to stare at her in the window's flat reflection.

"I know you can't remember," Deidre says. "But that's what happened."

"I didn't kill Mom," Jewel says as the typing resumes. "*You* did. I read your confession in chapter twenty-nine. You know, that was actually a pretty good twist. I didn't see that one coming. I knew the story about her having a ruptured appendix was bullshit. There were a lot of clues I should have picked up on. But it's hard to see things clearly in a flashback. Your perspective gets all distorted."

"You're right," Deidre says calmly. "The story about Mom's appendix bursting *was* a lie."

"I knew it!" Jewel laughs haughtily. "I knew you and Dad were lying to me about how Mom died."

"We had to lie," Deidre says. "Dad told the police that it was an accident. That Mom tripped and fell on the scissors as she was entering the bathroom. At first, we thought that's what had happened. You were in bed asleep. When we went to wake you up, you had blood all over your hands. We asked you what happened, but you wouldn't speak. You just kept staring into space. By the time you came out of it, you couldn't remember anything. You acted like you didn't even know that Mom had died. We had to tell you something. So Dad came up with the story about her appendix rupturing."

"Yeah, to keep me from going to the police and telling them that you killed her. But I wouldn't have done that, Dee. You should have told me the truth. I wouldn't have blamed you. Mom was trying to kill us. The muse possessed her. She had to be stopped before she hurt us. She was writing how she was going to kill us all in her manuscript."

"Wait," Deidre gasps, almost laughs. "Oh, no. Oh, Carol. Did you read that on her computer? About her wanting to shoot you in the head with a nail gun?"

The muse pauses typing to await Jewel's response, but before she can formulate one, Deidre says, "*I* wrote that, Carol! I wrote all that stuff about Mom wanting to kill us. I caught you sneaking into her office and wanted to teach you a lesson. I didn't think you'd actually believe all that crap. Well, I guess I did.

I wrote it to scare you, but . . ." Deidre shakes her head. "I was a horrible big sister. Trying to scare you all the time. Making you think Mom was a witch. Locking you in the cellar. I regret all of it. If I knew what it was doing to you, I never would have done those things."

The muse highlights the entire exchange about the death of Jewel and Deidre's mother and deletes it. Jewel stares at the last sentence before that and begins the scene from the top.

"'You're supposed to be scared,'" she reads aloud. "'This is a horror story, after all.'"

Deidre shakes her head, confused. "What?"

"Let's pick it up from there. From where Jewel says, 'You're supposed to be scared. This is a horror story, after all.'"

"You can't just delete scenes in life when they don't go your way, Carol."

"No. But I can delete them from this story."

"This isn't a . . ." Deidre lets out a frustrated sigh. "You need help, Carol. Let me call Dr. Leonetti. He can bring you some medicine."

"I don't need a doctor, Dee. I need a priest." Jewel glances back at Father Mattis. "And we're fresh out of priests."

The muse throws its head back and laughs, then bends to the laptop to add that line.

"Carol, listen to me."

"Stop calling me Carol," Jewel says. "You're going to confuse the reader."

"No one is going to read this . . . *Jewel.* It's madness! Just like all your other books. You get so caught up in the story that you forget yourself. This has happened before. Remember when you were writing that story about the woman who lost her eyesight in an explosion? You had hysterical blindness for over a week. Or the time you were writing about living next door to a serial killer and called the cops on Dad's neighbor? Or last year when you thought you were married and bought all those Christmas presents for your husband? You even wrapped them and put them under the tree."

"I *am* married, Dee. I'm married to Cal."

"Cal's a character in one of your books. Correction. In *all* of your books. You've killed him off and brought him back to life so many times I can't keep it straight. Sometimes in the same chapter."

Jewel disregards this with a tsk of her tongue. "Nice try. But I know Cal is real, Dee. We've spoken several times since I've been here."

"Then let's call him," Deidre says. "See how he's doing."

"I don't need to call him."

"Because you can't! You made him up just like you're making everything else up. It's all a figment of your imagination. I can prove Cal's not real. One of your books is over there on my shelf. Go look at it. Read the first page. It starts with the main character meeting a man named Cal in a bookstore. They reach for the same book at the same time. *Gone Girl*. I think. You go on and on about how you wished it were something more romantic. You list like a dozen titles. *Wuthering Heights*, *Pride and Prejudice*. *Anna Karenina*. I didn't know if I was reading a novel or a Google search."

"Of course you know how I met Cal, Dee. You're my sister. I told you the story of how we met."

"No. I know about it because I read about it in your novel. You kill him off a couple of chapters later. The main character, whom you never name, by the way, thinks a prowler has broken into her home and stabs Cal in the neck with a nail file."

Jewel frowns.

How could Deidre possibly know about that?

Jewel was alone in the apartment at the time. In the shower.

Thinking a prowler had broken into the apartment. Arming herself with a Sally Hansen nail file.

"Which didn't seem like an accident at all to me, but anyway," Deidre goes on. "The cop who's a reoccurring character in all your books comes to investigate. What's her name again?" Deidre looks up to think, then smiles as the name comes to her. "Oh, right. Officer Kerns."

The keyboard falls silent.

Jewel stares in disbelief at the name that was just typed out on the screen.

"How did you know her name?"

"Officer Kerns is always the cop in your novels. There's a running joke between her and the main character about not killing her off. But you always do." Deidre nods at the laptop. "She's probably in the novel you're working on right now, I bet."

"This isn't my novel," Jewel says. "It's yours."

"It's on *your* laptop, Carol."

"Yes, but I accessed the file through *your* cloud account." Jewel turns to look at Deidre. "It's the novel you were working on before your accident."

"*Blood Moon over Venus*?"

Jewel's right eye twitches as the title strikes a chord with her. F minor.

"No," she says, rubbing her eye. "The novel we've been talking about this entire time! *Unspeakable Demons*."

"*Unspeakable Demons* is *your* novel, Carol. *You* sent it to *me*. You wanted me to pass it on to my agent, but it was just too violent and disjointed. It was like a crazy person wrote it. Which, now I think about it, was probably the case."

Deidre covers a mewling cry with her hand as she looks down at the dead priest lying on the floor.

"I know you wrote *Unspeakable Demons*, Dee. I had never heard of it before Emily told me the title."

But Emily didn't mention the novel by name. Only the genre. Jewel had to search Deidre's cloud account for a title that fit the horror genre. She almost clicked on *Blood Moon over Venus* when she spotted a file named *Unspeakable Demons*.

"Emily?" Deidre gasps. "Oh, Jesus, Carol. Please tell me you haven't been speaking to Emily Channing. You haven't been telling her all this crazy stuff, have you?"

"I only told her about your accident."

The real Emily Channing, anyway.

Jewel closes her eyes against a crashing wave of confusion.

If the muse isn't real, and all this is a delusion brought on by a childhood trauma that has manifested into a full-blown psychotic break, why is someone pretending to be Deidre's agent? And even if she had written *Unspeakable Demons* in some sort of fugue state, Deidre just said that she never sent the manuscript to her agent.

So how did Fake Emily, who Jewel suspects might be Tabs, know about the muse?

We don't need a muse to kill you, she taunted. *Just ask your sister when she wakes up.*

Not *if* she wakes up. But *when*. As if it were a given that Deidre would awake from her coma at any moment. Jewel hadn't spoken to Fake Emily at length about Deidre's condition. Which should have been a red flag. Other than their initial call, Fake Emily never asked how Deidre was doing. Never wanted an update.

Was it a coincidence that Deidre awoke almost immediately after Jewel outed Emily as a fraud?

And what had Fake Emily meant by *we*? Her partner in crime has to be someone who is acquainted with the publishing industry. Someone intimately familiar with Deidre Baldwin's work.

The author herself, perchance?

48

"Why don't we give Emily a call?" Jewel says, snatching her bag off the kitchen counter. "Figure this out, once and for all." She reaches into the exterior pocket, pulls out Deidre's phone, crosses the room, and drops her bag on the floor by the desk. "I'll put her on speaker phone so we can both hear the conversation."

"Please don't bother Emily with this nonsense!" Deidre pleads. "It's so embarrassing."

"When she answers," Jewel says, ignoring Deidre's appeal and accessing the recent call log, "I want you to say exactly what I tell you to say, or I'm going to shoot you in the head. Got it?"

Deidre glances at the gun, lying on the corner of the desk, and nods.

"Say, 'Jewel's on to me. She knows everything. What do you want me to do?' Repeat it back to me."

Deidre reiterates her lines verbatim but adds a nonverbal eye roll.

"Make it sound good." Jewel taps the screen to redial. "Your life literally depends on it."

Deidre gives her lips a nervous lick as a phone rings through the speaker.

Another phone rings a second later.

Jewel looks down as the mouth of her purse lights up.

"What the hell?" she says as the line connects, and a familiar voice blares up from the phone in her hand.

"Hi, this is Carol. Sorry I missed your call, but leave a message and I'll call you right back."

"No," Jewel breathes, staring down at the screen. She ends the call as the *beep!* signals, then quickly redials.

"Hi, this is Carol—"

"No!" Jewel cries, disconnecting the line. "I know this is Emily's number. I called her on it just a few hours ago."

"What number are you calling?"

Jewel reads the phone number aloud to Deidre.

"That's *your* phone number, Carol!"

Jewel shakes her head, though she knows Deidre is correct. That *is* her cell phone number. But the name it's listed under doesn't belong to her. She holds the screen out for Deidre to see.

"Why do you have my phone number listed under Emily Channing?"

Deidre squints at the screen. "That's not the contact information I have for Emily. She's listed under Channing and Associates."

Jewel turns the screen around and cues up Channing and Associates. She taps the number she called from the café earlier, then places the phone to her ear. A message advises that the office has closed for the evening.

"She's already left for the day," Jewel says, setting the phone on the desk next to the gun. "But that doesn't matter. I know that's the real Emily Channing's phone number. The woman

I've been speaking to was just pretending to be Emily. I just don't know how my phone number got added under her name."

"I do," Deidre says.

Jewel looks expectantly up at her. "You do?"

"You entered it, Carol. You created a contact for Emily Channing using your phone number so you could pretend to call her."

"No! Emily called me first. She was trying to reach you, but I answered your phone. She told me about the deadline with your publisher. She asked me to hack into your laptop to find out if your novel was finished. When I told her it wasn't, she commissioned me to write the ending."

"You also said you've been speaking to Cal. And you know damn good and well that he isn't real."

Jewel covers her ears. "Stop trying to gaslight me, Dee!"

"I'm not. It all makes sense. You were so desperate to get published, to get an agent like Emily Channing to represent you, that you dreamed up a delusionary scenario where that might actually happen. That you could swoop in and save the day while I was in the hospital." Deidre covers a gasp with her hand. "Oh, my god, Carol! Did you hit me with your car to get me out of the way?"

"I wasn't even in Virginia when you got hit. I was in Hartford. I flew in as soon as I found out you were in the hospital. I'm driving a rental."

"You don't live in Hartford. And if you're driving a rental it's probably because your car got damaged when you hit me with it and had to find another ride."

Jewel stares at her sister a moment, then turns back to the laptop.

"I can prove what I'm saying is true. *You* wrote *Unspeakable Demons*, Dee. You wrote an entire section about throwing

Reggie down the elevator shaft. I didn't even know him, so I couldn't possibly have written how he died."

"You knew Reggie, Carol. Well, I don't know if you ever actually met him, but you knew who he was. You were upset that he was going to evict us. He wanted to turn the house into a bed-and-breakfast." Deidre's breath hitches. "Oh, Carol, did you kill Reggie so we could keep living here?"

"No!"

Jewel begins scrolling upward to find the chapter concerning Reggie, but it is closer to the beginning. She right-clicks on the vertical bar to jump to the top of the document. She's about to page down when her eyes fall on the opening paragraph.

The inexplicable opening paragraph.

A shriek burst through a set of swinging doors to Jewel's left and escaped down the hall on a fast-moving gurney. Spun around, the directions hastily spat at her by the front-desk nurse seemed incomplete. Jewel traced a hand across the achingly white walls and counted down the room numbers of the ICU at Ware Memorial Hospital.

Jewel leans away from the monitor.

"What the hell? This isn't how *the story starts*. Where's the preface?"

"What preface?" Deidre asks.

Jewel recites the first two lines from memory: "'*I'm afraid to write this. Afraid doing so will summon the muse.*' That's how *Unspeakable Demons* begins. Not like this!"

Heart sinking a little deeper into her stomach with every swipe of the trackpad, the weight of what's on the screen pulls Jewel's eyes forward until they almost cross on the words.

Jewel's knees faltered, then fainted out from under her midway across the hospital room as she spotted Deidre. She expected to be shocked by her sister's appearance. Deidre's face to be fractured and swollen . . .

"No," she whispers, scrolling farther down the screen.

"I need you to find out if the book is finished," Emily said. "It could be sitting in her outbox ready to send . . ."

Movement in her periphery causes Jewel to flinch, but she can't stop reading the incomprehensible document in front of her.

Jewel turned the page of the manuscript over, as if the joke would be explained on the other side, then flipped it quickly over again. She reread the passage with increasing unease . . .

Jewel cocks her head toward a strange scratching sound. She knows she should see what Deidre is up to but can't seem to unglue her eyes from the screen, the conversation she had with Dr. Leonetti the day Deidre flatlined.

"But we got her back. All her vitals look good . . . We expect her to make a full recovery . . ."

The scratching grows more frantic as Mrs. Willard backsteps into the open air of the stairwell. As Nicki places a hand on her solar plexus and switches her hips to a belly dance. As Officer Kerns says, "He choked on a bible." As Lyle moves deeper into the cellar.

Welcome to My Nightmare.

Jewel quickly scans the rest of the story. And though she can't recall beating Nicki to death with an iron mallet and hiding her body in the cellar with Lyle's, or touching a lighter to the corner of paperbacks as she skirted two dead bodies on the floor of Last Chance Books, the words she used to describe these horrors would have made the muse proud. Jewel's heart breaks anew as she relives the moment she realized Emily Channing was a fake. Skips worriedly as she receives word that Deidre has awoken from her coma.

It's all here.

A diary of the damned. One diabolical sentence after another. Chapters going forth by day, bringing Jewel to this exact moment in time. The cursor begins to swirl in a hypnotic circle in the center of the screen. Her eyes follow it around like a fly. She jabs the Enter key to squash it, and the cursor falls onto the next page. It lies there twitching for a stunned moment, then jumps to life as the scent of Mattis's blood, seeping into the area rug behind her, activates the muse's sixth sense for mayhem.

As new, filthy-fresh words ooze across the screen, Jewel reaches across the laptop with her left hand and grabs the gun off the desk.

It is time to write the ending of this nasty narrative.

49

As new, filthy-fresh words oozed across the screen, Jewel reached across the laptop with her left hand and grabbed the gun off the desk.

"What the hell's going on?" she said, as the scene played out in real time on the Word document before her, anticipating her words a second before they crossed her mind.

"What?" Deidre blinked as if coming awake, then reared from the gun pointed at her face.

"Where's the other manuscript? The one I was reading?"

"Beats me. I just got home."

"How did the story change?" Jewel asked, following the bouncing ball, or in this case, cursor, across the screen. "Did you install a dictation app on my laptop?" Jewel craned her neck and looked around the ceiling. "Do you have cameras installed? Is that how you knew everything that happened while I was here?"

Deidre turned her head with a preemptive wince as Jewel jabbed the gun at her face.

"Have you been gaslighting me this entire time?"

"Not me," Deidre said, a knowing lilt in her voice.

"The muse?" Jewel turned to look at the screen of the laptop as it captured their dialogue. "But how does the muse know what I'm going to say even before I say it?"

The smile that sneaked across Deidre's face had already sneaked across the page.

"Because we're in the story now," she said. "Can't you tell? Doesn't everything feel a little . . . fictionalized?" Deidre tilted her head, pityingly. "And the story didn't change, Carol. It's written exactly how it happened. Is happening. Word for word."

Jewel looked at her. "What do you mean?"

Deidre rolled her eyes. "*You're* the protagonist, Carol. The quintessential unreliable narrator. You didn't have the first clue what the story was about. That's what made it so interesting."

"But . . ." Jewel turned to stare at the computer screen. Words marched swiftly across the page and hopped into the total pool in the lower left-hand corner of the Word program. "If I'm the protagonist, then I should be able to control what's happening in the story."

"You're not in control of the story, Carol. You never were. *Unspeakable Demons* is the muse's novel. Not yours. Not mine. Not any of the protagonists'. We're just characters. Just as you suspected. I couldn't tell you that before. I didn't want to give the ending away. The muse wouldn't have liked that."

"So I really am just a character in a story?"

"No. You're *the* character. You're the author the muse has been searching for. Your story is its greatest work. A fully developed character from beginning to end."

"But this wasn't my story to begin with. It was yours, Dee."

"I played a part. Yes. But you were the star. Isn't that what you've always wanted? To outshine me?"

Jewel dropped her eyes so her sister couldn't see the truth

behind them, and spotted the corner of the printout through the opening of her bag on the floor by the desk. And though it had grown some since she printed it out, the beginning of the manuscript should still be the same. It should contain Deidre's contribution to the story. How she had summoned the muse in the bookstore. How the shirt box containing the manuscript had magically appeared on a folding table.

Jewel leaned over her knees and picked her bag off the floor.

A bit heavier than she remembered it being just hours before, her legs trembled slightly under the weight as she set the sack in her lap. No. It wasn't her legs that were trembling. It was the item her bag contained that was shaking.

With suppressed laughter.

It took all her restraint not to yank the abhorrent tome out by one of its dog-eared corners and tear it to shreds. Still, as she worked the manuscript gently around the teeth of the satchel's unzipped opening, flakes of old, disintegrating pages wafted into the air like ash. Jewel reared back as they rekindled in a sizzle of fiery sparks, then vanished, leaving only the stench of burned hair behind.

Jewel stared down at the sickly yellow top page, thick and brittle as mummified skin, and tried not to laugh.

The original manuscript had been right under her nose the entire time.

She flicked her eyes at the back right corner of the desk as a thought occurred to her. The work in progress she had brought with her in her laptop bag from home, and had set aside for safe keeping, was no longer there.

It was resting contentedly in her lap.

"But how did I end up with the original manuscript?" she asked, fondling its pages.

"I don't know," Deidre said. "You never told me where you found it."

"Because I didn't find it, Dee! You did! It was in the box that appeared when you summoned the muse at the bookstore. You wrote about it in *Unspeakable Demons*."

"I made that part up," Deidre said. "I wanted the start of my story to be a little more intriguing than it actually was. And I didn't want my fans to know that I had stolen the story from my poor, crazy sister."

"From *me*?"

"Mrs. Willard had been complaining about someone making noise in the cellar in the middle of the night, so I went to check it out. I don't know how or when you dragged Mom's old secretary down there, but I found the manuscript in the drawer. Along with some notes. Most of them were death scenes about me. Thank goodness you hadn't begun working on the manuscript in earnest or my head might be sitting in your freezer right now. I don't recall seeing a note about me getting hit by a car, but you must have jotted that down somewhere. Anyway. I was afraid that when you discovered the manuscript was missing, you'd go completely nuts, so I put a padlock on the cellar to keep you from going down there. You must have suspected that I had taken it, though. I caught you prowling around my apartment a couple of times. I didn't know how you were getting in. You must have made a copy of my key or something. I had Lyle install a slide chain on the door to try and keep you out. I must have forgotten to latch it the night of my accident, though. Or maybe you were already hiding in here when I went to bed. I don't know. But when I woke up to use the bathroom, I found you rooting around in my desk." Deidre rubbed her forehead. "I kind of remember that we struggled, but nothing after that. You must have chased me out of the house. Or maybe I chased you. I don't know. That part's a blur."

Jewel shook her head. "What did you care if I stole the manuscript back? You weren't working on it. You hadn't touched it for almost a month."

"I didn't want you working on it either."

"Why? Because you think I'm a bad writer?"

"I was trying to protect you."

Jewel rolled her eyes. "Yeah. Right."

"I was! I got scared after I killed Reggie. Then Keith. I was afraid I'd get caught—we'd get caught—if anyone else died. You can only explain away so many murders as accidents. But I was under pressure to finish it. So I handed a copy of the manuscript off to one of Emily's new, hotshot authors."

"Lisbeth Abbott?"

"Yes. What a total waste of time that was. She didn't even write anything. Just a bunch of gibberish."

A sad pang squeezed Jewel's heart as she recalled that part of the manuscript. Though she had never met Lisbeth Abbott, it broke her heart to think those nonsensical words might have been a cry for help.

"I don't know why she couldn't write anything coherent," Deidre went on. "Maybe it was because she was working off a copy. Maybe the muse didn't like that I had handed off the story to her midway through my section. Or maybe it didn't like where Lisbeth was taking its story. She wanted to contribute to it, but the muse wouldn't let her. No matter how slow she typed, her fingers would shift off home row by one key. She thought it could be translated easily enough, but Emily couldn't make sense of it either. Even when she tried to transcribe it by hand, it would turn out to be the exact same gibberish. When Emily told Lisbeth what she had written couldn't be used in the novel, Lisbeth went crazy. She almost killed Emily's daughter . . ." Deidre frowned to think. "I can't seem to remember her name."

"Jennifer," Jewel affirmed. "She was mentioned in an article I read about Lisbeth falling from Emily Channing's office window." Jewel scowled as a thought occurred to her. "But that happened in the *real* Emily Channing's office. I spoke to her. She didn't know anything about *Unspeakable Demons*. Whoever hired me to finish the manuscript was just pretending to be Emily Channing. She's been playing me from the start."

Deidre shook her head. "I don't know anything about that."

"Sure you don't."

"I don't! Swear to God, I don't."

Jewel chuckled. "That doesn't mean much coming from you. You fucked a priest, after all."

This gave the manuscript in her lap a giggle. Contagious, Jewel covered her mouth to hide a smile as Deidre cried,

"I did not!"

Deidre looked down at Father Mattis's body. "Mark was my friend." She sniffed away a tear and raised her chin as she turned her watery eyes at Jewel. "And very devout."

"Sure. Whatever."

"Look. I know I've done terrible things, but I'm not a terrible person."

"Just a terrible sister."

"I know. I *was* a terrible sister to you. But I've changed. I think being in a coma actually woke me up. I don't want anything more to do with the muse. I don't want it to try and tempt me, or anyone else, to write its filth ever again. I thought it would bring me success, but it's only brought me misery."

"What are you saying?"

"The story ends with you."

The manuscript gave a fearful shiver and burrowed against Jewel's thighs.

"You're the muse's final protagonist," Deidre explained. "Now that you've finished your part of the story, we have to destroy the original manuscript."

Jewel set a comforting hand on the quivering top page to settle it.

"*Can* it be destroyed?"

Deidre shrugged. "I don't know. I've never tried. But it's just paper. It should burn easily enough."

"The muse won't let us do that. It will kill us first. Make us turn on each other."

"Only if we write it. It can't make us do anything if we don't write it down."

Deidre flicked her eyes at the laptop to draw Jewel's attention to it.

The screen was dark.

Jewel reached out a finger to tap the space bar without thinking.

"Don't wake it up, for Christ's sake," Deidre growled. "And put that gun down before you shoot me."

Jewel tipped the gun in her right hand at Deidre to point out, "I thought you said the muse couldn't make us do something unless we wrote it down first."

Deidre raised her hand to protect her face. "No. But you could accidentally shoot me," she said, then winced as Jewel clunked the gun onto the desk next to the laptop. "Will you please be quiet?" She shot the laptop a worried glance. When the screen remained dark, she extended her hand to Jewel. "Okay. Give me the manuscript. I have some lighter fluid in the kitchen."

Worried the manuscript might try to bite her if she were to pick it up, Jewel lowered a casual glance at her lap.

And found the most beautiful sight.

A glossy, brand-new, honest-to-God hardback novel with her name on the cover.

AN EVIL PREMISE by JEWEL MAXWELL

"Oh," Jewel gasped. "That's much better!"

"What is?"

"*An Evil Premise*."

"What's an evil premise?"

"My novel!" Jewel cries. "I never much cared for *Unspeakable Demons* as a title."

She gazed in awe at her name for a moment, then gasped as she noticed the red banner across the top of the shiny black cover.

NEW YORK TIMES BESTSELLER

"I did it!" Jewel laughed through a stream of tears. "I wrote a bestseller!"

"Carol?" Deidre said measuredly. "Whatever you think you're seeing right now, it's not real."

"Yes, it is! You just don't want me to be successful. You've never wanted me to succeed at writing. You never supported me."

"That might be true." Deidre huffed a relenting sigh. "Okay. That is true. I should have supported you. And I promise I will. From now on. I'll see to it that your other novels get published. Just not this one."

"I don't need your help anymore." Jewel picked up the book and shoved it in her sister's face. "I already am published!"

"That's not a real book, Carol! It's the *manuscript*. The muse is making you see a bestselling novel. It's charming you. You have to fight it!"

Jewel yanked the book away a second before Deidre could snatch it out of her hand.

"Give it to me, Carol!" Deidre screamed, wheeling forward in her chair.

"Don't call me that!" Jewel grabbed the weapon off the desk and pointed it at Deidre. "You just want the story for yourself!" She tucked the book under her left arm and switched the weapon to her dominant hand. "Well, you can't have it! It's my novel! It's got my name on it!"

"No, it doesn't," Deidre said, voice breaking toward a scream as she eased the wheelchair forward. "You're seeing things. It's not a real book. It's the manuscript."

Jewel took a step back. She slipped the book out from under her armpit and opened it. The dedication she found inside brought a tear to her eye.

For my mother.

"I dedicated the book to Mom," Jewel gasped. "Oh, she'd be so proud of me, wouldn't she, Dee?"

"Please, Carol," Deidre pleaded, rolling slowly closer. "Don't make me hurt you."

"You can't hurt me anymore, Dee."

Deidre extended her arm. "I'm begging you. Give me the manuscript."

A click sounded as the weapon cocked.

"Sure," Jewel said. "Just let me sign it first."

"NO!" Deidre slammed the wheel of her chair with the palm of her left hand and rammed her outstretched casted leg into Jewel's knee.

Jewel screamed in pain as she stumbled backward over Father Mattis's dead body. She stagger-stepped sideways to keep on her feet and collided with the coffee table. She threw her hands up in a last-ditch effort to hold her balance, tossing the book into the air.

A tremendous crack sounded as the hardback hit the floor flat. But the plush, blood-soaked area rug broke Jewel's fall.

Shaken but unhurt, Jewel raised her hand to reach for the

edge of the coffee table to pull herself upright and stared in disbelief at the weapon still clutched in her hand.

Her mother's Montblanc pen.

She spread her fingers to drop it and looked up at her sister.

Slumped with her head down, blood dripped steadily into Deidre's lap. The gun dangled from her slack fingers beside the wheelchair, then clopped to the floor.

Jewel shook her head in disbelief, then looked around for her glossy bestselling novel. But it was nowhere to be seen amongst the old, loose sheets of paper still wafting to the floor.

"No, no, no," she cried, crawling forward to gather them together. Though some of the older pages nearly disintegrated at the touch of her trembling fingers, the last one she snatched up held strong.

A distraught cry escaped Jewel's lips as her eyes took in the words she had hastily penned across the yellowing flyleaf of the original manuscript.

Dear Deidre, I hope this blows your mind.

EPILOGUE

Emily Channing sets her purse on the floor and takes a seat in the chair across the desk from her client. Downy hair swept from her forehead, her concentration lines are filled to the max with liquid foundation. A gust of spearmint rattles from her pursed lips as she switches a mint from cheek to cheek.

"Hello, Carol," Emily says, plucking a hot flash from the front of her blouse. "I see you've lost more weight."

"Thank you," Carol says.

"It wasn't a compliment. You look positively bony."

Carol lets it go. That's just how Emily is. Honest to a fault. They don't have to like each other. Theirs is a professional relationship. Based on a contract, not mutual affection.

"So, how do you like my new office?" Carol says.

Emily glances around the fluorescently lit room. "It could use some sprucing up."

"I've ordered a few pieces of art. A lot of expensive squiggles. That should brighten things up a bit."

"I hear Rorschach's pretty hot right now," Emily says.

Carol laughs, then leans forward. "Okay. Enough small talk. Don't keep me in suspense. What did the publisher say?"

Emily holds Carol's avid stare for a beat. "They've agreed to publish all three of your novels. *Thunder Cove*, *Wretched Waves*, and *Beyond the Bluff*. They'll pay a lump sum for the lot. Fifty thousand dollars."

Carol shakes her head. "That's it? I was expecting it to be more like a million."

"In your dreams," Emily says. "You're lucky you got anything for them."

Carol nods. "Well, thank you for going to bat for me, anyway. Another agent might have gotten me more, but I didn't want anyone else to represent me. You were destined to be my agent."

"I suppose you're right there."

Carol takes in the moment with a contented smile, then asks, "What about *An Evil Premise*? Have you heard anything on that front? Am I going to receive credit for writing it?"

"The judge ruled that it's your intellectual property."

"So Deidre's name won't appear on the cover, right?"

"She won't be credited. But the publisher is going to dedicate a foreword to her. Depicting her accomplishments."

"Were they okay with the title change? I think *An Evil Premise* is better than *Unspeakable Demons*."

Emily nods. "It makes sense for the actual title not to be the same as the novel referenced in the book. They would like you to reconsider using a pseudonym, though. The name Carol Baldwin, or Jewel Maxwell, for that matter, might turn off some readers. Especially Deidre's fans."

"I'll think about it," Carol says. "And they're going to include the preface I submitted? I think I remembered it correctly from Deidre's transcription."

"It will be included."

"Great," Carol says, then raises her eyebrows. "So how much am I going to get for it?"

"Nothing. An author can't benefit financially from the crimes they committed. I've explained that to you several times."

Carol slumps back in her chair. "Well, at least Deidre won't get anything for it either. Have you spoken to her since the judge made his ruling?"

"No. I haven't spoken to her," Emily snaps. "Deidre's dead! You killed her. You shot her in the head."

"Deidre shot *herself* in the head, Emily. The muse made her do it. Didn't you read the book?"

"I didn't have to read the book to find out what happened. I heard all about it at the trial."

"That was a pretty good twist, though, wasn't it? When the weapon in Jewel's hand turns out to be a pen? And Deidre's actually the one holding the gun? Then Jewel signs the book and makes Deidre shoot herself in the head with the inscription she wrote? I still get goose bumps thinking about it."

"You honestly believe that's what happened, don't you? That Jewel and Deidre were just characters."

"That's my story." Carol smiles. "And I'm sticking to it. Maybe if you actually *read* the book you might understand things a little better."

"I'll read it. I just haven't gotten around to it yet."

Carol holds Emily's eyes until her agent looks away. "You're afraid to read it, aren't you?" When Emily admits nothing, Carol shakes her head to laugh. "Reading the book won't turn you into a bloodthirsty monster, Emily. You have to add to the story to become a part of the story. Reading the book will just make you *think* that you're turning evil. Or that the muse is possessing you."

"You sure about that?"

"The paranormal group Deidre sent a copy of the manuscript to didn't immediately start killing each other after they read it. It put bad thoughts in their heads. Made them paranoid. Made them wonder if they might have it in them to kill. But for the most part, they were able to resist the muse's influence." Carol shrugs. "I suppose if you already have evil in you, reading the muse's story could push things to the next level. But if you're basically a good person, you should be fine." Carol cocks her head. "You're a good person, aren't you, Emily?"

Emily blinks at her for a moment, then says, "We're not talking about me. We're talking about you. And I know for a fact that you're not a good person, Carol. You're a murderer. You did shoot Deidre. She was dead in her wheelchair when the police arrived at the apartment. And Father Mattis had a hole in his throat. They found you hunched over your laptop, typing like a maniac. Your neighbor, Mr. Willard, called 911. The police had to break down the door to get in. It took three cops to pry the laptop out of your hands. You kept screaming that the muse made you do it."

"If all that were true, Emily, I'd be in prison right now."

"You *are* in prison, Carol! You're serving five consecutive life sentences. My god, how deluded *are* you?"

"So, when do I get the money from the publisher? I want to start renovations on the house right away. I'm going to convert it back into a single-family home. The upstairs will be the living area. I want to turn the first floor into an arts center for aspiring authors. It might cost a little more than fifty thousand dollars to pull off, but I'm working on a new novel that should earn out in time to finish it. It's really good. I'll send you some sample pages. It's about an author who kills her agent for not getting her the book deal she wanted."

Emily leans slightly back in her chair.

"I'm just messing with you." Carol laughs. "Jeez. Lighten up. But seriously. When can I expect the fifty-thousand-dollar advance for my other novels? I have to put a deposit down on a new roof. I'm going to tear out the attic."

"It won't be fifty thousand all at once. They're breaking the advance into thirds. Approximately sixteen thousand for each novel. They're going to stagger their releases over a three-year period. You'll receive half of the partial advance once the contract for your first novel, *Thunder Cove*, is signed."

"So I'm only going to get eight thousand dollars right away?"

"Yes. But I'm sure your attorneys will take most of that." Emily holds up her hand as Carol's mouth drops open. "And before you ask again, any profits from *An Evil Premise* will go to the families of your victims. Lyle Riggs. Mark Mattis. William Sinclair. Kristen Lewis. Some of the money will go to Nicki Boyle's hospital bills. It's a miracle she survived the beating you gave her. They haven't been able to connect you to the orderly at the hospital, but they're pretty sure you were responsible for his death too."

"No, no, no." Carol shakes her head adamantly. "You're getting the story all wrong. I like the idea that Nicki survived, though. I wasn't sure if killing her off was the right call or not. But Father Mattis killed the orderly. Deidre was probably in on it. I mean, you don't stop being possessed by a demon just because you're in a coma. Which, if you didn't catch, she was faking the entire time."

"Did she fake getting run over by a car too?"

Carol blinks at her for a second, then changes the subject with a roll of her eyes. "Do you think they'll want me to go on a book tour? I'll have to check with my husband, but I'm sure Cal will be okay with it. He's going to be so excited when he finds out I'm going to be published."

"You don't have a husband, Carol. Cal isn't real. He's just part of your delusion."

"He is real, Emily. We just had lunch together. He stopped by to surprise me. Oh. Wait! You're talking about the story. No. Deidre just wanted Jewel to think Cal wasn't real. She was gaslighting her. Trying to make her think she was crazy."

"I think it worked."

Carol dismisses the joke with a wave of her hand and clangs her bracelet against the metal desk. "So, when will *An Evil Premise* be released?"

"In a couple of months. They want books on the shelves by Halloween."

So readers can devour them like pieces of tampered candy, Carol thinks.

"Before I go," Emily says, "the publisher wanted me to ask you about the original manuscript of *Unspeakable Demons* again."

Carol shrugs. "What about it?"

"Where is it?"

"I don't know what happened to it. I don't think we're supposed to know. Jewel didn't even know she had it the entire time. That's what she pulled out of her laptop bag in the beginning. The pages that spilled to the floor? The work in progress she mentioned? That *was* the original manuscript. She set it on the back of the desk. It was right under her nose the whole time. That's what she had in her purse. What kept wiggling around and laughing at her. It turned into an actual novel when she discovered it in the end."

"And then what happened?"

"Seriously, Emily." Carol shakes her head. "You really need to read the book. It would make things so much easier."

"Just tell me what happened to the original manuscript! After you finished the story."

"I don't know what happened to it after that. The muse probably took it back to the hell from whence it came." She snorts a laugh. "It's probably looking for another author to write a sequel. It will probably just materialize in another bookstore one day." Carol tilts her head to smile. "Does that help you any?"

"Not in the slightest." Emily shakes her head wearily. "I didn't want to have to do this, but I'm running out of time. And patience. I need to jog your memory somehow."

Emily stands and walks to the door. The echoing rap of her knuckles on metal makes Carol's teeth hurt.

A uniformed man peeks his head inside the room. "You all set?"

"I need a few more minutes," Emily says. "Could you please ask Ms. Baldwin's other visitors to join us?"

"Other visitors?" Carol stands to receive them. The chain of her bracelet catches on the edge of the desk and sits her quickly back in her chair. "I wasn't prepared to meet with anyone else today, Emily. I have a lot of work to do."

"This will only take a moment," Emily says, returning to her seat.

"You have fifteen minutes," the doorman says, escorting a man and a woman into Carol's office. The man is tall, completely bald, and has a silver, manicured goatee. The woman has shoulder-length brown hair and looks completely different in her street clothes.

"Officer Kerns!" Carol exclaims, then flinches as the office door clangs shut.

Officer Kerns gives her a little wave. "Hey, Jewel. I mean, Carol."

"It's so good to see you," Carol says. "I've been meaning to call, but things have been so hectic lately."

"That's okay. I get it."

"Hello, Carol," the man says in a low, bedside voice. "How are you feeling today?"

"Dr. Leonetti?" Carol gasps. "I didn't recognize you without your . . ." She flushes. It isn't nice to point out someone's physical deficiencies. Though he does look a million times better without that awful toupee. He wasn't fooling anybody with that thing.

"Hair?" Dr. Leonetti offers, running a hand over his waxed cue ball.

"Yes. Sorry. But it really wasn't very flattering." Carol looks between him and Officer Kerns. "It's so good to see you both. I'd offer you a seat, but I only have one guest chair at present."

"That's all right," Dr. Leonetti says. "We won't be staying long."

"God, I hope not," Officer Kerns says, slinging the knapsack on her shoulder to the floor and leaning against the wall. "Prisons give me the creeps."

Carol laughs. "I know. This office building does have an institutional vibe to it. But it's only temporary. Until I finish renovating the apartment house. But who knows how long that's going to take."

"At least five lifetimes, I'm sure," Emily quips.

"Yeah," Officer Kerns laughs. "I'd get used to being here if I were you."

"So she's still completely deluded?" Dr. Leonetti asks.

"Crazier than a loon," Emily says.

"More like a jailbird," Officer Kerns adds.

Carol frowns. "That's not very nice. I don't appreciate you coming into my office and insulting me. I think it might be best if you left. I'll have my assistant validate your parking."

Emily looks over her shoulder at Dr. Leonetti. "See what I'm dealing with?"

"Just get on with it," Officer Kerns urges.

Emily nods. "Why don't we start with some introductions."

"We don't need to be introduced," Carol says. "We've already met."

"You haven't been *properly* introduced, though." Emily touches Dr. Leonetti's arm as he steps beside her. "I'd like you to meet a dear friend of mine. Parapsychologist, and amateur actor extraordinaire, Mr. Christopher Arnold."

"Don't forget Prelate of the Satanic Order of Baal, my dear," he says.

"How could I?" Emily beams up at him.

"Wait," Carol gasps as the rug is pulled out from under her. "What?"

Emily gestures to Officer Kerns. "And this bundle of joy is none other than my daughter, Jennifer. Say hello to the nice crazy lady, Jennifer."

Jennifer gives Carol a laconic wave.

A dark edge begins to creep across Carol's vision like a fungus. She blinks fast to bat it away before the nebula can black out her mind, then switches her eyes between the new character developments standing before her.

"I'm confused," she says.

"That's painfully obvious," Emily gibes. "That's why I invited them here. To force you to see things a little more clearly."

Carol looks at Christopher Arnold. "So you're not a real doctor?"

"No, but I play one on TV," he jokes. "I might have made the role look effortless, but believe me, a lot went into it. I had to remember a lot of complicated medical terms. Most of what I told you about Deidre's condition came from Dr. Phelps. He'd tell me, then I'd tell you. I almost had him believing I was Deidre's primary care physician. Visiting from New York to ensure my famous patient got the best care possible. I had to call in a few favors to gain access to the ICU. The hospital administrator's cousin was a part of my Satanic warren in college."

Jesus, the world is crawling with them, Carol thinks.

"He was more than happy to vouch for me," Christopher continues. "Assured them that my paperwork would be forthcoming. Dr. Phelps wasn't thrilled about the situation, but he kept his mouth shut. In the beginning. I'm not sure what suddenly made him suspicious of me. Nurse Ingram probably ratted me out about something. She was always looking at me sideways. I thought for sure I'd have to kill her too. But you can only push your luck so far."

"I told you shoving that bible down that orderly's throat was a mistake," Jennifer says. "It drew too much attention. Couldn't you just kill him like a normal person?"

"I honestly couldn't resist. I kept finding him in Deidre's room reading to her from the bible. I warned him that I was going to shove it down his throat the next time I found him in there. It's not my fault he didn't take me seriously."

"You're lucky he didn't report you before you got the chance to kill him," Jennifer says.

Carol looks at her. "Let me guess, you're not really a cop."

Jennifer rubs a snigger from her nose. "Not even close."

"But you wore a uniform. You had a badge. And a gun!"

"You don't have to be a cop to carry a gun. I got the badge and uniform on eBay. They don't sell police cruisers, though. I can't believe you bought that story about mine being in the shop." Jennifer laughs, then shakes her head. "I thought Mom was crazy when she told me to pretend to be a character from one of your novels. I thought you'd bust me as soon as I told you my name was Officer Kerns, but you didn't even bat an eye."

Carol turns her frown on Emily. "Are you going to tell me that you're not the real Emily Channing either?"

"Oh, no." Emily fluffs the back of her hair. "I'm the real deal."

"Then who was Fake Emily? The one Jewel was talking to on the phone."

"That would be me," Jennifer says, whipping up a head cold and congesting her voice with a nasal tone.

"Huh." Carol tilts her head in wonder. "I thought for sure Tabs was Fake Emily."

Jennifer holds up a finger, then bends to the knapsack she set on the floor when she arrived. In a sweep of blond hair, Tabs stands upright. "Ta-da!" She turns her head side to side, then struts an imaginary catwalk. "I really can't pull Tabs off without platform heels and fake eyelashes, but you get the idea."

"I knew you were goading me that night we ran into you in the elevator," Carol says. "All that stuff about Nicki getting *hammered* and meeting a *hot* date at the bookstore."

"I was just having a little fun. I knew shit was about to hit the fan. Deidre was home. And you were on to me. Or at least on to the fact that the Emily you were talking to was a fraud. You scared me with all that talk about turning your phone over to the police so they could trace my phone number. I changed the number in Deidre's phone from mine to yours while you were at the hospital. I had to dig Lyle's keys out of his pocket to get into the apartment. Ugh. That was awful."

"But why have Jennifer impersonate you?" Carol says, turning back to the agent. "You are Emily Channing. You could have just called me yourself."

"I couldn't be directly connected to this," Emily says. "I have a reputation to uphold. And my assistant is a bit of a helicopter. I couldn't risk Margo being in the room if you were to call. She would have wanted to know who you were and what book we were working on and why I didn't tell her about it and blah, blah, blah."

"Was Deidre in on this too?"

"She's the one who told me about the manuscript. How it had possessed her mother. Drove her to murder their neighbor. I was intrigued. I called Christopher right away. Deidre worked on the novel for a while, but then things started to get weird. Her behavior became erratic. To put it mildly." Emily glances up at Christopher Arnold. "We were very encouraged. It was working. The muse was taking hold of her. It was everything we had hoped for. But Deidre was not, as they say, a happy camper. She became extremely upset after she killed that second man. Keith, I think his name was. She refused to work on the manuscript another second. She sent me what she had transposed so far. I handed it off to one of my new authors, but that didn't work out so well."

"Yeah," Carol sighs. "I know about Lisbeth Abbott. She threw herself from your office window."

"Sort of," Emily says. "It really was a tragedy, though. Lisbeth's star was on the rise. Her writing was super edgy. Like her. She had piercings in places I don't want to think about. Tattoos neck to toe. I thought she would be able to handle the muse. It seemed like she was. She turned in the manuscript in just under a week. But the ending she wrote was complete gibberish. It looked like something a monkey might bang out on a typewriter. When I told Lisbeth I couldn't use it, she went completely insane. She came to my office and almost killed Jennifer."

"She was strong as shit," Jennifer says, working discomfort from her jaw. "She got in a few good ones before I managed to push her out the window."

"After that, I didn't know what to do," Emily says. "I couldn't risk having another one of my authors take it on. The police were investigating Lisbeth's death. Her sister was convinced that I was somehow involved with what happened to her."

Emily tilts her head to smile at Carol.

"Then I remembered Deidre telling me about her crazy little sister. A wannabe author who'd do just about anything to get published. So consumed by her own stories that she actually thought they were real. You and the muse sounded like a match made in heaven."

"I think you mean hell, dear," Christopher Arnold chuckles.

"Deidre said no as soon as I brought up your name," Emily goes on. "She didn't think you'd be able to connect with the muse. Only someone with true talent can bring out its evil genius. I thought it was worth a shot, though. I asked her to show you a sample page to see what happens. You must have had some sort of psychotic break or something. The next thing I know Deidre's in the hospital." She rolls her eyes at her daughter. "Jennifer was supposed to be keeping an eye on things for me at the apartment house. I guess she slipped past her that night."

"I *was asleep*, Mom," Jennifer snits. "I have to sleep sometimes, you know. I'm not a fucking robot."

Emily shrugs. "It all worked out in the long run, I guess."

Carol looks at Jennifer. "Did Nicki know who you were?"

"No. I was just going to rent an apartment from Deidre, but then I ran into Nicki when I entered the apartment house that day. She and Tabs hit it off right away. She said she was looking for a roommate. I thought that might be better. I wouldn't have to deal with Deidre directly. She probably wouldn't have recognized me, though. I was a gawky teenager when I saw her last. But I thought, why chance it?"

"Was Deidre really in a coma? Or was that just an act?"

"She was definitely in a coma," Christopher says. "I tested her to make sure. She would have cried out if she could have."

"Her falling into a coma was a stroke of luck," Emily adds. "It allowed us to work with you without her intervening.

Everything was going according to plan until you realized you were being duped. I shouldn't have answered the phone the day you called my office, but Margo would have wondered why I didn't want to take your call."

"Things were already going sideways by then," Jennifer says. "That old bitch, Mrs. Willard, kept running her mouth about Deidre being a Satanist to anyone who would listen. After what happened to the orderly in Deidre's room"—she rolls her eyes at Christopher Arnold—"the local cops called in the FBI. I tried to point them toward Father Mattis, but he had an alibi for that morning. I was worried they might question you. They just needed to get one look at you to know that you were a fucking demon. You were literally oozing evil."

"The rash," Carol says, touching her pitted cheek.

"An unfortunate side effect of the muse," Emily says. "The human body doesn't react well when an evil spirit inhabits it. Lisbeth developed a rash too. Nothing compared to yours and Deidre's, though. An adaptation of the manuscript isn't as strong."

"Which is precisely why we need the original," Christopher says.

Carol shakes her head, confused. "Why do you need the original manuscript? The book is finished. The story's over."

"We have to protect it," Emily says. "We're not the only ones who have an interest in the muse. The Catholic Church has been looking for its original manuscript for years. We thought they had tasked Father Mattis with finding it. That's why we were in such a panic for you to finish it. We were afraid he might locate it before you could flesh out an ending and somehow destroy it."

"I tried to take him out of the equation," Christopher admits. "But the lucky bastard escaped the fire. I wanted to take another shot at him, but Emily thought it was too risky."

"You missed your shot, Chris," she admonishes. "His death had to look like an accident. If Mattis turned up dead right after the church burned, the Vatican would have sent a team of priests to investigate. You couldn't kill them all."

"No. But I would have had fun trying."

"The church is trying to stop the publication of *An Evil Premise*," Emily says to Carol, ignoring him. "They won't be successful. Free speech and all. And they can't exactly say a demonic muse is possessing the book. They might draw undue attention to it. And open themselves to ridicule. No. Their only option is to find the original manuscript and destroy it. Take away the muse's power. Without the original manuscript, your book is nothing. Just words on paper."

"And with it?" Carol asks.

"A movement."

"Toward what?"

"Hell on earth," Christopher says. "Your novel is just the spark we need. Once it catches fire, there will be no stopping us. It can turn average readers into mindless killing machines. Naturally, they'll look for a leader. Who better than the man who possesses the muse's original manuscript? It will be our bible, of sorts. And I'm going to thump it until it bleeds."

Jennifer pushes off the wall, slams her hands on the table, and gives Carol her best hard-boiled cop look. "Tell us where it is, Carol. Or Jewel. Or whoever the fuck you think you are today."

"I honestly don't know where it is."

Jennifer slaps the table to emphasize, "Bullshit!"

"I'd tell you if I knew," Carol says. "You can have it. I want nothing more than to be rid of this nightmare. I want the muse to leave me alone. I'm sick of it. Always whispering in my ear. Horrible things. I hate it!"

Emily's expression brightens. "The muse is still with you?"

"Yes. I was kind of joking before about the original manuscript just materializing in a bookstore someday. I don't know if that is true or not. But I do know you won't find the manuscript unless the muse wants it to be found. Until then, I guess I'm stuck with it."

"I knew she wasn't going to tell us anything," Jennifer says. "Coming here was a waste of time."

"Look, I want someone to find the manuscript," Carol says to Emily. "I don't care if it's you or somebody else. Maybe once another author starts working on it the muse will leave me alone. But only the muse knows where the original manuscript is."

"Can you talk to it?" Christopher asks.

"I tell it to get the hell out of my head all the time. Which it doesn't seem to hear. But I've never asked it a direct question before."

"Ask it about the manuscript."

Carol concedes with a shrug, then closes her eyes. "Okay, muse. What did you do with the original manuscript of *Unspeakable Demons*? Where can we find it?"

"Did it answer?" Emily asks after a moment.

"*Shhh*," Carol hisses. "I'm listening."

"She's fucking with us," Jennifer says.

"Give her a second!"

"We don't have a second." Jennifer checks her watch. "We've already been in here ten minutes. The guard's going to kick us out anytime now. We need to make her talk."

Carol flinches as if she just heard a sudden noise, then snaps her fingers. "Quick! Give me something to write with!"

"Just tell us what it said," Emily groans.

"It doesn't work that way. I have to write down the muse's words. Give me a pen! Quick! Before I lose it."

"They told us not to give her anything sharp," Jennifer warns.

"I don't care what they said!" Emily exclaims. "Give the woman a damn pen!"

"Here!" Christopher Arnold extracts a fountain pen from the inside pocket of his suit jacket and sets it on the table.

Jewel snatches it up, then slaps the table to demand, "Paper! Paper!"

"Oh, for fuck's sake," Emily cries. "Give her something to write on!"

Christopher pats himself down. "I don't have anything."

"Mom, you've gotta have some paper in your purse."

"Oh, of course." Emily collects her bag from the floor. She searches the contents of the damn bottomless pit packed with so much crap she can't find what she's looking for half the time. She mutters a few expletives as she unzips interior pockets, then whips out a folded envelope. "Will this do?"

"Yes!" Carol fingers the electric bill forward as Emily sets it on the table. She flips it over and begins scribbling tightly fitted words across the back.

"Well?" Emily tilts her head to try and read upside down. "What is it saying?"

"Give me a second!" Carol pulls the envelope closer and crouches over it. "It's giving me some sort of directions."

As Carol transposes the muse's communiqué, Emily leans back and places her hand on top of Christopher's as he gives her shoulder an encouraging squeeze.

Carol blinks through a spray of blood as Emily's forehead explodes against the metal table. Again, and again, and again . . .

"Chris!" Jennifer cries. "What the hell are you doing? Stop it!"

"I can't!" he screams as Emily's head turns to mush under his hand. "I'm not doing it! I can't control it!"

"Oh, shit!" Jennifer grabs Carol by the wrist, her ironclad wrist. "Stop writing!"

"Go fuck yourself," Carol growls in a dark voice, bending deeper to her work and spelling "J-E-N-N-I-F-E-R" aloud.

As the pen scratches quickly across the envelope, Jennifer stands bolt upright and spins rigidly around.

"What's happening!" she cries, swinging her head back and forth to locate the invisible force driving her forward. The soles of her shoes squeak across the floor as she tries to brace her heels. "NO!" she screams as her head is lowered to waist level and aimed at the wall. "HELP ME!" is her final plea before her head cracks in two against the cinderblocks.

An alarm sounds as the door slams open and three guards rush into the room. Weapons drawn, they gaze in horror at the wet chunks of fractured melon spilled across the metal table, the pool of blood around the head of the girl sprawled out on the floor, then turn their sights on Christopher Arnold, who is trying his very best not to rush at them with his bloody hands extended.

"STOP!" he screams at Carol as he races by, toes skittering against the floor. "STOP WRITING! STOP—"

As his body convulses with a barrage of bullets, Carol leans over the blood-speckled envelope in front of her and smiles. She closes her eyes to think for a second, then jots down the last six letters she will ever be allowed to write.

YJR RMF

ACKNOWLEDGMENTS

A most heartfelt thank-you to my agent, Zoe Sandler at Sanford J. Greenburger Associates, for championing me through multiple attempts to have a second novel published. Her belief that we would be able to get some version of this story into print kept me going. Without her confidence in me and enthusiasm for my work, this novel might not have found its way.

I cannot express how grateful I am to everyone at Blackstone Publishing for the warm welcome I received upon joining their incredible team, and how supported I have felt ever since. Their graciousness is second only to their professionalism. A special thanks to my senior acquisitions editor, Dan Ehrenhaft, for seeing promise in my manuscript and for shepherding us so effortlessly to publication. To my editorial director, Josie Woodbridge, thank you for overseeing the entire process and being there for all of us every step of the way. Many thanks to Candice Edwards, art production manager, for bringing my story to life with such an amazing cover. And to Lysa Williams for all her efforts and support. And though I write these acknowledgments in advance of publication, I have no doubt that I will owe my publicity manager, Sarah Bonamino, and her team a huge debt of gratitude for all they did to make this novel a success!

I was beyond fortunate to have worked with two of the most outstanding copyeditors in the business today. Toni Kirkpatrick, my developmental editor, was nothing short of extraordinary. She challenged me to solve problems I didn't know existed and transformed my pretty good story into a great novel! Her insight into my characters, and eye for the plot holes they had scattered around, was truly amazing. As were the instincts of my managing editor, Ananda Finwall, who earned all my admiration for her meticulous attention to detail and knowledge of pretty much everything under the sun. I can't thank you both enough for caring for my novel as if it were your own.

And a very special thanks to my husband, Jamie, and all my friends and family who encouraged me to keep at it over the years. Your belief powered me forward. My accomplishments are yours, as yours are mine, and in celebration of this, all of our dreams are realized.